Text Book of

PHARMACEUTICS

For

First Year Bachelor of Pharmacy

Dr. R. S. GAUD
M. Pharm. Ph.D., F.I.C.A., F.I.C.
Dean of Pharma Sciences,
NMIMS University,
Vile Parle (West)
MUMBAI 56.

Dr. P. G. YEOLE
M. Pharm., Ph. D.,
Principal,
Institute of Pharmacy,
Borgaon (Meghe).
WARDHA 442001.

Dr. A. V. YADAV
M. Pharm. LL.B., A.I.C.
Ex. Head of Pharmay Dept.,
Govt. College of Pharmacy,
KARAD 415124.

S. B. GOKHALE
M. Pharm. A.I.C.,
Ex. Co-ordinator
R.C. Patel College of Pharmaceutical
Education and Research
SHIRPUR Dist. Dhule 425405.

NIRALI
P R A K A S H A N
ADVANCEMENT OF KNOWLEDGE

N1621

F.Y. B. Pharmacy - Pharmaceutics   ISBN 978-81-85790-41-1

Fifteenth Edition : July 2015

© : **Authors**

Published By :

NIRALI PRAKASHAN

Abhyudaya Pragati, 1312, Shivaji Nagar,
Off J.M. Road, PUNE – 411005
Tel - (020) 25512336/37/39, Fax - (020) 25511379
Email : niralipune@pragationline.com

☞ **DISTRIBUTION CENTRES**

PUNE

Nirali Prakashan : 119, Budhwar Peth, Jogeshwari Mandir Lane, Pune 411002, Maharashtra
Tel : (020) 2445 2044, 66022708, Fax : (020) 2445 1538
Email : bookorder@pragationline.com, niralilocal@pragationline.com

Nirali Prakashan : S. No. 28/27, Dhyari, Near Pari Company, Pune 411041
Tel : (020) 24690204 Fax : (020) 24690316
Email : dhyari@pragationline.com, bookorder@pragationline.com

MUMBAI

Nirali Prakashan : 385, S.V.P. Road, Rasdhara Co-op. Hsg. Society Ltd.,
Girgaum, Mumbai 400004, Maharashtra
Tel : (022) 2385 6339 / 2386 9976, Fax : (022) 2386 9976
Email : niralimumbai@pragationline.com

☞ **DISTRIBUTION BRANCHES**

JALGAON

Nirali Prakashan : 34, V. V. Golani Market, Navi Peth, Jalgaon 425001,
Maharashtra, Tel : (0257) 222 0395, Mob : 94234 91860

KOLHAPUR

Nirali Prakashan : New Mahadvar Road, Kedar Plaza, 1st Floor Opp. IDBI Bank
Kolhapur 416 012, Maharashtra. Mob : 9850046155

NAGPUR

Pratibha Book Distributors : Above Maratha Mandir, Shop No. 3, First Floor,
Rani Jhanshi Square, Sitabuldi, Nagpur 440012, Maharashtra
Tel : (0712) 254 7129

DELHI

Nirali Prakashan : 4593/21, Basement, Aggarwal Lane 15, Ansari Road, Daryaganj
Near Times of India Building, New Delhi 110002
Mob : 08505972553

BENGALURU

Pragati Book House : House No. 1, Sanjeevappa Lane, Avenue Road Cross,
Opp. Rice Church, Bengaluru – 560002.
Tel : (080) 64513344, 64513355,Mob : 9880582331, 9845021552
Email:bharatsavla@yahoo.com

CHENNAI

Pragati Books : 9/1, Montieth Road, Behind Taas Mahal, Egmore,
Chennai 600008 Tamil Nadu, Tel : (044) 6518 3535,
Mob : 94440 01782 / 98450 21552 / 98805 82331,
Email : bharatsavla@yahoo.com

niralipune@pragationline.com | www.pragationline.com

Also find us on [f] www.facebook.com/niralibooks

PREFACE TO THE FIFTEENTH EDITION

We are pleased to release the revised Fifteenth edition of **Pharmaceutics** within a span of thirteen years only.

The contents of the chapters "Introduction to Dosage Forms", History and Development of Profession of Pharmacy and Introduction to Alternative Systems of Medicines" have been revised, while additional information and new figures have also been included to other chapters.

We hope to receive the same over-whelming response from the students and colleagues in future as received in the past.

July, 2015

Gaud
Yeole
Yadav
Gokhale

PREFACE TO THE FIRST EDITION

Pharmaceutics is the branch of Pharmacy that carries the impression of Pharmacy Profession in general. It encompasses whole area that involves designing, formulating and presenting a therapeutically useful chemical entity in a most appropriate drug delivery system. The comprehensive study of this subject necessitates integration of physical, chemical and biological principles, as applicable to all the components of Drug Delivery Systems. Presenting information on such a subject, that too, to the beginners is rather a herculian task. With this awareness in mind an attempt has been made here in the form of this book.

Inspite of our sincere efforts in presenting the information, we believe that, there always exists a room to improve. We shall highly appreciate constructive suggestions including criticism from the readers.

We wish to put on record our thanks to Shri. S. V. Sandhansive, AM, CTC, Kaliyoga Arts, Asoda Jalgaon, for preparing the cover design of this book. Our sincere thanks are also due to Shri. D. K. Furia, publisher and the staff members of Nirali Prakashan for timely publishing the book.

December 1999   **Authors**

SYLLABUS

1. **Introduction to Pharmaceutics and its Scope.**

2. **Development of a new drug.**

3. **Introduction to Dosage Forms of Drugs.** Their classification and applications. Sterile and none sterile products.

   Drug Delevery Concept and Drug Delivery Systems. Concept of formulation. Development of various dosage forms.

4. **History and Develpoment of Profession of Pharmacy** and Pharmaceutical Industry in India. Introduction to pharmacopoeias and other compendia.

5. **Introduction to Pre-formulation Studies.**

6. **Biopharmaceutics.** Introduction to Bioavalability and Biopharmaceautics.

   Concept of Drug Efficiency and Dose Responce.

   Drug Administration, Physiological considerations for various routes of administration.

   Introduction to Absorption, Drug distribution and its fate.

7. **Introduction to Good Manufacturing Practices and Quality Assurance.**

8. **Introduction to Alternative Systems of Medicines -** Ayurveda, Homeopathy, Unani and Siddha.

9. **Drug Delivery Systems.**

   (I)   Non-sterile monophasic liquids :

   (a)   Aromatic waters and concentrated aromatic waters, (infusions & decoctions)

   (b)   Glycerites

   (c)   Solutions - factors affecting rate of solution - Pre-formulation - formulation development- vehicles and excipients - manufacturing process and equipments, packaging and quality control standards(including controls on raw material, inprocess controls and finished product control) of pharmaceuticals like syrups, elixirs, linctuses, ENT Preparations and paints, mouth washes, Ayurvedic and Homeopathic liquids, cosmetics preparations after shave lotions, hair care solutions.

   (d)   Unit processes and equipments used for manufacturing of non-sterile monophasic liquids.

   Liquid mixing : Mechanism of mixing, Impeller and propeller type mixers, Tanks, Baffles, Prevention of aeration and foam.

   (e)   Filtration and Clarification : Factors affecting rate of diffusion – Filter media – Filter aids – Nutsch filter, Plate and Frame filter. Leaf filter, Rotary Vacuum filter, Basket centrifuge.

   (f)   Equipments used for manufacturing and packaging of liquids, Bottle washing and filling equipments, Belt conveyor, cartoning and batch numbering machines.

II. **(a)** **Powders and Granules :** Formulation, preparation and evaluation of various powders and granular products like dusting powders, oral rehydration powders, dry syrup formulations, talcum powders, tooth powders.

Equipments used in the production of powders.

(b) **Size reduction :** Importance in Pharmacy, Factors influencing size reduction, Grinding mills of various types like Hammer Mills, Multimill, Conico-cylindrical Ball mill, Edge and End runner mills, Fluid energy mill.

(c) **Size separation :** Sieves, Size gradation, Size distribution – Methods for determining size distribution.

(d) **Powder mixing :** Mechanism of mixing, Various types of trough mixers, Sigma and ribbon blenders, Paddle mixer, Tumblers like cubes and double cone, Planetary mixer.

(e) **Granule manufacturing :** Environmental controls – Pouch filling machine.

10. **Biological Products :** Introduction to

(A) **Immunology –** Immuity and its classification, antigens, antibodies and vaccines and sera.

Preparations and quality control of the following :

Vaccines and Sera – Bacterial, viral as exemplified by BCG, Typhoid A and B, small pox, and poliomylitis.

Toxoid – Tetanus and old tuberculin.

(B) **Blood and Blood products :** Whole human blood collection and regulatory controls, dried human plasma, plasma substitutes (e.g. dextran), fractionation of blood plasma.

(C) **Sutures and Ligatures :** Classification into absorbable and non-absorbable materials. Types, processing and manufacturing, sterilization, packaging and quality control tests of materials like calgut and nylon.

Introduction to official surgical dressings and bandages.

11. **Packaging of Pharmaceuticals :** Primary and Secondary packaging materials : Components of packages and various accessories – Packaging material selection – Their evaluation – closures – child resistant packaging.

CONTENTS

***

Chapter ... 1

INTRODUCTION TO PHARMACEUTICS AND ITS SCOPE

Drugs which are obtained from various sources are rarely administered in their pure chemical form. Generally, drugs are combined with other inert substances (excipients or additives) and converted into suitable form of administration, commonly termed as **dosage** form. It is observed that dose response relationship depends on route of drug administration, type of dosage form, mechanism used to make the dosage form and physico-chemical nature of the drug and response is not the same in all cases. Drugs given by parenteral route will respond earlier than the drug given by oral route. If same drug is given in tablet or solution dosage form, effect will again vary. Sometimes we see different response in the same dosage form manufactured by the different organisations and it is due to difference in the physico-chemical properties of the drugs and additives used and method of formulation of the dosage form. Sometimes the same drug is available in different dosage forms and is known as multiple dosage form.

Selection of dosage form depends on number of factors, the most important is the route of administration. Majority of drugs are administered orally. Sometimes body cavities are used to have local or systemic effect. In case of emergency, parental route is preferred for prompt action. External application is also one of the major routes for localised action.

DESIGNING OF DOSAGE FORMS

Dosage form is designed considering various factors which affect the patient acceptance as well as the drug efficacy. Dosage form should have the colour, flavour, odour, taste and appearance which will not affect the patients acceptance. On the other hand it should be manipulated and presented in a way which is easily acceptable to patient. e.g. Calcium tablets for children are available in different colour, flavour with a sweet taste and sometimes even packed in a toy like container to encourage children acceptance. At the same time the dosage form should be such that patient should not feel any difflculty in the proper use by the desired route. Cost of the dosage form should be justified and undue profit should not be charged to patient.

All precautions should be taken so that the effectiveness of the drug is maintained throughout the shelf life and when administered it gives the therapeutic effect, in the manner desired by the physician. The dose varies with age, sex, severity of the disease and the physician should have flexibility to advise the required dose from the same dosage form as per his intentions.

Pharmaceutics is a branch of pharmacy which includes the study of formulation of a drug into a dosage form. It is a systematic approach to get an effective and stable formulation considering all aspects required to maintain its quality. It also deals with technology involved in large scale manufacturing of these dosage forms. It is the responsibility of manufacturing chemist to formulate a dosage form which is uniform, effective, stable and safe along with the information about its storage, use, precautions to be taken while it is administered and associated side effects. Thus, *pharmaceutics is a branch which imparts the knowledge required to meet out all these responsibilities to formulate a suitable and standard dosage form as needed.*

Dosage forms which are commonly dispensed in retail or hospital pharmacy are tablets, cachets, mouth washes, gargles, capsules, solutions, suspensions, emulsions, aerosols, aromatic waters, dentifrices, ear drop, eye drops, enemas, nasal drops, cones, throat paints, gels, implants, inhalations, injections, jellies, linctuses, spessaries, spirits, tinctures, suppositories, glycerines, granules, elixirs, syrups, dry syrups, ointments, lotions, liniments, dusting powders, applications etc.

The details of these **dosage forms** are as follows:

1. **Aerosols:**

A system that depends on the power of a compressed or liquefied gas to expel the contents of the container in the aerosolised form (fine spray or foam) is called aerosol or pressurised package. Aerosols are used for internal or external use with the help of atomisers.

Internally, it is used for administrating drugs like anti-asthmatic drugs like salbutamol, epinephrine and isoproterenol, steroids ergotamines etc. These drugs are dispensed in the form of fine spray of solid particle (size less than 5 microns) to the desired site such as respiratory tract or nasal passages. These preparations are used for their local action in the nasal areas, throat and lungs.

Externally, it is used for the treatment of dermatological diseases, inflammation, muscular pain and for antiseptic action. The formulation or product concentrate enclosed in the pressurised container is a simple formulation and may be solution, suspension, emulsion or powder form. The components of the aerosols are propellent, container, valve and actuator and product concentrate. Propellent is the most important component being responsible for its operation. Containers used are of best quality and strong enough to bear the pressure inside the container. Valve and actuators are designed as per requirement of the product.

Aerosol dosage form is advantageous as it is safe due to dosage accuracy, free from contamination, easy to use, maintains the stability of the product, avoids the loss of product as delivers directly at the required site and has facility of dispensing the product as per the desire of manufacturer by providing suitable valve. It is easy to withdraw if toxicity or allergic symptoms appear. Dose involved is very less and is in the range of 70-80 microns. It also helps in external applications as can be applied to broken skin without irritation and to intact skin in thin uniform film easy to spread over the large surface area which is otherwise difficult. Thus, it helps in faster absorption. It can be used to instil the formulation to the different sites using body cavities which is not possible by other dosage forms. Due to available pressure and micronised size it is promptly absorbed by the bronchial tree or the desired site and immediate relief is achieved.

Many antiasthmatic, cardiac, antimigraine, antiseptic preparations are available in the market are widely used due to the prompt relief to the patient.

2. Applications:

Applications are biphasic preparations intended for external application to the skin. It may be liquid or viscous in nature (emulsion or suspension). Most of the official preparations contain paraciticides and are intended for only a limited number of formulations. For dispensing of application coloured fluted bottles are used. The bottle should be labelled as **"For External Use only,"** and also **"Shake well before use."**

e.g. Calamine application compound BPC , Dicophane application BPC.

3. Aromatic Waters:

Aromatic waters are saturated aqueous solutions of volatile oils or other aromatic or volatile substances. An aromatic water may be used as a pleasantly flavoured vehicle for a water soluble drug or as aqueous phase in an emulsion or suspension. If a large amount of water soluble drug is added to an aromatic water, an insoluble layer may be formed at the surface due to salting out effect. In this case, molecules of water soluble drug have more attraction for the solvent molecule of water than volatile oil molecules. It should be stored in tight, light resistant bottles to reduce volatilisation or degradation of active constituents.

e.g. Anise water, Chloroform water, Camphor water, Cinnamon water, Peppermint water etc.

4. Cachets:

Nauseous or disagreeable powders are enclosed in a moulded rice paper and converted in dosage form suitable for administration. Cachet consists of drug powder enclosed in a shell, usually prepared by pouring a mixture of rice flour and water between two hot, polished revolving cylinders. The water evaporates and a sheet of wafer is formed. Before taking the cachets should be immersed in water for few seconds and then taken with a draught of water. e.g. Sodium aminoglycolate cachets, sodium amino salicylate and isoniazid cachets. Due to limitation of handling, patient acceptance and stability problems, this form has become obsolete.

5.   Capsules:

Capsules are solid dosage forms in which one or more medicinal or inert substances are enclosed within a small gelatine shell. The shell of the capsule must dissolve at 37°C to release medicaments completely. The potent medicament in small doses are mixed with an inert diluent before filling into capsule.

Gelatine capsule may be hard or soft. Hard gelatine capsule shell are manufactured from a mixture of gelatin, colorant and sometimes an opacifying agent such as titanium dioxide. The U.S.P. also permits addition of 0.15% sulphur dioxide to prevent decomposition of gelatine during manufacture. Capsule shells are prepared by dipping cold metallic moulds or pins into a gelatine solution maintained at a unifomm temperature.

Soft gelatine capsules are prepared from gelatine shells to which glycerine or polyhydric alcohol (such as sorbitol) is added. These shells also contain preservatives such as methyl and propyl parabens and sorbic acid to prevent the growth of fungi. Soft gelatine shell may be oblong, elliptic or spherical in shape and contains liquid, suspension, polishing material, dry powder or palletised material. Soft gelatine capsules are usually prepared by the plate process using a rotary or reciprocating productive die.

e.g. Tetracycline capsules, Ampicillin capsules, Vit. A and D capsules, etc.

6.   Draughts:

Draught (Haustus) is a liquid oral preparation taken as only one or two large dose. If several doses are prescribed, each of the dose is dispensed in separate container. It must be freshly prepared. Ipecacunha emetic paediatric draught is an exception of draught preparation which are prescribed in a multiple dose container.

e.g. Male fern extract draught, Paraldehyde draught, Tetracycline draught etc.

7.   Dusting Powders:

Dusting powders are very fine powders intended for external use. It is meant for application on various parts of the body as lubricants, antiseptics, antipruritics, antibromhydrosis agents, astringents and antiperspirants. Commercially, dusting powders are available in sifter top containers or as aerosols. They may also be supplied in wide mouth containers and applied with powder puff, a soft brush or a sterile gauge pad. Effectiveness of powder is enhanced by the micronized size of the powder obtained by passing through sieve no.120. Dusting powders should not be applied to open wounds as it is highly contaminated with soil organisms due to wide use of minerals.

e.g. Zinc oxide and Salicylic acid dusting powder, Zinc oxide, talc and starch dusting powder.

8.   Dentifrices:

Dentifrices are fine powders or pastes applied with soft brush or finger on the teeth surface and cleaned with the water.

e.g. Tooth powders, Tooth pastes etc.

9.   Eye Drops:

Eye drops are liquid preparation of drugs dissolved in aqueous vehicle. It should be free from microbial contaminants. Hence, should be prepared with aseptic precautions. A suitable fungistatic should be used in the preparations liable to support the growth of moulds. For oily eye drops, the oily vehicle which has been previously sterilised by heating at 160°C for one hour must be used.

Eye drops should be made approximately isotonic with lachrymal secretions by the addition of sodium chloride or other suitable substance. *Once opened should be used within a month.*

e.g. Antazoline eye drops, Streptomycin eye drops, Pilocarpine eye drops, Sulphacetamide eye drops etc.

10. Ear Drops:

Ear drops are liquid preparations of drug(s). The drugs are dissolved or suspended in the vehicle such as water, dilute alcohol, glycerin or propylene glycol and administered into the ear with the help of dropper. 3-4 drops of the preparations are instilled in the affected ear. Generally used for cleansing the ear, drying weeping surfaces, softening the wax and treating mild infections. The container should be labelled **"For External Use Only"**.

e.g. Hydrogen peroxide ear drops, Phenol ear drops, Boric acid ear drops, Chloramphenicol ear drops.

11. Elixirs:

Elixirs are pleasantly flavoured hydro alcoholic solutions intended for oral use. The alcohol content of elixir varies from 5 to 40%. Sufficient alcohol is added to maintain the drug in solution. Most elixirs become turbid when moderately diluted by aqueous liquids. Elixirs containing therapeutically active compound are known as medicinal elixirs. The medicinal elixirs usually contains very potent drugs such as antibiotics, antihistaminics and sedatives. The non-medicated elixirs are used as flavours and vehicles.

e.g. Chlorpheniramine elixir, diphenhydramine elixir, ephedrine elixir, paracetamol elixir, paediatric-piperazine citrate elixir etc.

12. Emulsions:

An emulsion is a heterogeneous system consisting of atleast one immiscible liquid with another liquid or dispersed in the form of droplets (droplet diameter usually exceed 0.1 Nm). These two immiscible liquids are made miscible and stable dosage form is obtained by the addition of third substance known as emulgent or emulsifying agent. Emulsions are mainly of two types-oil in water and water in oil. This dosage form helps us in improving the palatability of oily material meant for oral use and also improves miscibility and spreadability of the material to be applied externally.

It should be supplied in wide mouth container and should be labelled **"Shake well before use."**

e.g. Castor oil emulsion, Liquid paraffin and phenolphthalein emulsion etc.

13. Enemas:

These are aqueous or oily solutions or suspensions meant for rectal administration.

Many drugs are administered rectally for localised or systemic action as they have undesirable effects if taken orally. e.g. aminophylline and theophylline. The required therapeutic levels can be obtained within 30 minutes immediately after rectal administration. Corticosteroide like drugs are also given by this route due to gastro intestinal tract problem. Rectal enemas are used for evacuating the bowels and for purgative, sedative, anthelmentic, nutritive and anti-inflammatory effects. They may also be used for X-ray examination of the lower bowel. Enemas are usually given at body temperature in quantities of 500-1000 ml and are available commercially in disposable plastic squeeze bottle.

e.g. Paraldehyde enema, Soap enema, Glycerine and arachis oil enema etc.

14. Gargles:

Gargles are aqueous solutions used for treating the pharynx and nasopharynx, used for prevention or treatment of throat infections. Gargles are usually diluted with water prior to its use. Gargles should not be swallowed but should be thrown out after rinsing the oral cavity.

e.g. Phenol gargles, potassium chlorate and phenol gargles, potassium permanganate gargles etc.

15. Gels:

Generally gels are the aqueous colloidal suspensions of the hydrated forms of insoluble inorganic drugs. It should be stored in tight closed container preferably at a temperature above freezing and below 35°C which helps in the formation of gel structure.

e.g. Aluminium hydroxide gel, Milk of magnesia etc.

16. Glycerines:

Glycerines are also known as glycerites. They are viscous preparations in which drug is mixed with or without heat. These preparations generally are used as antiseptic, anti-inflammatory preparations.

e.g. Ichthammol, Glycerine, Phenol glycerin, Borax glycerin, Starch glycerin, Tannic acid glycerine etc.

17. Granules:

Granules are the solid dosage form of medicament in which the powdered drug or drugs are mixed with sweetening, flavouring and colouring agents. These ingredients are mixed in suitable quantity and then moistened with the granulating agent and properly mixed. Wet mass is passed through suitable sieve and dried at a temperature 60°C. Granules are more stable than powder dosage form.

Sometimes effervescent granules are preferred due to the pleasant taste of Carbon-dioxide evolved during effervescence. They are prepared by mixing citric acid, tartaric acid with sodium bicarbonate and drugs. Other additives such as sweetening agent may be incorporated if necessary.

18. Implants:

Implants are sterile dosage forms which are inserted under the skin by surgery. Drug is released for long time about 3 to 6 months or even a year. These tablets are commonly used in animals and human beings.

e.g. Steroidal harmones, testosterone, stilbesterol etc. employed as implants.

19. Inhalations:

Inhalations are liquid preparations containing volatile substances. These preparations are used to relive nasal congestion and inflammation of the respiratory tract. They may be placed on pad like fabric face mark or handkerchief or added to hot water (below boiling) and the vapour is inhaled about 5-10 minutes. **"For external use only."**

e.g. Benzoin inhalation, Menthol, Inhalators, Eucalyptus, Oil inhalations etc.

20. Injections:

Injections are the sterile liquid preparations and are administered by the parentral route under or through one or more layers of skin or mucous membrane. Injections may be classifled as solutions ready to use, suspension ready to use, dry powder to be solubalised prior to its use, dry powder to be suspended prior to its use and emulsions. It may be small volume or large volume parenteral. This dosage form is preferred in case of emergency when prompt action is desired.

e.g. Ampicillin injection, Gentamycin injection, Sodium chloride and dextrose injection etc.

21. Jellies:

Jellies are transparent or translucent, non-greasy, semi-solid preparations mainly used externally. They are used for lubrication or medication purpose. It contains antimicrobial agent along with the drug to prevent the microbial growth during storage. It should be stored in tightly closed container as it has tendency to lose water to the air and dry out.

e.g. Proflavin jelly, Lidocaine hydrochloride jelly, Pramoxine hydrochloride jelly, cyclomethyvaine jelly, contraceptive jellies etc.

22. Linctuses:

Linctuses are sweet viscous liquid usually containing medicinal substances. It is employed for the relief of coughs and also used as demulcent, sedative or expectorant properties.

e.g. Codeine linctus, Noscapine linctus etc.

23. Liniments:

Liniments are liquid or semisolid preparations intended for external application. It is applied by rubbing or friction but should not be applied to the broken skin. They are dispensed in coloured fluted bottles with label **"For External Use only"** and **"Shake the bottle before use."**

e.g. White liniment, Camphor liniment; Turpentine liniment etc.

24. Lotions:

Lotions are liquid suspensions or medicated dispersions meant for external use. It is applied on the skin without friction. After application it dries forming a thin film of medicament over the affected area. After application of the lotion the skin should be covered with suitable dressing or water proof material to reduce evaporation. It should be shaken vigorously before each application to have homogeneity and container must bear a label. **"For External Use Only."**

e.g. Calamine lotion, Sulphurated lotion etc.

25. Lozenges:

(Trouches) Lozenges are disc shaped solid dosage forms mainly meant for slow dissolution in the mouth. These dosage forms are made up of mainly sugar, gum and medicaments.

e.g. Bismuth lozenges, Liquorice lozenges etc.

26. Mixtures:

Mixtures are liquid dosage forms in which drug or drugs are in solubalised or dispersion form. It contains medicament and various other additives required to make them in a suitable form acceptable to patient and also to have proper homoginity. They are freshly prepared and used within few days. The container should be labelled **"Shake well before use."**

e.g. Aluminium hydroxide mixtures, Kaolin mixture, Magnesium sulphate mixture. etc.

27. Ointments:

Ointments are semisolid preparations intended for external use. They are easily spread on the skin. Their plastic viscosity is controlled by modifications of additives.

Generally, they are used as emollients, protectives, as a vehicle etc. Simple ointment is the preparation which can be used as a base for other medicaments. Eye ointment use the pure ointment base free from contamination and irritants present as impurity in the additives.

e.g. Benzoic acid ointment, Chloromycetin eye ointment, Atropine eye ointment etc.

28. Pessaries:

Pessaries are solid or semisolid mass meant to be inserted into the vagina. They are oval in shape and weigh about 5 g. Drugs administered by this route are intended to have local effects but systemic effect may occur. They may be prepared by moulding or by compression.

e.g. Lactic acid pessaries, Nystatin pessaries, Trichomonal pessaries, Monilial pessaries etc.

29. Powders:

A pharmaceutical powder is a mixture of finely divided drugs or chemicals in dry form meant for internal or external use. Substances incorporated in this dosage forms are frequently milled to reduce particle size. After milling various substances are mixed as needed. Milling helps in having better absorption and patient acceptance.

e.g. Rhubarb oral powder, Compound sodium chloride powder, Dextrose oral powder, Talcum dusting powder etc.

30. Solutions:

Solutions are sterile or non-sterile liquid preparations meant for external or internal use. These preparation contains one or more than one ingredient usually dissolved in water.

e.g. Strong ammonium acetate solution, Aqueous iodine solution, Cetrimide solutions etc.

31. Spirits:

Spirits are alcoholic or hydro alcoholic preparations of volatile substances containing 50% or 90% alcohol. Some spirits are medicinal spirits. It should be stored in tight containers to reduce loss by evaporation.

e.g. Chloroform spirit, Lemon spirit, Orange spirit, Aromatic ammonia spirit etc.

32. Sprays (Aerosols):

Sprays are the liquid preparations in which drug(s) are dissolved in water, alcohol or glycerine used on mucosae of the nose or throat with the help of an atomiser or nebulisor.

e.g. Compound adrenaline spray, Atropine spray, Isoprenaline spray etc.

33. Suppositories:

A suppository is a solid or semisolid mass meant to be inserted into body orifice (the rectum, vagina or the urethra) to provide either a local or systemic therapeutic effects. Suppositories are frequently used for local effects such as relief of haemorrhoids or injection in the rectum, vagina or the urethra.

(a) Rectal suppositories: It is usually cylindrical, tapered to a point forming a bullet like shape. An adult suppository weighs about 2 g.

(b) Vaginal suppositories: They are oval shaped and typically weighs about 5 g.

(c) Urethral suppositories: They are long and tapered, about 10 to 60 mm long and have diameter of 4 to 5 mm.

e.g. Nitrofurazone urethral inserts.

34. Suspensions:

It is a two phase system composed of a solid material dispersed in a liquid. The particle size of the dispersed solid is usually greater than 0.5 Nm. The liquid may be oily or aqueous in nature.

e.g. Barium sulphate suspension, Kaolin suspension etc.

35. Syrups:

A syrup is a concentrated or nearly saturated aqueous solution of sugar. Syrup NF contains 850 g of sucrose and sufficient purified water to make a litre. They are used as sweetening and flavouring agents.

e.g. Lemon syrup, Raspberry syrup, Tolu syrup etc.

36. Tablets:

Tablets are most commonly used solid dosage form. An ideal tablet should be free of defects such as cracks, chips, discoloration and contamination. Tablet may be manufactured by various methods viz. dry granulation, wet granulation or direct compression depending upon the nature of medicament.

e.g. Aspirin tablets, Paracetamol tablets, Chloroquine tablets etc.

37. Tinctures:

Tinctures are alcoholic or hydroalcoholic solutions of chemicals or soluble constituents of crude drugs. Tinctures are prepared by an extraction process of maceration or percolation. Tinctures must be stored in light resistant containers.

e.g. Belladona tincture, Aromatic cardamom tincture, Nux vomica tincture etc.

NEW DOSAGE FORMS

Some important novel drugs delivery systems are as follows:

1. **Transdermal Drug Delivery System:** Skin patches containing drug molecule in the desired concentration are used for percutaneous absorption. The advantage of the system is that the drug is not exposed to gastrointestinal tract and that the drug release rate can be controlled. Many products are available in the market under the brand name NitroDur, Nitrodisc, Catapress TTS etc.

2.   Ocuserts: These are the preparations meant for controlled drug delivery from a unit containing drug placed in the cul-de-sac of the eye. Each epilliptically shaped unit contains a core reservoir of the drug and alginic acid surrounded by hydrophobic ethylene or acetate copolymer membrane that controls the drug release in eye at a constant rate for a week. The alginic acid remains in the core. The rate can be controlled as per the intention of the formulations.

3.   Resealed Erythrocytes: In this system, erythrocytes are used as a drug carrier cell. Pores of size (200-500 A° diam.) are created in the cell membrane and after allowing the drug to enter the pores are resealed. It is advantageous in targeted drug delivery to liver or spleen.

4.   Liposomes: Liposomes are similar to cell membrane and are used to enclose the drug in required concentration to be released at desired site. Thus, mainly it is used as a drug carrier and lacks the toxicity which the conventional dosage form may have due to its site specific nature. Number of drugs are under clinical trials and few are being marketed.

5.   Nanoparticles: These are career drug molecules having very small particle size in the range of 10-100 Nm. These are used for making 'site specific' drug delivery. This helps in overcoming the toxic effects due to contact of the drug with other sites. Many anti-cancer drugs are being formulated in this dosage form along with the drugs that require liver specific drug delivery.

6.   Osmotic pump: Osmosis principle is being used in this system. It helps in controlling the rate of drug release in the desired concentration.

Depending upon the sterility, dosage forms can be classified as under.

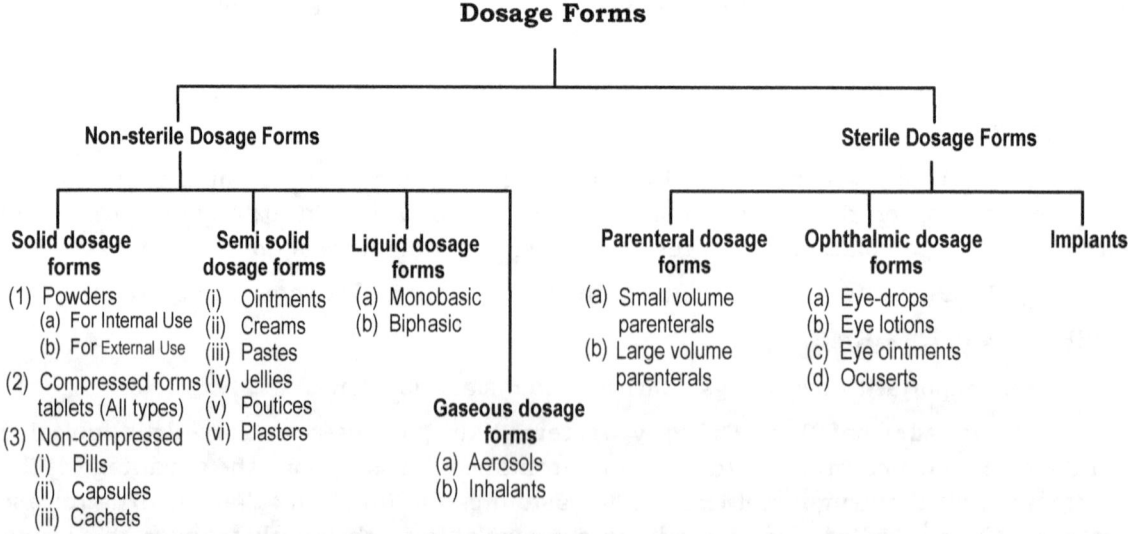

A broad classification of dosage forms as per their physical nature.

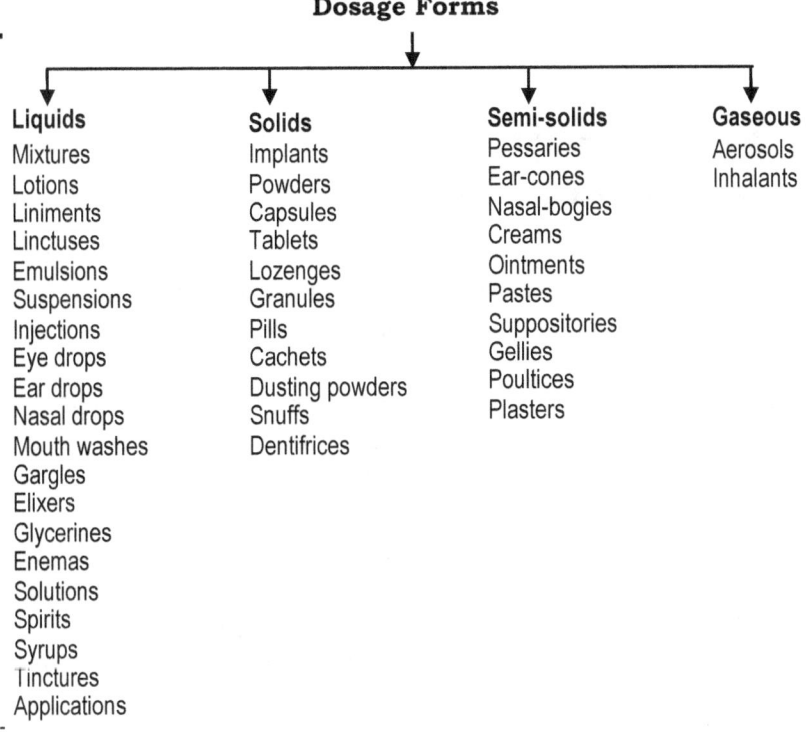

Dosage Forms

Liquids	Solids	Semi-solids	Gaseous
Mixtures	Implants	Pessaries	Aerosols
Lotions	Powders	Ear-cones	Inhalants
Liniments	Capsules	Nasal-bogies	
Linctuses	Tablets	Creams	
Emulsions	Lozenges	Ointments	
Suspensions	Granules	Pastes	
Injections	Pills	Suppositories	
Eye drops	Cachets	Gellies	
Ear drops	Dusting powders	Poultices	
Nasal drops	Snuffs	Plasters	
Mouth washes	Dentifrices		
Gargles			
Elixers			
Glycerines			
Enemas			
Solutions			
Spirits			
Syrups			
Tinctures			
Applications			

✱✱✱

Chapter ... 2

DEVELOPMENT OF A NEW DRUG

Throughout history the major source of new drugs has been the natural products of plant and animal origin. Some of the worth mentioning examples includes Reserpine, a tranquilizer and hypotensive agent, the Digitoxin a cardiotonic agent, the antineoplastic vinca alkaloids and the endocrine secretions such as insulin, thyroid extract and pituitary hormone obtained from cattle, sheep etc. The production of various biologicals including serums, antitoxins and vaccines using animals are even today contributing significantly in modern drug therapy. With the advent of laboratory techniques in isolation, structural identification, the organic chemists have contributed significantly in synthesizing drugs in laboratories. Many of the antibiotics have been produced through induced proliferative growth of micro-organisms. In addition, a host of semi-synthetic antibiotics have resulted through the knowledge of chemical structure and activity of these compounds. Thus, from about 3rd century BC to the early 20th century most useful drugs were derived from natural sources and their therapeutic uses were based on ancient serendipitous discoveries. The advances in chemical research on isolation, identification and synthesis of drugs, coupled with developments in biological sciences on understanding of mechanisms in health and disease, in the latter part of 20th century has yielded many important drugs which are both effective and specific. Thus, the search for new drugs gradually took on a more rational basis.

No matter how a drug arises whether as a serendipitous finding or as a planned long-term tireless efforts on rational basis; it requires a overall evaluation to prove its effectiveness and safety for being used in clinical practice.

The history has witnessed and taught us the need of overall evaluation of drug product. Then the new wonder drug sulfanilamide; solubilised in diethylene glycol was prepared and distributed for use in 1930s. The toxic effects of the solvent diethylene glycol took about 100 lives, before the product was withdrawn from the market. The well known drug tragedy of 1960 is the thalidomide disaster happened in Europe. A new synthetic drug called thalidomide was sold for sedative and tranquilizing effects. Thalidomide given to women during pregnancy produced phocomelia or arrested development of the limbs of the newborn infant. Thousands of children were affected to various extent. These teachings of the history are clearly indicative of the need to evaluate thoroughly the drug product in its development process. In this chapter "the development of a new drug" is discussed in details.

In the stages of drug development, the investigational drug requires to be evaluated in animals prior to its evaluation in human beings for legal, regulatory and scientific reasons. Such studies in animals are designated as pre-clinical studies. After successful performance of pre-clinical studies and on gathering necessary information from such studies; the investigator has to apply to FDA for permission to administer such unapproved drug product to human beings. This application is called as Investigational New Drug Application (IND). The application shall be forwarded to review committee consisting of physicians, pharmacologists, chemists, statistician and other consultants. On reviewing the file the FDA may permit the investigator to proceed. However for reasons stated below the FDA may withhold the permission to initiate the study.

1. That the subjects are or would be placed at an unreasonable and significant risk of illness or injury.

2. That the clinical investigators are not qualified to perform the proposed study.

3. That the investigators brochure is misleading, erroneous or materially incomplete and

4. That the IND does not contain sufficient information to assess the risk to the subjects.

Although there are guidelines for the review committee to follow; the reviewers shall review the IND with emphasis on the following details.

1. Basically, animal studies are designated to ascertain the safety of investigational drug. Hence, for assessing toxic potential of drug; whether investigators have exposed the animals to a dose size sufficiently high to produce toxicity or not; shall be critically examined.

2. Whether proposed protocol for clinical trials is suitable to follow it practically and safely or not shall thoroughly checked.

3. In addition to toxicity studies, the pharmacokinetics (ADME) of drug product (parent drug and its metabolities) has been studied and recorded showing plasma levels of both parent drug and metabolites.

4. Characterization of drug substance used in terms of its purity quality, identity, strength and stability.

After submission of IND application and on reviewing the data submitted therein, if there is no objection by the FDA within 30 days the work described in IND may begin. The processes of running clinical trials to qualify a drug for sale to the public has been classified by the FDA into three stages. These are referred to as Phase I, II and III. The post approval trials fall into a category known as Phase IV.

Phase-I:

After very extensive pre-clinical safety testing has indicated that the toxicity of the material is low enough to justify careful small scale clinical testing, the Phase-I trials begin. Phase-I represents the initial but most critical phase of development. Phase-I trials are usually very small involving as few as 4 to 10 subjects. Studies generally correspond to the first administration to humans.

The initial studies consists of administering a single dose of the test drug and closely observing the subject. If no adverse reaction occurs, the dose is increased progressively until a predetermined blood level is reached or toxicity supervenes. If no untoward effects result from single doses, short-term multiple does studies are performed. During Phase-I, these cautious small sample tests may employ gradually increasing sample sizes. The total number of subjects or patients in Phase-I is generally not more than 20 to 80. The sample commonly consists of healthy volunteers rather than patients, although either might be used.

The emphasis is upon safety of increasing doses, metabolism and pharmacologic action of the drug. These trials should emerge out with the information that decides the most appropriate dosing regimen to be employed in the further trials. The study identifies a dosing regimen having optimum efficacy and at the same time with minimum untoward effects. The additional information to be gathered from this study includes the pharmacokinetic profile of parent drug as well as its active metabolites. The kinetic profile includes determination of the metabolic fate, the site of metabolism, the enzymes involved degree of protein binding etc. The effect of food on absorption of oral dosage form is also studied in this phase. It is here in this phase the complete characterization of drugs pharmacokinetic/pharmacodynamic relationships is done.

As phase-I trials are performed on limited number of healthy volunteers, the information accumulated is not complete. It is therefore, further necessary to perform large scale clinical trials in relatively large number of patients suffering from the disease of interest. Especially, it is necessary to evaluate the pharmacokinetic parameters of drug as evidenced in large number of patients.

If in this series no serious safety effects are found, the investigator may continue to Phase-II trials. Just as for Phase-I, a complete outline of the experimental work planned must be or have been submitted. If within 30 days, the FDA makes no objection that would delay or cancel the proposed work the investigator may begin Phase-II.

Phase-II:

Phase-II trials emphasize both safety and efficacy and are well controlled. Usually, these are double blind, closely monitored and randomized. These trials are substantially larger, extensive and involve several hundred patients. The sample size (i.e. the number of patients) may vary with condition under study, but will commonly range from as few as 20 to as many as 150 to 200 or more. The information to be gathered during these trials includes the further details of dosing regimen, tolerability of drug in patient population and additional pharmacokinetic assessments.

Prior to efficacy evaluation *in-vitro* experiments should be conducted to determine which formulation provides the most uniform and complete availability. During the Phase-I, investigations more than one form might be evaluated for *in-vivo* availability to select the most promising for efficacy evaluation. If these steps have been taken, the investigator is relieved of the problems during Phase-II. However, he should be aware that any change in formulation may require re-evaluation for availability.

Several designs are used and the investigator shall consult statistician for deciding the design of studies. Usually, the following questions shall be considered while deciding the design of studies.

1. How many subjects should be involved ?

2. What controls should be used ?

3. What is the measure of effectiveness ?

4. What are the criteria for admission to the study ?

5. What happens if subjects drop out ?

6. How long should the study run ?

7. How can it be analysed when the data are in ?

8. Will the study answer the appropriate questions ?

Usually five different designs are used. These are as follows:

1. Placebo concurrent control:

Here in this design the test drug is compared with placebo. Two methods are used for this purpose viz. Parallel group trial and counter balanced cross-over trial. In parallel group trial patients are randomized to treatment with either drug or placebo. The study is double blind and outcome of treatment in patients with drug is compared with patients with placebo. In counter balanced cross-over trial, patients are randomized to a sequence of treatments. For example, patients are randomized to one of two sequences placebo-drug or drug-placebo. In this design since every patient receive both treatments, the outcomes can be compared in each patient.

2. Dose comparison concurrent control:

This design aims at studying the correlation between dose given and treatment outcome. The patients are randomized to receive one of the fixed doses of treatments. These studies may also include placebo group and active treatment group. Recently rather than randomizing patients to fixed doses; these are randomized to fixed plasma levels (ranges), but the study needs frequent monitoring of plasma levels and corresponding adjustments in dose which it practically somewhat difficult. The study provides more information about effect of different doses (plasma levels) on treatment outcome than single dose studies.

3. No treatment concurrent control:

These studies are performed rarely. Here neither placebo nor active treatment (standard) is involved. The patients are randomized to test treatment or no treatment and the objective measure of outcome are compared.

4. Active treatment concurrent control:

The patients are randomized to receive either test drug or standard drug (known to be active in the given clinical situation). The study may also include placebo and different doses of either of the drugs. Usually, these trials are aimed at establishing therapeutic equivalence of a test drug to the standard drug. Of course the final interpretation in this regard depends on satisfaction of the statistical criteria.

5. Historical control:

Here the outcome of the new drug treatment in a group of patients is compared with similar group of patients in the historical cohort. As the historical control data is usually collected from literature, one can't be sure that the patients in historical cohort are truely comparable to the patients receiving new drug. For this and many other reasons the historical control trials are generally considered inappropriate.

It should be remembered that Phase-II trials are not conclusive but are designed to establish different aspects of further trials that would be conducted with greatest likelihood of success. The limitations of Phase-II trials are as follows:

1. Subjects (patients) enrolled in these trials might be surprisingly different than the general population suffering with condition under study.

2. Patients enrolled are generally those with narrow range of severity of illness.

3. Patients taking concomitant medications or suffering with other diseases simultaneously are generally excluded from this study.

4. Sometimes the duration of trials is inadequate.

5. Sensitivity of outcome measures needs to be critically examined.

At the end of Phase-II, the investigator meets the appropriate review division (FDA), to discuss in details the acceptability of past studies, the design of further studies, and further development plan. In late Phase-II and early Phase-III, then, the definitive efficacy trials are performed. Such trials are rigorously performed experiments and requires great attention to their design, review of the designs and conduct. The investigators on submitting the protocols to FDA, may initiate further trials on receiving the comments from FDA. On receiving the protocols; the review division of FDA consisting of pharmacologist, chemist, clinical reviewers and statistical reviewers in consultation together decide whether the trial as designed is capable of answering all the questions asked or not. Non-compliance to this may form basis for imposing hold on these controlled trials. In addition the regulations in this behalf may also permit the imposition of hold on further studies if the protocol for investigation is clearly deficient in design to meet its stated objectives. The reviewers examine the following information provided in the protocols.

1. Inclusion and exclusion criteria.

2. Dosing regimens.

3. Methods and timing of collecting; safety and effectiveness data.

4. Duration of treatment.

5. Plans for maintenance of blind.

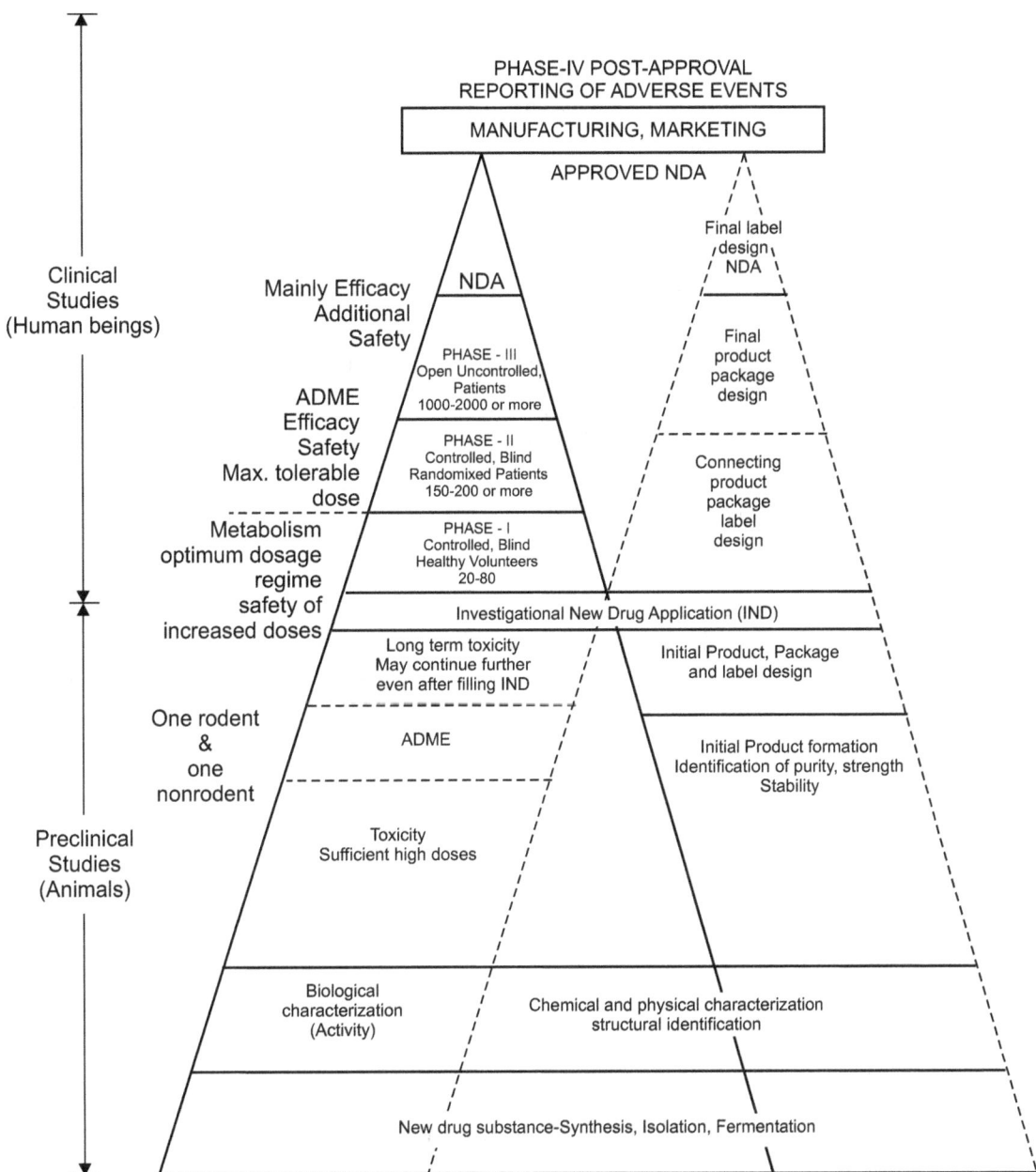

Fig. 2.1: Schematic representation of development of new a drug

6. Plans for recording and encouraging compliance with protocol.

7. Identification of the primary outcome variables and time of assessment.

8. Statistical and analytical plans.

9. Methods of randomization.

10. The primary populations to be included in the analysis.

11. Accounting of dropouts.

Phase-III:

On establishing effective dose range and confirming that no serious adverse reaction occur; large numbers of patients can be exposed to the drug. Thus, Phase-III of human assessment correspond to the larger trials.

Since by this stage of development the controlled trial data indicates that the test drug is effective; in Phase-III, data is obtained in open, uncontrolled trials. However, in this phase not only effectiveness trials but also the additional controlled trials may be performed to obtain information on safe use of drug. The investigator intends to collect information about safe and effective use of product according to the conditions of use that would be included in the proposed labelling. The number of patients to be exposed to the treatment should be typically in the range of 1000 to 2000 at least 300 or so who has received the drug at an appropriate dose for 6 to 12 months.

At the end of Phase-III trials; before submitting New Drug Application (NDA), it is necessary for the investigator to get the information (outcomes of trials) reviewed by Review division of FDA.

NDA Phase:

When investigator believes that a sufficient information regarding safety, effectiveness and composition of test drug have been generated to fulfill the statutory and regulatory requirements; it submits an NDA. The following information must be included in NDA.

1. All reports of studies indicating safety and effectiveness of test drug.

2. A list of components and composition of drug.

3. A full description of methods, facilities and controls used for manufacturing, processing and packaging of drug.

4. Samples of the drug.

5. Copies of labelling.

There are regulatory provisions to withhold approval to the application for the following reasons:

1. The application does not contain results of tests to show whether or not the drug is safe for the use recommended in the labelling.

2. The results show that the drug is unsafe or do not show that it is safe.

3. The methods, facilities and controls used for manufacturing, processing and packaging of such drug are inadequate to preserve its identity, strength, quality and purity.

4. There is insufficient information to determine whether drug is safe.

5. There is lack of substantial evidence that the drug will have the effect described in the proposed labelling.

If there are no deficiencies stated above, the application is to be approved within 180 days of the submission of the application. If any of the deficiencies exist the application is not approved within 180 days of its submission. If the application is accepted, the detailed review continues. After the division has reviewed the data submitted; the NDA will be presented to the relevant Advisory Committee. If the office director concludes that the application is approvable, a letter is sent to investigator indicating this is so. The letter may include requests for additional information and/or draft labelling for the product. Approvable letter means that the application contains sufficient information to conclude that the application can be approved soon and subsequently the FDA approves it.

Phase-IV (Post Approval):

Table 2.1: Phases of Clinical Investigation

Phase	Number of human subjects	Purpose
Phase-I	20-80	First administration to humans. To establish safety.
Phase-II	20-200	Administration to patients. To establish efficacy and dose.
Phase-III	300-2000	Larger number of patients, open, uncontrolled trials. To verify efficacy and detect-adverse effects.
Phase – IV	Therapeutic use in many patients	To obtain additional data.

Investigators of approved NDA's are required to submit reports of adverse events that occur during the marketing experience. The reports of adverse events which are serious and unexpected should be submitted within 15 days of the investigators receipt of information. In addition the investigators must review periodically the incidence of adverse events that are serious and expected. For the first three years the investigators have to report the adverse event data quarterly and thereafter annually.

Developing a promising chemical entity into a useful therapeutic tool through laboratory synthesis, pre-clinical and clinical trials is a complex process that needs huge expenditure and long period of time.

Chapter ... **3**

INTRODUCTION TO DOSAGE FORMS OF DRUGS

Dosage forms can be classified in various ways depending upon nature of formulation, route of administration, site of application, release pattern, release site, designing of formulation, sterility etc.

Depending on its sterile nature, it can be classified as sterile or non-sterile dosage form.

Sterile dosage forms are those dosage forms which are administered by other than oral/topical route, directly into internal body fluids such as parenteral, ophthalmic, implants and surgical powders and need to be free from any sort of contamination.

Non-sterile dosage forms are those dosage forms which are administered orally or applied topically on intact skin. In this case, sterilization is not required due to acidic nature of stomach and also it is not applied to broken skin or introduced into body fluids.

CLASSIFICATION OF DOSAGE FORMS OF DRUGS

1. NON-STERILE DOSAGE FORMS

(A) Solid Dosage Forms

(I) Powders:

    (a) Internal use:

        1. May be simple powders or compound powders.

        2. Bulk powders - effervescent powders or granules, non-effervescent-antacids, laxatives and dietary powders.

    (b) External use:

    Dusting powders, snuffs, insufflations, sprays, aerosols, dentifrices, tooth powders.

(II) Compressed Forms:

(a) Tablets:

    (i)   Oral - Dispersible tablets, Standard compressed tablets (CT), multiple CT (Layered tablets, Compressed coated tablets), Sustained release tablets, Enteric coated tablets, Sugar coated tablets, Chewable tablets, Film coated tablets

    (ii)   Lozenges (trouches)

    (iii)   Buccal

    (iv)   Dental cones

    (v)   Sublingual

    (vi)   Vaginal

    (vii)   Soluble

    (viii)   Hypodermic

    (ix)   Effervescent.

(III) Non-compressed Forms (Other solid dosage forms):

    (a)   Pills.

    (b)   Capsules – Soft capsules-oral, ointments, Hard capsules - oral.

    (c)   Cachets – Dry seal cachets, Wet seal cachets.

(B)   Semi-solid dosage forms

    (a)   Ointments – Oleoginous, water washable

    (b)   Creams

    (c)   Pastes

    (d)   Jellies

    (e)   Poultices

    (f)   Plasters

(C) Liquid dosage forms

(I) Monophasic:

    (a)   Internal use: Simple mixtures, solutions, draughts, linctuses, syrups, elixirs, drops.

    (b)   External use: Liniments, lotions, collodians, applications.

    (c)   Special use:

        (i)   Used in oral cavity   - Glycerites, throat paints, gargles, mouth washes, throat spray.

        (ii)   Other than oral cavity - Douches, enemas, ear drops, nasal drops, applications, inhalations, spays, aerosols.

(II) Biphasic:

    (a) Emulsions: (Liquid in liquid):

        (i)   o/w emulsion - Internal, external

        (ii)   w/o emulsion - Internal (rarely), External (mainly) - ointment, creams, pastes.

    (b) Suspensions - (solid in liquid):

        (i)   Internal

        (ii)   External.

(D) Gaseous dosage forms

    Aerosols, inhalants

2. STERILE DOSAGE FORMS

(I) Parenteral dosage forms

1. Small volume parenterals may consist of:

    (a)   Powder to be suspended in vehicle prior to its use.

    (b)   Powder to be solubilised in solvent prior to its use.

    (c)   Readymade suspensions.

    (d)   Readymade solutions.

    (e)   Emulsions.

2. Large Volume parenterals:

    (a)   Infusions.

(II) Ophthalmic dosage forms

    (a)   Eye drops: Solutions and suspensions

    (b)   Eye lotions

    (c)   Eye ointments

    (d)   Ocuserts.

(III) Implants

DRUG DELIVERY CONCEPT

Whenever drug is administered orally or by any other route, it gets absorbed into the circulatory system and then excreted through the kidney or may be excreted as metabolite (Fig. 3.1).

Drug may or may not be absorbed after administration as its absorption depends on number of physico-chemical and biological factors. The drug having different brand may differ in the drug response. The availability of drug at absorption site is its bioavailability. However, *it is the concentration of drug available in absorbable form* and not the drug available at biological site, governs the absorption rate.

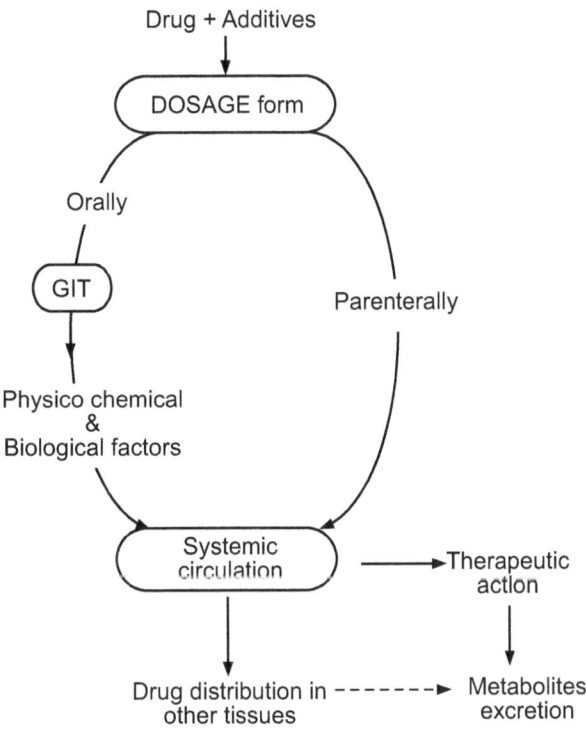

Fig. 3.1: Fate of drug after administration

DRUG DELIVERY SYSTEMS

NOVEL DRUG DELIVERY SYSTEMS

These are also referred to as 'Non-immediate Drug Delivery Systems' or Sustained Release Dosage Forms. The aim of formulating and designing such dosage forms is to prolong the action of drugs for longer periods than that achieved by conventional dosage forms such as tablets, capusles or ointments. These dosage forms release the drug to the biological system (i.e. human body) over a prolonged period of time thus reducing toxic manifestations due to over dosing, reduce the frequency of dosing and maintaining therapeutic concentration of drug in the body for better efficacy and bioavailability.

Novel Drug Delivery Systems can be classified broadly as follows:

1. Oral Sustained or Controlled Release Drug Delivery Systems.

2. Parenteral Controlled Release Drug Delivery Systems.

3. Occular Controlled Release Drug Delivery Systems (for eyes).

4. Intravaginal Controlled Release Drug Delivery Systems.

5. Intrauterine Controlled Release Drug Delivery Systems.

6. Magnetically controlled Drug Delivery Devices.

7. Transnasal Drug Delivery Systems.

8. Implantable Therapeutic Systems.

9. Transdermal Therapeutic Systems (for skin).

10. Microparticulate Drug Carriers such as Nanoparticles, Liposomes.

11. Pumps and implantable infusion systems.

12. Iontophoretic Devices.

Administration of drugs in conventional dosage forms except intravenous infusion at constant rate result see-saw fluctuations (peak and valley pattern) of drug concentrations in systematic circulation and body tissues. The magnitude of these fluctuations depends on the rates of absorption, distribution and elimination of drugs and the dosing interval or dosing frequency. This "peak and valley" pattern is more striking for drugs with a biological half-life of less than four hours, since prescribed dosing intervals are rarely less than four hours. On the other hand, a drug with a long half-life has the drawback that rapid termination of therapy is very difficult.

A well designed controlled release drug delivery system can significantly reduce the frequency of drug dosing and also maintain a more steady drug concentration in blood circulation and target tissues.

e.g. controlled release of a contraceptive drug.

Medroxy progesterone acetate from medicated vaginal rings.

CONCEPTS OF FORMULATION

As previously pointed out, it is always preferred to use inert substances, the number of which should be kept minimum, to convert pure drug into suitable dosage form.

Formulations:

While formulating a dosage form a drug is rarely prescribed alone. It is mostly combined with other non-medical adjuvants (Pharmaceutical aids). These adjuvants may serve varied functions. They may be the bases, fillers or diluents, vehicles, stabilisers, anti-oxidants, binders, lubricating agents, disintegrants, organoleptic additives i.e. colours, flavours and sweetening agents, buffers and tonicity agents. They may control and sustain the release medicament. A single drug may be given in the form of a liquid, a tablet, an injection or an ointment having different requirements of adjuvants. Choice of a proper dosage form and selection of an appropriate pharmaceutical aid is domain of pharmacist.

Table 3.1: Commonly used additives (Pharmaceutical aids)

Types of ingredients	Examples
Adsorbants	Bentonite, kaolin, magnesium carbonate, magnesium oxide.
	Powdered cellulose, activated charcoal.
Antioxidants	Ascorbic acid, butylated hydroxyl anisole, propyl gallate, sodium meta bisulphite, tocopherol, lecithin, gallic acid, thiourea, citric acid.
Buffers	Potassium meta phosphate, potassium phosphate, sodium acetate.
Chelating agents	Ethylene diamino tetra acetic acid (EDTA).
Preservatives Bactericides and bacteriostatics	Benzoic acid, sodium benzoate, methyl and propyl paraben, nipagin, nipasol, phenol, phenyl mercuric nitrate, cresol, chlorocresol, benzyl alcohol, **benzalkonium chloride**.
Colours	Certified and permitted food colours (green, red, yellow, orange) caramel, **amaranth**, indigo, ferric oxide, eosine, chlorophyll, cochincal alizarine, tartrazine.
Emulsifying agents	Acacia, sorbitan **mono-oleate**, polyoxyethylene stearate, triethanolamine oleate and stearate monovalent and divalent soaps.
Flavours	**Anise oil, cinnamon oil, cocoa, menthol, orange oil**, lemon oil, pepermint oil, vanillin.
Humectants	Glycerin, sorbital, polyethylene glycol.
Ointment bases	Paraffins, waxes, lanolin, PEG, polysorbate, Emulsion bases.
Solubilising agents	Tween 20, 40, 60, 80 polyethylene glycol – 400 triethanolamine oleate.
Solvents	Alcohol, glycerine, mineral oil, water, oleic acid, isopropyl alcohol.
Suppository bases	Cocoa butter, glycero gelatin, PEG (mixture).
Surface active agents	Sodium lauryl sulphate, polysorbate – 80 benzalkonium chloride.
Suspending agents	Agar, bentonite, C.M.C. sodium, tragacanth veegum.
Sweeteners	Aspartame, sacharin sodium, sucrose.
Tablet antiadherants	Magnesium stearate, talc.

Types of ingredients	Examples
Tablet binders	Acacia, gelatin, ethyl cellulose, methyl cellulose, sodium alginate, starch tragacanth.
Diluents, fillers	Micro-crystalline cellulose, lactose kaolin, mannitol, dicalcium phosphate.
Tablet coating agents	Corn starch, sodium alginate, effervescent base.
Tablet glidants	Colloidal silica, talc, corn starch.
Tablet lubricants	Calcium stearate, magnesium stearate, stearic acid.
Tablet polishing agents	Carnauba wax, white wax.
Tonocity agents	Dextrose, sodium chloride.
Vehicles	Acacia syrup, aromatic elixirs, orange syrup, mineral oil, sterile water, propylene glycol glycerin.

The type of formulation depends on various factors viz. nature of drug, mechanism of absorption, route of administration, dose, stability, side effects onset of action, economy, patient acceptance etc.

Solid dosage forms are preferred as it maintains dosage accuracy, stability, convenient to administer, easy to transport and store.

Solid dosage formulations cannot be preferred as

1. They may cause gastric irritation.
2. They may be hygroscopic or delequescent in nature.
3. They may have large dose.
4. If bulky difficult to swallow.
5. They may be difficult to convert in compact solid dosage form.
6. Few drug ingredients are in liquid form only.

Liquid dosage forms are prefered as:

1. Their absorption is very fast and give quick response.
2. They are easy to swallow.
3. Better patient complience.
4. Few drugs available in liquid form only.
5. Suitable for paediatric/geriatric preparations.

Limitations of liquid dosage forms:

1. Stability problems.
2. Dose inaccuracy.
3. Complicated formulations.

4.   Drug interaction in multiple drug formulations.

5.   Microbial contamination.

6.   Bitter or nauseous substances are not palatable.

7.   Storage problem.

8.   Breakage and packing problems.

9.   Sorption and leaching problem in packing.

10.   High packing and transportation cost.

Parentral dosage forms are preferred due to its immediate onset of action, dosage accuracy and when patient is not co-operative. It has limitation that the toxicity is very high, allergy if any, can not be checked immediately, self administration is not possible, technology is very costly and needs special environment for proper storage. It is also not acceptable to patient due to pain in administration. It is life saving dosage form and needs special precautions in manufacturing and its use.

DEVELOPMENT OF VARIOUS DOSAGE FORMS

Thus, one has to consider number of factors before deciding the proper dosage form. Mainly there are two types of drug delivery systems-conventional and novel drug delivery system.

Conventional drug delivery system includes tablets, capsules, ointments, solutions, suspensions, emulsions, colloids, parenterals, powders, granules etc.

Novel drug delivery includes transdermal products, lipozomes, ocuserts, implants, resealed erythrocytes, nanoparticles, niasomes, microspheres etc.

The details of the some of the conventional dosage forms, most frequently used, are given below for better understanding of these dosage forms.

SOLUTIONS

The solution is a homogeneous mixture obtained by dissolving solid or liquid or gases in another liquid. In this system, molecules of solute or dissolved substances are dispersed in the molecules of solvent. The solvent may be aqueous or non-aqueous.

Advantages of Solutions:

1.   It can be formulated for different routes of administration viz. oral use, introducing in the body cavities or for external use.

2.   It is easy for adjusting the dose by simple dilution particularly in case of children.

3.   It is very convenient for oral route in case swallowing is a problem.

4.   Sometimes it reduces the gastro-intestinal irritations e.g. potassium chloride.

5.   It is most convenient and acceptable dosage form to patients.

Disadvantages of Solutions:

1. Solutions are excellent growth media for bacteria and microbial contamination, if any, leads to spoiling of the preparation. The water used in the process should be handled with care as it is most common source of contamination. Equipment should be thoroughly cleaned before use. Environment and personnel should be considered for avoiding the contamination.

2. Some drugs are not stable in liquid form due to environmental effects or reaction between the ingredients used, during storage, which limits their use. e.g. antibiotics.

3. As these preparations occupies more volume than solid form and are packed in bottles, transportation becomes the main problem.

4. It is not economical as it is multidose preparation and many times dosage accuracy may not be maintained.

Classification:

1. **Aqueous solutions:** (a) Solutions: Simple solutions, Solution by chemical reaction, Solution by extraction.

   (b) Aromatic waters

   (c) Douches

   (d) Gargles

   (e) Mouth washes

   (f) Juices

   (g) Nasal solutions

   (h) Otic solution

2. **Other viscid aqueous solutions:** Syrups, mucilages, jellies etc.

3. **Non-aqueous solutions:** Collodions, elixirs, glycerines, inhalations, liniments, spirits, toothache drops.

AQUEOUS SOLUTIONS

Solutions may be classified on the basis of physical or chemical properties, method of preparation, use, physical state, number of ingredients used and particle size. e.g. aromatic waters, aqueous acid solutions etc.

Solutions:

A solution is a liquid preparation that contains one or more soluble chemical substances dissolved in water. These solutions exhibit specific therapeutic pattern and are meant for external or internal use. Solvents used are mostly polar or non-polar in nature. Polar solvents include water, hydrogen peroxide and non-polar solvents include vegetable oil, mineral oil, benzene etc.

Solutions are classified on the basis of method of preparation.

1.   Simple solutions: They are prepared by dissolving the solute in a suitable solvent. In addition, it may contain additives which helps in solubilizing or stabilising the active medicament.

e.g. Strong Iodine Solution, Iodine solution, Aqueous, Weak iodine solution, Liquid potassium permanganate, Calcium hydroxide topical solution, Sodium phosphate oral solution, Solutions for eye drops, Sodium chloride solution, Chlorinated soda surgical solution

Calcium Hydroxide Topical Solution: It contains Calcium hydroxide 140 mg in each 100 ml of water. The solution is prepared by shaking 3 g of calcium hydroxide with 100 ml cool and purified water. Excess amount of calcium hydroxide is allowed to settle down and supernatant liquid is filtered and used. The official solution is prepared at 25°C as excess temperature decreases the solubility.

As this solution reacts with carbon dioxide of atmosphere hence should be stored in well filled air tight container at 25°C.

Strong Iodine Solution:

It contains 4.5 to 5.5 g of iodine and 9.5 to 10.5 g of potassium iodide in 100 ml of water. It is prepared by dissolving 5 g of iodine in 100 ml of purified water containing 10 g of potassium iodide. Volume is adjusted by additional water to make one litre solution. A solution of iodides dissolve large quantities of iodine. Hence, potassium iodide is included in the preparation. Strong Iodine solution is thus, a solution of polyiodides in excess iodine.

It is used as anti-goitre drug with a dose of 0.3 ml/t.i.d.

Some antibiotics viz. vancomycin, cloxacillin, nafcillin are also used in solution form. These antibiotics are prepared as dry powders or granules in combination with suitable additives. Upon dissolving, pharmacist add appropriate amount of water. This solution is stable only for 14 days if stored in refrigerator.

2.   Solution by chemical reaction: It is prepared by reacting two or more solutes with each other in a suitable solvents.

e.g. Aluminium Sub-acetate Topical Solution: It contains aluminium sulphate 145 g, precipitated calcium carbonate 70 g, acetic acid 160 ml, cold water to 1000 ml.

Aluminium sulphate is dissolved in 1000 ml of cold water. Solution is filtered and precipitated calcium carbonate is added in several parts and mixture is set aside for 24 hours. Product is filtered and magma on the filter is washed till it measures 1000 ml. The 0.9 gm boric acid can be used to stabilise the product. The bicarbonate formed in the reaction is removed as carbon-dioxide. This solution is used in the solution of aluminium acetate in approximate 5% by weight of acetic acid in water.

Aluminium Acetate solution:

It contains glacial acetic acid 15 ml, aluminium subacetate topical solution 545 ml, water to make 1000 ml.

It is stabilised by adding 0.6% boric acid.

3. Solution by Extraction: Drugs or pharmaceuticals obtained from vegetable or animal sources are extracted using suitable solvents, generally water or water containing substances. They may be included in this class.

AROMATIC WATERS

Aromatic waters are saturated aqueous clear solutions of volatile oils or other aromatic or volatile substances. They are also known as **medicated water**. Aromatic water have odour and colour similar to volatile substances or drugs. They are free from foreign particles like smoke or turbidity. Some times an insoluble layer may be seen at the top which may be attributed to excess amount of water soluble drugs. The volatile oil used in making aromatic water is of pharmacopoeial standards.

Method of preparation:

Aromatic water may be prepared by the following methods:

(a) **Distillation:** It is universal method, but it is very costly or complicated. This is the reason why it is only used to prepare very few preparations. e.g. Rose Water NF and Orange flower water NF.

(b) **Solution Method:** Volatile oil or volatile substance is agitated with sufficient water to make one litre of solution. This solution is kept for 12 hours and then filtered through the wetted filter paper to prevent the excess passage of oil into the filtrate and to eliminate adsorption of dissolved aromatics.

(c) **Alternate solution method:** It is the most commonly used method for the preparation of aromatic water. The volatile substance is thoroughly mixed with an inert substance like talc or purified siliceous earth and water is added and agitated for some time. The solution is filtered until a clear filterate is obtained.

The volatile substance is adsorbed by the inert agent, which also acts as clearifier as the undissolved materials remain adsorbed and does not pass through the filter.

Official Preparations:

1. Cinnamon water BP

2. Peppermint water BP

3. Chloroform water (single strength) BP

4. Concentrated Dill water BP

5. Concentrated Peppermint water BP

6. Concentrated Cinnamon water BP.

GLYCERINES

They are also known as Glycerites. Glycerites are viscous mixtures or solutions of medicated or non-medicated preparations which contains not less than 50% by weight of glycerine. These preparations have jelly like consistency used in their original form as medicinal agents while other glycerites are used to prepare aqueous and alcoholic dilution of substances which are not easily soluble in water or alcohol.

Preparations:

Phenol Glycerine BPC:

    Phenol   -   160 g

    Glycerine - 840 g

    Phenol is dissolved in the glycerine.

Phenol Ear Drops BPC:

    Phenol   40 ml

    Glycerine q.s.   100 ml

Mix phenol glycerine with glycerine. Water should not be added to this preparation because it reacts with phenol to produce a caustic preparation and consequently damaging the area of application.

Some aqueous and non-aqueous preparations are used to remove the wax from ear. These preparations contain some chemicals such as benzocaine, chlorbutol, p-dichlorobenzene and turpentine, olive oil, dioctyl sodium sulfosuccinate or triethanolamine polypeptide oleatecondensate etc.

e.g. Sodium Bicarbonate Ear Drops BPC:

    Sodium bicarbonate - 5 g

    Glycerine   - 30 ml

    Purified water q.s.   - 100 ml

In this preparation, one additive is glycerine but this preparation is not of glycerites category. Glycerites are hygroscopic and should be stored in tightly closed containers.

Official Glycerites:

Borax Glycerine	–	Bacteriostatic
Starch Glycerines	–	Emollient base
Tannic acid glycerine	–	Antiulcer preparation
Phenol glycerine	–	As paint in mouth ulcer and tonsillitis
Ichthammol glycerine	–	For lymphanblenitis and thrombo phlebitis.

SYRUPS

A syrup is concentrated or nearly saturated aqueous solutions of sugar such as sucrose in water or other aqueous liquid. In addition to sucrose some other polyols such as glycerine, dextrose, sorbitol may be incorporated to increase the solubility of added substances or retard the crystallisation of sucrose.

Classification:

Simple syrup: When sucrose is dissolved in the purified water, the preparation is known as syrup or simple syrup. A concentrated syrup contains 85% w/v or 65% w/w sucrose in purified water with a specific gravity of 1.30. The higher sugar content gives syrups a moderately high viscosity and have a high specific gravity.

Medicated syrup: Aqueous saturated solution of sugar which contains a medicinal substance is known as medicated syrup.

Flavoured syrup: A flavoured syrup is one which, usually does not contain medicinal substance but have various aromatic or pleasantly flavoured substances. It is used as a vehicle or flavour for prescriptions.

Invert syrup: According to BPC, invert syrup is prepared by hydrolysing sucrose with hydrochloric acid and the solution is neutralised with calcium or sodium carbonate. Invert syrup contains 66.7% w/w solution of sucrose. When it is mixed with suitable proportions with syrup, it prevents the decomposition of crystals of sucrose during storage. The levulose formed during inversion is more sweeter than sucrose. The relative sweetening of levulose, sucrose and dextrose is in the ratio 173 : 100 : 74. The invert sugar is 1.23 times sweet as sucrose. The levulose is formed during the hydrolysis and the colour of the solution is darkened. It is sensitive to heat and darken very fast particularly, when it is in solution form.

Functions of syrup:

1. As a vehicle.
2. Sweetening agent.
3. Masking of bitter taste e.g. Glycyrrhiza syrup.
4. Masking the saline taste e.g. Cherry syrup, raspberry syrup.

5. As an anti-oxidant.

6. As a preservative.

7. As a flavouring agent.

8. As a demulcent and soothing agent.

9. Medicinal preparations e.g. chlorpheniramine maleate, ephedrine sulphate syrup.

Categories of drugs used in syrup form:

1. Antibiotics

2. Antitussive

3. Antihistaminics

4. Sedatives

5. Vitamins

6. Alkaloids

7. Analgesics/Antipyretics.

Method of preparation:

Syrups may be prepared by any of the following methods:

1. Agitation: Sugar with water is agitated in a suitable container to produce an odourless, colourless, viscous syrup. This is used to prepare syrups containing thermolabile or volatile substances. As sugar dissolve and saturation takes place, the dissolution rate and concentration gradient decreases. Thus, the agitation is a slow process.

2. Agitation with heat: By this method, the solution of sugar in water produces a pale yellow coloured viscous syrup because the solution of sucrose is hydrolysed to dextrose and fructose in presence of heat. With excessive heat the sweet taste is destroyed and dark brown liquid results. This method is not suitable for the preparation of syrup containing a thermolabile or volatile ingredient.

3. Percolation: It is an extraction process in which the active contents are dissolved from powdered or granulated drug packed in a column and the extract is obtained by the suitable solvents.

(a) Percolator is a cylindrical or tapered vessel with a lower outlet having a controlled flow. It is made up of glass or stainless steel.

(b) Powdered drug: It is packed in the percolator which has a layer of loosely packed cotton covering the lower outlet, to which suitable solvent is added.

When all the sucrose is dissolved the required liquid is added to the percolator to remove the syrup from the cotton into percolate. It also helps in adjusting the final volume.

Official preparations:

Non-medicated syrups:

Simple syrup IP	Orange syrup IP
Lemon syrup IP	Tolu syrup IP

Medicated Syrups:

Paracetamol syrup	125 mg/5 ml
Piprazine citrate syrup	500 mg/5ml
Psudoephedrine syrup	IP 30 mg/5ml
Promethazine hydrochloride syrup	IP 5 mg/5ml
Ipecac syrup	21 mg/15 ml
Guifensin syrup	100 mg/5 ml
Ferrous sulphate syrup	90 mg/10 ml

ELIXIRS

Elixirs are clear, pleasantly flavoured sweetened hydro-alcoholic liquids intended for oral use. Due to its hydroalcoholic nature, they can maintain water soluble as well as alcohol soluble ingredients in solution. This is not possible in aqueous syrups. They are also more stable and simple to prepare than syrups. Elixirs are less sweet and less viscous than syrup and hence not better in masking the taste of bitter drug.

Usually, they are used as flavouring agent or as a vehicle in medicinal preparations. The main ingredients in elixirs are alcohol and water Alcoholic content varies from 5-40%. The other ingredients used are glycerine, sorbitol, propylene glycol, flavouring agent, preservatives and syrup. Medicaments may or may not be present. Elixirs containing 10-12% of alcohol are stable and do not require addition of any preservative.

Classification:

It may be classified as per alcohol content or presence of medicinal substances.

(A) Classification based on alcohol content of the preparation:

(i)   Low alcoholic elixirs: It consists of 8-10% of alcohol.

(ii) High alcoholic elixirs: It consists of 75-80% of alcohol. By mixing of appropriate volume of two elixirs, an alcoholic content, sufficient to dissolve the drug, can be obtained.

(B) Classification based on presence of medicinal substances:

(i)   Non-medicated elixirs: Elixirs which does not contain any therapeutic compound are included in this category. They are used as a vehicle, flavouring agents or preservative in the formulations.

(ii) Medicated elixirs: Elixirs containing therapeutically active compounds are known as medicinal elixirs. e.g. Phenobarbital elixirs.

Additives used in Elixirs:

1. **Chemical stabilisers:** pH stabilisers, sequestering agents. e.g. EDTA.

2. **Colouring agent:** Amaranth, compound tartrazine, greens and tartrazine.

3. **Flavouring agents:** Black current syrup, conc. raspberry, lemon spirit, compound orange spirit.

4. **Sweetening agent:** Syrup, Glycerol, Sorbitol solution, Invert syrup, Sodium saccharine.

5. **Preservatives:** Ethanol, propylene glycol, glycerol, syrup, methyl paraben, propyl paraben, benzoic acid, double strength chloroform water.

Categories of drugs used in Elixirs:

Antibiotics, Antihistaminic, Sedatives, Expectorant etc.

Method of preparation:

They are prepared by simple agitation or by mixing of liquid ingredients together. It is advisable that all the ingredients soluble in water should be dissolved in water and then the other ingredients soluble in alcohol be dissolved in alcohol so as to have a homogeneous mixture. Then add aqueous solution to alcoholic mixture so as to have maximum alcoholic strength which aids in keeping alcohol soluble ingredients in the system else the separation may occur. Once these two solutions are mixed completely, make up the volume with the vehicle. Solution may appear turbid due to presence of some of the aromatic oil separated from the system, due to decrease in alcoholic concentration. In such case, keep the preparation aside for prescribed number of hours so that hydroalcoholic solvents becomes saturated and oil globules will coalesce and can be removed by filteration. Addition of talc to the solution helps in removing these oil globules. However, excess quantity of filter aid should not be used as it may adsorb the colour and oil present in the system.

Official preparations:

Ephedrine elixir, BPC

Dexamethasone elixir USP

Aromatic elixir USP

Benzaldehyde elixir

Terpine hydrate elixir

Paracetamol elixir

Phenobarbitone elixir.

EMULSIONS

When two immiscible liquids are mechanically agitated both the phases are converted into droplets and are distributed through out the system. When the agitation is stopped these droplets quickly coalesces and two liquids are again separated. For stabilising this product third compound is added, known as emulsifier.

An emulsion is a heterogeneous liquid preparation in which two immiscible phases viz. Internal phase or dispersed phase (converted into globules by mechanical agitation) and external phase or continuous phase (in which internal phase is dispersed) are present.

The system of two immiscible liquids is stabilised by the presence of an emulgent or emulsifying agent. The globule diameter of the dispersed phase generally extends from 0.1 to 10 nm, smallest diameter of globule is 0.01 nm and as large as 100 nm. Spherical droplets of internal phase in close pack gives monodisperse and internal phase can not accommodate more than 74% of the total volume of an emulsion. However, if these droplets are not of same size then it can exceed this limit.

Emulsifiers are responsible for stabilising the globules of internal phase and depending upon their structure may be described as molecules of both lipophillic and hydrophilic portion and hence this group is known as amphiphilic.

Classification:

Emulsions are classified based on the type of preparation or the way they are used.

Broadly, it is classified in two categories, Oil in Water (o/w) and Water in Oil (o/w). In oil in water type of emulsion, oil is in dispersed phase and water in continuous phase while reverse is the case in water in oil type of emulsion. Occasionally, the one form of the emulsion is changed in to other and this phenomenon is termed as *phase inversion*. This additional types of emulsion oil in water in oil (o/w/o) or water in oil in water (w/o/w) are classified as multiple emulsion. They also have tendency to revert but results in simple emulsion. Thus, generally w/o/w emulsion gives an oil in water emulsion.

The radius of emulsion globules in an opaque, usually white emulsion ranges from 0.25-10 micron. Dispersed particles with diameter less than $1/4^{th}$ wave length of visible light (> 120 nm) do not refract light and hence appear transparent to us. They are known as microemulsions or micellar emulsion. The globule size lies in the range from 10-75 nm.

They can also be classified as,

1. Cosmetic emulsions: Creams.
2. Pharmaceutical emulsions:
   (a) Oral emulsions,
   (b) Topical emulsions,
   (c) Parenteral emulsions.

Priorities for the dosage form:

1. Many drugs having objectionable odour or taste can be made more palatable in this form. e.g. oil soluble drugs like vitamins, oil based laxatives, high fat nutrients etc.

2. Most of the drugs are absorbed in the emulsion form only. e.g. insulin, heparin etc.

3. Patient acceptance for topical application is improved as it is easy to apply and easy to wash and has higher degree of elegance.

4. Formulator has control over viscosity, appearance, feeling after application of cosmetic or external application.

5. Thixotropic emulsions helps in the process of penetration to the skin and gives faster absorption.

6. Lipids in emulsion form are more convenient for I.V. administration.

7. Prolonged drug action is obtained by altering the bioavailability, e.g. w/o emulsions helps to disperse water soluble antigenic material in oil for I.V. depot injections.

8. Solubility of drugs is enhanced in this dosage form and results in improved absorption.

9. Most of the drugs which are not stable in aqueous solutions but are required in solution form for its therapeutic effect, can be given in this dosage form.

10. Emulsions are more economical as compared to costly lipids and its solvents meant for external use can be diluted with water maintaining the efficacy and behaviour of the preparation.

Identification tests:

Type of emulsion can be identified in various ways. The tests used are as follows:

1. Dilution Test (miscibility): It is based on the principle that addition of continuous phase will not disturb the system but adding internal phase results in breaking of emulsion. Oil in water type of emulsion can be diluted with water and water in oil emulsion by oil without any significant change.

2. Dye Test (staining): Water soluble dye like amaranth when added to o/w emulsion, as oil is in the dispersed phase it will appear as colourless and water will acquire the colour and if a drop of this solution is observed under the microscope disperse phase will be colourless with coloured background of external phase.

Instead if oil soluble dye like Sudan III or scarlet red is added to o/w emulsion, in background will be colourless with coloured spots of dispersed phase. This test may fail if ionic emulsifiers are used in the preparation.

3. Cobalt-chloride filter paper: Filter paper impregnated with cobalt-chloride solution and dried, appears to be blue but when it is dipped in o/w emulsion, it changes to pink. This test may fail if emulsion is unstable or breaks in presence of electrolyte.

4. Fluorescence Test: Many oil produce florescence in presence of UV light. Oil in water emulsion exhibits spotty appearance while in case of w/o emulsion entire field fluorescences. This test is not always applicable.

5. Conductivity: This test is based on the fact that electric current passes through water. Hence, if a circuit is made and current is passed through the emulsion, light will glow only if water is in external phase due to presence of ionic species in water. This test is not applicable for non-ionic o/w emulsions.

Emulsifying agents:

Substances which lowers the interfacial tension and form a film at an interface can function as an emulsifying agent. The effectiveness of these agents depends on chemical structure, concentration, solubility, physical properties, pH and electrostatic effects.

CLASSIFICATION OF EMULGENTS

1. Hydrocolloids:

    (a) Natural:

        (i)   Vegetable : Acacia, tragacanth, sodium alginate, starch, chondrus, pectin, guar gum, agar etc.

        (ii)   Animals : Gelatin, casein, wool fat, bees wax, egg yolk.

        (iii) Minerals : Bentonite, veegum etc.

    (b) Inorganic:

        Colloidal alumina

        Milk of magnesia

        Magnesium oxide

        Magnesium trisilicate.

    (c) Synthetic:

        Carbapol

        Colloidal silicon dioxide

    (d) Semisynthetic:

        Methyl cellulose

        Sodium carboxy methyl cellulose

        Hydroxy methyl cellulose

        Microcrystalline cellulose

2. Surfectants:

(a) Anionic Group:

(i)	Carboxylic acid	:	Soap, lactylates, polypeptide condensate.
(ii)	Sulphuric acid esters	:	Sulphurated monoglycerides alkyl sulphates.
(iii)	Alkyl and aryl sulphonates	:	Dodecyl benzene sulfonate.
(iv)	Phosphoric acid esters	:	Trioloyl phosphate.
(v)	Hemisters	:	Sulfosuccinate.
(vi)	Substituted alkyl amides	:	Sarcosinates taurates.

(b) Cationic Group:

Amines	:	Alkoxyalkyl amines.
Quaternaries	:	Benzalkonium chloride.

(c) Amphoteric Group:

Ammonium carboxylate	:	N alkyl amino acids.
Ammonium phosphate	:	Lecithin.

(d) Non-ionic Group:

(i)	Polyalkoxy ethers	:	Polyoxyethylene alkyl/aryl ethers. Polyoxyethylene Polyoxypropylene block polymer.
(ii)	Polyalkoxyesters	:	Polyoxyethylene fatty acid esters. Polyoxyethylene sorbitan acid esters.
(iii)	Polyalkoxyamide	:	Sorbitan esters Glyceryl esters Sucrose esters.
(iv)	Fatty alcohol	:	Lauryl alcohol.

Formation of Emulsion:

Emulsion formation requires breaking up of the internal phase into droplets and then immediately stabilising them in the external phase so as to avoid coalescence. In laboratory this can be achieved using mortar and pestle.

Laboratory methods:

1. **Wet gum method:** In this method, two parts of water and one part of acacia is triturated using mortar and pestle until a mucilage is forrned and oil is added

droply with continuous stirring until a primary emulsion is formed. Other ingredients and additives are then added and volume is adjusted with external phase.

2. **Dry gum method:** This method is also known as continuous method. A primary emulsion of the fixed oil, water and acacia (4 : 2 : 1) is prepared as follows:

    The oil is added to acacia and the mixture is triturated until the powder is distributed uniformly throughout the oil and the water is added at once with continuous titurating to form the primary emulsion. Remaining additives are then mixed and volume is adjusted with external phase.

3. **Bottle method:** The ratio of oil, water and acacia is 3 : 2 : 1 or 2 : 1 : 1. This is a modification of above methods. In this method, oil is added to the acacia in a bottle and water at once and bottle is shaken vigorously until emulsion is formed.

4. **Nascent soap method:** A soap is formed by mixing relatively equal volume of an oil and aqueous solution containing a sufficient amount of alkali. The soap thus formed acts as an emulsifying agent.

Industrial methods utilise the same principle, but using mechanical stirrers, homoginizers, colloid mill, ultrasonifier like equipment to deal with large volume and to have droplet break-up and complete emulsification.

Stability of Emulsion:

Creaming, aggregation and coalescence and inversions are the instability factors involved in the stability of an emulsion. When suspended particle is moved upward or downward creaming occurs. It depends on the specific gravity of the phases. Large particles have more tendency to form cream due to its higher sedimentation rate. Thus, formation of larger aggregates by coalescence, accelerate creaming.

If creaming is formed without any aggregation, the emulsion can be reconstituted by shaking or mixing.

In coalescence emulsified globules are aggregated to each other and form a larger particle. This tendency to form aggregates of large particles is termed as coalescence.

The major factor preventing coalescence is mechanical strength of interfacial barrier. This is true for o/w system containing non-ionic surfactant and for w/o emulsion in which electrical effect are negligible. Formation of a thick interfacial film is essential for minimal coalescence.

Inversion is a process in which conversion of one type of emulsion occurs into other due to change in physico-chemical parameters of the system. Under the controlled condition this results into stable emulsions else it gives phase separation.

Presence of light, air, contaminating microbes can adversely affect the stability of an emulsion. Appropriate steps should be taken while making or packing the product to minimise possible hazards to stability. Many molds, yeast and bacteria decompose the emulgents and cause disruption of the system. It also adversely affects the efficacy of the product.

Combination of methyl and propyl parabens are frequently used to protect the system. Alcohol (12 to 15%) of external phase is frequently added to orally used emulsion.

SUSPENSIONS

Suspensions are heterogeneous system consisting of finely divided insoluble material dispersed in a liquid medium. It consists of continuous or external phase, generally a liquid or semisolid and internal phase or dispersed phase, which is solid insoluble in continuous phase.

The particle size of dispersed phase varies in the range of 1 to 100 microns. It is generally a powder mixture containing drug along with suitable suspending and dispersing agents which upon dilution and agitation with the required quantity of vehicle, gives a suspension ready to use. If it can not withstand for extended period for its efficacy, then it is supplied as dry powder mixture to be suspended prior to its use.

Need for Suspension:

Suspensions are required due to many reasons. Many drugs are not stable in solution form are suspended to maintain the chemical stability and its efficacy. Many times it is desired to have controlled release effects of soluble drugs which can be modified in suspension dosage form. Drugs having solubility problems can be formulated using biphasic liquid dosage form.

Patient acceptance is also affected due to bitter or nauseating taste of most of the drugs and these drugs can be converted into insoluble form and then converted in a suspeuition. It has also added advantage of liquid dosage form such as ease of swallowing liquid, convenience in adjusting unusual large doses, safety and convenience of liquid dosage form in making paediatric formulations.

Desired Qualities:

It is always desired that all dosage forms should maintain ellegancy and therapeutic effect through out the shelf life. The same is applicable to suspension along with few additional features due to its typical system.

1. As it is a biphasic system, there is always tendency of settling of dispersed phase and ideal suspension should not create any problem in redistributing the dispersed system by shaking the container.

2. It should maintain the particle size during its shelf life as it causes problem in homogeneity and dosage accuracy of the suspension.

3. The dispersed particle should remain free and should not have particle-particle interaction. This type of preparation is also known as monodispersed suspension.

4. Suspension should not have any problem for its withdrawal from the container. It should maintain its flow properties.

5. It should not be affected during the process of sterilisation, which may be required in parentral preparation.

6. Parentral products should not have problems in syringibility and in case of eye drops it should not block the eye dropper.

7. It should remain free from microbial growth and should be stable at room temperature.

8. It should be compatible with excipients or additives used within the system.

Suspension Parameters for stability:

1. Particle size: Particle size plays an important role in making stable suspension. Hence, small particle size is preferred to have proper uniformity and desired flow properties in the suspension.

2. Surface area: Surface area is also equally important in the formulation of suspension and is related with the particle size. Reducing the particle size, it can be increased and hence surface free energy is also increased.

W = Y* A. According to this mathematical expression surface free energy (w) is increased by the increase in surface area (A) and particle-particle interaction increases due to sedimentation process. Hence, suitable particle size is required for making a stable emulsion. Y is interfacial tension in between two phases.

The other way of having stable suspension is reducing this interfacial tension. The surface free energy can be reduced by using wetting agents which is responsible for reducing the interfacial tension due to its addition in between two phases.

3. Sedimentation: Rate of sedimentation of particle depends on the size of the particle in the suspension. It can be determined using Stoke's law.

$$V = \frac{2r\ (\sigma_s - \sigma_1)\ g}{g_n} = \frac{D\ (\sigma_s - \sigma_1)\ g}{18\ n}$$

Where, V = velocity of sedimentation in cm/sec

r = particle radius

D = particle diameter in cm

σ_s = density of dispersed particle (g/ml)

σ_1 = density of continuous phase (g/ml)

n = viscosity of the medium in poises (g cm sec.)

The Stoke's law states that rate of settling is directly proportional to diameter of the particle and inversely proportional to the viscosity. The Stoke's equation can not be applied directly to pharmaceutical suspensions, but still the basic concept of this equation gives a valid indication of factors concerned to particle suspended and the way to accommodate them properly in the formulation.

4.   Surface Potential: Dispersed fine particles of powder have electric charge on the surface, therefore more particles are attracting or repel to each other. Dispersed particle are surrounded by two charged layers.

(a)   Stationary layer

(b)   Diffusible layer.

The difference in potential on stationary layer and diffusible layer are known as **zeta potential**. When zeta potential is high, particles repel from each other and suspension is deflocculated.

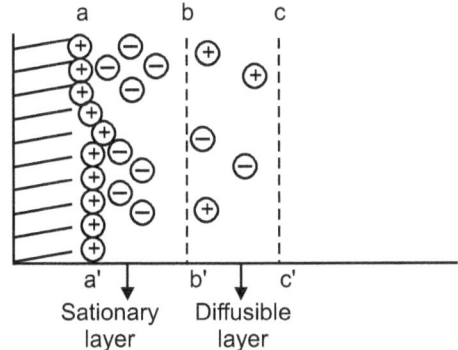

Fig. 3.2: Particles behaviour in suspension

5.   Cementation or caking of suspension: Particles of the suspension are aggregated and form indispersible solids which are difficult to redistribute even after shaking are called caking or cementation of suspension.

Types of Suspensions:

Suspensions are mainly of two types and dependent on sedimentation rate of particles.

1.   Flocculated suspensions.

2.   Deflooculated suspensions.

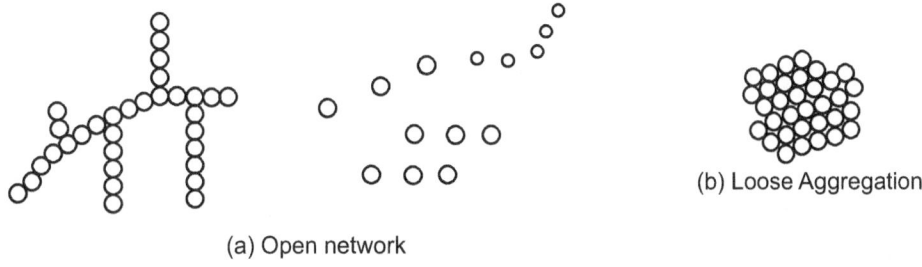

(a) Open network

(b) Loose Aggregation

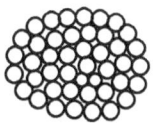

(c) Closed Aggregates

Fig. 3.3: Types of suspensions

1. Flocculated Suspension:

In flocculated suspension, the individual particles are in open network (Fig. 3.3 (a)) or loose aggregation between the particle - particle (Fig. 3.3 (b)). As aggregates are sedimenting together, sedimentation rate is very high and as they are loosely held together, redisperse very easily, just by shaking the container.

2. Deflocculated Suspension:

In this type of suspension the dispersible particle has separate entities. Sedimentation rate is very slow but the closed aggregation is formed (Fig. No. 3.3 (c)) and difficult to redistribute, even after shaking the container.

Table 3.2: Difference between Flocculated and Deflocculated Suspension

Flocculated System	Deflocculated System
1. Particles form loose aggregation called flocs	1. Particles exists as separate entities.
2. Formation of sediment is fast.	2. Formation of sediment is slow.
3. Rate of sedimentation is very high.	3. Rate of sedimentation is very slow.
4. No cake formation.	4. Hard cake is formed.
5. Sediment is redispersed uniformly by shaking the container and accuracy of dose is maintained.	5. Redispersion is not possible even after shaking and dosage accuracy cannot be maintained.
6. Some flocs stick to wall of the container.	6. No such sticking is found.
7. Suspension is not pleasant because two separate layers, one of supernatant clear continuous phase and other sedimented dispersed phase is clearly visible as particles settle down in flocs.	7. Product is elegant as it is through out turbid and hence, appears similar, due to settling of indivdiual particles in the medium and some still floating in the system.

Formulation Additives:

There are various additives required to form a stable suspension and their selection mainly depends on the type of suspension one want to formulate. The additives frequently used are as follows:

(I) Flocculating Agents:

Addition of surfactant to the system results in the proper distribution of particles in the vehicle as it reduces the interfacial tension between the dispersed and continuous phase. e.g. sodium lauryl sulphate, tweens, spans, carbowax, protective colloids etc.

(II) Suspending Agents:

Suspending agents or thickening agents used to stabilise the suspension are hydrophobic colloids. These substances form colloidal dispersion with water due to its affinity with both the phases.

There are various types of suspending agents and used according to the desired formulation properties.

1.   Polysaccharides:

   (a)   Natural – Acacia, Tragacanth, Starch, Sodium alginate, etc.

   (b)   Synthetic – Methyl cellulose, Hydroxy methyl cellulose, Sodium carboxy methyl cellulose, microcrystalline cellulose.

2.   Inorganic agents:

   (a)   Clays – Bentonite, Hectorite, Aluminium magnesium silicate.

   (b)   Aluminium hydroxide.

3.   Synthetic compounds:

   (a)   Carbomer (carboxy vinyl polymer).

   (b)   Colloidal silicon dioxide.

(III) Wetting Agents:

During the formulation of suspension complete wetting of solid is required so that all the particles can be suspended in the system. It depends on the contact angle of the particle with the vehicle. The particle may be wetted completely or partially or may float on the surface depending on its nature. As vehicle is mostly aqueous in nature, hydrophobic material floats on the surface and hydrophilic material dragged in the vehicle.

From formulation point of view, one has to deal with the particle which is not readily wetted by the vehicle is mainly due to presence of air in between particle and vehicle. This air can be replaced using wetting agent which has affinity for both, vehicle and hydrophobic material. Hydrophilic polymers like sodium carboxy methyl cellulose and other material like bentonite, colloidal silica, and aluminium magnesium silicate are used for this purpose. It also has thickening effect and helps in improving the flow properties as per requirement. Alcohol, glycerine span 20, span 40 can also used for aiding the penetration of vehicle to powder mass. These substances help in improving the wettability of solid particle are termed as wetting agents. They are basically surfactant having HLB value in the range of 7 to 9. It should be used in quantity sufficient to give the desired effect as excess amount may change the organoleptic properties.

(IV) Dispersing Agents:

For stable suspension, it is desired that each particle should remain dispersed. The surface energy of individual particle is not sufficient to separate the particle and hence, they interact to form large particles.

To overcome this type of difficulty dispersing agents are used. They have ability to increase the zeta potential and thus are responsible for avoiding the particle interactions e.g. Darvans, Daxads, Maraspheres etc.

(V) Preservatives:

The presence of suspending agent and medicaments may promote the growth of micro-organisms due to their presence in the atmosphere. Hence, to safeguard preparations, it is necessary to incorporate preservatives in the suspension which inhibits or protect the preparation from the microbial growth. e g. Benzoic acid, sodium benzoate, methyl paraben, propyl paraben etc.

(VI) Organoleptic Additives:

To have patient acceptance, the colour, flavour and taste of the preparation is improved by adding the suitable additives. The bitter taste can be overcome by adding sweetening agents such as syrup or coating the particle with suitable polymers and then suspending it. The fruit flavours can be used for suspension meant for internal use and cosmetic flavours for external preparations. The proper match between the colour and flavour should be managed so as to have better elegance and patient acceptance.

General method of Preparation:

1.   Transfer the previously milled drug and excipients in the clean container. All ingredients should be in fine powdered form as particle size plays an important role in the stable suspension.

2.   Mix all the additives along with drug in mortar to have a homogeneous mass. This is important specifically in case of potent medicaments where amount of drug to be handled is very small.

3.   Add the vehicle slowly with proper trituration sufficient to form smooth paste. This is required to have complete wettability and thorough mixing of all the ingredients.

4.   Volatile materials or insoluble materials are mixed with or without vehicle.

5.   The paste is further diluted with vehicle in geometric dilution until pourable.

6.   If any foreign particles are present same can be removed using appropriate aid or passing through muslin cloth.

7.   Add other volatile substances, diluted previously if required, preferably in the same vehicle.

8.   Add any liquid ingredient if remaining, and mix well.

9.   Rinse the mortar and pestle with vehicle and add to the preparation.

10. Adjust the final volume as per requirement and shake thoroughly.

This preparation can further be passed through homogeniser to have better mixing. For industrial preparations, tanks fitted with stirrers or turbine impellers can be used. Then with the use of colloidal mill or homogenisers proper mixing can be achieved.

Official Preparations:

Examples of Oral Suspensions (O.S.)

1. **Antacids:**	Aluminium hydroxide O.S. USP/IP	
	Magaldrate O.S.	USP/IP 80 mg/5 ml
	Milk of Magnesia USP/IP	
2. **Analgesic preparations:**	Acetaminophen O.S.	USP 100 mg/ml
	Paracetamol O.S.	IP 125 mg/5 ml
3. **Antiamoebic/Anthelmentics:**	Thiabendazole O.S.	500 mg/5 ml
	Metronidazole Benzoate O.S.	IP 100 mg/5 ml
	Furazolidone O.S.	IP
4. **Antiboitics:**	Chloramphenicol Palmitate O.S.	USP 150 mg/ml
		IP 125 mg/5 ml
	Chloroquine Suspension	IP 50 mg/5 ml
	Cloxacillin Sodium O.S.	IP 125 mg/5 ml
	Oxytetracycline Calcium O.S.	125 mg/ml (syrup)
		100 mg/ml (drops)
	Tetracycline O.S.	125 mg/5 ml
	Erythromycin estolate O.S.	125 mg/5 ml
5. **Antibacterial (other than antibiotics) preparations**	Nitrofurantoin O.S.	25 mg/5 ml
	Sulphamethoxazole O.S.	500 mg/5 ml
	Sulphamethoxazole with	200 mg/5 ml
	Trimethoprim	40 mg/5 ml
6. **Antiflatulent**	Semithicone O.S.	40 mg/0.6 ml
7. **Antifungal preparations**	Mycostatin O.S.	100,000 unit/ml
	Griseofluvin O.S.	125 mg/ml

8.	Antimalerial preparations	Quinine sulphate O.S.	110 mg/5 ml
9.	Antospamodic	Decyclomine HCl O.S.	IP 10 mg/5 ml
10.	Antipsychotic preparations	Triflupromazine O.S.	50 mg/5ml
		Haloperidol O.S.	1 mg and 2 mg/ml
11.	Diuretics	Chlorthiazide O.S.	250 mg/5 ml

Dry powder for Oral Suspensions (USP):

1.	Ampicillin	2.	Becampacillin
3.	Cefaclorclor	4.	Cephedrine
5.	Cephalaxin	6.	Colistin sulphate
7.	Cyclacillin	8.	Dicloxacillin
9.	Doxicycline	10.	Erythromycin
11.	Hetacillin	12.	Penicillin V.

COLLOIDS

Colloid is a Greek word for glue and was used to describe polypeptides, vegetable gums and inorganic compounds which had similar behaviour. A substance is said to be colloidal when its particles have a range between 1 mμ to 500 mμ or 0.5 μm. Colloidal dispersion, besides its abnormal particle size also have optical properties which a true solution lacks. They are turbid in nature and this turbidity can be seen even after dilution. But in pharmaceutical preparation most of the colloids have high concentration of particles with this range which is sufficient to show turbidity. In many products, variation in particle size gives opaque appearance (coarse particles here are visible to naked eye. These particles are usually larger than atoms, ions and molecules and generally consists of aggregates of molecule. Sometimes single large molecule may fall in this range and form colloidal dispersion.

Thus, blood, cell membrane, milk represent the colloidal system. Serum albumin, acacia and povidone form true or molecular solution in water still, due to its particle size, fall in colloidal system. They are visible in ultramicroscope.

Most stable substances can be prepared either as low molecular weight solutions or colloidal dispersion depending on the choice of dispersion medium and dispersion technique.

Pharmaceutical Applications:

Colloidal nature, sometimes, ulter the therapeutic properties. e.g. silver chloride, silver iodide and silver protein in colloidal form are effective germicide and it lacks irritation assisted with the silver salts. It also changes the absorption properties.

e.g. sulphur in colloidal form has faster absorption which may be more than needed. Colloidal copper can be used as a diagnostic agent for paresis and colloidal mercury for syphilis. Proteins are natural colloids. Plasma protein may bind drugs and affect the therapeutic activity. Many synthetic polymers are used in coating to solid dosage form. Colloidal electrolyte/surfactants are used as additives in pharmaceutical preparations.

Classification:

It can be classified in three groups based on the interaction of particle of dispersed phase with those of dispersion medium.

Lyophillic colloids: System with colloidal particle which interacts with dispersion medium are called as lyophillic colloids. They easily form colloidal dispersion and are obtained simply by dissolving the material in solvent being used. e.g. dissolution of acacia or gelatine in water or celluloid in amyl acetate.

The property of attraction between the dispersed phase and dispersion medium results in the salvation. Mostly they are organic molecules. e.g. gelatine, acacia, insulin, albumin, rubber and polystyrene. They are also termed as lipophilic colloids. Change in dispersion medium may not form the colloidal system.

Lyophobic colloids: In this system, colloidal particles have little attraction for the dispersion medium. These are lyophobic (solvent hating) colloids and have different properties. They are generally composed of inorganic particle dispersed in water. e.g. gold, silver, sulphur, arsenous sulphide and silver iodide.

It requires special technique for its preparation and it may be prepared by reducing the size (dispersion method) or causing the aggregates of particles of sub-colloidal dimensions into colloidal size range (condensation method). High intensity ultrasonic generators may be used for its preparation. Other method involves use of an electric arc in liquid. Due to its heat, some of the metal of electrode is converted into vapour and then condenses to form colloidal particles. Milling and grinding procedures may be used for its preparation. But its efficiency is low. These colloidal mill reduce only a small portion of total particles to colloidal size range.

It involves high degree of initial supersaturation followed by formation and growth of nuclei. Supersaturation can be obtained by reduction in temperature. e.g. Dissolving sulphur in alcohol in excess amount of water forming many small nuclei giving supersaturated solution, which further grow to form colloidal solution.

Other condensation methods depends on a chemical reaction such as reduction, oxidation, hydrolysis or decomposition. e.g. Neutral/slightly alkaline solution of noble metal salts when treated with reducing agents (formaldehyde) from action that gives changed aggregates. Oxidation of hydrogen sulphate leads to formation of sulphur atom and gives sulphur solution. If solution of ferric chloride is added to large volume of water, hydrolysis occurs and a red solution of hydrated ferric chloride is obtained.

Double decomposition between hydrogen sulphide and arsenous acid gives arsenous sulphide solution Excess of Hydrogen Sulphide gives large negative charge on particle and form a stable sol.

Associated Colloids: It has been observed that some molecules have two distinct regions of opposing solution affinities in same molecule or ion are termed as **amphiles** or **surfectants**. At low concentration in liquid medium they are independent and in subcolloidal range. But by increase in concentration, aggregates are formed which may again become independent after a particular value. These aggregates are known as micelles and are made up of 50 or more monomers and the concentration at which this happens is called Critical Micelle Concentration (CMC). Due to its size 50 A°, it is termed as colloidal system. Formation of associated colloid is also spontaneous if the concentration exceeds the CMC.

Amphiles may be anionic, cationic or non-ionic or zwitter ionic in nature.

Anionic	–	Sodium lauryl sulphate,
Catinoic	–	Cetyl trimethyl ammonium bromide
Non-ionic	–	Polyoxyethylene lauryl ether.
Ampholytic	–	Dimethyl dodecyl ammonio-propane sulfonate.

TABLETS

As oral route is most convenient and effective mean for administration of drugs, the most of the dosage forms are formulated either in solid or liquid dosage forms. Tablet is one of the most popular solid unit dosage forms.

- Temperproof dosage form.
- Convenient to all age groups and easy to swallow.
- Highly stable.
- Bitter and nauseous drugs can be administered by coating.
- More stable as a compact dosage form.
- Suitable for all ranges of dose to be administered.
- Easy to handle, transport and store.
- Economic.
- Action can be enhanced by additives. e.g. dispersible tablet.
- Drug release can be sustained or released at specific site.
- Local action in oral cavity.
- Product identification is easy by embossing/engraving /using colours.
- Easy to manufacture on large scale.
- Less microbial contamination.

Limitations of this dosage forms are:

- Bulky or highly amorphous drugs can not be converted into compressed tablets.

- Drugs having limitations of solubility or producing any uncomfortable effect in gastrointestinal tract are difficult to formulate.

- Coating becomes necessary where taste or odour is to be masked to make it palatable.

- Drugs with hygroscopic/delequescent nature can not be compressed into tablet form and require special additives.

- Sophisticated tablet press is involved which require technique in handling and maintenance.

- Liquid drugs can not be formulated in tablet.

Formulation:

Drug can not be used in its pure form due to many reasons. Various additives are required along with the drug due to the following reasons.

1. Low dose,

2. Compressibility,

3. Flow properties required to feed material into machine,

4. Sticky material,

5. Hygroscopic/deliquescent material,

6. Controlling of release rate,

7. Releasing the drug at specific site,

8. Enhancing absoption of poorly soluble drugs,

9. Taste or odour masking

   To protect drug from atmosphere.

These additives can be catagorised as:

1. Diluents:		Lactose, starch, microcrystalline cellulose, dextrose, calcium sulphate, sucrose, dibasic calcium phosphate, sorbitol, mannitol etc.
2. Binders:		Starch paste, acacia, tragacanth, gelatin, PVP, sodium alginate, glucose, alcohol, cellulose derivatives.
3. Disintegrants:		Soluble starch, aerosil, avicel, etc.

4.	Lubricants:	Magnesium stearate, talc, stearic acid, polyethylene glycol, surfectants, waxes etc.
5.	Glidents:	Talc, corn starch, silica derivatives etc.
6.	Colour, flavour, sweeteners:	Approved colours and flavours, natural, artificial and synthetic sweetners.

Method of Preparation:

During compression drug along with additive cannot be directly compressed into tablet form as a regular flow is required to feed the material uniformly in the dies. It is always converted into granules so that the required flow properties can be maintained and there will not be any separation of ingredients due to vibration of machine. Also it will provide the sufficient hardness and uniformity in the drug content.

Tablets can be prepared by wet granulation, dry granulation and direct compression.

1. Wet granulation: Drug along with additives are mixed homogeneously using batch mixer and granulating fluid is added with constant mixing, sufficient to convert into dough mass and passed through granulators so as to get the homogeneous granules. It is dried at suitable temperature in dryers. After mixing lubricants, glidents and other ingredient required for proper compression, material is added to feeder of the tablet machine and compressed into tablet form (Fig. 3.4).

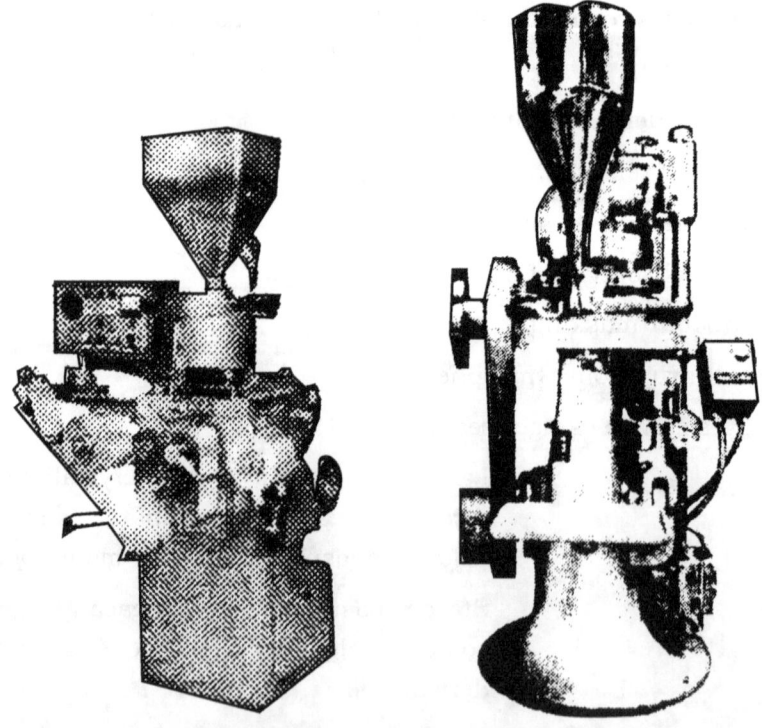

Fig. 3.4 : Tablet machines

2. Dry granulation method: Drugs and additives which can not be directly compressed or sensitive to the additives used for wet granulation, are converted into big tablets (slugs) by directly pressing it in the tablet press and then passed through mill to convert it into granules. These granules are then mixed with other ingredients required for proper compression and feed to tablet press.

3. Direct compression: Drugs and additives, due to their nature, can be directly compressed into tablet press does not require any pre-treatment and can be feeded to press by mixing additives for proper compression.

Tablet Characteristics:

1. Shape, size and appearance: The tablet should have uniform size and shape. Its surface should be smooth and coloured, if any, should be properly distributed over the surface without causing any mottling. Thickness of the tablet can be determined by using sliding Caliper scale or Vernier callipers using 5-10 tablets (Fig. 3.5). Tablet thickness should be controlled within +5% variation of a standard value.

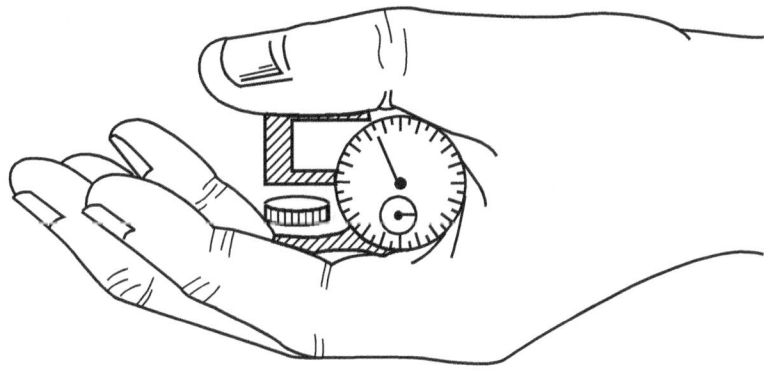

Fig. 3.5: Tablet thickness gauge

2. Organoleptic properties: The tablet produced should not have any objectionable taste, odour or appearance which affects the palatability and patient complience.

3. Hardness: Tablet should have sufficient hardness so that it will maintain its shape and appearance during handling, transportation or any type of mechanical shock. It can be determined by using any of the hardness testers such as - Monsanto Tester, Strong Cobb Tester, Pfizer Tester, Erweka tester and Schluniger Tester. (Fig. 3.6). Generally, hardness should be in the range of 5-8 kg.

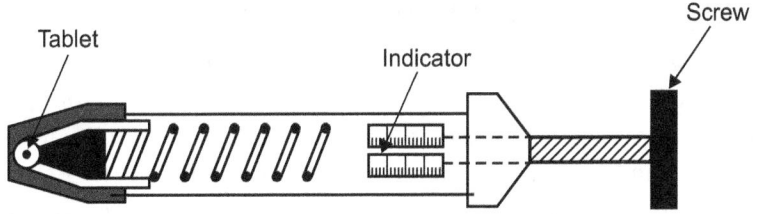

(a) Monsanto tablet hardness tester

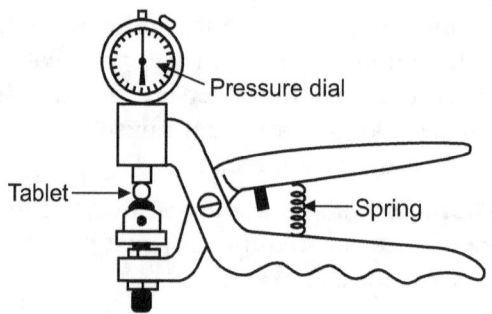

(b) Pfizer Tablet Hardness Tester

Fig. 3.6

4. Friability: Tablets have tendency to cap during handling and transportation which affects its quality, appearance, drug content, coating requirement, and patient acceptance and hence, the friability test is to be carried out. The apparatus used is Roche Fribilator, which consists of a rotating disk 12 inch in diameter, rotating at speed 25 rpm.

Tablets to be evaluated are added into disc and is rotated for 100 revolutions. Friability is calculated using formula,

$$\text{Percent Friability} = \frac{\text{Initial weight of tablet} - \text{final weight of tablet after 100 revolutions}}{\text{Initial weight of tablet}} \times 100$$

The tablet should not have friability more than 1% and it can be improved by using proper additives friability is determined by using tablet friabilator (Fig. 3.7).

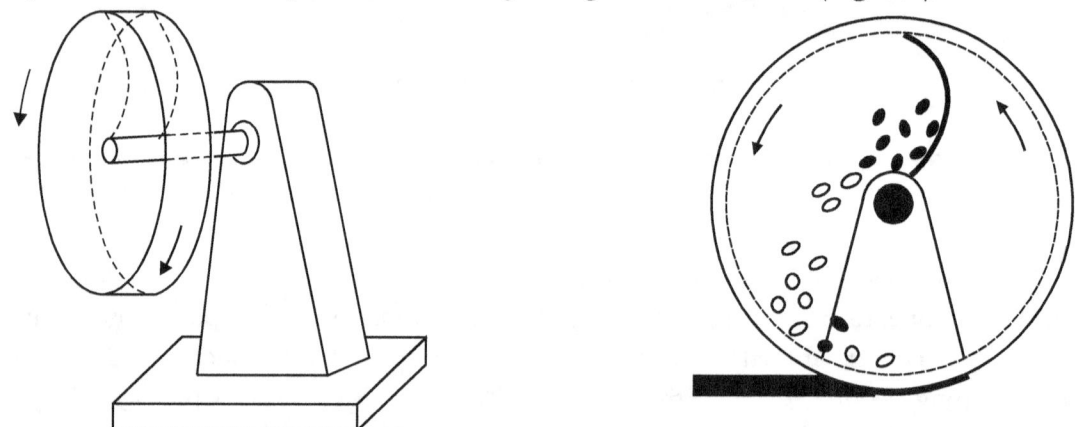

Fig. 3.7: Tablet friabilator

5. Disintegration: Tablet should disintegrate after administration. Too hard tablet may not disintegrate in the body and may affect the absorption. Disintegration is a process in which the tablet is broken into small pieces so that it can be dissolved for rapid absorption. Official apparatus consists of six glass tubes of 3" long, open at top and bottom contain 10 mesh screen (Fig. 3.8). For testing disintegration time one tablet is to be placed in each basket and the basket is placed in a one litre beaker containing water, simulated gastric or intestinal fluid at 37°C ± 2°C. The movement of basket is adjusted such that when it is immersed in the liquid, it should be 0.5 inch outside the surface of the liquid and when moved up, it should be 0.5 inch immersed in the liquid. Thus it moves a distance of 5 inch in up and down direction. (Fig. 3.8). Its rate of movement should be 28-32 cycles/minute. The time required for complete release of tablet through 10 mesh screen is noted. This time is called disintegration time. Generally, disintegration time for uncoated tablet may be in the range of 5-30 minutes. For enteric coated tablets, it should not be more than one hour in simulated gastric fluid and two hours in simulated intestinal fluid.

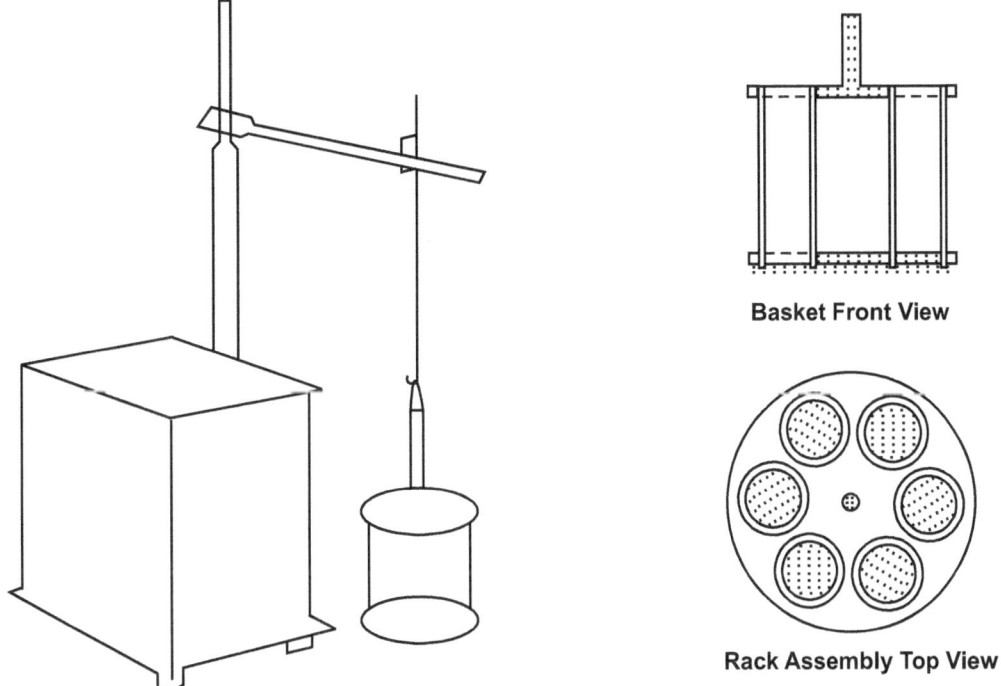

Basket Front View

Rack Assembly Top View

Fig. 3.8: Tablet disintegration tester

6. Weight variation: Dosage accuracy is the main advantage of the tablet formulation and hence uniformity in this dosage form should be checked by taking samples from the lot to be tested and average weight is to be determined. Usually 20 tablets are used for this test and the test should be repeated throughout the compression. The variation in the weight is permissible within a limit considering the machine variation and other factors affecting weight of the tablet. Not more than two tablets should deviate from the percent as mentioned in the Table 3.3.

Table 3.3: Weight variation of tablets

Average weight of tablet	Percent deviation
10 mg or less	10
More than 80 mg and less than 250 mg	7.5
250 mg or more	05

7.   Dissolution: Dissolution test is not essential for those drugs which are freely soluble in water. However, sometimes the dosage form disintegrates but gives no guarantee to dissolve due to its poor solubility or particle size, are to be tested for dissolution.

The apparatus used for this purpose is standardised and described in official pharmocopoeias. (Fig. 3.9). T 90% in 30 minutes is considered as ideal condition for carrying out this test. But it should not dissolve less than 75% in 45 minutes. The limit for dissolution should comply with the value given in the individual monograph of the drug to be tested.

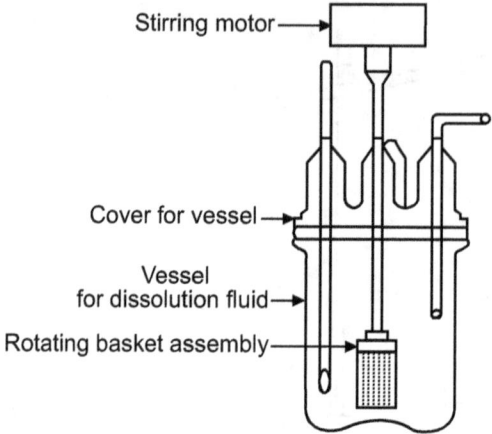

Fig. 3.9: Dissolution test apparatus

8.   Drug content: The drug content should be uniform in all tablets and is to be tested by taking sample and carrying out assay of the same. The drug content should comply with the value given in the individual monograph in pharmocopoeia. Generally tablets drug content limits are in between 90 and 110%. For limit less than 90 or greater than 110 % proportionately larger allowance should be made.

Tablet defects:

1.   Lamination: When tablet gets separated into two or more desecrate layers, the effect is called as lamination. It may be due to lack of proper binding or due to internal pressure or entrapment of air. Pre-compression, decreasing punching rate and decrease in compaction pressure may solve this problem.

2.   Capping: If top or bottom crown of the tablet is removed completely or partially, the effect is known as capping. It may be due to entrapment of air, high or high pressure. This effect may be observed immediately after compression or after few days. It can be corrected by slowing the speed of the compression, reducing pressure and increasing the moisture contents.

3. **Picking, sticking and chipping:** Picking is the process in which the material sticks to upper punch and tablet gives pitted surface. It may be due to engraving or embossing or special letters like S, P, W where it is difficult to clean the punch. Special care in these aspects may remove this problem. Sticking is the process in which material adheres to the die wall which requires the higher pressure for ejection of the tablet from die. This may lead to chipping. It gives tablet with rough surface. It may be due to excess of moisture, improper mixing or due to typical letters ingraved on the punches. Use of lubricants can minimise the chipping and sticking.

4. **Mottling:** Unequal distribution of colour on the tablet surface is known as mottling. This is not a serious problem but it affects the patient compliance. Improper mixing, excessive dry granules, use of dry colour materials may be the reason for mottling. It can be reduced by selecting proper solvent for the colours, reducing the drying temperatures, changing the binders, changing the particle size and proper mixing.

5. **Double impression:** During compression if punches are not operating properly, then engraved punches are rotated while dropped down and causes double impression. This can be improved by using proper tools and maintenance of the machine. This problem is not related to the formulation but is related to the efficiency and performance of the machine.

CAPSULES

Capsules are solid unit dosage form which consists of one or more than one active substances with or without additives in a compact shell. This shell is known as capsule shell and prepared by using suitable form of gelatin. It is obtained from hydrolytic extraction of treated animal collagen from animal bone, hide portion and frozen pork skin. Commercially, gelatin is available in the form of fine powder, coarse powder, thread, flakes and in the form of sheets. It is stable in air when dried, but is susceptible to microbial contamination when it contains more moisture or is in the form of aqueous solution. Gelatin is insoluble in cold water. It is soluble in hot water and in gastric fluid.

Capsule dosage form is very popular in drug delivery system due to -

1.   Easy to swallow

2.   Needs minimum additives.

3.   High elegancy.

4.   Testless shell suitable for hygroscopic substances.

5.   Special treatment to capsule shell gives improved drug delivery.

6.   Suitable for unpleasant, bitter and nauseous drugs.

7.   Suitable for patients of all ages.

8.   Manufacturing time is less.

9.   Can be given in different colours or shades.

This dosage form has the following limitations:

1.   Needs gelatin shell.

2.   High microbial contamination.

3.   Softness or brittleness due to excess or low moisture respectively, causing serious problem in handling and storage.

4.   Not suitable for highly soluble substances.

5.   Needs special techniques for filling.

6.   Breakage of shell in filling process or storage.

7.   High cost.

8.   Drug release depends on disintegration of shell.

Capsule dosage form can be classified according to the nature of gelatin and their compositions such as

1.   Hard gelatin capsule

2.   Soft gelatin capsule

Hard gelatin capsules:

Majority of the drugs are formulated using hard gelatin capsules. Empty hard gelatin capsule shells are manufactured by the following methods:

1.   Dipping cool stainless steel mold pins into warm homogeneous gelatin solution.

2.   Centrifugation casting method.

Physicochemical characteristic of gelatin shell is based on:

1.   Viscosity of gelatin.

2.   Source of gelatin.

3.   Extraction method of gelatin.

4.   pH of gelatin (acid or alkali treated).

5.   Speed of rotating pins.

6.   Dipping time.

7.   Solidification temperature.

8.   Size of capsule.

9.   Composition of gelatin mixture.

10.   Method of preparation.

Generally, hard gelatin capsule consists of moisture between 13-16%. If empty capsule shell is not stored in proper environmental controlled conditions like temperature and moisture. Humidity softens the capsule shell which becomes difficult to handle and gets agglomerated. At high temperature, moisture content of capsule shell is reduced and capsule shell becomes brittle and is not suitable for use.

Hard gelatin capsule consists of two parts. First part in which powder material is filled is called body and the other part which covers the body is known as cap. Body of the capsule shell is larger and less in diameter than the cap. Capsules are always transported in sealed form and it can be opened by applying slight pressure, for filling the material.

Body and cap of the capsule are plain and cylindrical in shape. Other types of capsule shells are coni-snap and coni-snap supro (Fig. 3.10). Empty capsules are sold by the size range and are manufactured in varying in length, diameter and capacity. The type of capsule to be used is not mentioned. It can be decided by trial and error method and suitability of the dose of the drug.

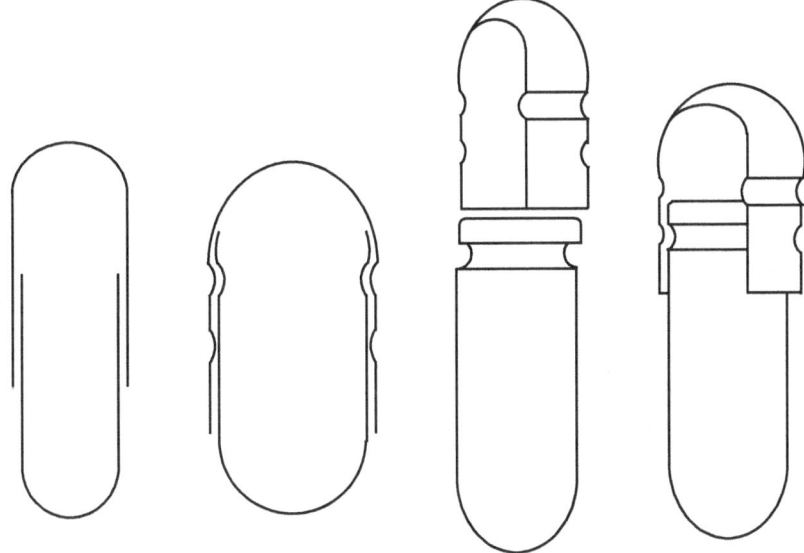

Fig. 3.10: Parts and types of hard gelatin capsules

Capsule shells are mainly of eight types ranging from 000 to 5. Out of which 000 is the largest size which is not suitable for human being and used for animals. Capsule size five is the smallest size (Fig. 3.11) which accommodates 65 mg of the drug or used for potent drug substances which have very low dose. (less than 65 mg).

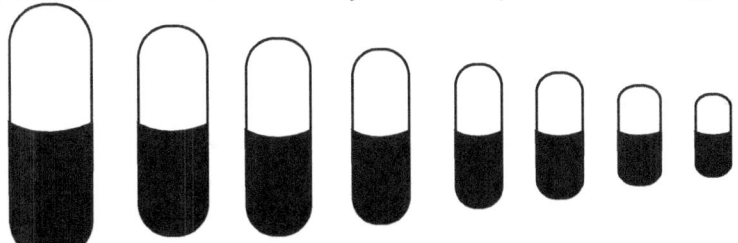

Fig. 3.11: Sizes of hard gelatin capsules

Preparation of hard gelatin capsules:

Following steps are involved in the preparation of hard gelatin capsule. (Fig. 3.12)
1. Mixing the drug and additives thoroughly.
2. Selection of size of capsule to be prepared.
3. Filling operation.
4. Cleaning, polishing and packaging of capsules.

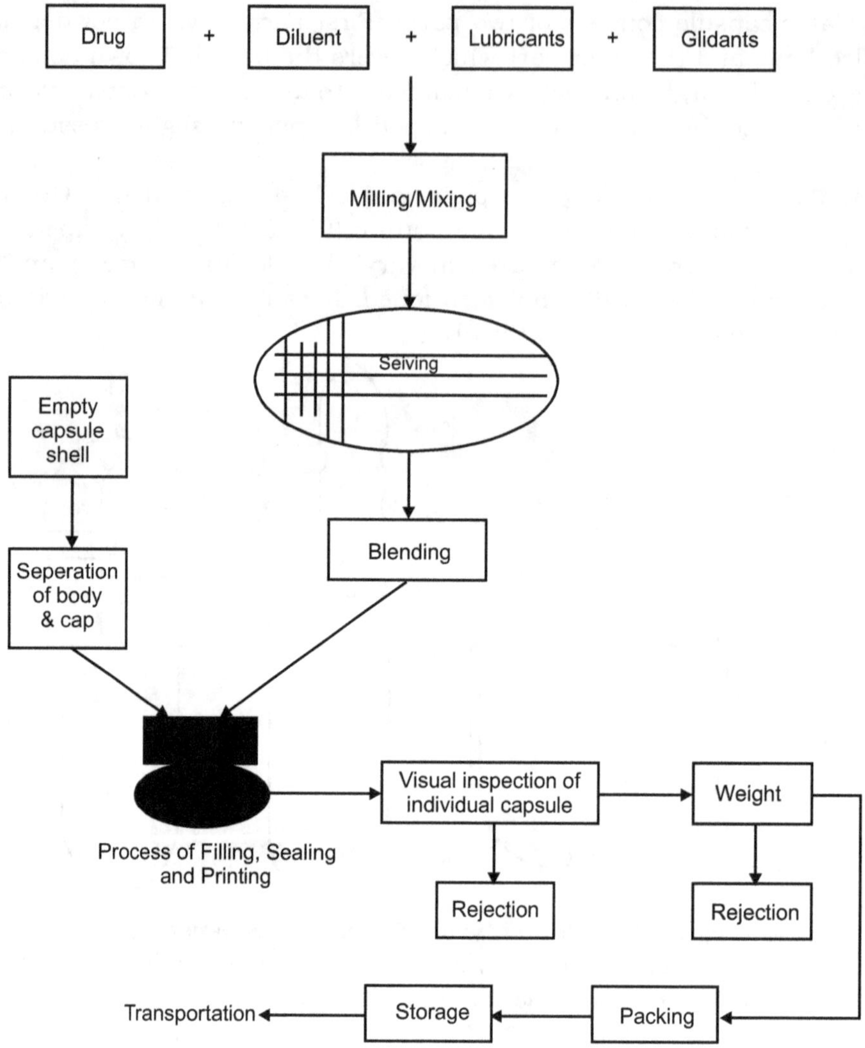

Drug	+	Diluent	+	Lubricants	+	Glidants

Milling/Mixing

Seiving

Empty capsule shell

Seperation of body & cap

Blending

Process of Filling, Sealing and Printing

Visual inspection of individual capsule

Weight

Rejection

Rejection

Transportation ← Storage ← Packing ←

Fig. 3.12: Flow diagram of capsule formulation

Soft Gelatin Capsules:

These capsules are manufactured from gelatin shell in which some elastic or plastic light material is added such as glycerine and polyhydric alcohol (sorbitol).

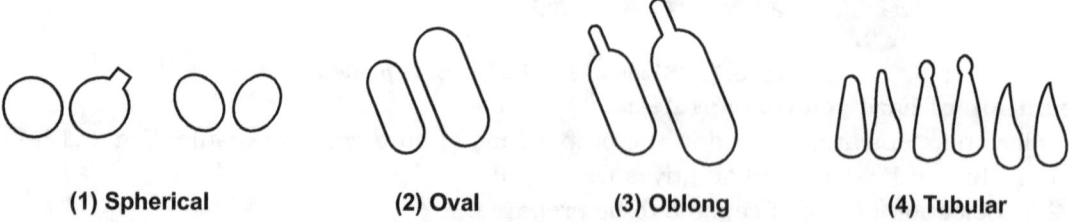

(1) Spherical   (2) Oval   (3) Oblong   (4) Tubular

Fig. 3.13: Shapes of Soft gelatin capsules

It is classified according to shapes (Fig. 3.13) such as oblong, elliptical, spherical, cylindrical etc. These capsule may contain liquid, suspension, pasty material, oily substances, dry powder etc.

Soft gelatin capsules are prepared by continuous process in which at a time formation of gelatin shell, filling, sealing, cutting, finishing and printing processes are carried out simultaneously. (Fig. 3.14).

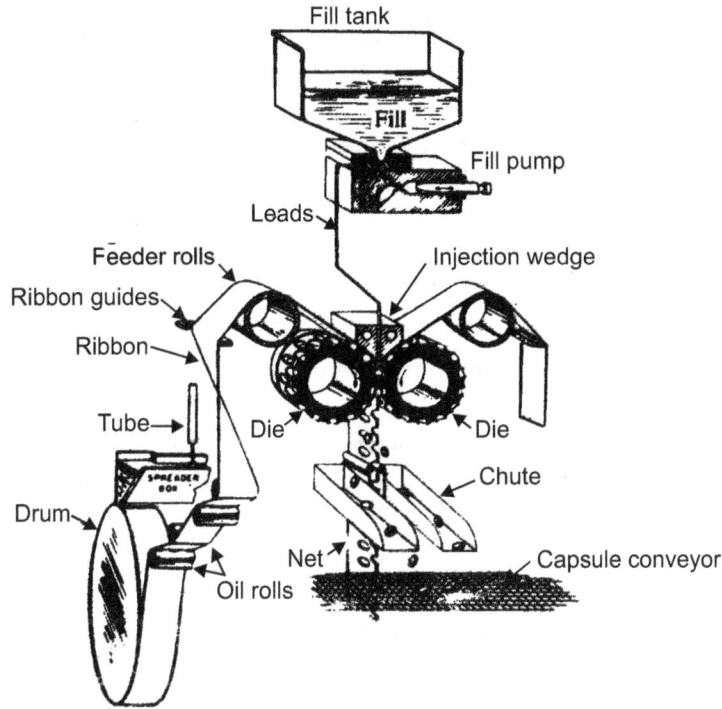

Fig. 3.14: Preparation of soft gelatin capsules by continuous process

Soft gelatin capsules are very useful for those substances which degrades in presence of air e.g. liquid, semisolid, volatile, bitter in taste, have unpleasant odour, oils etc. It is more elegant and easy to swallow than hard gelatin capsule.

It is prepared by plate and die process. In plate process, a plane warm gelatin sheet is kept on the surface of the plate, which consists of mold and the warm liquefied gelatin solution is poured into the mold. Then an another sheet of prepared gelatin is carefully laid at the top of the medication and then entire pressure is applied. It forms a cavity in which the material is filled and capsule is sealed simultaneously. These sealed capsules are removed and polished or washed with the solvent to remove harmless material adhering on its surface. For this purpose, highly automatic machine is required.

The die process is same and gives gelatin ribbon to encapsulate the material.

Chapter ... 4

HISTORY AND DEVELOPMENT OF PROFESSION OF PHARMACY

'Bheshaj' is a term used in India since last four thousand years which is equivalent to Greek term 'pharmacon' (means-drug) from which the word 'pharmacy' has been derived. It was since then, that pharmacist is held responsible for making the drug into a suitable form acceptable to patient. At the same time, he was also involved in procurement of the drug from various available sources. Thus, pharmacy is a science imparting the knowledge required to identify, procure, formulate, standardise the drug and provide the necessary environment to maintain its therapeutic activity and to regulate drug distribution. In the ancient days, the senior people from tribes used to exercise their own experineces in the hours of need and repeated practice of such happenings resulted into compilation of all such knowledge into the apothecary. There was a common belief that a person involved in this profession was associated with some spiritual power and that drug along with its natural effect had some magical involvement in curing the disease. It was due to this reason that tribal apothecary was treated as a different society. This era was followed by the involvement of apothecary in priestly activities due to the belief that they are near to God due to their spiritual power.

Archaeologist discovered most of the material related to the historical part of this aspect and one of which was *Papyous Ebers*, 16th century document, named after the person who discovered it. It contain drug formulae and drugs mainly of vegetable origin, e.g. fennel, acacia, castor bean, sodium carbonate, sulphur etc. Then came the era of indivisuals who due to their constant involvement in the profession, contributed for deveolopment in the science which in turn affected pharmacy profession.

Hippocrates, Dioscorides, and **Claudius Galen** were the authorities responsible for such advancement in the field.

Hippocrates (c.a.466-377 BC) systematised the knowledge available and linked it with ethics. His concepts were then accepted worldwide and still utilised by health professionals.

Dioscorides, a Greek physician linked botany to this field and wrote *materia medica*, which included various drugs of vegetable origin. He described opium, hyoscyamus and other naturally occurring drugs and provided the basic information regarding its identification, cultivation, collection and storage.

Galen, who was a physician known for his medical literature carrying description of number of drugs, their formulae and method of preparations. His work is still known as 'Galanical Pharmacy'. Until 1240 AD, pharmacy remained linked with medicine, but when it became difficult to be handled simultaneously due to increase in number of drugs pouring in, it was separated. German Emperor Frederick II felt that field of pharmacy is altogether different than the medicine and hence he implemented this separation. Further the involvement of botany as a base for pharmacy was changed to chemistry by **Paraselsus**, a Swiss physician. He is responsible for developing the basic thinking of using individual chemical moiety for the treatment of diseases. Then further contribution was made by number of scientists by developing new drugs from different sources and Europe was exporting drugs through out the world, which was then shifted to USA, as they could establish pharmaceutical unit. In India, however the ayurvedic medicines were used as per the ancient books written by **Charaka**, a physician, which was gradually replaced by allopathic medicines in the regime of British rule. After independence the further development in pharmaceutical industries fulfilled the need of our country.

Pharmacopoeias and their Importance:

To maintain the uniformity and to control the standards of drugs and devices available in the market, each government has to make some laws and the standards are to be specified so as to avoid the availability of substandard or adulterated drugs. Each country has its own book of standards which includes the list of the drugs/articles along with its complete protocols viz. descriptions, tests and formula for its preparations, storage, use, dose and all other information which is essential for its proper manufacturing and safe use. Thus, the book which mentioned, stall these standards is known as pharmacopeia. Each country has its own pharmacopoeia as the stability and efficacy of drug is affected by environment, the population in which it is used, geographical climate, source and many other factors. Each country has its own procedure to involve scientists in preparation of these standards as per their country's requirement. It is amended from time to time depending upon the changes in the drug list (deletion and addition) as per the current need. Monograph and standards of the existing drug may also change due to new findings or change in the dosage form or change in the analytical techniques.

Indian Pharmacopoeia:

The first edition of Indian Pharmacopoeia was published in 1955, but actually the process of which started as early as 1944. In 1944 Government of India asked Drugs Technical Advisory Board to prepare the list of drugs in use, in India, having sufficient medicinal value to justify their inclusion in official pharmacopoeia.

The list of drugs which were not included in the British Pharmacopoeia alongwith standards to secure their usefulness, tests for identity and purity was prepared by the committee and was published by the Government of India under the name **The Indian Pharmacopoeial List 1946.**

The committee constituted under the chairmanship of COL. **Sir R. N. Chopra** alongwith other nine members, prepared the list of drugs with the following details.

1. Substances included in the British Pharmacopoeia, 48 monographs for crude drugs, chemicals and their preparations.

2. Substances not included in the British Pharmacopoeia:

    (a) Drugs of plant origin   : 90

    (b) Drugs of animal origin   : 10

    (c) Biological products   : 05

    (d) Insecticides   : 07

    (e) Colouring agents   : 03

    (f) Synthesis   : 05

    (g) Miscellaneous   : 15

    (h) Drugs for veterinary use   : 02

The Indian Pharmacopoeial List 1946, was prepared by Department of Health, Govt. of India. Delhi in 1946 and having a price of ₹ 5-8 or 8s 6d. It was reprinted in 1950.

Most of the crude-drugs included in this list, are still official in Indian Pharmacopoeia.

Indian Pharmacopoeia 1955:

After the publication of Indian Pharmacopoeial List 1946 and in order to undertake the preparation of the Indian Pharmacopoeia on the lines of Pharmacopoeias existing in other countries, a permanent Indian Pharmacopoeia Committee was constituted by Government of India on 23rd November 1948, under the Ex-officio chairmanship of Director General of Health Services, Ministry of health New Delhi. Chairman of Drugs and Pharmaceuticals committee, CSIR Delhi, was ex-officio member alongwith other nine renowned scientists. The tenure of the committee was five years. Several other sub-committees were appointed to assist the Pharmacopoeial Committee.

Clinical sub-committee, Pharmacology sub-committee, Biological sub-committee, Pharmacognosy sub-committee, Pharmacy sub-committee and Pharmaceutical sub-committee were important amongst the committees helped in compilation of draft-monographs of the pharmacopoeia. Subsequently the durations of the pharmacopoeial committee was extended by one year and Dr. B. N. Ghosh was appointed as chairman of the committee. Thus, first edition of Pharmacopoeia of India was published in 1955 and is written in English. The official titles of the monographs are given in Latin and covered total 986 monographs. It includes crude-drugs, chemicals biologicals and several formulae derived from them. It costs ₹ 21 or 31 sh.

Supplement to first edition of Indian Pharmacopoeia 1955, since many new drugs were introduced to the market, it was felt necessary to provide standards for these drugs and as such the first supplement to first edition of Indian pharmacopoeia was published in 1960.

Indian Pharmacopoeia Second Edition 1966:

The second edition of Indian pharmacopoeia contains 890 monographs and 41 appendices several changes have been made. The titles of monographs are written in English (not in Latin) and style naming the monographs has also been changed. Titles contain the name of the drug first, category of the drug has been indicated at the end and doses given in metric system. Preparations of the drugs are followed immediately after the parent monograph of the drug. For tablets and injections "Usual Strength" have been given. Non-aqueous titrimetry, column chromatography, compleximetry have been included under new analytical technique, pills, pellets and lamellae have been deleted from the pharmacopoeia.

After the death of Dr. B. N. Ghosh the chairman of 2nd Pharmacopoeial committee in 1958, Dr. B. Mukharji was appointed as chairman and who expedited the revision process and completed the compilation work and second edition was published in 1966.

274 monographs from IP 55 and its supplement of 1960, were deleted from the 2nd edition of Indian Pharmacopoeia. Where 93 new monographs neither official in IP 55 nor in its supplement of 1960 were added to 2nd edition.

Addition of monographs consists of vegetable drugs like Jatamansi, Rasna and Vidang, while antibiotics like Bacitracin, Neomycin were also added. Amongst the chemicals and pharmaceuticals of importance are Amylobarbitone, Bemegride Tolbutamide, Tolazoline HCl and others. Doses were expressed on Metric system only. Column chromatography, non-aqueous titrimetry and complexometry are the new analytical techniques that were adapted. Usual strength for the preparations like tablets and injections was given, when no specific strength is mentioned by prescriber.

Pharmacopoeia of India Supplement 1975:

This is the supplement of Indian Pharmacopoeia second edition 1966. Since many new drugs were introduced in the medical practice after the publication of second edition of IP, it was very essential to provide them the official standards and also to amend IP 1966, where so ever necessary.

Thus, in the supplement 126 new monographs have been included and also 250 monographs of 2nd edition have been amended. Only one monograph Cholera vaccine formolised has been deleted.

Many appendices giving the detailed analytical procedures have been re-written and some appendices have been added. Monographs on capsules and eye ointments have been rewritten and sterility test for eye ointments has been incorporated for the first time. TLC, GLC and IR spectrophotometry have been adopted as new analytical techniques where so ever applicable.

Indian Pharmacopoeia III Edition 1985:

After the publication of second edition of Indian Pharmacopoeia 1966 and its supplement in 1975, Indian pharmacopoeia committee for the preparation of third edition was reconstituted under the chairmanship of Dr. Nitya Nand, Director of Central Drug Research Institute, Lucknow, in June 1978. Third Indian pharmacopoeial committee consisted of 13 members alongwith member secretary and assistant secretary. The committee was assisted by 10 sub-committees in the compilation work.

Third edition of Indian pharmacopoeia has been published in 1985 in two volumes along with the nine appendices. 261 new monographs have been added to this edition, which were not included in second edition. 450 monographs included in second edition have been deleted from this edition. Following are the important salient features of this edition:

1. As far as possible IUPAC system of nomenclature of organic chemical drugs has been used.

2. Analytical techniques like electrophoresis, flurometry, flame photometry, photometric haemoglobinometry have been given the official recognition for the first time.

3. Instrumental techniques i.e. IR and UV spectroscopy, gas liquid chromatography, fluorescence and atomic absorption spectrophotometry have been used where so ever applicable.

4. To ensure the dissolution of contents, dissolution test has been made applicable to six tablets.

5. Limit test for microbial contamination has been mentioned for few frequently used pharmaceutical aids and some oral liquid preparations.

6. The appendices for pharmceutical containers, water for pharmaceutical use design and anlaysis of biological assays have been annexed.

(a) Addendum (I) to Indian Pharmacopoeia 1985 third edition: This is a supplement to Indian pharmacopoeia third edition 1985, published in 1989.

This provides the official standards for several new drugs introduced in medical profession. It has added 46 new monographs and amended 126 monographs of third edition.

(b) Addendum (II) to Indian Pharmacopoeia 1985 third edition: Addendum (II) to IP third edition was published in 1991 and is effective from 1st January 1992.

It provides the official standards to the new drugs which came into use after the publication of first addendum to third edition. Addendum II covers 62 new drugs and amendments to 110 monographs of the third edition. An appendix on high performance liquid chromatography (HPLC) and determination of water by azotropic distillation have been added.

Indian-Pharmacopoeia Fourth edition 1996:

Fourth edition of Indian Pharmacopoeia i.e. Indian Pharmacopoeia 1996, has been made effective from 1st December 1996. It supersedes the 1985 edition and its addenda.

Fourth edition has 1149 monographs and 123 appendices. This edition includes 294 new monographs not included in third edition while 110 monographs have been deleted.

A good number of general monogrpahs like creams, eye drops, gels, nasal preparations, oral liquids, pesseries, suppositories, have been incorporated.

Important among the new appendices added to the 4th edition are the Biological Indicators, jelly-strength, osmolarity, particulate matter, contents of packaged dosage forms etc.

Method of preparation and in-process control for many biological products, IR and UV absorption tests for identify have been added to many drug-substances.

Test for bacterial endotoxins as a substitute test for the pyrogens, and the extensive use of HPLC for analysis of drug-substances and few of the salient features of 4th edition of IP 96.

IP 1996, Addendum 2000:

In view in compliance of the WTO, IP committee decided that there is a need for normalizing and integrating the pharmacopoeial standards in India so as to bring it, on par with other pharmacopoeias. Thus, number of tests and standards for many monographs have been ammended.

42 new monographs have been added to IP 1996 through this addendum. The carbamazine monograph have undergone major changes while, bacterial endotoxin test for pyrogens has been replaced by extensively revised version to the earlier gel clot test. This has come into force from 31st December, 2000.

IP 1996, Addendum 2002:

This has came into effect from 30th June, 2003. new 19 monographs have been added through this addendum to IP 1996. Due to the rapid developments in the field of practical sciences, it was essential to update the official compendium. A new appendix on residual solvents has been added to monitor the content of organic volatile impurities which are used to produce in the manufacture of active pharmaceutic substance, excipients of medicinal products. The appendix for HPLC has also been replaced by a revised version covering ion chromatography.

Indian Pharmaceutical Codex 1963 (IPC, 53):

The pharmaceuticals and drugs research committee of the Council of Scientific and Industrial Research, in February, 1947 passed a resolution that a book containing detailed information on Indigenous drugs of India be compiled.

The work was entrusted to two important personalities Dr. S. Siddiqui, Director, Chemical Laboratories, Delhi and Dr. B. Mukarji, Director, Central Drugs Laboratory, Kolkatta. Dr. Siddiqui left for Pakistan and Dr. B. Mukarji was asked to complete it when he was Director of Central Drug Research Laboratory, Lucknow.

The work of this volume I was divided into two parts, Part I dealing with general monographs and Part II formulary of galenials and other preparations of vegetables and animal origin.

The work was undertaken with an intention.

1.   To focus the attention on the need for intensive research on indigenous drugs, and

2.   To serve as a guide for research on indigenous drugs.

The indigenous drugs were not prescribed by medical practitioners as no standards were laid down for them.

Since, the Indian Pharmaceutical Codex - Vol I got published in 1953, alongwith standards, methods of preparation, dosage and other details, it has served the purpose to a great extent.

National Formulary of India:

Multiplicity of drugs, their several preparations and continuous flow of new drugs in the medical practice has made it difficult even for a qualified and experienced physician to discriminate the choice of drugs. Drug interaction, resistance, cumulative effects are the other factors, which the physician has to take into consideration while treating the patients. Thus, for the guidance of medical practitioners, medical students and pharmacists in hospitals and in sales departments, National Formulary of India has been formulated.

The **first edition** of National Formulary was published in 1960 by Government of India, Ministry of Health.

Since, many new drugs had come into use, after the publication of first edition. It becomes essential to revise the formulary and bring it upto date. Thus, the second National Formulary committee under the chairmanship of Dr. B. B. Yodh consulting physician, was constituted and second edition was published in 1966.

206 formulations of first edition have been deleted and 219 formulations of new drugs have been added to **second edition**. Separate pediatric section and a chapter on Diet has been added to formulary. Methods of treatment of poisons, list of diagnostic agents, list of proprietary and trade names are the other features of second edition.

While compiling the valuable information, BP, USP, British National Formulary, NF of United States, BPC, several renewed teachers in the profession, consulting physicians have been consulted.

Revised **third edition** of the National Formulary has been brought up in 1979, under the chairmanship of Dr. Wig K. L. which has deleted 255 formulations of second edition, while added 342 new formulations.

Separate chapters on Drug-interactions, drug dependence, prescription writing are the special features of this edition.

United States Pharmacopoeia (USP):

First planning to create National Pharmacopoeia was originated in January 1817 by Dr. Lyman Speeding in Medical Society of New York. He divided United States into four districts viz. Northern, Middle, Southern and Western. The plan provided for calling a convention on medical societies and schools in each state to draft a pharmacopoeia and then all the four states with their four drafts were invited to General Convention held at Washington DC to compile it into a single National Pharmacopoeia. This resulted into first USP convention assembled on January 1, 1820 in Washington DC and first USP was published on 15th December, 1820 in both Latin and English. In all 217 drugs were listed which were worthy of recognition and were described in total 272 pages.

It also decided to revise pharmacopoeias after every ten years. Firstly, the committee was comprised of only physicians and in 1830 and 1840, prominent pharmacists were invited to assist new revisions. Then in 1850 convention, full membership was given to pharmacist. By 1870, pharmacopoeia was in hands of pharmacists and then efforts were made to revive the interest of physicians. Present plan provides that a minimum one third member of revision committee should be from medical profession.

In 1940 convention it was decided that revision of pharmacopoeia should be after every five years. USP VI published during 1880-90 decade, included the first time, test and assays to set the standards of strength and purity for drugs.

The technology of drug standardisation underwent a remarkable transition during 1950-60 decade. Need of radio-active drugs arose and it was introduced into drug analysis. From 1960, further advances in these techniques continued to revolutionise the approaches to test and standards.

In 1970 meeting it was decided to have revision on a five year basis including all pharmacopoeial activities which helped in getting more continuous representation and communication between convention official and its members.

Two individual compendia published at the end of 1974 were combined to one and included 200 more monographs to give USP XX (1980) emphasis was also given to GMP and bioavailability as apart to focus upon health care of the nation.

Revision of introduction of tests for content uniformity, microbial limit and dissolution rate, as well as, revision regarding container standards was also made. Thus USP and NF were revised continuously and published in a single volume. USP XXI-NF XVI (published in 1985) and USP XXIII-NF XVIII were the next publications which added 336 monographs and deleted 12 monographs.

The First National Formulary of United States was published in 1868 by American Pharmaceutical Association. The books of standards or drugs like Pharmacopoeia, codex, formulary are prepared and published by some recognized authorities in most of the countries but USP and USNF are published by private organization. In 1906, American Congress passed the first Food and Drug Act, and with this act only USP originally published in 1820 and National Formulary published received legal recognition by the U.S. Government. In 1974, United States Pharmacopoeial Convention purchased the National Formulary, and from supplement to 1975 edition of NF, United States Pharmacopoeial Convention accepted the responsibility of publication. Upto 1980, separate issues (i.e. 20th revision of USP in 1980 and 15th edition of NF in 1980) were published, but recently the combined issue (i.e. USP and NF together) has been published.

USP which now represents 25th revision of USP and 20th revision of NF has became official on January 2002. Starting with this edition, USP-NF will be published annually.

USP contains over 3,400 monographs for drug and sub products, together with over 160 general chapters that describe specific procedures to support monograph tests and other informations as well. USP also contains 16 monographs and 9 general chapters pertaining specifically to nutritional supplements. NF contains over 380 monographs for excipients and dietary supplements.

Eight supplements were published after the publication of main volume of USP XXIII-NF -18 published in 1995. First supplement released on November 1, 1994 and the eighth was released on March 15, 1998 which includes 71 new monographs. New general test chapters, radio pharmaceutical for positron emission, Tomography Compounding are the new features included in it. Titles of several injection dosage forms have been changed and new chapter on general information has been included.

European Pharmacopoeia (EP):

European Pharmacopoeia Commission started working since 1964 to prepare EP and first volume was published in 1969 and then in 1971. The supplement was published in 1973. USP has maintained contact and exchanged information with EP since its inception. Third volume of EP was published in 1975. The third edition supplement of 1999 has been recently launched. This supplement has added 105 new European standards or monographs and 124 revised monographs that incorporates latest scientific advances. It complements the third edition and is first publication on cumulative basis. It is applicable from 1st January, 1999, in all member states through out the European Economic Area as well as in about 10 other European countries superseding national standards on the same subject.

International Pharmacopoeia (I.Ph.):

WHO with the co-operation of United Nations published International Pharmacopoeia in the year 1951. The information contained in it has been widely utilised by the other countries for inclusion in their own pharmacopoeias. But it is not a legal document to any country. The efforts taken by scientists involved in safeguarding human health to provide this information is, however, has its own standing in the profession and hence the information is widely accepted.

Second volume was published in 1981 and third in 1988 comprises quality specification. The present volume contains four quality specifications for finished drug dosage form. These cover general requirements for dosage form, individual monograph for excipients, including solvents, acidifying agents, tablets and capsule binders, diluents, suspending agents, viscocity increasing agents, stabilisers and surfectants (which are termed as 'pharmaceutical aids') have been included.

Martindale's Extra Pharmacopoeia:

The first edition was published in July 1883. The aim was to provide practising pharmacist and physicians with unbiased evaluated information on drugs and medicines used through out the world. Squaire's Companion was incorporated in 23rd edition in 1952.

Present 31st edition has been published in 1996. It contains 283 new monographs in addition to previous 30th edition and 173 monographs have been deleted. It has also included description of those diseases, which are treated by drugs along with a review of the choice of treatment in such cases. The book has been divided in three parts. Part I contains 4458 monograph. Part II contains a series of 784 short monographs of new drugs, toxic substances and drugs not used clinically but still of interest. Part III contains proprietary preparation from a range of countries as well as official preparations from the current edition of the BP, USP, NF and BPC. It also includes list of 4800 manufacturers and distributors in it. It covers information from various pharmacopoeias viz. Austrian, Belgian, British, Chinese, Czecks, Italian, Japanese, Netherland, Portuguese, Swiss and USNF.

This edition also contains 11600 abstracts or reviews based on information in an ever widening range of publications. Over the last 110 years Extra Pharmacopoeia has developed through 31 editions from William Martindale's small pocket book to this large volume.

British Pharmacopoeia:

General Medical Council under the Medical Act 1858 was engaged in the publication of British Pharmacopoeia which was released in 1864. Prior to that Edinburgh, Scotland and Dublin had their pharmacopoeias and all were merged in the first BP.

Since 1948, the revision of BP was after every five years. After the publication of addendum II the responsibility of this publication was handed over to medical commission. The commission recommended the health ministers who then appointed a BP Commission on 1st March 1970. After 1973, BP was published in 1980 and 1988. Addendum were also published in between the regular publications. Earlier it included extracts, galanicals and other crude drugs but then there was revolutionary change due to discovery of new medicaments.

Latest edition of BP was published in 1993. It comprise of main volume and four addendum viz. 1994, 1995, 1996, and 1997. Addendum 1997 adds new drugs and preparations to amend the BP 1993. Major change includes the replacement of all the edited texts of the monographs of European Pharmacopoeia by entries in the form of cross references to the monographs published in the third edition of the European Pharmacopoeia. BP has provided authoritative standards for the quality of substances, preparations and articles used in medicine and pharmacy for some 130 years. There are two volumes. The first volume deals with medicinal and pharmaceutical substances. It also includes IR reference spectra needed for the identification of drugs. Volume II contains section on formulated preparation, blood products, immunological products, radio pharmaceutical preparation and surgical materials. This 15th edition contains 2040 monographs for substances and article used in practice of pharmacy. 800 monographs of the second edition of European pharmacopoeia also has been included in this edition. The side heading, definition and production have been introduced, where appropriate, through out the pharmacopoeia to provide clarity and consistence of approach. This is specifically useful for biological products.

British Pharmaceutical Codex (BPC):

With an intention to provide authoritative guidance to the persons engaged in the medical practice (physicians) and pharmacists in the British Empire, the Council of Pharmaceutical Society in 1903 proposed to produce a reference book.

This reference book was published for the first time in 1907 under the title British Pharmaceutical Codex. Since then, subsequent revised editions in 1911, 1923, 1934, 1949, 1959, 1963, 1968 and 1973 were published. British Pharmaceutical Codex (BPC) use to serve as supplement for the information in British Pharmacopoeia in several respects like actions of drugs, undesirable effects, standards, uses etc. Codex also furnished valuable information of medicaments and formulations not included in the BP. From 1963 BP and BPC use to get published simultaneously for the convenience of users. However, in 1972 **Medicines commission** stated that there should be only one book of standards for all medicines in UK, the provision of codex standards have been discontinued. 1973 edition of codex was 10th edition and 1979 edition revised with the desired changes in the 11th edition and is known as **"The Pharmaceutical Codex."**

The book is going to be an encyclopedia of drug information for medical practitioners, pharmacists, in hospitals and in pharmaceutical industry. This also gives references to the published literature including information on bioavailability.

British National Formulary:

This is a ready source of essential information on the drugs and medicinal preparations in common use. It is prepared and published by Pharmaceutical Society of

Great Britain and British Medical Association. It has arranged the preparations as per pharmaceutical forms and is of importance to Pharmacist. Pharmacological classification is given for the convenience of medical practitioners. It gives valuable information about actions, uses, dosage of drugs, and adverse reactions of drugs are also given. National Formulary also gives the vital information of the new drugs as they are included in the formulary before they achieve the status for incorporation either in Pharmacopoeia or codex. British National Formulary does not give any standards for drugs or their preparations.

Chapter ... 5

INTRODUCTION TO PRE-FORMULATION

While developing a new drug, first *in-vivo* studies on animals are carried out and if satisfactory results are obtained then it is evaluated for human use. Before formulating a dosage form of a new drug, it is necessary to study its physical, chemical and other parameters which are suitable to enhance the efficacy, stability and handling of drugs.

All these parameters are studied prior to the formulation and hence it is called as preformulation. It can be defined as a stage of development of a new drug and characterise the physicochemical properties of drugs. When these studies are completed, data obtained are compiled and utilised for the development of the formulation.

Following parameters are considered in pre-formulation studies:

1. **Physical parameters:**

   Characteristics of the drug

   Microscopy

   Particle size

   Partition coefficient

   Polymorphism

   Crystallinity

   Solubility

   Permeability

   Hygroscopicity

   Bulk density

   Flow properties

   Temperature effect.

2. **Chemical parameters:**

   Salt formation

   Hydrolytic degradation

   Oxidation

pKa determination

Common ion effect

Dissolution

Stability analysis

Solution stability

Solid state stability.

3. Formulation additives:

Antioxidents, adsorbants, binding agents, buffers, diluents, emulgents, glidants, colorants, flavours, lubricants, ointment bases, sweetening agents, vehicles preservatives etc.

The parameters which are most important in pre-formulation studies are only discussed in detail.

Characteristics of the Drugs:

As most of the drugs are supplied from different sources, their colour, odour, taste etc. are to be established well in advance to avoid any variation in the quality.

Sometimes physical properties are changed due to change in the method of its preparation, intermediates used or in the environment.

Microscopy:

Microscopic investigations give us particle size, particle shape, crystal habit of the substance, which can be viewed and can be compared with the sample to be standardised. Various types of microscopes are available and helpful in finding out the additional behaviour of the compound such as polymorphism, melting points, transition temperature and rate of transition etc.

Particle size:

Particle size of drugs affect properties such as dissolution rate, absorption rate, content uniformity, stability, colour, test, texture etc. Flow characteristics and sedimentation rate are also controlled by particle size. Therefore, it is necessary to study the particle size and its utility in the formulation and the product to be formed. Oral absorption of drugs are influenced by the particle size. e.g. griseofulvin, nitrofurantoin, spiranolactone and procaine penicillin etc. Absorption of poorly soluble drugs such as tolbutamide, sulphonamides also depends on the particle size. Dissolution rate can be enhanced by optimum particle size.

Techniques used for determining particle size and size distribution are microscopy, sieving, sedimentation, steam scanning, Coulter counter, Hiac counter etc.

Hygroscopicity:

Some drugs when kept in open container, absorb moisture from atmosphere and get converted in liquid form. Adsorption and equilibrium constant depend on humidity, temperature, surface area and exposure time of the compound. It affects the chemical stability, rheological properties, compactibility of the drugs. The moisture uptake by a compound can be determined by analytical method such as gravimetry, TGA, Karl Fischer titration, gas chromatography etc.

Bulk density:

It is dependant on crystallization, size reduction and method of formulation. Bulk density is a ratio of mass of power to its bulk volume. It can be determined using cylinder method. e.g. 20 g of drug, passed through 40 mesh sieve and poured into a graduated cylinder and measure the volume of the powder. Let us consider it as 28 ml. Hence, bulk density = mass of powder/volume = 20/28 = 0.71 g/ml. After tapping the volume becomes 22 ml. Hence, the tapped bulk density = 20/22 = 0.91 g/ml.

Polymorphism:

In Polymorphism, arrangement of a molecule is different in solid state and it exist in two different forms. It differs in physicochemical behaviours and has different melting point, boiling point, stability and solubility.

Geometrical isomer or tautomers differ from polymorphism. Two polytrophs may differ in crystal form but are same in liquid or vapour form. e.g. carbon in cubic form is known as diamond (vary hard), while in hexagonal state is known as graphite (soft). These two forms of carbon in solid state is known as polymorphs. It also affects the bioavailability and stability of the compound. Number of methods are available for determination of polymorphic forms. e.g. Hot stage microscopy, thermal analysis, infra-red spectroscopy, X-ray diffraction and dilatometry.

Partition coefficient:

When excess of liquid or solid is incorporated to a mixture of two immiscible liquids (organic and aqueous phase), it will distribute itself in between these two phases till each phase becomes saturated. If small amount of liquid or solid is added to a mixture of two immiscible liquids, it will distribute between the two layers in a definite concentration ratio.

Partition coefficient $P = C_1/C_2$

Where C_1 and C_2 are the equilibrium concentrations of the substance in first solvent and second solvent. It is a measurement of a drug lipophilicity and shows its ability to cross membrane in the oil/water partition coefficient in system such as octanol/water and chloroform/water. It affects absorption and bioavailability of the drug.

Flow properties:

Powders which are used in formulations for any pharmaceutical purpose may be classified as free flowing powder, non free flowing powder or cohesive or sticky powder. Flow properties of powders are significantly affected by the changes in particle size, shape, porocity, density, electrostatic change, surface texture and adsorbed moisture. It is important in tablet formulation, capsule filling, powder filling in containers, granulations, punching etc. and can be determined by angle of repose, dustability, compressibility etc.

Percent compressibility = $d_t - d_o / d_t \times 100$

Where d_o is the bulk density and d_t is the tapped bulk density.

Table 5.1: Flow properties of powder

Material	Percent compressibility	Flowability
Celutab	11	excellent
Star X – 1500	19	fair – passable
Lactose Monohydrate	19	fair – passable
Maize starch	16-27	poor
Dicalcium phosphate		
Dihydrate coarse	27	poor
Magnesium stearate	31	poor
Titanium dioxide	34	very poor
Talc	49	very very poor

Dissolution Studies:

It is very important in solid dosage form. Experimental data are obtained by *in-vitro* study, are utilised for the determination of bioavailability. Dissolution rate of a compound can be determined using,

Noyes – Whitney equation i.e. $d_c/d_t = DA/hV\,(C_s - C)$.

where,

d_c/d_t = dissolution rate,

D = diffusion coefficient

h = thickness of the diffusion layer

V = volume

C_s = concentration of saturated solution in dissolution medium

C = concentration of drug in solution

t = time

A = surface area

It affects various parameters such as particle size, crystal habit, surface properties, solubility, pH and type of dosage form.

Dissolution rate can be determined by using two types of equipments:

(i)   Dissolution apparatus containing basket and

(ii) Dissolution apparatus containing paddle.

✱✱✱

Chapter ... 6

BIOPHARMACEUTICS

The desired therapeutic effect of drug depends on:

(i)   Reaching the drug to its site of action,

(ii)   Achievement of its adequate concentration at that site and

(iii)   Maintaining that concentration for entire duration of therapy.

Upon drug administration variety of mechanisms are set in action; that affect favourably or adversely to satisfy above prerequisites. The administered drug is subjected to these mechanisms/processes. These processes involved are depicted in Fig. 6.1. These processes are absorption, distribution, metabolism and excretion of administered drug. All these processes together are responsible for transportation of drug to and achieving and maintaining its adequate concentration at site of action. All these processes are quite complex and basically dependent on Anatomical and Physiological (Biological) characteristics of body systems involved and Physiochemical (Physical and Chemical) characteristics of both dosage forms and drug incorporated in it.

Thus, these physiochemical and biological factors affect rate and amount of drug reaching to site of action; which finally determine the effect of administered drug. While describing this relationship, Milo Gibaldi has quoted that *"Biopharmaceutics is concerned with the relationship between Physiochemical properties of drug in a dosage form and the Pharmacologic, toxicologic or clinical response observed after its administration."*

Biopharmaceutics has also been defined as *"the study of factors influencing the rate and amount of drug that reaches the systemic circulation and use of this information to optimize the therapeutic efficacy of the drug products"*. Rather more comprehensive defination given by Gems Swerbrik is that *"Biopharmaceutics is concerned with understanding those factors that can affect the amount Vs. time profile of a drug at receptor site."* The study of biopharmaceutics thus, involves the application of physical, chemical and biological principles to drug, dosage form and drug action to optimize the therapeutic efficacy of drug products.

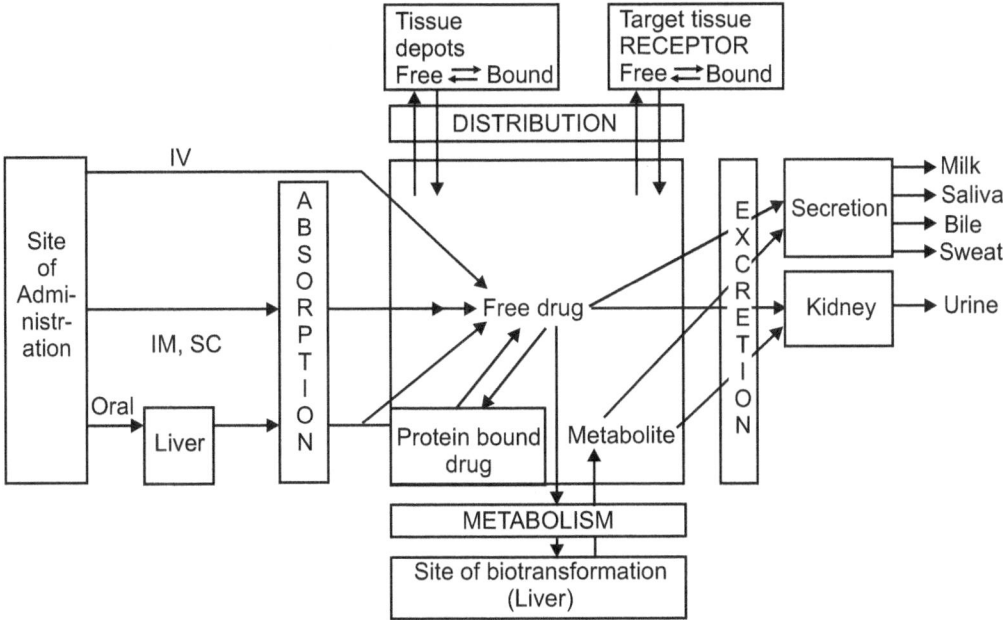

Fig. 6.1: Schematic representation of course of drug in the body following its administration

BIOAVAILABILITY

The most important property of a dosage form is its ability to deliver the drug substance to its site of action in an amount adequate to elicit the desired pharmacologic response. Thus, the onset of action, intensity and duration of action depends on this ability of dosage form. It has been variably referred to as its physiologic availability, biologic availability or bioavailability. It is defined as "the rate and extent (amount) of drug absorption from its dosage form in systemic circulation.

The quantitative response to a drug is highly dependent on the concentration of drug at the site of action. In most situations, it is quite difficult to quantify the drug concentration at actual site of action. Rather drug concentrations are measured in easily accessible site which is believed to be in equilibrium with the site of action. This site is the blood or one of its components, generally the blood plasma. It is generally assumed that the therapeutic effect of the drug is a function of the concentration of drug in patients blood plasma. The plasma concentration Vs. time profile of a drug gives valuable information about drug effect (see Fig. 6.2); as several parameters based on this profile are responsible for attaining and maintaining the optimum concentration of drug at the site of action.

1. **MSC (Maximum Safe Concentration):** The concentration of drug in plasma above which side effects or toxic effect of drug occur in patient.

2. **MEC (Minimum Effective Concentration):** Some minimum concentration of drug be achieved in plasma before desired therapeutic effect is achieved. It's value not only varies from drug to drug but from individual to individual and with the type and severity of disease state.

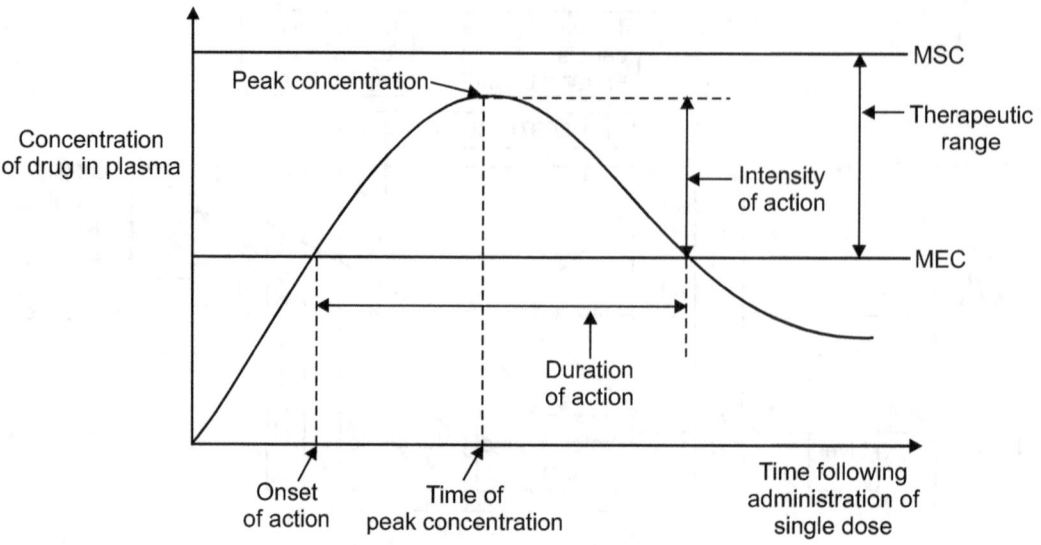

Fig. 6.2: Plasma concentration Vs. Time profile of a drug

3. **Onset of action:** Time required to achieve MEC following administration of dosage form.

4. **Duration of action:** It is the period during which concentration of drug in plasma exceeds MEC.

5. **Peak Concentration:** Highest concentration of drug achieved in plasma.

6. **Time of Peak concentration:** Time required to achieve highest concentration in plasma following administration of dosage form.

7. **Intensity of action:** In general the difference between peak concentration and MEC is relative measure of intensity of therapeutic response of drug.

8. **Therapeutic range:** The range of plasma drug concentration over which the desired effect is obtained yet toxic effects are avoided. The intention in clinical practice is to maintain plasma drug concentration within this range.

Earlier it was believed that the therapeutic response to a drug is an attribute of its intrinsic phamacologic activity. But today it is very much understood that the dose-response relationship obtained after drug administration by different routes e.g. oral and parenteal are not the same. Variations are also observed when the same drug is administered as different dosage forms or similar dosage forms produced by different manufacturers; which in turn depend upon the physiochemical properties of the drug, the excipients present in dosage form, the method of formation and the manner of administration. The plasma concentration Vs. time profile of drug indicating above variations (i.e. same drug in different dosage form or similar dosage forms from different manufacturers) are depicted in the following Fig. 6.3.

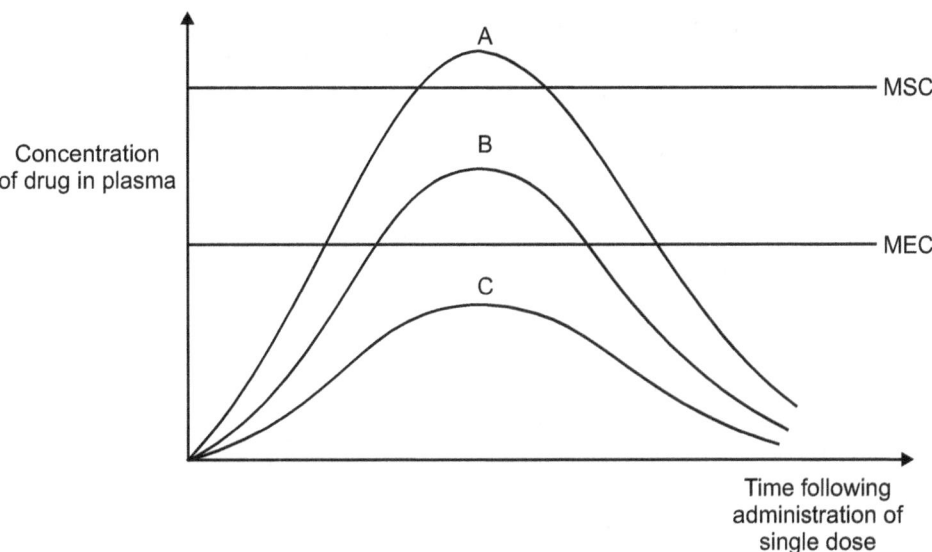

Fig. 6.3: Plasma concentration Vs. Time profiles indicating variations in response

1. **Drug Delivery System A:** The concentration of drug in plasma exceeds the MSC and hence, the drug toxicity will appear.
2. **Drug delivery system B:** The plasma concentration of drug is within therapeutic range and hence, the desired therapeutic response will appear.
3. **Drug delivery system C:** The plasma concentration of drug is below MEC (Subtherapeutic concentration) and hence desired therapeutic response will not appear.

For designating such variations shown by the Pharmaceutical products; in their rate and extent of appearance at active site (Bioavailability) different terms are used as follows:

1. **Chemical equivalence:** Pharmaceutical products are said to be chemically equivalent if they meet the chemical and physical standards as laid down in official books.
2. **Biological equivalence (Bioequivalence):** Pharmaceutical products are said to be biologically equivalent if they produce similar concentrations of the drug in blood and show nearly identical plasma concentration Vs. time profile.
3. **Therapeutic equivalence:** Pharmaceutical products are said to be therapeutically equivalent if they provide equal therapeutic benefit in clinical practice.

It has been clearly established that the bioavailability may vary for a number of reasons. Such variations have been identified as causative factors in certain failures in drug therapy. Moreover, clinical response to a given dose varies widely between and within individuals. The source of variation in human drug response is a twofold phenomenon viz. variation in plasma or tissue concentration and intensity of tissue response to given concentration. However, in most instances it is the plasma or tissue level which is responsible for variations. This variation can be explained in terms of four processes of pharmacokinetics; absorption; distribution, metabolism and elimination. Thus, pharmacokinetic principles can be applied to understand the reasons for this variation and means can be developed to rectify any problems arising from it. The use of drugs in treatment of diseases is thus, a multifaceted process. A pharmacologically active molecule synthesised, rationalised in terms of toxicity and potential benefits, has to be formulated in a suitable dosage form that will contain and deliver a recommended dose through a appropriate route of administration to the site of action. Further depending on physiologic, pathologic and clinical needs, the concentration of drug should be maintained by appropriately deciding the frequency of administration of dosage form (dosage regimen) in order to achieve the therapeutic goal (See Fig. 6.4).

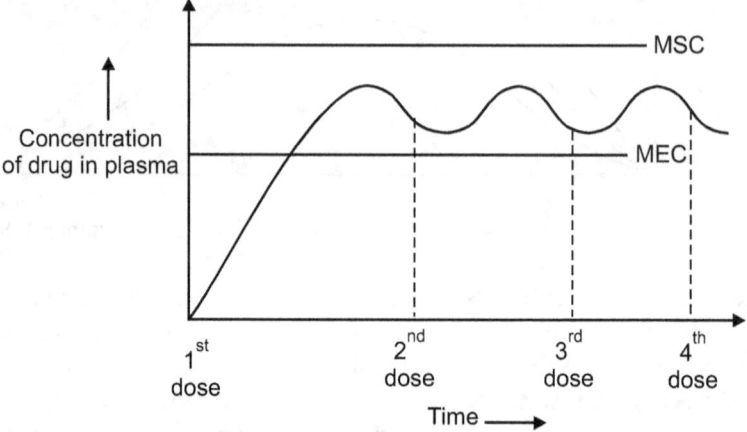

Fig. 6.4: Plasma drug conc. Vs. time profile showing dosing frequency (Dosage regimen)

Thus, a large number of factors play their roles in determining the activity of a drug and the successful integration of these factors results in successful drug therapy. These factors are summarised in Fig. 6.5.

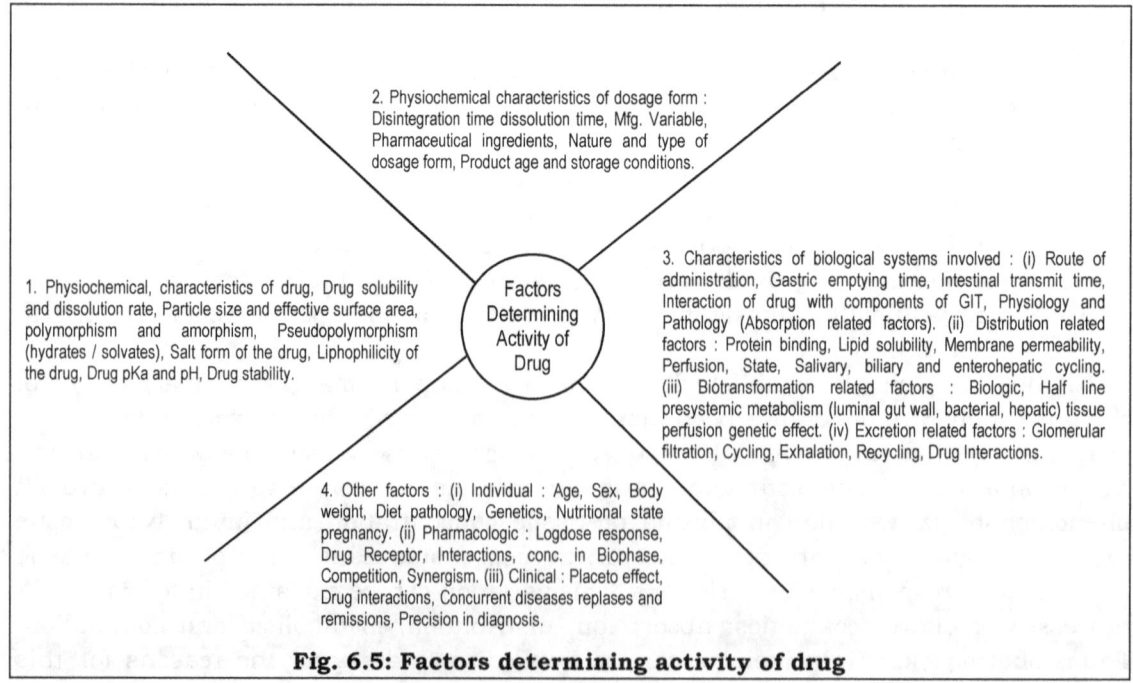

Fig. 6.5: Factors determining activity of drug

ABSORPTION OF DRUGS

Absorption, distribution, metabolism and excretion of a drug all involve its passage across cell membranes of the cell located at different sites in the body. The membrane characteristics of these membranes and the physiochemical properties of drug have profound effect on passage of drug. Despite the structural differences of various boundaries through which the passage of drug occur, they show many common characteristics and hence, plasma membrane is considered as a common barrier for passage of drugs. Since, this membrane is so important for many biological processes its structure has been the subject of considerable study and conjecture. Perhaps the best known model of cell membrane is the bimolecular leaflet structure postulated by Danielli and Davson in 1930's. This model with minor modifications persisted until 1960's when several proposals were advanced to account for new findings not explainable by the model. One model that has received considerable attention is the fluid mosaic model. Like bimolecular leaflet model the fluid mosaic model contains a bimolecular layer of phospholipids. However, instead of protein residing only on the surface of phospholipid layer, the fluid mosaic model also has protein incorporated into the lipid. Some of proteins float on the surface of lipid, while others either singly or in multimolecular clusters, penetrate the lipid to varying depths. Thus, the concept of cell membrane as a passive symmetric structure consisting of a sandwich of lipid and protein molecules has changed which can perform numerous metabolic and transport functions. Drugs are thought to penetrate these biological membranes (biomembrane) in two general ways:

1. Passive diffusion and

2. Specialised transport mechanisms.

1. Passive diffusion:

It refers to the movement of molecules from one region of higher concentration to other of lower concentration through barrier membrane. It does not require energy and participation of components of membrane. Such transfer is directly proportional to the concentration gradient across the membrane and the lipid: water partition coefficient of the drug. Higher partition coefficient favours the diffusion. Smaller lipid insoluble but water soluble drugs may pass across the membrane through numerous water filled pores.

Most drugs are either weak acids or weak bases and in solution show both ionised and non-ionised species. Cell membranes are more permeable to non-ionised forms of drug than ionised form because of lipid solubility of non-ionised form. The ionised fraction because of its poor lipid solubility is unable to penetrate the membrane. Moreover in association with water their hydrated ionic radia are relatively larger which further reduces their penetrating ability. The degree of ionisation of drug depends on the pH of the solution in which it is presented to absorbing membrane and pKa, the dissociation constant of the drug. As the pH of the body fluids varies (e.g. Gastric = 1.4,

Intestinal = 6.6 and blood plasma = 7.4) the absorption of drugs from various body fluids will differ and may dictate to some extent the type of dosage form and the route of administration preferred for a given drug. Absorption from the various sites can be favourably altered in some cases by adjusting the pH at the absorbing surface.

In case of absorption of drugs on parenteral administration, the bulk flow through intercellular pores of capillary endothelial membrane is the major mechanism by which diffusion across the membrane occurs.

2.   Specialised transport:

In this mechanism of transport, the membrane components are involved. The membrane component may be enzyme or any other substance that can form complex with drug. The complex then moves across the membrane, releasing drug to other side of membrane and the carrier returns back to the original surface. When all carrier molecules are bound by drug the process becomes saturated. The carriers in the membrane are specific for particular type of substance, so that if two substances are transported by the same mechanism. One may competitively inhibit the transport of other. In case of 'active transport', a type of specialised transport, the drugs are transported across the membrane against the electrochemical potential gradient. 'Facilitated diffusion' another type of specialised transport mechanism have all the characteristics mentioned above except that the solute is not transported against a concentration gradient.

Other transport mechanisms by which certain drugs are absorbed; include ion pair transport, Endocytosis (Pinocytosis and Phagocytosis) and ionic or electrochemical diffusion.

DRUG DISTRIBUTION

After drug is absorbed in systemic circulation, it may be distributed to tissue fluid (Interstitial fluid) and cellular fluids. The body's physiological characteristics and physiochemical properties of drugs affect and decide the pattern of drug distribution. Thus, the organs such as heart, liver, kidneys, brain receiving relatively high blood supply (Highly Perfused) shall receive most of drug after absorption within few minutes. Distribution of drug to muscles, most of visceral organs, skin and fat is slow and may require even several hours after absorption. Diffusion to tissue fluid component occurs rapidly as capillary endothelium is highly permeable (except brain). Depending on tissue characteristics such as lipid content, pH of environment, availability of binding sites; drug may accumulate in tissues. Such tissues may act as reservoir of drug and may affect duration of drug action. Distribution of drug to tissues may be limited by its binding to plasma proteins especially albumin. Protein binding of drugs may result in decreased concentration of drug at the site of action, as only free drug can penetrate through membrane. It also limits the glomerular filtration of the drug.

Distribution of drugs in brain tissue is quite unique, because of the anatomical characteristics of endothelim of capillaries in the brain. The endothelium there do not show the intercellular pores and pinocytotic vesciles, in addition there are more number of tight junctions. The aqueous bulk flow through capillary wall is thus severally reduced. Further the presence of pericapillary cells surrounding capillaries also prevent diffusion through capillaries. However, highly lipid soluble drugs (non-ionised) can penetrate this barrier but strongly ionised agents are normally unable to enter the CNS from blood circulation. This barrier to the distribution of substances to brain tissue is referred as 'blood brain barrier'.

FATE OF DRUGS

Drugs are foreign substances which the body always tries to eliminate. With few exceptions, all drugs are eliminated from the body in the form other than in which they are administered. Thus, the drugs undergo alterations in their chemical form in the body. The changes that the drug undergoes under the influence of enzymes in the body are known as biotransformation. The main site for biotransformation of majority of drugs is the microsomal enzyme system in the liver. Other tissues that metabolise drugs include kidneys lungs, GIT and blood plasma. The conversion of non-ionisable, lipid soluble drugs into more polar, water soluble metabolites constitute the major bio-transformation function. The lipid soluble non-ionisable drugs are not readily eliminated, while its water soluble polar metabolites are readily eliminated in urine.

Biotransformation of drugs result into one or more of the folloiwng effects:

1. Elimination of drug from the body.

2. Inactivation and termination of drug effect.

3. Activation of drug and

4. Intoxication.

1. Elimination:

Biotransformation of drug results into formation of its metabolites which are water soluble ionisable and hence, easily eliminated in the urine.

2. Inactivation:

Biotransformation results into inactivation of the compounds as the metabolite produced may not show the effects of parent compound.

3. Activation:

Certain drugs in the form in which they are administered, are not active but upon their biotransformation may be converted into their active metabolites (Such drugs are known as 'prodrugs').

4. Intoxication:

Although metabolism of drug tends to stop pharmacological activity; it is not correct to think of drug metabolism as detoxication process. Because in some cases the drug may be converted into a metabolite which show toxic actions.

The biochemical reactions involved in biotransformation of drugs are classified into two main categories:

(a) Non-synthetic reactions (Phase-I reactions) in which usually the drugs undergo oxidation, reduction, or hydrolysis converting it into more polar metabolite.

(b) Synthetic or conjugation reactions (Phase-II reactions) in which the drug or its metabolites undergo coupling with endogenous substances such as glucuronic acid, amino-acid, sulfuric acid or acetic acid.

Hepatic Microsomal Drug Metabolising Systems:

The enzymes present in hepatic microsomes catalyse glucuronide conjugations and most of the oxidation reactions of drugs. Many drugs and environmental pollutants may induce the activity of the enzymes. The drugs administered orally, upon absorption may be subjected to the action of these enzymes and adequate amounts of such drugs may not appear in circulation, resulting into poor bioavailability. The effect is described as the 'first pass effect'. On the other hand, con-current administration of two drugs may show competitive inhibition of microsomal drug metabolism resulting into high concentration of one of the drugs and its toxicity. Certain drugs undergo conjugation reaction with glucuronide and the conjugate may be eliminated in bile. In the intestine subsequently it may be hydrolysed by intestinal or bacterial β-glucuronidase and librated drug may be reabsorbed. This enterohepatic cycling may prolong the drug action.

Non-microsomal Drug Biotransformation:

The non-microsomal enzyme catalyse conjugation reactions except glucuronide formation and oxidation, reduction and hydrolysis reactions. These reactions primarily occur in liver but also in plasma and other tissues of the body.

Excretion of Drugs:

Drugs are eliminated from the body either unchanged or as metabolites. As discussed under biotransformation, the lipid soluble non-ionisable drugs do not get excreted while on biotransformation their water soluble polar metabolites are easily excreted in urine. The important channels of drugs excretion include the following:

1. Kidneys:

The processes involved in the elimination of drugs in the urine are passive glomerular filtration, active tubular secretion and passive diffusion across the walls of nephron. Majority of drugs are excreted in urine. Impairment in renal function may lead to increase in concentration of drug in the body; which prolongs the drug effect and may cause drug toxicity. The pH of urine affects the excretion of drugs. The weak acids are quickly excreted in alkaline urine and the weak bases in acidic urine. This fact is useful for immediate excretion of a drug to prevent drug toxicity in the drug poisoning cases.

2. Lungs:

These are related to the excretion of various gaseous inhalants. The volatile general anaesthetics are excreted by lungs. Certain substances like paraldehyde and alcohol are also excreted by lungs; which enables the physician to detect their presence in the body by the smell of the breath of the patient.

3. Intestines:

Metabolites of the drug formed in liver are excreted in the intestinal tract in the bile which are then excreted in the feces. The purgatives like cascara sagrada and senna are partly excreted in feces after their desired action on the large intestine.

4. Other routes:

Excretion of drugs in sweat, saliva and tears in quantitatively insignificant and hence, unimportant. The drugs or their metabolites may diffuse through epithelial cells of glands into such secretions. Sometimes concentration of drug in saliva may be significant and even equivalent to that in plasma. In such cases saliva may be useful biological fluid to determine drug concentrations. Excretion of drugs in milk may have significance while prescribing drugs to lactating women. Detection of toxic metals in hair and skin may have forensic significance.

The drug disposition/excretion mechanisms have their own limits upto which they effectively eliminate drugs and help in reducing the plasma concentration of drugs.

ROUTES OF ADMINISTRATION OF DRUGS

It is quite apparent that one of the factors deciding bioavailability is the site of administration of drugs. Anatomical and physiological characteristics of absorbing surface and the biological systems involved in transfer of drug from site of absorption to target tissue; greatly affect the bioavailability of drugs. Thus, one of the pre-requisites for successful therapy is that the drugs should be administered by most effective and appropriate route of administration. Although the selection of appropriate route of administration for a given drug depends on large number of factors; the most important of which are the Anatomical, Physiological and Pathological factors. Such factors applicable to various route of administration are discussed here.

1. Oral route of Administration:

More than 80% of drugs are administered orally in solid dosage forms since these are most stable, easily handled and formulated and provide a convenient mode of administration. Different dosage forms available for oral administration include tablets, capsule, suspension, elixirs, solutions, mixtures etc. On oral administration drugs may get absorbed from various sites of alimentary canal right from mouth cavity upto rectum. As the environment at various absorbing sites in GIT differ, drugs get absorbed to differing extent from these sites.

In case of sublingual tablets, the tablet is kept under tongue and allowed to dissolve and drug solution diffuses through mucous membrane into circulation. The lipid/water distribution coefficient is the prime factor deciding the absorption.

For drugs intended to be swallowed and absorbed from GIT, some specific features of absorption are given here.

1. Drugs may get changed in the form that affect absorption due to their interaction with food constituents or naturally occurring substances in GIT or concurrently administered drugs. e.g. Tetracycline absorption is greatly affected by presence of calcium which may be a constituent of food or other drug or formulation excipient.

2. Presence of food delays the absorption of drug from GIT. For rapid absorption it is preferable to administer drug on empty stomach.

3. Since, drugs are absorbed mainly from small intestine on oral administration, their onward transmission to small intestine depends on gastric emptying time. Factors that increase gastric emptying time such as ingestion of fatty food, lying on back when bed ridden, drugs reducing peristalsis etc. reduce onset of action of drugs.

4. pH of contents of GIT goes on increasing from stomach (pH = 1) to distal end of small intestine (pH = 8). It affects the degree of ionisation and hence, the penetration through lipid barrier. As a rule weak acids are largely unionised in gastric acidic medium and hence, are well absorbed from this site. On the other hand weak bases are highly ionised in this medium and are poorly absorbed.

5. The hepatic 'first pass effect' may hinder the availability of drug at its site of action.

2. Rectal Route of Administration:

Drugs are often administered into rectum in the form of solutions, suppositories and ointments for both local and systemic effects. Rectum and colon are capable of absorbing many drugs. Though the absorption is irregular and unpredictable, for the benefits mentioned below this route is utilized in practice.

1. Destruction and inactivation of drug in stomach and intestine is avoided.

2. Hepatic 'first pass effect' is avoided.

3. Can be employed in unconscious patients.

3. Parenteal Route of Administration:

Because of rapid onset of action, the parenteral routes are preferred in emergency situations. Absorption by the parenteral routes is not only faster than oral administration but is more predictable. The rate of drug absorption can be varied in parenteral products by selective combinations of drug state and supporting vehicle. Thus, instead of solution if suspension is administered the rate of absorption can be reduced similarly rather than aqueous solution, oily solutions would be much slowly absorbed. This fact is utilized in preparing depot or repository injections.

(a) Subcutaneous Injections:

The injected drug comes into immediate vicinity of blood capillaries and penetrate them and enter into blood circulation. The penetration depends on lipid/water partition coefficient. Another factor on which rate of absorption depends is the vascularity (blood supply) at the site of injection, more capillaries will enhance rate of absorption. Addition of vasoconstrictor (e.g. Adrenaline) in drug solution shall reduce the absorption conversely vasodilators may be used to enhance absorption by increasing blood flow to the area.

(b) Intramuscular injections:

Aqueous or oily solutions or suspensions may be used intramuscularly with rapid effects or depot activity selected to meet requirements of patient. With certain drugs sustained action upto ten days is possible by intramuscular injection.

(c) Intravenous injections:

Aqueous solutions of drugs are directly administered into vein in emergency situations where rapid action of drugs is desired. As the stage of absorption is skipped the onset of action is very rapid.

4. Topical Route of Administration:

Drugs applied to the skin can produce both local effects at the site of application and systemic effects on absorption into systemic circulation. Percutaneous absorption is better when drug is applied in solution form and has favourable lipid/water partition coefficient. Now-a-days, percutaneous penetration enhancers are used to enhance the penetration of drugs through skin for better absorption.

Chapter ... 7

GOOD MANUFACTURING PRACTICES (GMP)

From past experiences, it has been revealed that "despite increasing vigilance and conscientious anticipation of problems by administrators and scientists in both industry and regulatory agencies drugs will be produced which are not safe and effective". The reasons being varied and pertains to operating procedures, methods, equipments, premises and persons involved. Both regulatory authority (FDA) and industry are in agreement that, the consumers must receive safe, effective and quality drugs. For it is the mission and assignment of FDA and it is a matter of conscience and practical business outlook for the industry. Drugs are unique because their quality cannot be judged by the consumer. Moreover, their quality cannot be guaranteed by testing of the final product (the tests are performed only on a small sample of a batch). Obviously, then it becomes the responsibility of manufacturer to exercise control over all such factors that affect quality of the final product. A manufacturer's responsibility for control is founded today in the law. Schedule M of Drugs and Cosmetics Act, 1940, describes this law in the form of "Good Manufacturing Practices and requirements of Premises, Plants and equipments". The rule 71 of Drugs and Cosmetics rules 1945 clearly specifies the conditions for grant or renewal of a licence in form 25 (or form 25 F) in which one of the conditions is that "the licensee shall comply with the requirements of GMP" as laid down in Schedule M (w.e.f. 24.6.1988). It has been clearly specified that "each licensee shall evolve methodology and procedures, which should be documented and kept for reference and inspection".

It is the responsibility of manufacturer to exercise control over materials, methods, processes and activities in order to ensure identity, strength, quality and purity of the drug product. There shall be a quality control unit. The quality control unit/deptt. shall have responsibility and authority to approve or reject all components, drug product containers, closures, in process materials, packaging materials, labelling and drug products. It shall have authority to review production records to assure that no errors have occurred. Thus, quality control department can approve or reject the drug product manufactured by their organization. The concept of total quality control system thus includes all control measures contributing to the completed market dosage form. In this context, it shall be more appropriate to discuss as to what is quality ? Many attempts have been made to define the term quality. It has been defined by using the phrases such as "fitness for use", "compliance with specified requirements", "freedom from defects", "degree of excellence", "customer satisfaction", "ability to satisfy stated and implied needs of customer" etc. The definition given by "Swiss Standards Association" seems to be more comprehensive; it says "the degree to which the product characteristics conform to the requirements placed upon that product including reliability, maintainability and safety". The total control of quality as it applies to the drug industry is the organised effort within an entire establishment to design, produce, maintain and assure the specific quality in each unit of drug distributed.

The quality control is a plant-wide activity and presents the aggregate responsibility of all segments of a company. Hence, it is very clear that the quality control department does not merely perform the testing function. The term "quality assurance" is used to describe a discipline that includes the ability to ask the proper questions concerning functions responsible for various aspects of the drug production process in order to assure control. Thus, it should be clear that, while quality control refers to operational techniques and activities that are used to fulfill requirements for quality; the quality assurance means planned activities implemented within the system to fulfill requirements for quality. (The quality assurance is a post-operational activity). Thus, as a part of quality assurance steps; the GMP requirements should be included in the documented production and control operations.

Rather than reproducing the provisions made in the act; it shall be discussed with the emphasis on the intent of GMP regulations. Hence, the provisions made in the similar regulations viz. current good manufacturing practices promulgated by US FDA have also been considered here. US FDA has clearly described that the GMP regulations are intended to be general enough to be suitable for essentially all drug products, flexible enough to allow the use of sound judgement and permit innovation. It further states that the manufacture of Pharmaceuticals must be by current methods with current controls and hence, the name Current Good Manufacturing Practices (CGMP) regulations. The regulations places large burden on the manufacturer of Pharmaceuticals as it states that the standard is not only that practices be "current" but that they also be "good". Thus, the evaluation of compliance to regulations by the manufacturer shall be based on the measures taken by manufacturer to obtain knowledge, on a continuing basis, of both what is current and good and its incorporation in the present system of manufacture and control.

GMP – Factory Premises:

The location of factory premises should be such that the surrounding (External environment) should be free from unsanitary condition such as objectionable odour, air, water pollutants, sanitation hazards, insects and vermin. The premises should permit easy waste water removal and easy access to water, electricity fuel etc. The total area should be of adequate size so as to permit construction of building(s) that can ensure contamination free processing.

Buildings and Facilities:

The design and construction of buildings should be such that it facilitates cleaning and maintenance operations.

The walls, floors and ceilings shall be made of hard, non-porous and non-shedding materials and should be free from cracks and holes. The premises used for manufacturing, processing, packaging, labelling and testing purposes shall be compatible with other manufacturing operations that may be carried out in the same or adjacent premises. The buildings shall have adequate working spaces to allow orderly and logical placement of equipment and materials so as to avoid the risk of mix up between different drugs or with components and to avoid cross contamination.

Lighting, Ventilation, Air Filtration, Air Heating and Cooling:

Adequate lighting shall be provided as per the need of operations in all areas. Adequate ventilation and if necessary air conditioning to maintain a satisfactory temperature and relative humidity that will not adversely affect the drug during manufacturing and storage, shall be provided. Air filtration systems, including pre-filters and particulate matter air filters shall be used when appropriate on air supplies to production areas.

Disposal of Waste:

Waste water and other residues from the laboratory which might be prejudicial to the workers or to public health shall be disposed of after suitable treatment as per the prevailing requirements of the water pollution control authorities to render them harmless.

Water Supply:

The water used in manufacture shall be pure and of a drinkable quality, free from pathogenic microorganisms.

Requirements for Sterile Products Manufacturing Area:

Sterile manufacturing, filling and handling spaces requires special air processing. A separate enclosed areas specifically designed for the purpose shall be provided. For all areas where aseptic manufacture has to be carried out; bacteria retaining filters (HEPA filters) should be used for air supply and the air pressure should be higher than in the adjacent areas. The performance of the filters should be periodically checked and documented. In special areas, laminar flow units are to be used to avoid airborne contamination of the product. Continuous monitoring of air pressure and velocity should be considered for aseptic operations areas. Periodic monitoring for total particulate and viable micro-organisms must be performed.

Access to the manufacturing areas shall be restricted to minimum number or authorised personnel. Written procedures displayed at the entrance should be followed while entering and leaving the area.

Working Space and Storage area:

The manufacturer shall provide adequate working space (manufacturing and quality control) and adequate room for orderly placement of equipments and materials used for any of the operations. Generally, the requirements and utilization of space shall be as follows:

1. Appropriate spaces for equipments and materials in order to minimise or eliminate any possibility of mix-ups and cross contamination.

2. The receipt, storage and holding of all materials for a Pharmaceutical product prior to release for use.

3. Storage areas for materials designated as "under test", "approved", and "rejected."

4. Storage of finished products.

5. If needed suitable housing shall be provided for the care of any laboratory animals needed.

Health, Clothing and Sanitation of Workers:

To protect drug products from contamination by the personnel working in the manufacture, processing, packaging or holding of drug products; their periodic health check-up shall be performed. All personnel shall be free from contagious or obnoxious diseases. There shall be charge room (minimum 8 sq. m. area) separate for each sex with locker facilities and provided with items needed for personnel cleanliness. The personnel shall change their street clothes and wear clean clothing appropriate for the duties they perform. The workers engaged in the filling and sealing of containers of sterile preparations shall wear suitable sterile gowns headgear, footwear and masks made of synthetic fabrics to cover the nostrils and mouth during work.

Medical Services:

The manufacturer shall provide adequate first aid facilities. The workers periodic health check-up once in a year shall be performed and records thereof shall be maintained. Services of qualified physician shall be provided for assessing the health status of personnel involved in manufacturing and quality control of drugs.

Sanitation in the Manufacturing Premises:

The manufacturing premises shall be maintained in a clean and sanitary condition. There shall be written procedures describing in details the cleaning schedules, methods, equipment and materials to be used in cleaning. The personnel assigned to and responsible for cleaning shall be indicated in the written records. The manufacturing area shall not be used for storage of materials except for materials being processed. Eating, smoking or any unhygienic practices shall not be permitted in the manufacturing area.

Equipments:

1. Equipment used for the manufacture, processing, packaging, labelling, holding, testing or control of drug shall be maintained clean and orderly manner to achieve operational efficiency and desired quality of drug product.

2. The accuracy and precision of the equipment used for specific filling shall be checked and confirmed at regular intervals and its records shall be maintained.

3. The design and construction of equipment shall be such that all surfaces that come in contact with a drug product shall not be reactive, additive or absorptive.

4. The substances required for operation of the equipment such as lubricants or coolants should not contact drug products.

5. Specific written cleaning instructions for equipments should be readily available and followed by the operators.

6. Manufacturing equipment and utensils shall be thoroughly cleaned and if indicated should be disassembled and thoroughly cleaned to preclude the carry over of drug residences from previous operations.

7. Equipments used for critical steps in processing shall be monitored by devices capable of recording the permanent parameters or with alarm system to indicate malfunctioning.

Production and Process Controls:

There shall be written procedures for production and process control designed to assure that the drug products have the identity, strength, quality and purity. Such procedures should be drafted and reviewed by appropriate organisational units; and should be approved by quality control unit. The written procedures should be followed during various production and process control functions and should be documented at the time of performance. It is necessary that when each step is performed by a competent person; another equally competent persons verify that successful completion of sequential steps have occured. Thus, a concept of "doers and checkers" should be followed. When such concept is replaced by certain automated equipments, several quality control criteria should be considered regarding efficiency, accuracy, precision, standardisation, calibration and maintenance of records of equipment functioning and use. The drug components should be labelled whenever they are transferred to another container. The containers must be labelled with:

(i)   Component name or item code,

(ii) Receiving or control number,

(iii) Weight or measure in the container and

(iv) Batch for which the component is dispensed.

Further it is necessary that each component added to the batch should be certified by signature and date by the doer and verified by signature and date by the checker.

For issuing raw materials generally an order is initiated by a production planning and control section. A specialised raw material issuing section shall issue proper ingredients in proper amounts and records maintained by this section shall permit accountability of raw materials issued for specific lots and batches. A system of doers and checkers is utilized to verify amounts and identities of measured quantities. Signatures are recorded of all personnel handling or checking materials.

The compounding, storage containers and major equipments used during production of a batch should bear a label showing their status. The labels should indicate contents, phase of processing, name of product, lot number, total quantity, operators signature, date and last operation completed.

Precautions Against Contamination and Mix-up:

(i) The cross contamination with sex hormones, B-lactam antibiotics, antineoplastic drugs shall be prevented by appropriate methods utilizing separate building or adequately isolating the operations, adequate pressure differential in process area, suitable exhaust system and laminar flow air systems for sterile products.

(ii) The germicidal efficiency of UV lamps shall be checked and recorded. The water for injection IP shall be used immediately or stored at temperature not less than 80°C to prevent microbial growth.

(iii) Individual containers of liquid orals, parenterals and ophthalmic solutions shall be examined for freedom from foreign suspended matter.

(iv) All processes controls as required under master formula including room temperature, humidity, weight variation, disintegration time, mixing time, homogeneity of suspension, volume filled, leakage and clarity shall be checked and recorded.

Master Formula Records:

Written instructions relating to all manufacturing procedures for each product prepared and approved by competent technical staff (Head of production and quality control) shall be maintained. This record shall consists of:

(i) Name of the product, strength and dosage form.

(ii) Description of final containers, packaging materials and labels.

(iii) The identity, quantity, quality of each raw material to be used.

(iv) Description of all vessels, equipments with sizes to be used.

(v) Manufacturing and control instructions alongwith parameters for critical steps.

(vi) The expected theoretical yield at different stages of manufacture.

(vii) Precautions to be taken in manufacture and storage of drugs and of semi-finished products.

(viii) Requirements of in-process quality control tests and analysis to be carried out during each stage of manufacture.

Batch Manufacturing Records:

The licensee shall maintain batch manufacturing record as per Schedule U for each batch of the drug produced. It shall be a copy of the relevant parts of the master formula. It shows the complete manufacturing history of each batch of drug. Indicating that it has been manufactured, tested and analysed in accordance with the manufacturing producers and written instructions as per the master formula.

According to the Schedule 'U' the following particulars are to be shown in the manufacturing records.

(i)   Serial number.

(ii) Name of the product (name of pharmacopoeia as the case may be).

(iii) Lot/Batch size.

(iv) Lot/Batch number.

(v)   Date of commencement of manufacture and date of completion.

(vi) Name of all ingredients, quantities required for the lot/batch size, quantities actually used.

(vii) Control reference numbers in respect of raw materials used in formulations.

(viii) Reference to analytical report numbers.

(ix) Actual production and packing particulars including the size and quantity of finished packings.

(x)   Date of release of finished packing for distribution or sale.

(xi) Signature of the expert staff responsible for the manufacture.

Labelling and Packaging:

All labels for containers, carton and boxes and all circulars, inserts and leaflets shall be examined and released as satisfactory for use by the quality control personnel. Prior to packaging and labelling of a given batch of drug it must be ensured that the batch has been tested and duly approved and released by quality control personnel. Unused coded and spoiled labels and packaging materials shall be destroyed. Records shall be maintained for each shipment received of each packaging materials indicating receipt, examination relating to testing and whether accepted or rejected.

Distribution Records:

Records of distribution of finished batch of drug shall be maintained in order to facilitate prompt and complete recall of the batch if necessary.

Records of Complaints and Adverse Reactions:

The serious adverse reactions reported alongwith comments shall be informed to the concerned licensing authority.

QUALITY ASSURANCE AND QUALITY CONTROL

The quality of product is being approached through the concept of Total Quality Management (TQM). According to the changed emphasis the efforts are directed towards defect prevention (proactive) rather than defect detection (after the fact). The Quality assurance and Quality control develop and follow standard internal operating procedures directed towards assuring the quality, safety, purity and effectiveness of the drug supply. The Regulatory Authority (FDA) has issued the regulations viz. Good Manufacturing Practices (GMP), giving directions to the industry to plan for and to remain in compliance. Assurance of compliance to these government regulations and with internal policies and procedures shall be the responsibility of quality organisations in the industry.

The quality organisations consists of two different departments viz. Quality Assurance (QA) and Quality Control (QC) in the industry. The following chart gives idea about responsibilities of these departments.

Table 7.1: Responsibilities of Quality Assurance and Quality Control Departments

Quality Assurance	Quality Control
1. Responsible for assuring that the quality policies adopted by the company are followed.	1. Responsible for day-to-day control of quality within a company.
2. It helps to prepare standard operating procedures (SOPs) useful for control of quality. It determines whether the product meets all specifications and is manufactured according to internal standards and GMPs or not.	2. Responsible for analytical testing of raw materials and inspection of packaging components including labelling. It conducts in-process testing where required. It performs environmental monitoring operations and inspect operations for compliance.
3. It performs quality audits to determine whether the operations have adequate systems, facilities and written procedures and all these are followed by trained operators or not.	3. Selecting qualified vendors from whom raw materials are purchased.
4. It is the final authority for product acceptance or rejection.	

Chapter ... 8

INTRODUCTION TO ALTERNATIVE SYSTEMS OF MEDICINES

Diseases are as old as mankind and throughout history, human beings have been fighting against diseases. Research workers and scholars have tried to find out causes of diseases and means to cure them. Historic accounts indicate that magic and empiricism each played an important role in finding and employing remedies. However, man's instinct rather than magic and empiricism was responsible for internal employment of remedies. Instinct was affirmed or denied by increasingly self-conscious empiricism. This empiricism became the foundation of medical science. The systematized and purified observations were insufficient, and much of the sufferings remained beyond ordinary observations: explanations and control. Hence, for thousands of years the magical religious practices tended to prevade medical practices. As civilization advanced to a higher level and magical beliefs and animism were reduced to mere superstition religion became the vehicle for health. In early 20th century with the advent of the microbiology the germ theory of disease was putforth. The empirical cause of disease were replaced by different theories and factors with scientific basis. In consistent with the concept of health and diseases different therapies were evolved for treating diseases. Variety of such therapies include modern system of medicine; the allopathy and the traditional systems of medicine viz. Ayurveda, Homoeopathy, Unani and Siddha etc.

I. AYURVEDA

Ayurveda a traditional indigenous system of medicine is a part of the rich and vast Indian heritage. The word Ayurveda is derived from two words viz. Ayu means life and veda means ancient repository of knowledge. Thus, Ayurveda means the knowledge of life or the science of life. It considers both happiness and miseries of life and explains as to how a best life span can be achieved. It is not only a system of medicine, considering diseases and its treatment but also describes the maintenance of healthy and prosperous life.

The Indian tradition has recognised four primary objectives of life viz. Dharma, Artha, Karma and Moksha; attainment of which is necessary for well-being of individual and society. Health and longevity is considered essential for achievement of these objectives. According to Vagbhata, "A person who desires longevity which is a suitable vehicle for the achievement of dharma (religious virtues), artha (wealth and satisfaction of objects of senses) and Sukha (happiness) should observe with great respect the instructions prescribed in Ayurveda. Ayurveda is defined as, "the science through which the scholars could ascertain factors which are useful and harmful for life and causative factors as well as the treatment of diseases.

History of Ayurveda:

This traditional medical system was introduced early in the vedic age, and is claimed to be the first of its kind in the world. This science of medicine has taken the origin from the gods. According to Indian mythology, Ayurveda was first perceived by Brahma, and he taught this Science to Daksa Prajapathi, who taught it to the Aswini Kumaras and they taught it to Indra (God king). The Ayurvedic texts differ regarding further hierarchy of propounders of Ayurveda. The twin Aswinis have always been described as the physicians of the Gods. Many of their marvellous cures have been recorded in the Rigveda. It is evident that during vedic period medicinal herbs were known to the ancient Hindus. But it did not became a regular science till the Puranic age.

According to Sushruta the Indra taught this science to Dhanvantari. Dhanvantari taught Ayurveda to his eight disciples. Acharya Sushrata compiled all teachings of Dhanvantari in a classic text form named as Sushruta Samhita. The period of Dhanvantari is supposed to be 1000 B.C. just contemporary to Acharya Charaka. Thus, Charak Samhita written by Acharya Charaka, the Sushruta Samhita and Astanga Hridaya written by Acharya Vagabhatta are the three classic texts of Ayurveda.

The mythical account of Ayurveda indicates that it originated in the Kaliyuga; when Brahma, taking compassion on man's weak, degenerate and suffering state produced the Upaveda or commentary on the sacred vedas, which consists of four treaties. viz.

(1) Dharmashastra, (2) Dharmaveda, (3) Gandharva veda and (4) Ayurveda.

Branches of Ayurveda:

The original work of Lord Brahma is divided into eight parts as described below:

1. **Kayachikista (Internal medicine):** It concerns with the principles and methods of treatment of diseases primarily of endogenous origin.

2. **Salya (surgery):** It deals with the diseases that are treated with the surgical measures. It explains the methods used to remove foreign substances entered into the body, dead child from mothers womb and use of different surgical instruments.

3. **Shalakya:** It deals with the diagnosis and curing diseases of eyes, ears, mouth, nose and throat.

4. **Kaumarabhritya:** A branch of Ayurveda concerned with nutrition of child and cure of diseases of childhood.

5. **Agad Tantra (Toxicology):** It deals with the diagnosis and treatment of poisoning.

6. **Rasayan Tantra (Geriatrics):** Deals with the maintenance of optimum life span of the individual.

7. **Vijikaran Tantra:** It deals with the means of restoring the manhood and increasing the human race.

8. **Bhuta Vidya:** It concerns with the diagnosis and treatment of mental diseases, caused by evil spirits.

Some Concepts of Ayurveda:

Purusha Vichaya Sharir:

The similarity in structures and characters of body of individual and universe has been described in this subject. According to this concept the body of individual is composed of shad-dhatus. (6 elements) viz. Prithvi, Apa, Vayu, Teja, Akash and Braham. Body's form is simulated to the element Prithvi, moistness is Apa, Heat is Teja, Pranamal (life energy) is Vayu, the hollow spaces are Akash and Brahma is Antaratma (Soul).

According to Sushruta, "The aggravated dosas afflict the dhatus by its own tejas. It gets further aggravated by the association of the agni which is present in dhatus to produce a disease. Thus, Ayurveda has described the etiology of diseases on the basis of structure and characters of body individual.

Tridosa theory of Ayurveda:

Vat (Vayu), Pitta and Kapha are three dosas in the body. As long as they remain in definite proportion in the body, the body activities are regulated and health is maintained. But any change in this equilibrium results in disease.

Improper diet and disturbances in physical and mental activities may disturb this equilibrium and results into disease. All the measures including drugs, dietary restrictions, physical and mental exercises have been described to alleviate the aggravated dosas or to eliminate them from body. Moreover, the natural factors e.g. seasons affecting the equilibrium have also been described and the precautions to be taken to avoid disease by healthy person have been given in the form of ritu carya. It has been stated that the Ayurvedic medicines bring about equilibrium of dosas, that has been disturbed by pathogens and create a environment in the tissues in which the germs die their natural death.

II. HOMOEOPATHY

This peculiar Pharmacologic system was proposed around the turn of the 19th century by the German Physician Samuel Hahnemann (1755-1843). The implications of this new system of medicine were quite revolutionary that time. It had a strong appeal not only to the public but to many regular physicians and the system flourished in United States until 1900. However, new scientific developments greatly undermined the rationale of homeopaths and it had undergone a great decline in Europe and America. Once again during last decade it has gained acceptance from both doctors and patients.

Basic principles of homoeopathy:

1. The Simile principle:

The basis of homoeopathy is basic natural principle. In Latin this principle is stated as, "similia similibus curentur" and it means "let likes be treated by likes". The general idea of homoeopathy is to encourage the defence mechanisms of the body by irritation rather than to attack the disease as such. The substance which can produce specific symptoms in a healthy individual cure those same symptoms in a sick individual. Drugs are tested on healthy individuals to determine the type of symptoms they produce, and thus, their therapeutic indications. Hahnemann called his theory homoeopathy (from the Greek homoion-similar) as contrasted to traditional therapy using remedies with properties opposite to the symptoms of the disease which he called allopathy (from the Greek allion-different).

2. Principle of minimum dose:

The concept of encouraging body's defence provides rationale for the use of minute doses in homoeopathic practice. It is in consistant with the biologic fundamental law which states that, "minute stimuli initiate the activity of living organisms, and those of medium strength promote it, while strong stimuli slow it down and very strong ones stop it." Thus, in homoeopathy practitioners prescribe very small dose in order not to bring about an enormous aggravation of patient's symptomatology. Once the initial microdose has acted it will bring about a curative response, that follows. Hence, the remedy acts as a triggering and catalytic agent and needs to be administered in very small doses.

3. Principle of single remedy:

In homoeopathy, an ailment is treated according to its symptoms. To find out the symptoms of a medicine these are tested on healthy persons. This is known as "drug proving." Thus, for effecting real cure in the patient; the practitioner has to find out a single remedy that has produced in its proving the greatest similitude to the symptom complex existing in the patient. Any other remedy may not be effective in producing real cure. Dr. Hahnemann himself has insisted on the use of only a single active drug at a time.

Finding out such single remedy requires great deal of time, energy and dedication on part of the practitioners. Perhaps on this point depends the skill of practitioner and success of homoeopathic therapy.

4. Principle of individualisation:

In homoeopathy, every patient is considered as peculiarly individual. The human beings react differently from each other and this is true in case of both medicines and diseases. Therefore, each patient will have to be treated individually on the basis of his or her symptoms. The physician has to consider the whole range of mental, emotional and physical pathology in order to understand how a patient is reacting to his illness. Accordingly, he has to select the appropriate remedy that will further stimulate the patients defense mechanism to combat the disease.

Some facts and findings:

1. Homoeopathy has been found very effective especially in treating chronic diseases such as diabetes, arthritis, bronchial asthma, allergic conditions, epilepsy and psychological disorders.

2. Homoeopathy provides long lasting cure rather than only alleviating the symptoms; as it re-establishes internal order.

3. In homoeopathy, medicines have been tested on healthy persons and then validated making the system fool-proof and safe.

4. Homoeopathy can be used in undiagnosed cases which present scanty symptomatology.

5. As microdoses of medicines are utilized in homoeopathy the price of medicines and the cost of health is very low.

6. Experimental evidence to demonstrate the effectiveness of homoeopathy is lacking.

7. Well trained and dedicated practitioners of homoeopathy are rare.

8. The mental and physical symptoms created in a healthy person by administering a medicine are catalogue in the homeopathic materia medica.

III. UNANI SYSTEM OF MEDICINE

This system was developed during the Arab civilization. It is known as 'Unani Tibb' system of medicine. The system is based on the concept of 'four humors', putforth by Hippocrates. According to this concept the cause of health or sickness is the harmony or disharmony of the four humors. The four humours present in the body are blood, phlegm, yellow bile, and black bile. The balance and distribution of these humors is fundamental to the living organisms. Temperament (Mizaj) of individual depends upon the predominance of one of these humours. According to Galen's concept the temperament of individual may be Sanguine, Phlegmatic, Choleric or Melancholic. Any change in temperament causes change in health state of individual. Thus, in Unani Tibb system temperament of individual is considered as the basis of pathology, diagnosis and treatment of diseases.

The humours are assigned temperaments as shown in Fig. 8.1, thus, blood is hot and moist, phlegm is cold and moist, yellow bile is hot and dry and black bile is cold and dry.

Drugs are grouped according to temperament they can produce in the body. The abnormal pathological temperament resulting into disease is corrected by administering drugs.

Body's power of self-preservation and adjustment, which corresponds to defence mechanism is highly appreciated and hence, the aim of Unani system is to help in developing this power in the state of imbalance.

Every disease is fully described in Unani texts, with signs and symptoms, hints for diagnosis and any complications. For diagnosis the pathological examination of urine and stools is made. Body heat is measured by pulse, palpation and thermometer. Examination of tongue, eyes, lips, tonsils, throat and teeth all provide information useful for diagnosis. Emotions such as fear, grief, happiness or anger also are considered in diagnosis.

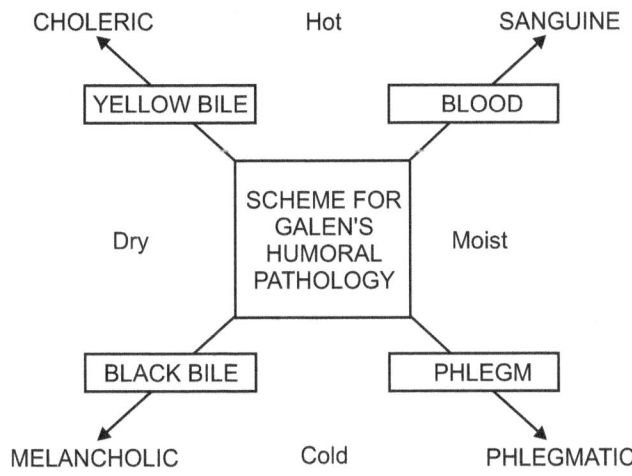

Fig. 8.1: Relationship of humor and temperament

The drugs utilized in therapy includes those of plant, animal, mineral and marine origin. The drugs may be prescribed either singly or in combinations. The traditional practitioner is known as the Tabib. The Tabib should ensure that the temperament of patient is allowed to function according to its own nature and speed; at the same time medicines should help its functioning.

IV. TRADITIONAL CHINESE MEDICINE AND KAMPOH SYSTEM

The Chinese system of medicine is still prevalent. This ancient system finds its references in the Yellow Emperor's classic of Internal Medicine (*Huang Di Nei Jing*) which is believed to be prepared between 200 BC and 100 AD. This herbal is based on the idea that all life is subject to natural laws. The hypothesis includes two quite different systems the *yin* and *yang* theory and the five elements (i.e. water, metal, earth, fire and wood). These two theories have been developed separately and differ in terms of diagnosis and treatment. The *yin* and *yang* theory says that everything in the universe consists of a dark (*yin*) and light side (*yang*). These are complimentary opposites like wet and dry, up and down or day and night. The five elements theory proposes that each element leads to the next in a continuous fashion like fire to metal, to wood, to earth, to water and so on. The elements are the five phases indicating the process of continuous movement of life. The elements play a dynamic role in the Chinese system of medicine like in making groups of herbal tastes and parts of body.

According to this system, diseased conditions are the expressions of imbalance in *yin* and *yang* like excess or deficiency of either of them. For example, shivering occurs due to excess of *yin* while excess of *yang* causes a fever. The treatment makes use of various herbs especially the formulations. The important herbs from this system are *Ephedra sinica, Rheum palmatum, Carthamus tinctorius, Clerodendron trichotomum, Panax ginseng, Schisandra, Chinensis, Schizonepeta tenuifolia, Agastache rugosa* etc.

The traditional chinese system of medicine has spread to Japan and Korea in a form called *Kampoh*, called as the traditional system of Japanese medicine. Although, it has developed its own characters, giving due importance to the Japanese style of simplicity and naturalness, still the basic ideas like *yin* and *yang* have a crucial role in *Kampoh* medicine. As compared to *Kampoh*, Korean system is very much similar to Chinese system and includes most of the herbs in it.

V. SIDDHA

The term Siddha means achievement. The saintly personalities known as 'Siddhars' in prevedic period have attained proficiency in medicine through practice of Bhakti and Yoga. Siddha system of medicine owes it's origin to the Dravidian culture. It is mainly therapeutic in nature. The principles and doctrines of this system, both fundamental and applied have a close similarity to Ayurveda. Hence, like Ayurveda this system also believes that all objects in universe are made up of five basic elements viz. earth, water, sky, fire and air. The diagnosis is made through pulse reading, body colour, voice, examination of urine and tongue. The medicines mentioned in Pharmacopoeia of Siddha include mainly the mercury, sulphur, iron, copper, bitumen, arsenic and vegetable poisons. This system of medicine is prevalent in southern states of India and in Sri Lanka, Malaysia and Singapore where Dravidian civilization was dominant. Most of the Siddha literature is in Tamil language.

VI. NATUROPATHY AND YOGA

Naturopathy is not merely a system of treatment, but also a way of life, which is based on laws of nature. The attention is particularly paid to eating and living habits, adoption of purificatory measures, use of hydrotherapy, mud packs, massage, etc.

The system of Yoga is as old as Ayurveda. The eight components of Yoga are restraint, observance of austerity, physical postures, restraining and sense organs, breathing exercises, contemplation, meditation and samadhi. Yoga exercises have potential in improvement of better circulation of oxygenated blood in the body, restraining and sense organs, improvement of social and personal behaviour and induction of tranquility and serenity in the mind.

VII. BACH FLOWER REMEDIES

Bach flower remedies were discovered by **Edward Bach**, a physician in the early decades of the twentieth century. These include 38 remedies prepared from flowers of wild plants, bushes or trees. The remedies are prescribed as per the patient's state of mind like, depression, anger, fear, worry, etc. The prescription is meant for achieving vitality and a harmonious state of mind, the lack of which causes sickness. According to **Dr. Edward Bach**, the remedies enrich the body with vibrations of human's superior nature, rather than attacking a disease. It is believed here that change of outlook and peace of mind have a major role in healing of a disease. Some of the remedies prescribed are white chestnut, wild rose, mimulus, agrimony, chicory, gentian etc. Some states of mind for which they are prescribed are worry, vague, fear of unknown origin, despair, extreme mental anguish, extreme fright, lack of confidence, etc. For the purpose of medication, the mother tinctures are prepared and dispensed in a diluted form as in homeopathic potentiation.

VIII. AROMATHERAPY

It is one of the most ancient healing arts and traces its origin to 4500 B.C., when Egyptians used aromatic substances in medicines. Greeks also used plant essences for aromatic baths and scented massage. In ayurveda, there is mention of scented baths (abhyanga). Prof. **Gantle Fosse**, a French cosmetic chemist coined the term *'Aromatherapy'* and described healing properties of essential oils. Many scientists at various universities are, now-a-days, investigating this method of healing. Different essential oils from various parts of plants are massaged into skin to treat a range of diseases, as well as, to have an effect on the mind and emotions. They are massaged into the skin or inhaled or taken as bath. They have been shown to heal wounds, promote formation of scar tissue, treat achne and skin problems, pre-menstrual tension, rheumatism, poor circulation and also nervine disorders like headache, stress, insomnia, etc. Various essential oils used in aromatherapy are basil, bergamot, black pepper, calendula, caraway, eucalyptus, fennel, garlic, geranium, ginger, jasmine, juniper, lavender, rosemary and sandalwood.

Chapter ... 9

DRUG DELIVERY SYSTEM

9.1 NON-STERILE MONOPHASIC LIQUIDS

(A) AROMATIC WATERS AND CONCENTRATED AROMATIC WATERS

Aromatic waters are clear, aqueous solutions, saturated with volatile oils or other aromatic or volatile substances. Their odours and tastes are similar to those of the drugs or volatile substances from which they are prepared.

Aromatic waters may be used for perfuming, flavouring or for special purposes like vehicle, stimulent, astringent etc.

Methods of Preparation:

Aromatic waters are prepared by any of the following three general methods:

(i)   Distillation method

(ii)   Solution method and

(iii)   Alternative solution method.

(i)   Distillation Method:

It is the most common method for the preparation of aromatic waters. It involves the placing of the coarsely ground odoriferous portion of the plant or drug from which the aromatic water is to be prepared in a suitable still with sufficient purified water. Most of the water is distilled over steam and the condensed distillate contains aromatic principles. Development of empyreumatic odour can be prevented by avoiding charming and scorching of the plant or drug material in the still. The excess oils collected with the distillate rise to the top of the aqueous product and is removed. The remaining aqueous solution, saturated with volatile material is usually clarified by filteration.

In some cases e.g. orange flower and rose waters which contain volatile principles in small quantities, it may be necessary to return the distillate several times to the still and redistill. Depending upon the number of distillations these products are known as double or triple distilled. The number of distillations carried out is indicated by Xs, on the labels of aromatic waters, each X represents one distillation like X, XX, XXX etc.

(ii) Solution Method:

These methods are simple, quick and economic as compared to distillation.

According to this method the corresponding essential oil from which aromatic water is to be prepared, should be shaken with 500 times its volume of purified water. Shaking is repeated several times during a period of about thirty minutes. The mixture is then set aside overnight and clarified by filtration.

(iii) Alternative Solution Method:

This method consists of incorporating 2 ml of volatile oil or 2 g of suitably comminuted aromatic solid with 15 g of powdered talc or a sufficient quantity of kieselghur or pulped filter paper. 1000 ml of purified water is added to this mixture and the resulting slurry is throughly agitated several times for about 10 minutes and filtered. More purified water is passed through the filter paper to make up the volume.

Powdered talc, kieselghur, pulped filter, paper and purified siliceous earth are act as filter aid and render the product more clear, and also act as distributing agents for the aromatic substances. In the latter capacity it serves to accelerate the rate of solution by permitting the aromatic substance to be adsorbed and spread over its entire surface, thereby increasing the surface area of the aromatic substance exposed to the solvent action of the water. It is for this reason that a saturated solution of the aromatic substance can be effected in short period.

Concentrated Aromatic Waters:

Volatile oil generally contains two types of chemical constituents:

(i)   Aromatic principles (oxygenated terpins) and

(ii)   Non-aromatic principles (terpins)

The flavouring property and the medicinal effect of volatile oil is mainly due to oxygenated terpin. Both the constituents are completely soluble in 90% alcohol but when the concentration of alcohol is reduced to about 55% the terpins gets precipitated, while oxygenated terpins remain in solution and this principle is used in the preparation of aromatic waters.

Following aromatic waters are official in pharmacopoeia:

Concentrated waters:	Anise water BPC
	Caraway water BPC
	Cinnamon water BPC
	Dill water BPC
Aromatic waters:	Camphor water IP, BPC
	Chloroform water IP
	Peppermint water BP
	Strong Rose water USP

Infusions:

Infusion is the process of extracting the vegetable drugs wherein water is used as menstruum. The process consists of treating vegetable crude drugs with boiling water but the drugs are not boiled with the menstruum. The entire mixture is allowed to cool, filtered and supplied. Infusion for use subjected to boiling process. The mixture is allowed to remain in a closed vessel for specified length of time. Freshly prepared infusions should be used. Coarse powder is used for the preparation of infusion. Water causes great expansion of ordinary vegetable tissues and it readily penetrates into it. Drug menstruum ratio is also large. This process is only applicable to those drugs which light structured without dense tissue and the constituents are water soluble. Too fine powder is used gives difficulty in filtration. If specific method or the preparation is not prescribed then the following general method be used.

General Method:

Moisten 50 gm of coarsely powdered drug in a suitable vessel with 50 ml of cold water and allot it to stand for 15 minutes. Then add 900 ml boiling water and keep the lid. Allow it to stand for 30 minutes the strain the liquid and add sufficient water to make the volume 1000 ml. If the active principles are more soluble in cold water then infusion should be prepared with cold water only.

Since, the active constituent of quassia i.e. quassin is more soluble in cold water, cold menstruum is used in the preparation of infusion of quassia.

These preparations quickly deteriorate as a result of microbial contanination and must be used within 12 hours after preparation. They have been now-a-days replaced by concentrated infusions which are made by cold extraction with 25 per cent alcohol. Alcohol preserves the product indefinitely. Dilution of 1 part of this product to 1 part with purified water gives a product resembling fresh infusion.

However, fresh infusions can be stored for fairly good length of time if it is stored below 10°C which retard the growth of micro-organism. Volatile oil present in the preparation has mild germicidial action.

Infusions are normally prepared easily from drugs of vegetable origin with water soluble active principles. However, these preparations have almost disappeared from use.

Fig. 9.1 shows the device used to prepare the infusion. This contains perforated earthen-ware tray at specific height over which drug is placed and menstruum poured.

Fig. 9.1: Infusion pot

Concentrated infusions:

These differ from the infusions in the respect that they either use alcohol as a menstruum or alcohol is used as a preservative. They are prepared by method of maceration similar to the tinctures.

Concentrated infusion preparations are actually liquid extracts which on dilution resembles fresh infusions. Normally, such dilutions are prepared with one volume of concentrated preparation and seven volumes of purified water. Such preparations should be used within 12 hours because low alcohol content has very little preservation action.

Following are the examples of concentrated infusions:

(1)   Concentrated Compound Chirata infusion IP, 66.

(2)   Concentrated Compound Gentian infusion BP, 1973.

(3)   Concentrated Buchu infusion BPC.

Concentrated infusions are prepared by double or triple maceration method, similar to tinctures.

Preparation of infusion by double and triple maceration process is carried out by the following general methods.

Double Maceration:

1.   Macerate the drug with part of menstruum for 48 hours and press the marc.

2.   Macerate the marc with remaining menstruum for 24 hours and press to express out the extract.

3.   Mix the liquids of both macerations. Allow it to stand for 14 days and filter.

Examples:

1.   **Concentrated Infusion of Orange BPC:** Dried bitter orange peel with 25 per cent alcohol as menstruum.

2.   **Concentrated Infusion of Clove:** Clove No. 10 powder with 25 per cent alcohol as menstruum.

3.   **Gentian Concentrated Compound Infusion:** BP.

Triple Maceration:

1.   Macerate the drug with part of menstruum for one hour and reserve the extract.

2.   Macerate the marc with second part of menstruum for one hour and

3.   Macerate it again for one hour with remaining menstruum.

      Press the marc lightly.

Combine second and third extract and evaporate it to specific concentration of extract. Mix it with the first reserve extract. Then add 90 per cent alcohol to one fourth volume of total volume. Adjust the final volume with water.

Examples:

Concentrated Infusion of Senega, BPC.

Concentrated Infusion of Calumba, BPC.

Decoctions:

Decoction is the process of extracting the hard and woody crude drugs wherein the water is used as menstruum and the crude drugs are boiled alongwith menstruum. Decoction differs from the infusion in the respect that the crude drugs in infusion are not boiled with the menstruum but only boiling menstruum is poured over the crude drugs. Freshly prepared decoction should only be dispensed, as it also extracts mucilageneous and albuminous matter as in infusions. This process is used for water soluble vegetable constituents for extraction, which are heat stable.

The general process involves the following procedures:

Place 50 gm of drug in a closed vessel and add 1000 ml cold water. Boil it for 15 minutes. Allow it to cool at 40°C. Press the marc and pass sufficient cold water to obtain 1000 ml.

Following are the examples of decoction:

(1)   Compound concentrated Aloe decoction BPC

(2)   Concentrated Cinchona decoction BPC

(3)   Prepared Coffee decoction BPC.

(4)   Decoction of Irish Moss BPC.

(B) GLYCERITES (GLYCERINES)

Glycerites are the solutions or mixtures of medicated substances in at least 50 per cent by weight of glycerine. Glycerine acts as vehicle for dissolving active principle. They

1.   Adhere to the surface of the skin especially mucous wall.

2.   Acts as preservative when not diluted.

3.   Give local soothing effect.

4.   Glycerines gives viscous stable solution. Thus, prolong the action.

5.   Medicaments which are comparatively less soluble in water are normally given with glycerine, thus, it is a good solvent.

They may be used such as or after dilution. Dilution may be effected by using purified water except for glycerine of phenol. Phenol glycerine if diluted by water gives irritation on application and hence diluted with glycerine only. These preparations are hydgroscopic and hence, must be stored in well closed container. They may be used as bacteriostalic, analgesic, astringent.

Examples of official glycerines are:

(i)   Glycero boxa IP.

(ii)   Glycerin of Phenol IP.

(iii) Tannic acid glycerin IP.

Glycerine of starch and glycerine of papain are the important official glycerines.

(C) SOLUTIONS

When two or more substances are mixed together chemically and physically homogeneous mixture is obtained. The mixture or the product is termed as solution. Sometimes, alcohol or glycerine is added as a preservative or to facilitate getting a clear solution.

It is presummed that the particles of the substances go to their molecular dimensions. Depending upon the size of the dispersed particles, the product is a true solution, colloidal solution or suspension.

Thus, in case of true solutions, the particles of dispersed phase will pass through parchament and particle size is 0.1 μ to 1.0 μ.

While in colloidal solutions the particles of dispersed phase do not pass through parchament paper. They are retained and their size is 10 to 100 mμ.

In case of suspensions the particles are so large that they are retained even an ordinary filter paper.

In a solution, the term solvent and solute are arbitary and normally express physical state of solvent. One which dissolves and is in continuous phase is a solvent, whereas one which gets dissolved and is in dispersed phase is a solute.

Sometimes this may go otherwise as in case of liquified phenol or solutions of chloral hydrate in water, wherein it is solution of water in phenol or solutions of water in chloral hydrate.

True-solutions can be of the following types:

(a)   Solution of solids in liquids.

(b)   Solution of liquids in liquids.

(c)   Solution of gases in liquids.

(d)   Solution of gases in solids.

(e)   Solution of gases in gases.

Factors affecting the rate of solution:

Several factors affect the rate of solution. The important of them are as follows:

1.   Temperature:

Usually, the rate of solubility goes on increasing with rise in temperature i.e. more the temperature more will be the solubility of solute, but in some cases temperature does not affect the rate of solution and exceptionally it has adverse effect. That is it goes on decreasing as is observed in case of paraldehyde or calcium hydroxide in hot water.

2.   Particle size of the solute:

Smaller the particle size more will be the rate of solution, since every small particle has got more area to get dissolved.

3.   Agitation:

In case of solution, the solute becomes concentrated in the nearby solvent and if it is dissolved it will proceed to saturation. Thus, agitation or stirring increases the rate of solution.

Vehicles:

The vehicles or solvents are used for the purpose of dissolving and rendering drugs more palatable and facilitating their administration. Important vehicles are waters, syrups and elixirs.

Excipients:

Apart from active or therapeutic ingredients, dosage forms of drugs contain a number of inert substances to produce the suitable formulation.

These inert substances themselves are known as excipients or additives each of which has a specific function or role to be played in the product, thus they are actually pharmaceutical necessities.

Excipients must be therapeutically inert, non-toxic and should not affect the stability of the product in which they are used.

Excipients commonly used are classified according to the part they play and fall within the following groups:

Table 9.1: Classification of excipients

	Types		Examples
1.	Diluents or bulking agents	–	Lactose, dextrose, dicalcium phosphate, sodium chloride etc.
2.	Adsorbents	–	Magnesium carbonate, Kaolin, Talc, MgO etc.
3.	Binders or adhesives	–	Guar gum, acacia, CMC, PVP, Polyethylene glycol.
4.	Lubricants	–	Magnesium stearate, Calcium stearate, Talc.
5.	Glidants	–	Boric acid, Sodium chloride, Calcium stearate, etc.
6.	Anti-adhesives or anti-sticking agents	–	Stearic acid, Coeol butter, Paraffin, etc.
7.	Disintegrating agents or disintegrators	–	Starches, CMC, Algins, Veegum, Sodium lauryl sulphates etc.
8.	Wetting agents	–	Sorbitan derivatives – SLS etc.
9.	Colours	–	Permitted and certified by FDA
10.	Flavours	–	Orange, Raspberry, Lemon, Pineapple etc.
11.	Sweetening agents	–	Sodium saccharate, Manitol, Sucrose etc.
12.	Granulating agents	–	Alcohol, Water etc.

(i) Syrups:

They are concentrated solutions (66.7% W/W) of sucrose in water. Such syrups are called simple syrups. When they contain some added medicinal substance they are called medicated syrups. e.g. chloral hydrate, piperazine citrate, etc. When they contain any flavouring substances they are called flavoured syrups. e.g. cherry, orange etc.

These are viscous oral liquids that may contain one or more active ingredients in solution. The vehicle usually contains large amounts of sucrose or other sugars to which certain polyhydric alcohols may be added to inhibit crystallisation or to modify solubilisation, taste and other vehicle properties.

Sugarless syrups may contain sweetening agents and thickening agents. Suitable for diabetic patients or for special purpose. Syrups may contain ethanol (95%) as a preservative or as a solvent to incorporate flavouring agents. Antimicrobial agents may also be added to medicinal syrups, generally they are propyl or methyl para amino benzoic acid or their sodium salts. They are used alone or in combination.

Method of Preparation:

Various methods are used for the preparation of syrups depending on the physical and chemical properties of the substances being used in their preparation. The methods are named as under:

(1)   Preparation of syrup by using heat.

(2)   Preparation without the use of heat and by agitation only.

(3)   Addition of medicinal liquid to the syrup.

(4)   By percolation method.

Simple syrup is prepared by heating, while ferrous sulphate syrup NF is prepared by agitation method.

Syrup of Balsam of Tolu and syrup of wild cherry are prepared by percolation method.

Uses of Syrups:

(i)   They act as demulcents in cough. They act by coating the mucous membrane and thus decrease pharyngeal irritation.

(ii)   They increase the viscosity of the solution; thereby help in suspension of insoluble substances.

(iii) They act as preservatives, because sugar in strong solution preserves many vegetables substances from decomposition.

(ii) Elixirs:

They are hydroalcoholic solutions of medicinal substances, sweetened and flavoured. They are excellent solvents for many drugs and mask the disagreeable odours and tastes of many substances dissolved in them.

Typical elixirs are:

(i)   Simple, Aromatic elixirs, Orange elixir, Benzaldehyde elixir etc.

(ii)   Medicinal elixirs e.g. Phenobarbital elixir, Terpin hydrate elixir, etc.

Elixirs are usually sweet, aromatic preparations, sometimes containing considerable proportion of alcohol and consequently require dilution at the time of use. Some elixirs are employed as flavouring agent. They differ from syrups in containing much less or sometimes no sugar. The preparations are made sweet by using soluble saccharin or glycerine.

Simple Elixir IP 1966

Orange tincture	....	75 ml
Syrup	....	400 ml
Chloroform water	....	to 1000 ml

Method of Preparation:

Mix all the ingredients with shaking to form sparkling clear liquid.

Use: Pharmaceutical aid.

Terpin Hydrate Elixir IP 1966

Formula:

Terpin hydrate	....	50 g
Orange oil	....	0.2 ml
Glycerin	....	400 ml
Alcohol	....	425 ml
Syrup	....	100 ml
Purified water	....	to 1000 ml

Method of Preparation:

Dissolve terpine hydrate in alcohol and add successively the orange oil, glycerine, syrup and sufficient purified water to make the product 1000 ml. Mix and filter if necessary.

Alcohol in the preparation, dissolves terpine hydrate and orange oil. Glycerine and syrup gives sweet taste. Glycerine also acts as preservative increases viscosity and adds to solvent action.

Use: Expectorant.

Piperazine citrate Elixir IP 1966.

Formula:

Piperazine citrate	....	180 g
Chloroform spirit	....	0.5 ml
Glycerine	....	100 ml
Orange oil	....	0.25 ml
Syrup	....	500 ml
Purified water	....	to 1000 ml

Method of Preparation:

Dissolve piperazine citrate in part of water. Then mix with agitation orange oil, glycerine, syrup in chloroform spirit and pour in watery solution of piperazine citrate. Adjust the volume with sufficient purified water.

Glycerine acts as solvent for oil and sweetening agent. Oil to give flavour. Chloroform spirit as flavouring and very mild preservative.

Storage: Preserve in well closed containers in cool place.

Use: As anthelmintic.

ENT PREPARATIONS

Various dosage forms used in the treatment of ear, nose, throat disorders or diseases are known as ENT preparations.

(i) Eye Drops:

Eye drops are aqueous or oily solutions. Ideal eye drops must have the following properties:

1.   They should be completely *sterile* at all times.

2.   They should be free from *suspended particles.*

3.   They should contain *preservative* to keep the solution free from growth of micro-organisms that may contaminate the drops during use.

4.   All eye drops must be *isotonic* with the lacrymal secretion.

5.   They should contain stable chemicals and solution must remain stable.

6.   They should have hydrogen ion concentration approaching the point of *neutrality.*

7.   A preservative must *not be present* in eye drops meant for injured eye, as preservatives are a source of irritation.

Preparation of Eye Drops:

Dissolve the active ingredients in water or oil with agitation. Add requisite quantity of preservative, adjust to the volume and filter suitably. Fill in the containers and sterilise by suitable method.

Preservatives:

(a)   Benzalkonium chloride in the concentration of 1 : 10,000 together with disodium ethylene diamine tetra acetic acid in the concentration 0.05 per cent may be used for preservation.

(b)   Chlorobutanol 0.5 per cent is another preservative of choice.

(c)   Sodium metabisulphate in the concentration of 0.1 percent is used as antioxident.

Other useful eye drop preservatives are 1 : 25,000 solution of phenylmercuric nitrate, methyl paraben and propyl parabens.

Containers:

The eye drops are sent out in vertically fluted bottles fitted with a bakelite cap carrying a dropper. The bottles are either amber coloured or green in capacities of 4 ml to 60 ml. These bottles must confirm to alkalinity limit test. The bottles must not impart particles to the contents and the closures should not absorb the active constituents or the preservative added to eye drops.

Hydrogen ion concentration of tears lie between 7.2 to 7.4. The irritation of the eye rises with rise in pH, while activity of some of the drugs, e.g. alkaloidal salt increases, with rise in pH. In such cases, a balance must be struck between higher activity and irritation. The adjustment is carried out by judicious use of buffer solutions. The commonly used buffers are solutions of phosphate buffers used in combination with normal saline.

The vehicle recommended for eye drops is normal saline or solution containing two per cent boric acid.

The eye solutions are prepared as follows:

All apparatus used must be sterile and filling in the final container is carried out aseptically. There sterilisation is effected by anyone of the following methods.

1.   Sterilisation of solution is carried out by filtration followed by aseptic transfer.

2.   Sterilisation is carried out in final container in an autoclave at 121°C for 15 minutes.

3.   Heat at 98°C to 100°C for thirty minutes after filtration and seal in the final container. The eye drops must be freshly prepared.

Base for Eye Ointment:

Normally, yellow soft paraffin containing 10% of wool fat is used as base. Before use, the base is melted and filtered to remove all particles of foreign matter and then sterilised for small scale.

The sterilisation of the base is carried out in an hot air oven. A little excess of base is taken. The collapsible tubes which serve as containers are well washed and wrapped in parchment paper.

The base and the collapsible tubes are heated until the thermometer registers 150°C and then maintained there for one hour.

The ointment is then prepared by using simple aseptic technique e.g. flamming scale, pan and spatula and using tile whose surface has been swabbed by acetone. When the ointment is completed, it is transferred to the jar in which the base was sterilised and it is warned gently in order to make pourable. The wapping from the collapsible tube is removed. It's mouth is tightly closed and then it is placed cap-downwards into containers containing cold water. Using a spatula the ointment is poured into the collapsible tube. It is allowed to solidify and then the tube is closed. It is labelled.

(ii) Eye solution:

Extemporaneous procedures:

I.   Solutions for applications to traumatized eyes:

All drugs used in traumatized eye, by accident or surgery should be compounded with 2% boric acid solution. All solutions intended for use during surgery should be filtered free of lint or other particulate matter and should be prepared without the addition of a preservative since all preservatives at bactericidal concentration are irritating to the inner structure of the eye. All such solutions should be dispensed in small containers (5-10 ml glass bottles) with screw caps for single patient only. The closed bottle and a separate dropper, should be packaged in a container that can be autoclaved.

II. Solutions intended for application to the eyes with an intact corneal epithelium:

(1)   Such solutions may be packaged in multiple dose containers for general patients.

(2)   Stock bottles of sterile purified water, isotonic sodium-chloride solution, 2% boric acid solution, and phosphate buffer at pH 6.8 to which preservatives have been added should be available for the compounding of prescriptions to be used in the intact eye.

(3)   All containers intermediate, final containers and closures should be treated by boiling or sterilised with a suitable disinfectant.

(4)   The solutions should be made free of suspended particles by any equipment which has been cleaned and sterilise previously.

(iii) Eye Lotions:

Eye lotions should be prepared with distilled water which has been boiled for about 30 minutes, and the measure, funnel and bottle should be well rinsed with a portion of the water before use. Eye lotions which contain only soluble substances should be sent out clear and bright. To achieve this lotion, before adjustment to volume should be filtered through filter paper and sufficient boiled water passed through the filter paper to produce the required volume.

Isotonicity of Ophthalmic Solutions:

(1)   An isotonic ophthalmic solution causes less discomfort than one that is paratonic.

(2)   Sterility and clarity is essential.

Ophthalmic solutions are required to be sterilised when prepared and great care must be exercised subsequently to prevent contamination in use. The common methods of sterilisation are:

(1) Autoclaving, (2) Bacterial filtration.

Preservation:

Preservatives are not to be used when solutions are intended for installation or injected into the chamber of the eye.

(iv) Nasal Drops:

Generally these are solutions of antibacterial substances, decongestants or substances which reduce mucous production.

Containers:

These are same as for eye and ear drops.

Nasal drops containing ephedrine as decongestant, atropine sulphate to change the mucous production are the common examples.

(v) Throat Paints:

Throat paints are required for their local action on the throat. It is, therefore, necessary that these solutions adhere to the affected portion for a reasonable time. It is for this reason that throat paints are solutions of drug in thick, viscous liquids like glycerin or liquid paraffin.

Containers:

Wide mouthed bottle, are used where the paint is to be used with a brush or swab. If the paints contain a *poison*, vertically fluted bottle may be used in order to distinguish it from ordinary medicine bottle. A few of the glycerities are also used as throat paints.

Mouth Washes and Gargles:

These are simple solutions intended to wash oral cavity and impart a deodorising and antiseptic action. The vehicle may be water or a combination of water and alcohol.

Gargles differ from mouth washes in that they are highly medicated.

Solution of potassium permangnate and dilute solution of phenol are the typical examples of mouth wash while 2.0% aqueous alum solution is the example of Gargle.

Dilute one Tablespoonful with a pint of warm water and gargle, morning and night.

AYURVEDIC LIQUIDS

In India various systems to medicines are being used for treatment of human-beings and animals. The important of them are Allopathic, Homoepathic, Ayurvedic, Siddha or Unani. All these medicines have been defined technically or legally where so ever desired. For their preparation and standardisation number of recognised and authoritative books like pharmacopoeias, codices, formularies are available depending upon the system of medicine. Before going to the details of the various types of dosage forms of Ayurvedic drugs one must know the definition of Ayurvedic medicine. Thus, an Ayurvedic medicine as defined in the Drugs and Cosmetic, Act, 1940, includes all medicines intended for internal or external use, for or in the diagnosis, treatment, mitigation or prevention of disease or disorder in human beings or animals and manufactured exclusively in accordance with the formulae described in the authoritative books of Ayurvedic systems of medicine specified in the first schedule of the Act.

The first schedule has a list of 53 Ayurvedic books:

Ayurveda is the science of health and healing practiced by ancient. Aryan which is based on the Atharva-veda, one of the oldest scriptures of Hindus, about 3000 years old.

The object of Ayurveda is to counteract the imbalance of three very essential elements, *vata, pitta* and *kapha* (air, bile and phlegm respectively), which constitute the *Tridosh* from which the body originates. It is the *Tridosh* which regularises the normal working of the human body.

The Ayurvedic drugs are obtained from natural source only i.e. from plants, animals or from minerals.

Similar to allopathic dosage forms, Ayurvedic dosage forms (formulations) can also grouped into four types depending upon their physical forms i.e.

    (a) **Solid dosage forms**   : Pills, Gutika, Vatika.

    (b) **Semi-solid dosage forms** : Avicha, Paka, Lepa, Ghrit, (Snehakalpa).

    (c) **Liquid dosage forms**   : Arista, Asava, Arka, Taila, Dravaka.

    (d) **Powder dosage forms**   : Bhasma, Satva, Mandura, Pisti, Parpati, Lavana, Kshara, Cuma (Churna).

Like allopathy, drugs or medicinal substances from plant, animal and mineral sources are used as raw materials (ingredients) for the formulations.

To extract the above mentioned natural products of various origins, various solvents (menstrum) are used in Ayurveda such as water, oils, milk, ghee, cow's urine etc. To convert them into suitable form and also to stabilise them various adjuvants are used. The use of sweetening agents, binding agents, colourants, flavouring agents is also very common in Ayurvedic formulae.

Following are the important dosage forms of Ayurvedic drugs:

1. Asava and Arista:

Asavas and Aristas are the medicinal preparations prepared by soaking the drugs in the powdered forms or in the form of their decoction (known as 'Kasaya in Ayurveda), in a solution of sugar or jaggery (Gur) as may have indicated, for a specified period of time.

During this soaking it undergoes fermentation, generating alcohol, thus, facilitating the extraction of the active constituents contained in the drugs. Alcohol so generated also serves as a preservative in the product.

Examples:

Kumariasav, Madhukasav, Punernavasav, Arvindasav, Chandanasav, Kanakasav, Lohasav, Kutjarista, Draksharista, Dashmularista, Vidangarista, Ashokarista, Khandirarista.

Absolute cleanliness is maintained during the preparation of Arista and Asava. The wooden pots (vessels) are fumigated with Pappali curna and also smeared with ghee before the fermentation liquids are poured into them.

Table 9.1A: Difference between Arista and Asava

Arista	Asava
The crude-drugs as mentioned in the formula (Patha) are coarsely powdered and decoction (Kasaya) is prepared. The decoction is then strained (filtered) and transferred to fermentation vessel (wooden), sugar, honey or jaggary are added, dissolved and boiled. Dravyas and other finely powdered ingredients are added. Then dhataki-puspa (Dhayati-flowers) if mentioned in the formula is added.	According to formula (Patha), required quantity of water alongwith jaggery (Gur) or Sugar is taken and boiled and cooled. Then it is taken to the fermentation vessel or barrel. Fine powdered crude drugs and ingredients as mentioned in the formula are then added to it. The container is then covered with the lid and the edges are sealed with clay-smeared cloth, wound in seven consecutive layers.
The opening of the vessel is then closed with lid and edges are sealed with clay smeared cloth, wound in seven consecutive layers. Normally, the vessels used for Arista and Asava are placed in underground cellar so as to maintain the temperature for specified period. After the specified period, the contents are examined to ascertain the completion of process of fermentation (Sandhana). The liquid is then stained after 2/3 days and bottled.	The further process is then completed as mentioned in Arista.

Filtered Asava and Arista should be clear and without any froth (foam) at the top. It should not become sour. It has characteristic aromatic and alcohol odour.

2. Arka:

It is the liquid preparation obtained by distillation of certain liquids on crude-drugs soaked in water using the distillation unit (Arkayantra).

The coarsely powdered crude-drug is soaked in adequate quantity of water and kept overnight, which soften the drug and releases the volatile principle during distillation.

Arka is a suspension of the distillate in water, having slight turbidity and colour, depending upon the nature of crude drug undergoing the distillation. It has characteristic aromatic odour.

Examples:

Ajmodarka, Karpuradiarka, Jatamamsyarka.

3. Taila (Oils):

Tailas are the preparation in which Taila (Fixed Oil) is boiled with specified decoction and fine paste (Kalka) of drug as mentioned in the prescribed formula.

The process of manufacturing Taila ensures the absorption of therapeutically active constituents of the ingredients used in the formula.

Tailas are prepared similar to ghrtas. Tailas are normally liquid preparations. Tailas can be used internally and topically as well.

Tailas retain their potency for about sixteen months. If taken internally, they are taken with warm water or warm milk.

Tailas are preserved nicely in glass or aluminium or polythene containers.

Examples:

Bhrangaraja taila, Maha Narayan taila, Laghu Visagarbha taila, Anu-taila, and Jyotismati taila.

COSMETIC PREPARATIONS

Before dealing with the cosmetic preparations, it is very essential to know technical and legal definition of the word cosmetic preparation as given in the Drugs and Cosmetics Act 1940.

Cosmetics means any article intended to be rubbed, poured, sprinkled or sprayed on, or introduced into, or otherwise applied to the human body or any part thereof for cleansing, beautifying, promoting attractiveness or altering the appearance and includes any article intended for use as a component of cosmetics, but does not include soap.

These preparations are classified according to their uses as:

1. Skin cosmetics.

2. Hair cosmetics.

3. Eye cosmetics.

4. Nail cosmetics.

Shampoos:

Shampoos are the formulations for clearing hair and conditioning effects. The shampoos are used for removal of accumulated sebum, scalp debris and residues of hair grooming preparations. The shampoo should be selective in the coat of natural oil on hair and scalp i.e. it should only remove excessive oil from the hair. Hair conditioning is necessary to give hair life, softness, volume, body sheen, a silky touch, fly-away control and ease of styling.

The shampoos should have the following properties:

(i) It should spread easily over the hair and should not immediately sink into the hair.

(ii) It should produce easily a lather having sufficient stability.

(iii) It should efficiently remove excess oil and scalp debris.

(iv) It should rinse away easily.

(v) It should not give roughness and tangling tendency to hair.

(vi) It should make hair feel and smell clean and fresh. There should not be loss of lustre of hair.

(vii) It should not affect ease of combing and setting of the dry hair.

(viii) It should not produce irritation or reddening of the scalp.

Ingredients of Shampoos:

The common ingredients in shampoos are classified as follows:

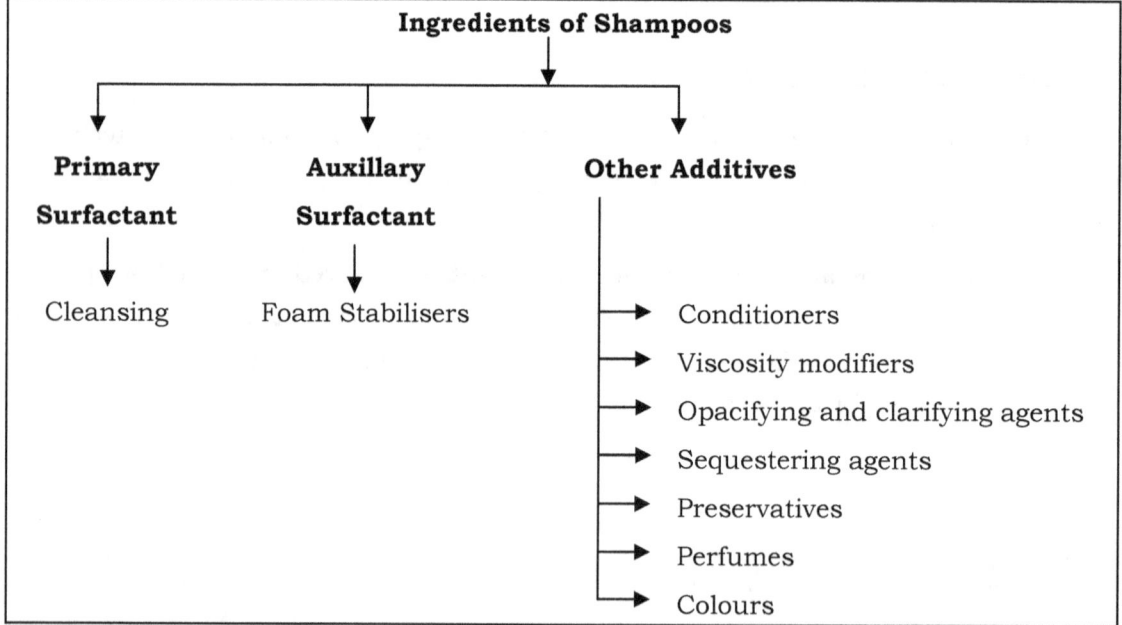

(A) Primary Surfactants:

Anionic surfactants are widely used as detergents in shampoos. Triethamine dedecyl benzene sulphonate is used in shampoos for oily hair. Lauryl sulphates are also used in combination with myristyl sulphate. Sodium lauryl sulphate is a popular foaming agent. It is used in concentration 7-15%. It is most suitable for powder or cream shampoos. Ammonium lauryl sulphate is preferred over sodium salt due to its stability at lower pH.

Alkyl either sulphate show stability over wide pH range, less irritancy, mildness, reduced keratin degradation and are suitable detergents in shampoos for dry hair. Sulphosuccinates are suitable for mild shampoos like baby shampoos.

Amphoteric Surfactants:

These are used as primary surfactants for mild shampoos. They are β-amino acid derivatives, asparagine derivatives, long chain betains and long chain imidazoline derivatives. Amphoteric surfactants allow large flexibility in their use.

Cationic Surfactants:

Have low cleansing and foaming properties as compared to anionics cetylpyridinum salts, distearyl dimethyl ammonium salts etc. are used as additives in small quantities.

(B) Auxilliary Surfactants:

Non-ionic surfactants are used in combination with surfactants. Lauric monoethanoamide and diethanoamide is commonly used. They form complexes with lauryl sulphate ions at air-water interface and improve lather qualities.

Ethylene oxide and propylene oxide derivatives common auxillaries, emulsifiers and opacifying agents.

(C) Additives:

1. Conditioners: Conditioners smooths, softens, texturizes and restores the protective shealth on hair. The agents used as conditioners are lanolin, mineral oil, polypeptides, harbal additives, egg derivatives and some synthetic resins.

2. Viscosity modifiers: Various thickness used are 1-4% w/w ammonium and sodium chloride, alginates karaya gum, tragacanth, carboxymethyl cellulose, hydroxyethyl cellulose and carboxyvinyl polymers.

3. Opacifying and clarifying agents: Opacity and pearlescerce is provided by finely dispersed zinc oxide, titanium oxide, glycerol monosterates and palmintates. Magnesium, calcium or zinc salts of stearic acid, latexes, magnesium aluminium silicate etc.

4. Preservatives: Milder surfactants are not effective against bacteria. Natural additives make shampoos prone to microbial attacks. Therefore, preservatives like hydroxybenzoate esters, quaternary ammonium surfactants, formaldehyde etc.

5. Sequestering agents: These are required to prevent the formation and deposition of calcium and magnesium soaps onto the hair; while rinsing with hard water. EDTA and pyrophosphates are generally used.

Formulations of Shampoos:

Different types of formulations on the basis of physical properties are:

(i) **Clear liquid shampoo:** Which contain amine (TEA) lauryl sulphate or lauryl either sulphate as detergent.

(ii) **Liquid cream shampoo:** Where opacifiers like glycol distearate and magnesium stearates are used to make the liquid shampoo a creamy one.

(iii) **Solid cream shampoo:** Which are packed in jars, tubes and are gelled with sodium sterate.

(iv) **Oil shampoo:** Contains sulphonated oils.

(v) **Powder shampoo:** Consists of detergent powder with easily soluble non-hydroscopic substances. But they are not popular as they do not have good conditioning power.

(vi) **Aerosol shampoo:** These are clear liquid shampoos with medium viscosity mixed with the propellant.

(vii) **Dry shampoos:** These are powders which are sprinkled on greasy hair, leaving it for about ten minutes and then brushing if off. They do not involve use of water. But they are not efficient. These contains boric acid, starch, timely divided silica, talc etc.

According to their functions shampoos are classified as:

(i) Conditioning shampoos:

Conditioning shampoos are aimed at cleansing hair and shampoo conditioners are for improving manageability and to promote desired feel and appearance of hair. Synthetic catonic polymers deposit a thin film on hair surface. Conditioning shampoos may incorporate oils like olive, oil, mineral oil in conc. 0.5-1.5% with amphoteric surfactants and quarternary ammonium compounds.

(ii) Baby shampoos:

It is a shampoo employing a very mild detergent. It mainly include amphoteric imidazole derivatives, fatty sulphosuccinate esters and amides. It should have no action on eye and skin. It is completely free from irritation.

(iii) Anti-dandruff and medicated shampoos:

Dandruff is a chronic, non-inflammatory scaling of the scalp caused due to microbial proliferation. The common micro-organism associated with drandruff is *Pityrosporum ovale.* Thus, these shampoos contain germicides like thymol, quaternary ammonium surfactants, chlorinated phenols, zinc undecylenate, PVP-iodine complex, selenium oxide and selenium sulphide are also effective against dandruff.

(iv) Acid balanced shampoos:

Low pH shampoos are used to minimise damage to their hair and skin. The low pH shampoos are acid-balanced shampoos. Low acidity shampoos seem to improve sheen of hair. But many surfactants are not stable at low pH. Lactic acid and citric acid are commonly used.

HAIR DRESSINGS

Hair dressings are the cosmetic formulations intended for:

(i)   To impart lustre,

(ii)   To maintain hairstyle,

(iii) To improve control and manageability of hair.

Hair dressing for women are less oily or greasy whereas men's hair dressings are oily.

Women's Hair Dressings:

Hair setting lotions which are used to strengthen and maintain the deformation given to the hair during waving. They deposit a polymeric film on the hair surface which remains unaffected by external environment for sufficient period. It is applied on wet hair. These are available as clear lotion or aerated gel. They contain film forming polymers, plasticizer, perfumes colouring agent another additives to increase sheen, softens and discent agling of hair. All these components are present in a hydroalcoholic solution. Cationic polymers are widely used.

Hair Sprays:

These are the preparations which quickly dry when sprayed on hair and impart rigidity to the set. This helps to keep the set hair in place and control the loose ends during activities. These are sprayed once combing is complete. The spray should be fine and gentle. It should dry the wide area. The film formed by the spray should not be sticky and should keep the hair free to move. The polymers include shellac PVP-vinyl acetate co-polymers etc. Spraying systems include hydrocarbons (liquidifiable and compressible gases) and carbon dioxide.

Men's hair dressings:

These are required to set the hair and to enhance hair lustre. Men's hair setting involves initial setting and then to keep it in the same style for longer period time. For the initial setting water can be used but as water will be lost the hair will get disturbed again. If only oil is used large amount of oil is needed for initial setting of oil. Therefore, pomades or Brilliantines are used. Sometimes, a mixture of oil and water is also suitable. It is used in emulsion form water will cause initial setting and oil will help to maintain it.

Different hair dressing formulations for men's uses vegetable oil, mineral oils, deodorised kerosene, caolin, cationic compounds, leathins, vitamins, propylene glycol etc.

Brilliantines is the oldest type of men's hair dressings. They may be:

(a)   Solid brilliantines or pomades;

(b)   Liquid brilliantines;

(c)   Alcoholic brilliantines;

(d)   Separable brilliantines.

Solid brilliantines are stiffened or thickened and perfumed mineral or vegetable oil. The stiffening agents used are different waxes such as bees wax, ceresn, carhuba wax, paraffin wax, spermaceti etc. Aluminium tristerate is used as gelling agent for transparant brilliantines.

Liquid brilliantine consists of a mineral oil with deodorised kerosene or isopropyl myristate.

Alcoholic brilliantine is a alcoholic solution of oils. It spreads easily, gives the feeling of freshness and stimulating effect for the scalp. Caster oil, almond oil etc. instead of castor oil isoproplyl myristate may be used.

Separable brilliantines are two layers systems prepared by addition of a perfume in alcohol to non-miscible mineral or vegetable oil. This mixture may be shaken vigorously before applying to the hair. The non-oily fixative preparations use gums like tragacanth, or sodium CMC etc. but they are not widely used. Aerosol sprays containing resins are used.

Creams are used as hair dressings. The emulsions may be o/w or w/o type. The brilliantine gels which are microgels (o/w type emulsion or true gels which are aqueous solution of PEG thickened with cellulose derivatives.

After Shave Lotions:

As the name indicates these are to be rubbed after shaving. These are meant for antiseptic, astringent for sensation of well being or for cooling effect. Following are suitable examples.

After Shave Lotion Formula 1:

Ethyl alcohol specially denatured	–	60%
Propylene glycol	–	3%
Water demineralized	–	36%
Perfume	–	1%

Method of Preparation:

Perfume and propylene glycol are dissolved in alcohol. Add the water slowly with stirring to avoid locally high concentrations of water precipitating the less soluble components of the perfume. Keep the solution for several hours at about 4°C and then filter.

Use:

Relieves the slight irritation and confer a pleasant feeling of comfort and well being after shaving.

Note:

These preparations are used for the above purpose and normally contain astringents, emollient, anaesthetics, cooling and antiseptic ingredients.

Formula 2:

Ethyl Alcohol (90%)	–	50 ml
Sorbitol	–	2.5 ml
Rose oil	–	0.1 ml
Menthol	–	0.5 gm
Boric acid	–	2.0 gm
Amarnath solution	–	q.s.
Water purified	– to –	100 ml

Method of Preparation:

Dissolve Boric acid, Sorbital, Rose oil and Menthol in alcohol. Add Amarnath solution and adjust the volume with purified water to 100 ml.

Leather Shaving Cream

Formula:

Stearic acid	–	36%
Coconut oil	–	9%
Potassium hydroxide	–	8%
Sodium hydroxide	–	1%
Sorbitol (70% solution)	–	3%
Water	–	43%
Perfume	–	q.s.
Preservative	–	q.s.

Method of Preparation:

Heat the coconut oil to 75°C to 80°C. Alkalies are dissolved in half of the water and add to the coconut oil. When saponification is complete, add melted stearic acid (70°C) in thin stream followed by the sorbital solution, preservative and the remainder of the water. The mixture is then cooled. The perfume may be added at 35°C or after the emulsion has cooled to room temperature. A check is carried out for completeness of saponification and the free fatty acid content is adjusted to 3 and 5 per cent. The product is eventually packed into tubes.

Use:

Shaving cream.

Hair Cream

Formula:

Lanette wax	–	3 g
Liquid paraffin	–	30 g
Distilled water	–	66.5 g
Sodium benzoate	–	0.5 g
Perfume	–	sufficient

Method of Preparation:

Lanette wax and liquid paraffin are heated to 80°C. Sodium benzoate is dissolved in distilled water and heated to 80°C. Add it slowly to melted Lanette wax Liquid paraffin with constant stirring. Incorporate perfume at 40°C. Homogenise properly and fill in the containers.

Storage:

In well closed container in cool place.

Use:

Cosmetic.

EVALUATION OF LIQUID DOSAGE FORMS

Liquid formulations can be evaluated on the following parameters:

1. Density:

Weight per millilitre of the solution can be determined and variation if any should be accounted for, so as to find out the reason for such behaviour. It depends on the particle size, homogenity, temperature, nature of solute and solvent.

Density = Mass/volume. It can be determined by using pyknometer or density bottle.

2. Viscosity:

Viscosity of liquid is an important characteristic as it affects rheological behaviour of the product and directly affects the patients acceptability. It depends on temperature, density, concentration of solute and solvent and nature and additives etc. It can be determined by Ostwald viscometer, Redwood viscometer, Falling ball viscometer, Cone and plate viscometer etc.

$$\eta_1 = \frac{\delta_1 \times t_1 \times \eta_2}{\delta_2 \times t_2}$$

where,

η_1 and η_2 are the viscosities of liquid and water respectively.

δ_1 and δ_2 are the densities of liquid and water at same temperature.

t_1 and t_2 are the time taken to flow of liquid and water between two fixed points.

3. pH:

Sometimes, pH affects the stability and absorption. Hence, it should be tested during evaluation and a variation if any should be checked to rectify the same. It can be determined by pH meter.

4. Organoleptic properties:

Colour, flavour and odour should be acceptable which can be tested applying usual means. Lot to lot uniformity is to be ascertained and maintained.

5. Sedimentation pattern:

The sedimentation rate can be determined by using Anderson pipette method. It depends on the particle size, nature of additives and solvent in the formulation. The rate can be determined using Stock's equation.

6. Stability:

Some substances are unstable in aqueous form due to incompatibility of additives or solvents. It should be checked in the formulation.

(D) UNIT PROCESSES AND EQUIPMENTS USED FOR MANUFACTURING OF NON-STERILE MONOPHASIC LIQUIDS

Liquid Mixing:

The process of mixing is one of the most commonly employed operations in everydays life.

Mixing is defined as a process that tends to result in randomization of dissimilar particles within a system. In mixed condition each particle lies as nearly as possible in contact with the each particle of other ingredient.

The mixed condition is not difficult to achieve with two or more mobile liquids or with mobile liquids and solids. The mixing of liquid and solid is likely to be permanent. The mixing operation has two requirements.

(i)   Localised mixing, sufficient to apply shear to the particles of fluid.

(ii)   A general movement, sufficient to take all parts of the bulk and the material through the shearing zone and to ensure that a uniform final product is obtained.

Mixing mechanism:

There are four categories of fluid mixing.

1.   Bulk transport

2.   Turbulent flow

3.   Laminar flow

4.   Molecular diffusion.

1. Bulk transport:

The movement of relative large portion of the material being mixed from one location in the system to another, constitutes bulk transport. A simple circulation of material in a mixer, does not result in efficient mixing. For effective bulk transport it must result in a rearrangement of the various portion of the material to be mixed. This is usually accomplished by means of paddles, revolving blades or other devices within the mixer arranged.

2. Turbulent flow:

The phenomenon of turbulent mixing is a direct result of turbulent fluid flow which is characterized by a random fluctuation of the fluid velocity at any given point within a system. The fluid velocity at a given instant may be expressed as the vector sum of its components in the x, y and z directions, with turbulent, these directional components fluctuate randomly about their individual mean values, as does the velocity itself.

In the case of turbulent flow in a pipe the mean velocity in the direction of flow through the pipe is positive, of course, and varies some what depending on the distance from the pipe wall.

Turbulent flow can be conveniently visualized as a composite of eddies of various sizes. An eddy is defined as a portion of fluid moving as a unit in a direction often contrary to that of the general flow, large eddies tend to break-up, forming eddies of smaller size until they are no longer distinguishable.

3. Laminar mixing:

Laminar flow is frequently encountered when highly viscous fluids are being processed. It can also occur if stirring is relatively gentle and may exist adjacent to stationary surface in vessels in which the flow is predominantly turbulent. When two liquids are mixed through laminar flow, the shear that is generated stretches the interface if the mixer employed folds the layer back upon themselves, the number of layers and hence, the interfacial area between them, increases exponentially with time.

4. Molecular diffusion:

The primary mechanism responsible for mixing at the molecular level is diffusion resulting from the thermal motion of the molecules. When it occurs in conjunction with laminar flow, molecular diffusion tends to reduce the sharp discontinuities at the interface between the fluid layers, and if it is allowed to proceed for sufficient time, result in complete mixing.

Fick's first low of diffusion:

$$\frac{dm}{dt} = -DA \frac{dc}{dx}$$

Where the rate of transport of mass, dm/dt across an interface of area A is proportional to the conc. gradient dc/dx across the interface.

D = Diffusion coefficient.

The sharp interface between the dissimilar fluids, which has been generated by laminar flow, by the ensuing diffusion considerable time may be required, however, for the entire system to become homogeneous.

Equipments for Mixing:

When the material to be mixed is limited in volume to that which may be conveniently contained in a suitable mixer, batch mixing is most flexible. A system for batch mixing usually consists of two primary components.

1. A tank and other container suitable to hold the material being mixed.

2. A means of supplying energy to the systems. So as to bring about reasonably rapid mixing. The power may be supplied to the fluid mass by means of an impeller, air streams and liquid jets. Baffles, vanes, and ducts also are used to direct the bulk movement of material in such mixers thereby increasing their efficiency.

Impellers:

The distinction between types of impellers is often made on the basis of types of flow pattern they produce, and on the basis of the shapes and pitch of the blades.

Three basic types of flow may be produced.

1. Radial

2. Axial

3. Tangential.

This may occur as single or in various combination.

The Fig. 9.2 (a) and (b) are diagrammatic representation of cylindrical tank in which **tangential** and **radial flow** occurs respectively and Fig. 9.2 (c) side view of a similar tank in which only one type of flow occurs.

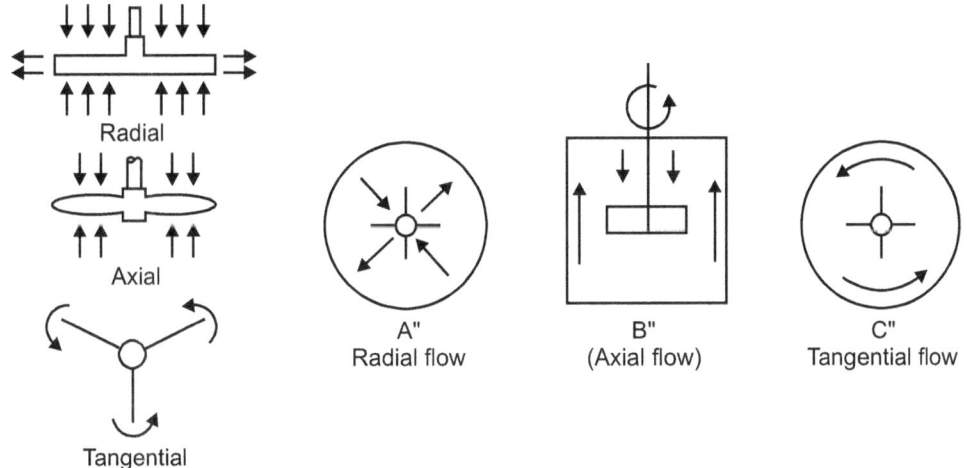

Fig. 9.2: Types of flow pattern

Propeller mixers: Propeller mixers are probably the most widely used form of mixer for liquids. The propellers usually resembles the ordinary mixing propeller in shape, is small in relation to the container and operate at high speed up to 8000 r.p.m. The propellers accentuates the longitudinal movement of the liquid and is therefore, most suitable when energy imposed by the propeller to the fluid is sufficient to set up a satisfactory flow pattern and while little shear is needed.

The propeller mixer is not normally effective with liquids of viscosity greater than 5 Ns/m^2 which is somewhat greater than the viscosity of glycerin and castor oil.

Prevention of Aeration:

To avoid undesirable **vortexing** and **aeration** (air bubbles may be difficult to remove from the product and the air may encourage oxidation in some cases). The propeller should be deep in the liquid and symmetry should be avoided. This can be done in a number of ways.

1. The propeller shaft may be offset from the centre.

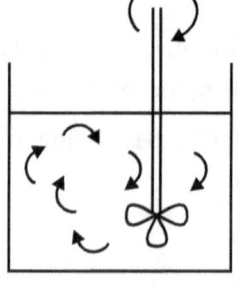

Fig. 9.3

2. The propeller shaft may be mounted at an angles.

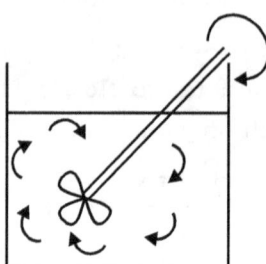

Fig. 9.4

3. The shaft may enter the side of the vessel and or vessels of a shape other than cylindrical may be used.

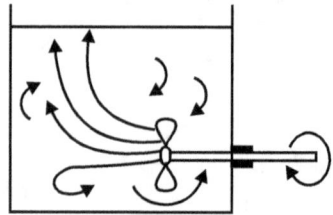

Fig. 9.5

4. Vortexing may be avoided by the use of a **Push Pull** Propeller, in which two propellers of opposite pitch are mounted on the same shaft, so that the rotatory effects are in opposite direction and cancel each others.

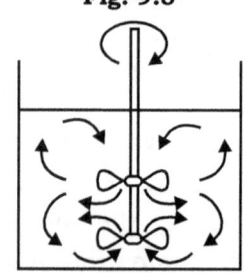

Fig. 9.6

5. The simple way to avoid the formation of a vortex is to use one and more baffles which are usually vertical strips attached to the wall of the vessel, the baffles direct the rotating fluid from its circular paths into the centre of the vessel and avoids the deep vortex.

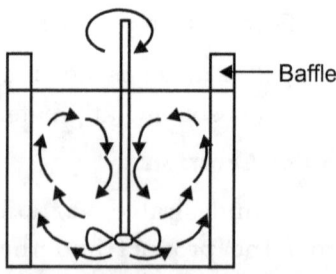

Baffle

Fig. 9.7

A propeller has angled blades which causes the circulation of the fluid in both the axial and radial direction. A vortex is formed when the circumferential motion imparted to the liquid by the propeller causes at to back-up in a circular motion and form a depression around the shaft. As the speed of rotation is increased, air may be sucked into fluid with frothing and possible oxidation.

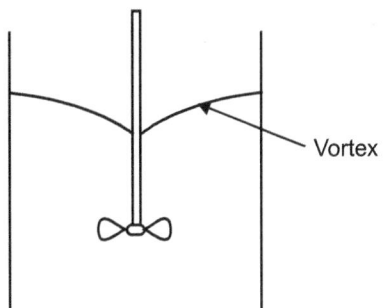

Fig. 9.8

Turbine mixers: These mixer consists of a circular disc impeller to which a number of short, vertical blades, which may be straight and curved, are attached. Turbine mixers are operated at a lower speed then the propeller type. Since, these mixers possess flat impellers, a little axial to tangential flow is obtained. The liquid is moved rapidly in a radial direction, Turbine – type gives rise to greater shear forces then the propeller.

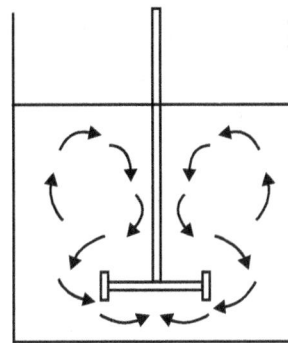

Fig. 9.9

Baffles: Bulk transport is important in mixing. For bulk fluid flow to be most effective, an intermingling must occur between material from remote regions and in the mixers. To accomplished this, it is frequently necessary to install auxillary device for directing the flow of the fluid, usually baffles. Baffles placement depends largely on the type of agitator used.

Centrally mounted vertical shaft impellers tend to induce tangential flow, which is often manifested in the formation of a vortex about the impeller shaft. This is particularly characteristics of turbines with blades arranged perpendicular to the impeller shaft.

Side wall baffles, when vertically mounted in cylindrical tanks, are effective in eliminating excessive swift, and further aid the overall mixing process by inducing turbulence in their proximity.

Baffled Pipe Mixers:

Tanks:

To ensure good mixing efficiency, such devices as vanes, baffles, screws, grids and combination of these are placed in mixing tube. Mixing tanks places mainly through mass transport in direction normal to that of the primary flow. Mixing in such systems require the careful control of the fccd ratc of raw materials if a mixture of uniform composition is to be obtained.

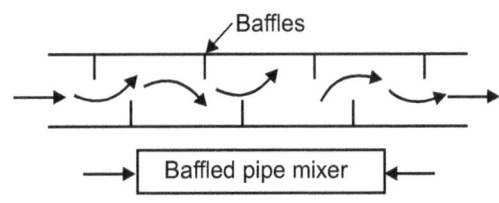

Fig. 9.10: Arrangement of baffles

Continuous Mixing:

The process of continuous mixing produces on uninterrupted supply a freshly mixed material and is often desirable when very large volumes of material are to be handled. To ensure good mixing efficiency, devices such as vanes, baffles, screws, grids combinations e.g. these are placed in mixing tube. Mixing in such systems requires the careful control of the feed rate of raw material if a mixture of uniform composition is to be obtained.

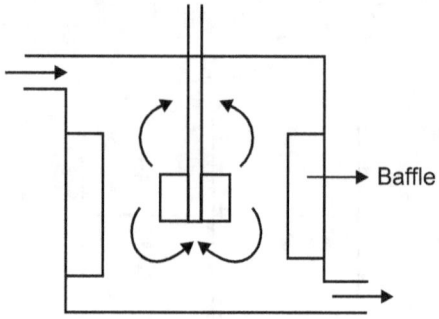

Diagram of a turbine agitated continuous mixing tank with vertical side wall baffles. Two cones of mixing are shown above and below the impeller.

Fig. 9.11: Mixing tank with baffles

Diffusion:

Penetration of one substance into the other under the potential of concentration gradient is known as **diffusion.**

Diffusion takes place in the direction opposite to the direction in which concentration gradient exists.

Factors affecting rate of diffusion:

Diffusion is governed by two laws known as Fick's First Law and Fick's Second Law which are stated as under.

1. The amount of soluble material that flows in unit time across a plane of unit area in a direction perpendicular to it is called **flux** and flux is proportional to the concentration gradient.

2. Concentration of the solute at the plane across which diffusion takes place may vary with time.

Fick's first law refers to the rate of diffusion through unit area, while the second law states for change in concentration of solute (diffusant).

Thus, it is observed that the diffusion is dependent on density (molecular weight), time and the concentration of the diffusant.

In pharmaceutical sciences, the free diffusion (or passive transport) through lipids and membrane is of vital importance.

(E) FILTRATION AND CLARIFICATION

Filtration may be defined as the separation of a solid from a fluid by means of a porous medium that retains the solid but allows the fluid to pass.

It will be realised that the term fluid includes liquids and gases, so that both these may be subjected to filtration.

In the filtration of liquid the following terms are useful:

1. The suspension of solid into liquid to be filtered is known as **slurry.**
2. The porous medium used to retain the solid is described as **filter medium.**
3. The accumulation of solids on the filter is referred as **filter cake.**
4. While the clear liquid passing through the filter is **filtrate.**

Factor affecting filtration:

The unit operation of filtration is affected by the characteristics of the slurry, including:

- The properties of the liquid, such as density, viscosity and corrosiveness.
- The properties of the solid, for example, particle shape, particle size, distribution of particle size.

Clarification:

It is the process of separation of separating the solids from liquid, wherein solids are not more than 1.0% while filtrate is elegant and also is the desired product.

Rate of filtration:

The factors affecting the rate of filtration were studied by Dorcy in 1830 in an investigation of the flow of water through beds in the public fountain at Dijon.

For this reasons, the equation correlating the rate of filtration is known as **Dorcy's law** and may be expressed as

$$\boxed{\frac{dv}{dt} = \frac{KA\,\Delta P}{\mu l}} \qquad \dots (9.1)$$

where,

v = volume of filtrate

t = time of filtration

k = constant for filter medium and the filter cake

A = area of filter medium

ΔP = pressure drop across the filter medium and filter cake

l = thickness of cake

μ = viscosity of fluid.

Following are the **factors that affect the rate of filtration**:

1. Properties of filter medium and filter cake:

The constant, K, in equation (9.1) represents the resistance of the filter medium and filter cake. Although the resistance of the filter medium is of significance on the laboratory scale, it is relatively less important on the large scale and can usually be neglected. The magnitude of the resistance of the filter medium will change due to the early layer of solids which may block the pores and may form bridges over the entrances to the channels. For this reason the pressure, should be kept low at the start, to avoid the pores **"Plugging"** and increased as the cake builds up.

Although the factor is referred to as a constant in the equation, it is of course, a constant only for a particular set of circumstances. Thus, any decrease in the resistance of the cake will show as an increased value of K, so increasing the rate of filtration.

2.   Area of filter:

It will be obvious that the total volume of filtrate flowing through the filter will be proportional to the area of filter. Hence, this rate can be increased by using larger filters, but the area can also be increased by using a number of small units in parallel.

3.   Pressure drops:

The rate of filtration is proportional to the overall pressure drop, that is, across both the filter medium and filter cake.

This pressure drop can be achieved in a number of ways.

(a)   Gravity: A simple method of obtaining a pressure difference is by maintaining a head of slurry above the filter medium. The pressure developed will depend on the density of the slurry, but as a rough guide, a head of 10 metres of water will create a pressure difference of 1 bar. At one time, the method was used in pharmaceutical manufacturing, with a long tube enclosing a filter by-passing through a several floors of a factory.

(b)   Reduced pressure: The pressure below the filter medium may be reduced below atmospheric pressure by connecting a filtrate receiver to a vacuum pump and creating pressure difference across the filter. This method has the disadvantage that the pressure difference is limited to about 1 bar, since it cannot be greater than the pressure exerted by the atmosphere on the surface of slurry.

Another disadvantage is that reduction of pressure lowers the boiling point of liquid. So that it is possible that the filtrate will boil in the receiver. Apart from the loss of liquid, which may be undesirable, the vapours may be damaging to the vacuum pump.

(c)   Increasing the pressure: Probably the commonest method in practice is to obtain a suitable difference by applying pressure to the surface of the slurry, the simplest method being to pump the slurry into the filter under pressure.

This has the advantage that greater pressure difference is possible than that obtainable with reduced pressure.

(d)   Centrifugal force: From the same way that gravitational force could be replaced by centrifugal force in particle separation, so use can be made of centrifugal force in filtration processes.

4. Viscosity of filtrate:

Increase in the viscosity of the filtrate will rise on the resistance to flow, so that the rate of filtration is inversely proportional to the viscosity of the fluid. It must be emphasised that it is the viscosity of the liquid and not of slurry that is important, since the resistance to flow occurs as the **filtrate** flow through the filter cake.

The rate of filtration may be increased by raising the temperature of the liquid, which lower its viscosity. This may not be practicable if thermoliable materials are involved and if the filtrate is volatile.

5. Thickness of filter cake:

The filtrate must flow through the filter cake formed on the filter medium as the filtration progresses hence, the rate of flow will be inversely proportional to the thickness of the cake. In some slurries containing high proportion of solids, it may be advantageous to reduce the rate at which the cake accumulates. This may be done by preliminary decantation without stirring which will lower the solid contents of slurry.

Filtering Media:

The filtering media is composed essentially of countless channels which imparts porosity to the medium. The properties of the filtering media should be such that:

(a) It should not interact chemically or physically with the components of the filtrate.

(b) It should have desirable retention power.

(c) It should offer minimum resistance to the flow of the filtrate.

(d) It should be mechanically strong.

Variety of filtering media are available but the selection is frequently based on experience.

1. Filter paper:

Filter papers are most commonly used for the retention of very fine solids and for the clarification of liquids containing only small amount of solids. Rapid filtrate is obtained because of the pores on paper are small and in a large numbers. Disadvantage is that we can not reuse it.

2. Membrane filters:

These are employed for micro-filtration e.g. in the preparation of sterile solutions. These are made of pure cellulose and cellulose derivatives and from nylon, telfon, polyvinyl chloride etc. Absence of fibre and particle in the integral structure is a particular advantage, useful for ophthalmic preparations.

3. Cotton filters:

Large particles of extraneous matter from a clear liquid may be removed by loosely inserting a small plug of absorbent cotton wool in the neck of funnel. This is sometimes necessary to recycle the filtrate a number of times.

4. Viscosity of filtrate:

Increase in the viscosity of the filtrate will rise on the resistance to flow, so that the rate of filtration is inversely proportional to the viscosity of the fluid. It must be emphasised that it is the viscosity of the liquid and not of slurry that is important, since the resistance to flow occurs as the **filtrate** flow through the filter cake.

The rate of filtration may be increased by raising the temperature of the liquid, which lower its viscosity. This may not be practicable if thermoliable materials are involved and if the filtrate in volatile.

5. Thickness of filter cake:

The filtrate must flow through the filter cake formed on the filter medium as the filtration progresses hence, the rate of flow will be inversely proportional to the thickness of the cake. In some slurries containing high proportion of solids, it may be advantageous to reduce the rate at which the cake accumulates. This may be done by preliminary decantation without stirring which will lower the solid contents of slurry.

4. Glass wool:

Filter paper and cotton wool etc. are not suitable when solution of highly reactive and corrosive substance such as acids alkalies, and oxidising agents are to be filtered. Although it provides very effective filtration, glass-wool may contaminate the filtrate with glass-fibres.

5. Asbestos:

Asbestos pads are also used for the reasons stated above and placed under glass-wool. It is prepared by compressing asbestos, tightly under pressure and variable in various size ranges.

Disadvantages:

(a) They often impart an alkaline reaction to the filtrate.

(b) Calcium and magnesium ions released from the pads may cause incompatibility.

(c) Substances like alkaloids may often be adsorbed on them.

6. Sintered glass filters:

These are made from borosilicate glass and the filtering medium is a flat convex. Depending upon the powder size used during sintering, these filters are available in different pore size.

7. Other filters:

Sand filters consists of large bed of properly arranged layers of sand, stone, and gravel and are used for large scale operation such as municipal purification of drinking water etc.

Filter Aids:

The resistance to flow due to the filter medium itself is very low, but will increase as a layer of solids builds up, blocking the pores of the medium and forming a solid.

The objects of the filter aid is to prevent the medium from becoming blocked and to form an open, porous cake, so reducing the resistance to flow of the filtrate. Thus the filter aid must be a light, porous, inert solid.

Kieselguhr is very successful filter aid and instance has been reported where as little as 0.1% added to a slurry with about 20% solids.

Other examples of filter aids are purified talc, siliceous earth, magnesium carbonate, bentonite, silica gel etc.

Industrial Filters:

Filter leaf:

The filter leaf is the simplest form of filter consisting of a flame enclosing a drainage screen or grooved plate. The rotate unit being covered with filter cloth. The outlet for the filtrate connects to the inside of the frame so that the general arrangement is as shown in the Fig. 9.12. The frame may be of any shape circular, square or rectanglar shapes being used in practice.

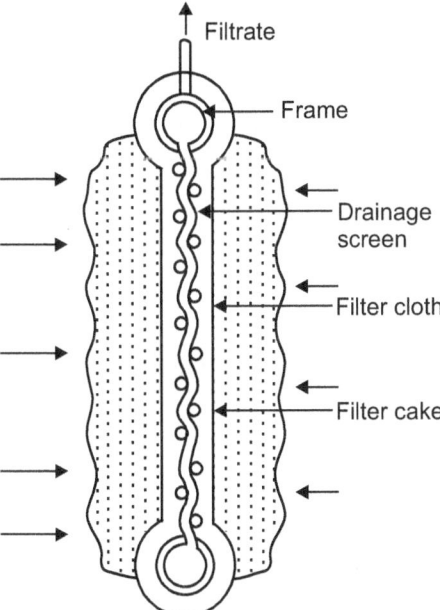

Fig. 9.12: Filter Leaf

In use, the filter leaf is immersed in the slurry and a recesser and vacuum system connected to the filtrate outlet. The method has the advantage that the slurry can be filtered from any vessel and the cake can be washed simple by immersing the filter in a vessel of water. Removal of cake is facilitated by the use of reverse air flow.

An alternative method is to enclose the filter leaf in a special vessel into which the slurry is pumped under pressure. In this any number of filter leaves (upto 100) can be enclosed in a special vessel housing column discharge and which provides large filter area and the assembly is called as filter basket. The material to be filtered will be pumped under pressure in the fils of a row of rectangular tank. The filter basket lowered in the tank and suckers applied. When a cake of the desired thickness has been formed the whole basket alongwith a cake is lifted without interfering the suckers and lowered into the neck stand containing wash solution. For each number the basket was lifted and transferred to the neck stand. Finally the basket is transferred to an empty tank and cake was removed by reverse air flow.

Advantages:

1. Slurry can be filtered from any vessel.

2. Cake can be tested simply by immersion the filter leaf in a vessel of water.

3. Cake can be removed by the use of reverse air flow.

4. Less flow space, minimum labour and efficient washing.

5. Area can be varied by employing suitable number of units.

Disadvantage:

Not useful if the solid content of slurry is high or more than 5%.

Nutsch Filter:

Batch vacuum filters are developed from gravity filter and Nutsche type filters used in industry are similar to gravity filters, except that they need a vacuum pump or some other vacuum generating equipment to reduce the pressure under the filter medium, thereby increasing the driving force across the filter medium. Pressure filters are usually discontinuous, vacuum filters are usually continuous. A discontinuous vacuum filter, however, is more useful tool. A vacuum Nutsch is little more than a large buchner funnel 1 to 3 m (3 to 10 ft.) in diameter and forming a layer of solids 100 to 300 mm (4 to 12 in.) thick. Because of its simplicity, a nutsch can readily be made of corrosion – resistant material and is valuable where experimental batches of a variety of corrosion material are to be filtered. Nutche are uncommon in large scale processing because of the labour involved in digging out the cake; they are however, useful as pressure filters in combination filter dryers for certain kinds of batch operations.

Plate and frame press:

As the name implies this process is made up of two types of units, known respectively as

1. Plates and

2. Frames.

With filter medium usually filter cloth between the two.

The frame is open, with an inlet for slurry, while the plate has a grooved surface to support the **filter cloth** and **outlet** for filtrate.

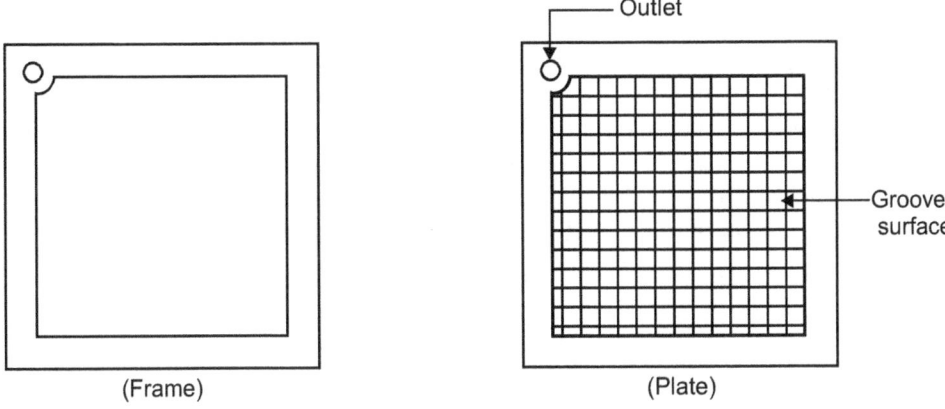

(Frame)   (Plate)

Fig. 9.13: Frame and plate arrangement

The material to be filtered enters the equipment under pressure through a pipe at the bottom and is forced into one of the many chambers. The filtered cloth is positioned over each plate, but not over the frame. As the material passes through the filtering clothes, solids remain behind in the chambers and the clear filtrate passes through the openings located on top of the plates are so constructed that the filtrate enters the outlet from both sides of the plate.

The viscosity of the fluid can be controlled by incorporating **heating** or **cooling coils.** Plate and frames are constructed of cast iron, gun metals and bronze. In pharmaceutical operations, stainless steel and silver plated steel are used. Material of construction should provide resistance to corrosion and prevent metallic contamination of the product.

Moulded polyester plates used in new filter presses as they provide improved chemical resistance, low cost and light weight.

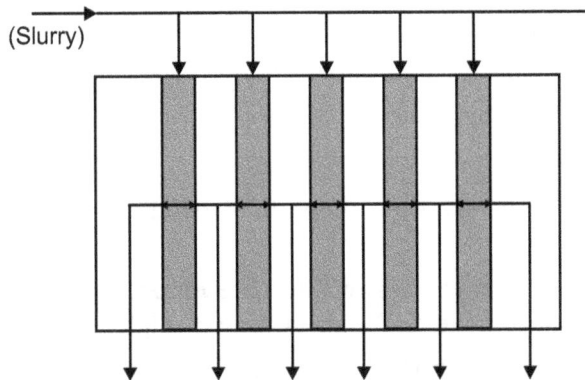

Fig. 9.14: Plate and frame filter press: principles of operations

The thickness of the cake can be varied by using frames of different thickness and in general, these will be on optimum thickness of filter cake for any slurry, depending on the solid contents of the slurry and the resistance of the filter cake.

Washing plate and frame press:

It is necessary to wash the filter cake, the ordinary plate and frame press is unsatisfactory, from the description and the operation of the filter press, it will be recalled that two cakes build up in the frames, meeting eventually in the middles. This means that flow is brought virtually to a stand still, hence washing by the following filtrate through the wash water is very inefficient, if not impossible. A modification of the plate and frame press is used, if it is required to wash the filter cake.

The difference in design is that special plate and frames are used, having an additional channel to carry wash water. In half the plates there is a connection from the wash water channel to the surface of the plate and these special plates are identified with three dots.

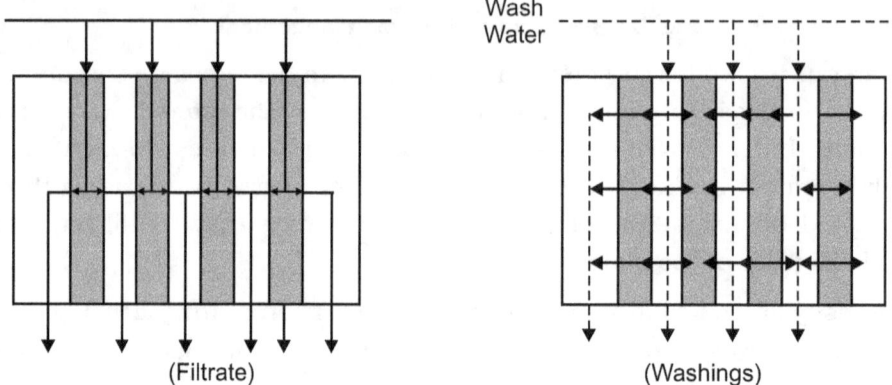

Wash Water

(Filtrate)   (Washings)

Fig. 9.15: Mechanism of filtration

Advantages:

1. Construction is very simple and available in a wide range of materials.
2. A large filtering area is produced in a small spaces.
3. The capacity is variable according to the thickness of the frames and plates.
4. Efficient washing of the cake is possible.
5. Operation and maintenance are simple.

Disadvantages:

(a) It is a batch filter, so that there is a good deal of "down-time" which is "non-producting".

(b) The filter press is an expensive filter the emptying time, the labour involved, and the wear tear on the clothes resulting in high costs.

(c) Operation is critical, as the frame should be full, otherwise it is inefficient and the cake is difficult to remove.

Rotary drums filter:

The first rotary continuous filter was built in 1906 by the Oliver. Since then, several forms of rotary drum filters have been developed using Oliver's principle and differing only in structural details.

When a continuous operation is desirable and the slurry contain a high proportion of solids where filter leaf and filter press are not suitable, rotary filters are useful. These are suction filters in which filtration, washing, the partial drying and the discharge of the cake takes place, automatically.

Rotary drum filter consists of a sheet metal drum. It may be from 1 to 15 ft. in diameter and 1 to 20 ft. in length. The drum is provided with automatic filter valve, filter tank with slurry agitator and the scrapper or doctor blade for cake discharge.

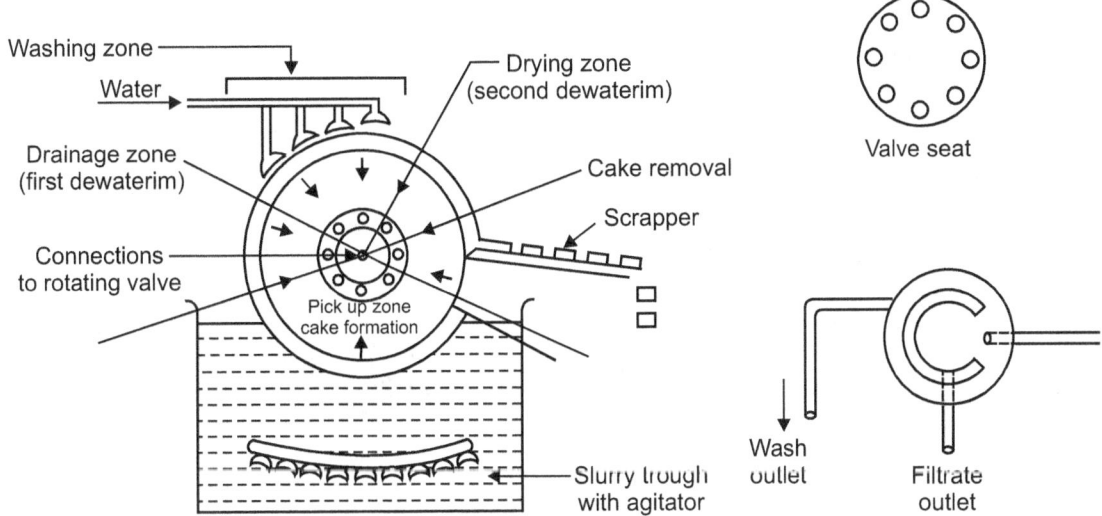

Fig. 9.16: Rotary drum filter

Rotary filter operation:

Zone	Position	Service	Connected to
Pick up	Slurry trough	Vacuum	Filtrate receiver
Drainage	–	"	"
Washing	Wash sprays	"	Wash water receiver
Drying	–	"	Wash receiver
Cake removal	Scraper knife	Compressed oil	Filter cake conveyor

Advantages:

(a) The rotary filter is automatic and is continuous in operation, so that labour costs are very low.

(b) The filter has a large capacity, infact, the area of the filter as represented by area "A" of Darcy's low is infinity.

(c) Variation of the speed of rotation enables the cake thickness to be controlled and for solids they form an inpreventable cake the thickness may be limited to less than 5 mm.

Disadvantages:

(a) The rotary filter is a complex piece of equipment with many moving goods, and is very expensive.

(b) Being a vacuum filter, the pressure difference is limited to 1 bar and hot filtrate may boil.

(c) The cake tends to crack due to the air drawn through the vacuum systems, so that washing is proper.

Basket Centrifuge: (Hydro extractor)

It consists of a perforated basket which supports the filter media. The working principle of basket centrifuge is very simple. The basket revolves inside the casing and slurry in spread form into the basket in which the centrifugal action forces and filtrate is passed through media on which cake gets deposited. Basket centrifuge is advantageous when very fine particles are to be separated from the substance. This method is a another alternative method of filtration.

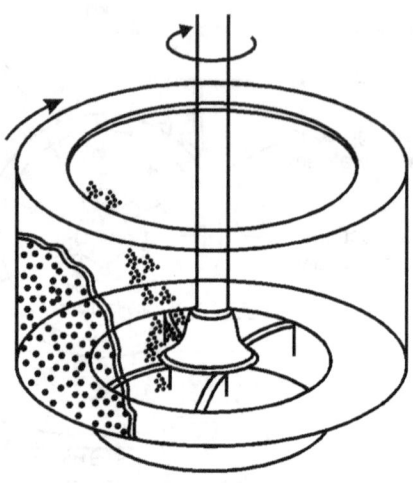

Fig. 9.17: Basket centrifuge

(F) EQUIPMENTS USED FOR MANUFACTURING AND PACKAGING OF LIQUIDS

Bottle Washing and Filling Machines:

1. Bottle washing machines:

It is provided with soaking tank containing the cleansing solution. Self-rotating brushes two in number are arranged on shaft, which clean the bottles and rinsed with water jets under pressure. If required brushing and rinsing operations are repeated.

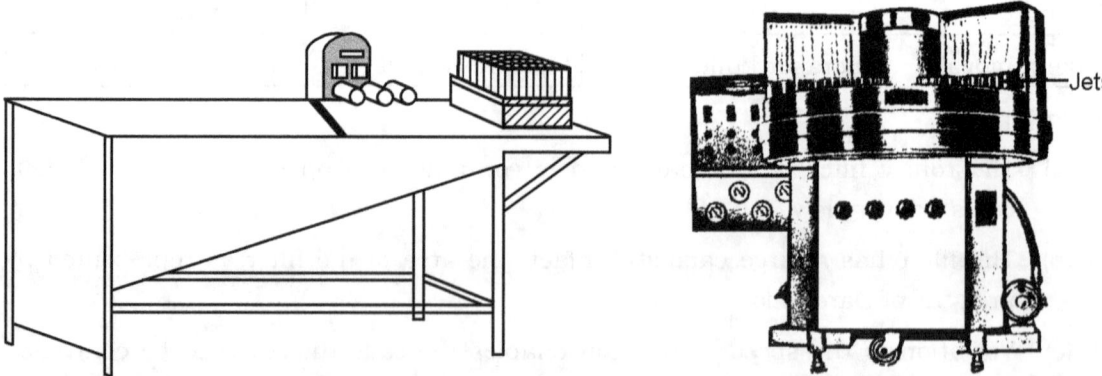

Fig. 9.18: Bottle washing machine   Fig. 9.19: Rotary bottle washing machine

The bottles can be washed with manually or by automatic machines. Bottles are washed by detergent and rinsed with purified water 2-3 times and ensured for absence of any detergent residue inside the container. After washing thoroughly it is protected from dust and any other contamination. Bottle should be completely dried before filling operation.

In automatic machines, the bottles are inverted on the spindle and rotated along with detergent solution and then rinsed with purified water 2-3 times and dried automatically. After washing it should be stored properly so as to avoid contamination.

2.   Rotary bottle washing machine:

It can operate 500-4000 bottles per hour. It is provided with two stainless steel tanks and four separate stations for jet wash. Detergent solution demineralised water and compressed air. It works automatically.

Bottle filling machines:

Liquid filling depends on the characteristic of the liquid such as viscosity, surface tension, foam producing and compatibility of the material. Gravimetric, volumetric and vacuum filling methods are available for filling liquid in the container.

1.   Gravimetric method: Liquids which are less viscous can be easily filled by the gravimetric method. This method is most commonly used for batch filling operations. This can be done either manually or by machine.

2.   Volumetric filling method: It uses the principle of positive displacement by piston action. Every station have a independent piston and cylinder. Accuracy is controlled by the piston and cylinder designs.

They are either automatic or semi-automatic, suitable to fill the two bottles each of 30 ml, 60 ml, 110 ml 500 ml or 1000 ml capacity can operate 1000 to 1200 bottles per shift, depending upon the capacity or the material to be filled.

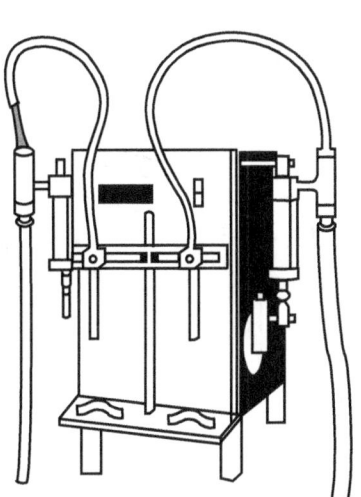   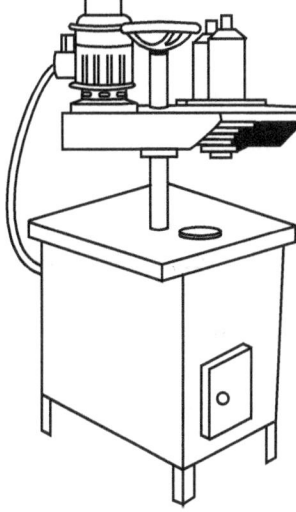

Fig. 9.20: Volumetric bottle filling machine   **Fig. 9.21: Vial cap sealing machine**

3.   Vacuum filling method: A seal is made in the container so that vacuum can be easily created in the container. The method is highly beneficial to fill viscous liquids accurately and speedly.

4.   Vial cap sealing machine: Semi-automatic motorised unit, can fill 30-40 vials per minute, can operate the vials of 2 ml to 30 ml. Machine is ideal for leak proof and accurate sealing. Suitable for saline. Bottles are pedal operated (Fig. 9.22).

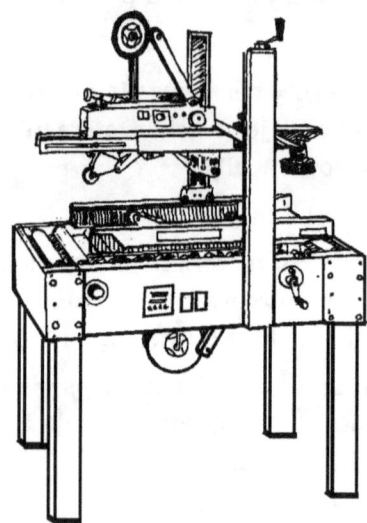

Fig. 9.22: Carton sealing machine

Equipments for Liquid Processing:

Carton Sealing Machine:

Carton sealing requires the fixing of glue tape over the closure of the package and has to be opened prior to the removal of product from the carton. The quality of paper should be of high density with poor tear strength. It can also be perforated prior to its fixing, to make it easy for tearing by pressing over the lines (Fig. 9.22).

The machine available in the market is designed for closing uniform cartons (with same heights and widths) and excellent for any low and high volume closure needs. It seals both top and bottom simultaneously and fast. It has adjustments for different box sixes.

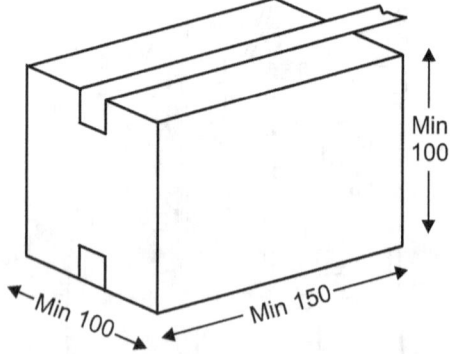

Fig. 9.23: Box sizes

Table 9.2: Packaging Specifications

Carton Size					
Width (mm)		**Length (mm)**		**Height (mm)**	
min	max	min	max	min	max
100	500	150	α	100	500

It has automatic box centering arrangement by the side drive and uses single motor drive which helps in synchronisation of the system. Its conveying speed can be adjusted upto 20/min.

Box Strapping Machine:

The carton and boxes after sealing requires strapping for additional safety and protection of the product. Different types of semi-automatic machines are available in the market which can handle package size from 60-900 mm × 570 mm × 750 mm and weight ranging from 85 kg to 100 kg. Width of the tape to be used ranges from 6 to 15 mm. The capacity of machine is 12-15 straps per minute. The strip is fixed by the machine and by changing the box position, cross stripping can be carried out.

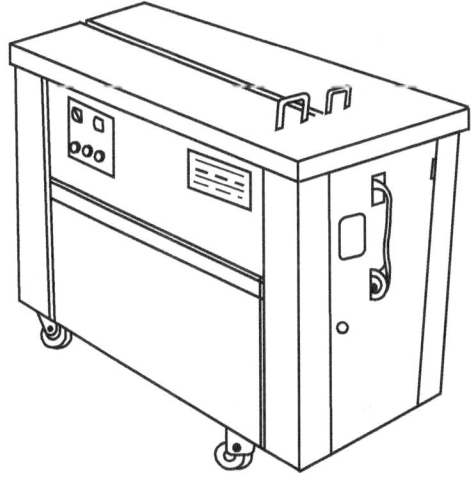

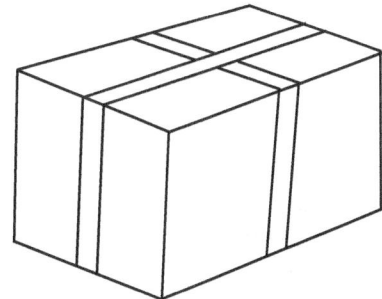

Fig. 9.24 (a): Box-strapping machine   **Fig. 9.24 (b): Strapped-carton**

Carton sealing and box strapping machines are very frequently used suitably in the tablet, capsule, vial and other parenteral departments.

Medicaments packed in pouches, sachets, strip-packs, and blister packages are conveniently transported by using these machines from Pharmaceutical manufacturing units to the market without any loss or damage, at the reasonable rates.

Belt conveyors: Conveyors are devices commonly used to move uniform loads continuously from point to point over fixed paths. The function of the conveyor is to move materials when the loads are uniform and paths do not vary. The movement, rate and direction is usually fixed. These are normally used to transport materials from storage area to processing section and finished product to storage area.

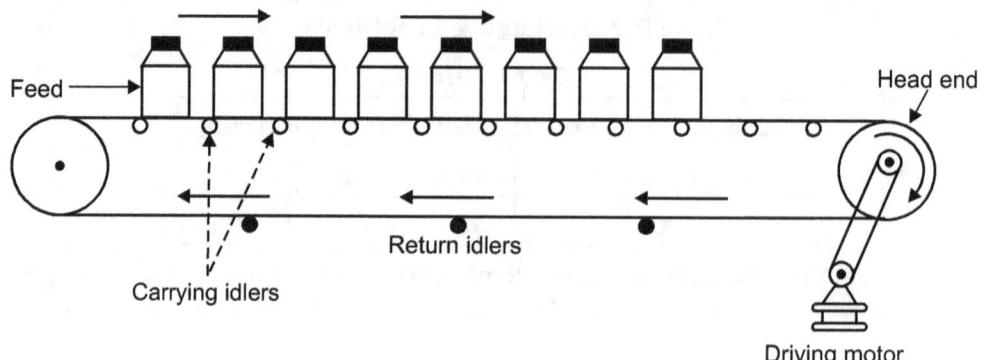

Fig. 9.25 (a): Belt conveyor

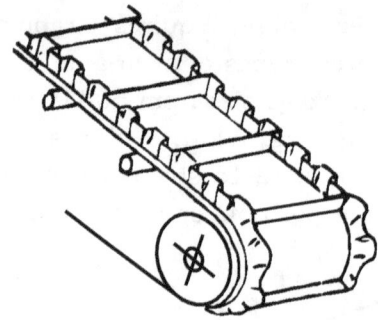

Fig. 9.25(b): Side walled belt conveyor

Belt conveyors consists of an endless moving belt of flexible material streched between two pulleys or drums and supported at intervals on idler rollers. Belt consists of single solid ply of suitable thickness cotton, nylon, polyester textile yarns are usually used. Belt covering is made of natural or synthetic rubber that protects the belt from any damage. Depending upon the material to be moved, the belts may be prepared by using metal sheets.

In Pharmaceutical factories, the conveyor belts are normally used in packaging and bottling departments to move the bottles for sealing, labelling etc. They are also used conveniently in tablet inspection and parenteral departments suitably.

Side walled belt-conveyors are perfectly suitable to carry near glass bottles of saline or other injectables.

Batch Numbering Machines:

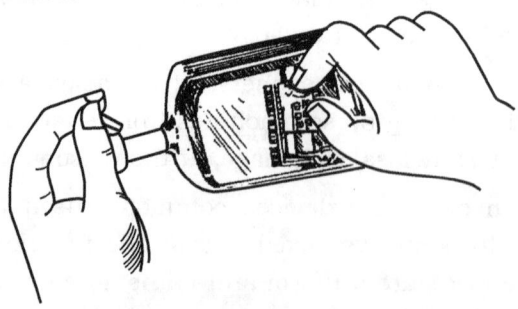

Fig. 9.26: Batch numbering machine

Good number of batch numbering machines with various functions are available today. They can be classified as automatic or hand operated. Automatic batch numbering machines are provided alongwith strip-packing or blister packing machines themselves. They are adjusted in sequence of the cycle of movements so that each strip get the printed information as desired in the drug-rules. These machines are self inking with easily interchangeable type sets so as to compose the desired information.

Normally, batch no., month and year of manufacture, expiry date, MRP, are provided by using these machines. Machines are suitable and especially designed for printing cartons, card boards, poly packs, HDPE sacks, plastic containers, cosmetic articles, aluminium foils and tin containers.

The working of hand operated batch numbering machines is described below.

Removable type holder and felt pad carrier are provided in these machines.

Press the knob to the highest extent which will allow the felt pad carrier (providing ink) to go aside and will print the information on the surface which comes in contact with it. When the knob is released the type holder comes in contact with the felt pad carrier so as to ink it, which is the resting position of the machine in the sequence of cycle, the knob is to be operated as desired to get the number of labels required per minute.

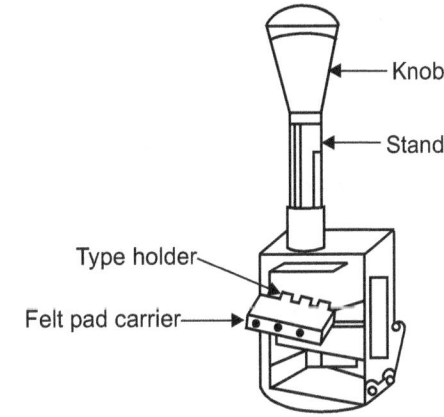

Fig. 9.27: Hand operated batch numbering machine

9.2 POWDERS AND GRANULES

A. POWDERS

Powders are a useful dosage form. The size of the particles of powders range from 10,000 microns to 0.1 micron depending upon the method employed for grinding. The size of the particle determines the effectiveness of physiological properties of medicinal powders.

They may contain single ingredient or may be the combination of many ingredients. They may be used internally or externally. Most of the basic chemicals, drugs and pharmaceuticals are available in the form of the powders only.

Following are the few examples of medicinal powders.

(i)   Purified talc

(ii) Precipitated sulphur

(iii) Precipitated chalk

(iv) Bleaching powder

(v)   Acacia powder

(vi) Tragacanth powder

(vii) Compound powder of Glycyrrhiza

(viii) Compound barium sulphate powder

(ix) Cosmetic powders.

As a dosage form, powders have certain advantages.

Advantages of Powders:

1. The dose variation depending on the condition of the patient is possible.
2. Powders are more stable than liquid dosage forms.
3. Many times the effect desired depends on the particle size and where a diffusion is desired a powder meets the required need i.e. it diffuses more rapidly than e.g. tablets and pills.
4. Relatively easy to swallow.

Disadvantages of Powders:

1. Bitter powders cause discomfort.
2. Powders which are affected by atmospheric conditions cannot be safely handled.
3. Time consuming.

Evaluation of powders:

As a dosage form many powders are being used since antiquity and several medicinal powders are official in various pharmacopoeias apart from cosmetic powders.

Taking into consideration their evaluation can be framed; as adopted in case of other formulations like tablets or capsules.

However, the following parameters will provide the guidelines for their evaluation.

(1) Organoleptic characters : colour, odour, taste etc.

(2) Nature : Crystalline or amorphous

(3) Reaction : Acidic or alkaline

(4) Solubility : In various solvents

(5) Identification : Chemical / microscopic for herbal or animal drugs

(6) Extractives : Water, alcohol, ether soluble / insoluble

(7) Loss on drying :

(8) Ash content : Acid insoluble ash or sulphated ash

(9) Limit tests : Arsenic, lead or heavy metals

(10) Limits for foreign organic matter

(11) Microbial growth

(12) Assay

POWDERS FOR INTERNAL USE

Oral Rehydration Salt Powders (ORS powders):

These are the dry homogenously mixed powders containing dextrose, sodium chloride, potassium chloride and either sodium citrate or sodium bi-carbonate for oral use in rehydration therapy.

Since, sodium bi-carbonate is unsuitable for use and being very unstable, sodium bi-carbonate may be dispensed separately for proper stability. If necessary, flavouring agents and suitable flow agents may be incorporated in the formulae.

Oral rehydration salts normally do not contain any artificial sweetening agents like saccharin or aspartame.

The usual strengths and formula used in India are given below :

	ORS – A	ORS - citrate
Sodium chloride	01.2 g	03.5 g
Potassium chloride	01.5 g	01.5 g
Sodium citrate	02.9 g	02.9 g
Anhydrous dextrose	27.0 g	20.0 g
or		
Dextrose monohydrate	29.7 g	22.0 g
Purified water	1000 ml	1000 ml

Formula ORS–A is for non-choleraic diarrhoea treatment while formula ORS–citrate is recommended by diarrhoeal disease control programme of WHO and UNICEF.

Storage:

They are supplied in tightly closed containers preferably in sachets and aluminium foil.

If the rehydration solution remains unused after 24 hours of preparations should not be used and be discarded.

Effervescent Powders:

As the name indicates, a powder of this type effervescences on coming in contact with moisture.

Obviously, it will be mixture of acid and substances like sodium bicarbonate. Generally, medicaments may also be incorporated. Effervescent granules effectively mask the taste of a nauseous drug.

The commonly used acids for preparation of effervescent granules are citric and tartaric acids together with sodium bicarbonate. The acids are slightly more in quantity than is necessary to neutralise the bicarbonate. This imparts pleasant sour taste.

If a medicament is being incorporated it is best to heat it at 100°C in order to let it loose water of crystallisation because the effervescent granules are required to be treated at 100°C.

Laboratory Method of Preparation:

Preheat a porcelain dish over a boiling water bath. Finely powder the acids and bicarbonate of soda in ascending order of weight.

Place the mixture in the preheated procelain dish. The citric acid looses the molecules of water of crystallisation and this is sufficient to make mixture of powders, moist and coherent. This operation takes about five minutes. As soon as the powder mixture halls into the hand, pass it through a No. 9 sieve superimposed by No. 20 sieve. The finer granules will fall through number 20 sieve. Collect these granules and place them in a warm place for drying.

Pack the granules in a wide mouth bottle for easy removal and dispense.

POWDERS FOR EXTERNAL USE

Powders are of the following types:

1.   Dusting Powders:

The characteristics of these powders is that the powders are in the state of very fine particles capable of passing through and required to pass through a No. 80 sieve. They are mixture of such substances as zinc oxide, starch, boric acid kaolin and talc. The last two are obtained from mineral sources and generally expected to contain the pathogentic organism viz. *Clostridium tetani.* Hence, when Kaolin or talc is included in a formula, they must be sterilised by dry heat (150°C) for one hour (from the time that the powder attain 150°C temperature) before use. The dusting powders are not meant to be applied to open wounds.

2.   Insufflations:

These powders are intended for body cavities or areas where direct access to affected part is not possible. They are sent out in wide mouth bottles from which the required quantity is removed and transferred to an insufflator (a device to blow the powder) for use.

3.   Foot Powder:

Formula:

Thymol	–	1%
Boric acid	–	10%
Zinc oxide	–	20%
Talc	–	69%

Method of Preparation:

Prepare fine powder and mix.

Use:

Sprinkle on the feet to avoid foul odour formation when socks and shoes are used.

Note:

Skin of foot have innumerable sweat glands and inhabitant organisms on foot surface decompose the sweat with foul odour. Ingredients of foot powder contain astringents and antibacterial agents. Thus, it minimises the sweat formation and its further decomposition.

4. Tooth Powder:

Formula:

Dicalcium phosphate dihydrate	–	79%
Precipitated calcium carbonate	–	20%
Sodium lauryl sulphate	–	1%
Flavour	–	q.s.
Sweetener	–	q.s.

Method of Preparation:

Grind all the solid ingredients to fine powders. Mix them thoroughly. Sprinkle the flavouring agent on the powder and mix thoroughly. Then pack the powder in a suitable container.

Use:

For cleaning the teeth.

Storage :

Store in well closed container. Avoid excessive heat.

Note:

Tooth powder contains abrasive agents such as calcium carbonate, calcium hydrogen phosphate dihydrate, aluminium oxide trihydrate, charcoal etc. for cleaning the tooth surface. Surface active agents are many a times included in the formulation to clean the unaccessible surface and formation of frothing. Saccharin is a sweetener of choice. The various flavouring agents used in tooth powder are spearmint, peppermint, menthol, vanillin, eugenol, anethole, oil of anise, wintergreen, eucalyptus, cinnamon etc.

5. Talcum Powders:

It is a skin cosmetic. In order to impart natural fresh look to the facial skin, face powder is used. It is applied with powder puff. The preparation has ability to complement skin colour by imparting a velvet like finish. It also masks the excessive shine of the skin due to secretion of sebaceous and sweat glands.

A powder should pass the properties such as good covering power, slip (feel), adhesiveness, absorbancy and bloom.

Covering power: It is the ability to mask skin defects as minor imperfections, pores and shine.

Slip: It is the spreading of powder giving smooth and natural feel.

Adhesiveness: It is the ability to remain on the skin surface.

Bloom: It is the ability to give velvety finish to skin.

In order to obtain these characteristics, different ingredients are incorporated in the face powder formulation.

Talc:

It is the magnesium silicate that has ability of spreading (slip) and can be used as the base for incorporation of other powders. It should be white, odourless with smooth greasy feel with particle size of 200 mesh screen.

Kaolin:

Which is hydrated aluminium silicate has good covering power, adhesion and body secretion also has adsorbent properties. Kaolin helps to remove shine of the talc and gives smoothing effect to the skin. It is hygroscopic in nature. Hence, its use in face powder normally does not exceed 25 per cent by weight.

Precipitated chalk:

This helps in balancing the required property of slip, adhension, covering power and transparency. It reduces shine of the talc and helps in retaining the perfume. Magnesium carbonate is also used for the same purpose. It possesses good absorbent property.

Zinc and magnesium stearates:

These are used for their adhesion to skin and water proofing quality. Zinc and titanium oxides are used as opacifiers. These mask the minor imperfections of the skin, impart little astringent action and helps to clear up minor skin disorders.

Starches:

Rice starch is used in face powder but it gives rise to stability problems.

Silicon and silicates:

In order to give free flowing and perfume retention power to the powder these ingredients are incorporated in the face powder.

Colours:

Only permitted and light fast organic or inorganic pigments are used. Intensity and the amount to be incorporated depends on the shade required.

Perfume:

This is one of the most important ingredients of face powder. It plays a key role in the sale potential of the product. Perfume should be non-irritating, non-sensitizing, harmless and stable especially in mild alkaline conditions.

Formulae:

Talc	–	75%
Kaolin	–	05%
Chalk precipitated	–	05%
Zinc sterate	–	05%
Zinc oxide	–	10%
Perfume and colour	–	q.s.

Method of Preparation:

All the solid ingredients are finely powdered and sieved to remove any gritty particles. Perfume is mixed with precipitated chalk and macerated. Then all the ingredients are mixed as per ascending order of their weight. Ribbon mixer is used for large scale production. The powder is then transferred in the plastic or tin container with sealed perforated mouth, closed with air tight lid.

Use:

As a cosmetic for facial skin.

Storage:

Store in well closed container.

Few other formulae are given below. The method of preparation is essentially the same as described above.

1. Talc 75%
   Zinc oxide 10%
   Rice starch 10%
   Perfume sterate 5%

2. Talc 50%
   Kaolin 15%
   Zinc oxide 25%
   Titanium dioxide 05%
   Perfume and colour ...... q.s.

3. Talc 60%
   Titanium dioxide 05%
   Zinc oxide 15%
   Chalk precipitated 13%
   Zinc stearate 07%
   Perfume and colour ...... q.s.

4. Talc 70%
   Kaolin 10%
   Chalk precipitated 10%
   Zinc oxide 05%
   Magnesium stearate 05%
   Colour and perfume ...... q.s.

Few Patented Market Products are:

1. PONDS DREAM FLOWER TALC
2. LIRIL
3. CINTHOL.

(B) SIZE REDUCTION OR MILLING

Size reduction or comminution is defined as reduction of materials to small pieces, coarse particles or fine powder.

It is the mechanical process of reducing the particle size of solids. Various terms e.g. crushing, disintegration, dispersion, grinding and pulverisation have been used synonymously with comminution depending on the product, equipment and the process.

Pharmaceutical Applications:

1. **To increase the acting surface area:**

   The surface area per unit weight, which is known as the specific surface is increased by size reduction which affects the therapeutic efficiency of medicinal compounds that posses a low solubility in body fluid.

2. **For extraction of crude drugs:**

   Extraction or leaching from animal glands (liver and pancreas) and from crude vegetable drugs is facilitated by comminution. The time required for extraction is shortened by the increased area of contact between the solvent and solid and the reduced distance, the solvent has to penetrate into the material.

3. **For quick dissolution:**

   The time required for dissolution of solid chemicals in the preparation of solutions is shortened by the use of smaller particles. Larger particles are more closely related to the process by which comminution is accomplished by which size reduction begins with the opening of any small cracks that were initially precise.

4. **To facilitate drying of wet masses:**

   The drying of wet masses may be facilitated by milling, which increases the surface area and reduces the distance. The moisture must travel within the particle to reach the outer surface. Micronization and subsequent drying increases the stability because the occluded solvent is removed.

5. **In the manufacture of compressed tablet:**

   The granules of the wet masses results in the more rapid and uniform drying. The dried tablet granulation is then milled to a particle size and distribution that will flow freely and produce tablets of uniform rot.

6. The efficiency of lubricants in compressed tablets and capsules depends on their fine size state or sub-division.

7. Dusting powders and snuffs causes less irritation due to fine state of sub-division.

8. The texture, appearance and physical stability of ointments, creams and pastes is improved by milling.

9. Stability of emulsion and suspension is influenced by the size of dispersed phase by decreasing the rate of setting/or creaming.

10. In sustained release preparations, the drug must be within a particular size range if its effects are to be prolonged over a period.

Factors Influencing Size Reduction:

1. **Hardness:**

   It is defined as resistance to scratching or indentation. It is basically a surface property and it is expressed in terms of Moh's scale. It is an arbitrary scale on which a sense of mineral substances has been given hardness numbers between 1 and 10, ranging from graphite to diamond. Upto 3 are known as soft, above 7 they are hard and the remaining are described as intermediate.

   In general, the harder the material more difficult to reduce the size.

2. Toughness:

Toughness is defined as impact resistance. The property of toughness is more important than hardness. A soft but tough material may present more problems in size reduction than a hard but brittle substance e.g. a stick of blackboard chalk is harder than rubber, but it can be broken more easily than rubber. Some thing about green twig and dry twig.

3. Abrasiveness:

The property of abrasiveness must be considered in the selection of machine. A material is said to abrasive if it can remove the fine powders from a solid surface when it is rubbed against that surface. This can cause two major disadvantages.

(a) The abrasive material which is to be powdered may get contaminated with metallic impurity from the surface of machine.

(b) The life of machine being used will decrease and it becomes weaker.

4. Moisture content:

The moisture content itself does not affect size reduction but it can alter other properties which affect size reduction i.e. hardness and toughness. In general, materials should be dry or wet and not merely damp. Usually, less than 5% of moisture is suitable if the substance is to be ground dry, or more than 50% if it is being subjected to wet grinding.

5. Softening temperature:

The softening temperature is that at which solid material becomes soft and resembles semisolids where a quite sufficient amount of heat is generated during the size reduction, the temperature is likely to be more. The materials like waxes, stearic acid etc. becomes soft at this temperature and choke or block the machine. In this case, the machine should be surrounded by a cooling system so the temperature will not rise to higher value.

6. Physiological effect:

Some substances are very potent. e.g. (podophyllum resin or hormone drugs) and their small amounts of dust may have an effect on the operaters. Since, very fine powder which may fly in air is likely to be inhaled by the operator. In such cases the machine should be completely covered to avoid inhalation.

7. Stickness and slipperiness:

Pharmaceutical substances that are gummy or resinous may cause difficulties in size reduction, particularly if the methods for size reduction generate heat. They may adhere to the grinding surfaces or the meshes of screens may become block. The slippery material lowers the efficiency of the grinding surfaces.

8. Material structure:

Some substances are homogeneous in nature, but majority show some special structure e.g. mineral substances may have lines of weakness along which the material splits to form flake-like particles, while vegetable drugs have a cellular structure made-up of long fibrous particles, which affects the size reduction.

9.   Ratio of feed size to product size:

The size reduction also depends upon

$$\text{Reduction ratio} = \frac{\text{Average diameter of feed}}{\text{Average diameter of product}}$$

Generally, machine that produces a fine product require a small feed size. Thus, it may be necessary to carry out the size reduction process in several stages with different equipment.

10. Bulk density :

If all other factors being equal, the output of machine is related to the bulk density of the substance.

Mechanism of Size Reduction:

1.   Cutting:

In this process, the material is cut by means of sharp blade or blader. e.g. scissors, shears, Guillotine.

2.   Compression:

The material is crushed by pressing in between two surfaces. e.g. Nut crackers.

3.   Impact :

When the material is more or less stationary and is hit by an object moving at high speed or when the moving particle strikes a stationary surface. In both, the case size reduction is said to caused by impact. e.g. Hammer.

4.   Attrition or shearing:

In this method, also the material is broken between two surfaces but one of the surfaces is moving relative to other i.e. nibbing action. e.g. file.

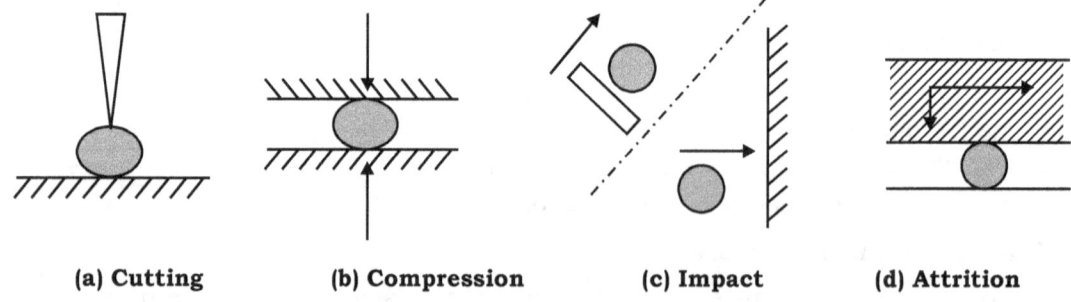

(a) Cutting   (b) Compression   (c) Impact   (d) Attrition

Fig. 9.28: Mechanism of size reduction

GRINDING MILLS

The term mill is used normally for machines for size reductive. It may be divided into three classes :

1.   **Coarse crushers:** The size of the particles to be powdered may be from 2" onwards and they yield a product generally greater than 1000 µm in diameter. e.g. Jaw crusher, Gyratory crusher, Brodford breaker, Tooth roll crusher.

2. **Intermediate machine:** Size of feed – 1" to 3" in diameter, size of yield about 100 μm to 1000 μm in diameter. e.g. stone crusher, crushing rolls, hammer mill, disintegrator, end runner mill.

3. **Fine size reduction:** Size of feed - 0.25" to 0.5", yield - 1 μm in diameter or below. e.g. Roller mill, Ball mill, Rod mill, Tube mill.

4. **Altrafine size reduction:** Particles pass through 500 mesh no. e.g. Colloid mill, fluid energy mill.

1. Cutter Mill:

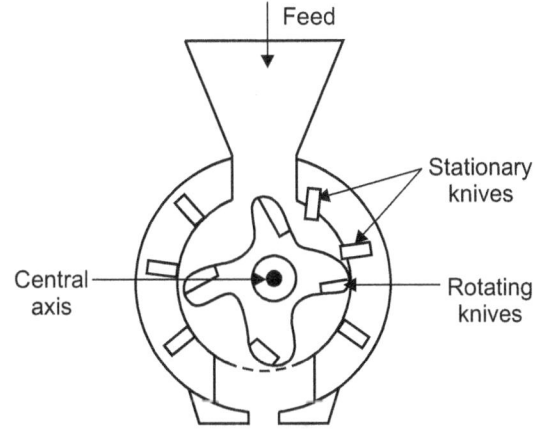

Fig. 9.29: Cutter mill

This is used for coarse crushing, generally for fibrous materials like roots, seeds or woods. It involves the mechanism of cutting.

Cutter mill consists of a stationary cylindrical vessel which is provided with feed hopper at the top and a sieve at the bottom. In the centre of vessel, there is central shaft with raised portion on which knives are arranged. On the inner surface of the vessel there are stationary knives. The material which is feed from the top is broken into small pieces by cutting and when the pieces are sufficiently reduced then pass through the sieve and are collected below the sieve.

2. Roller Mill:

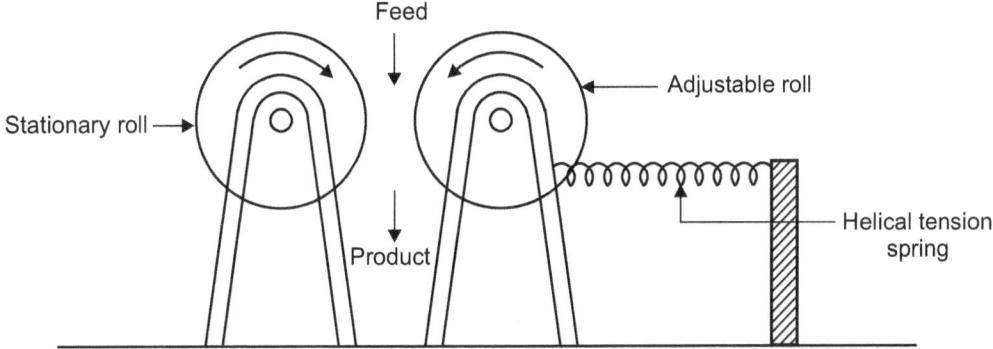

Fig. 9.30: Roller mill

The mechanism of operation in roller mill is compression. The Roller mill has two cylindrical rolls. The rolls are made up of stone or metal mounted horizontally. They are capable of rotation on their longitudinal axes. One of the rolls is driven directly while the second runs free. The material is placed above the rolls, it is drawn in trough, the nip and second roll is rotated by friction. The diameter of rolls may be from few centimeter to metre or more. The gap between the rolls can be adjusted to control the degree of size reduction.

The roller mill is used for crushing, such as cracking seeds and brushing soft tissues.

3.   Hammer Mill:

Mill uses principle of impact. It is used in all the stages of size reduction i.e. coarse intermediate and fine only, the construction of machine differs in different stages. The mill consists of a cylindrical vessel, the lower part of which is made of a sieve and the upper side consists of a strong metallic plate, which may be having undulating surface. In the centre of the vessel there is a revolving disc which is moved by means of a central shaft. Metallic hammers (which may be simple metallic rod) are attached to the revolving disc by means of swivel joints so that the hammers suing out a radial position means of swivel joints so that the hammers suing out a radial position when the shaft is rotated. Thus, the damage of machine can be prevented.

The material to be crushed is taken to the machine by means of a spiral conveyor, the revolving hammer strike the particles. Due to strikes the impact of the hammer the particles breaks. The broken particles strikes the undelating surface which increases the number of impact and thus, increases the efficiency of machine. When the particles are quite small they pass through the sieve since they come near the sieve tangentially the particle size of the product is always less than the operature size of sieve.

In fine size reduction the speed of the hammers may be 1000 to 5000 rpm while in the coarse and intermediate size reduction may be 70 to 100 rpm. In order to prevent the increase in temperature the machine may be cooled by circulation of cold water.

Advantages:

(a)   Rapid in action and capable of grinding different types of materials.

(b)   The product can be controlled by variation of rotor speed, hammer types, and size and shape of machine.

(c)   Operation is continuous.

Disadvantages:

(a)   High speed of operation causes generation of heat.

(b)   If rate of feed is not controlled properly, the mill may get choked. It also decreases the efficiency of machine.

(c)   Because of high speed of operation, the mill may damage by foreign objects like stones and metal pieces in feed.

(d)   Little contamination of the product with metal particles.

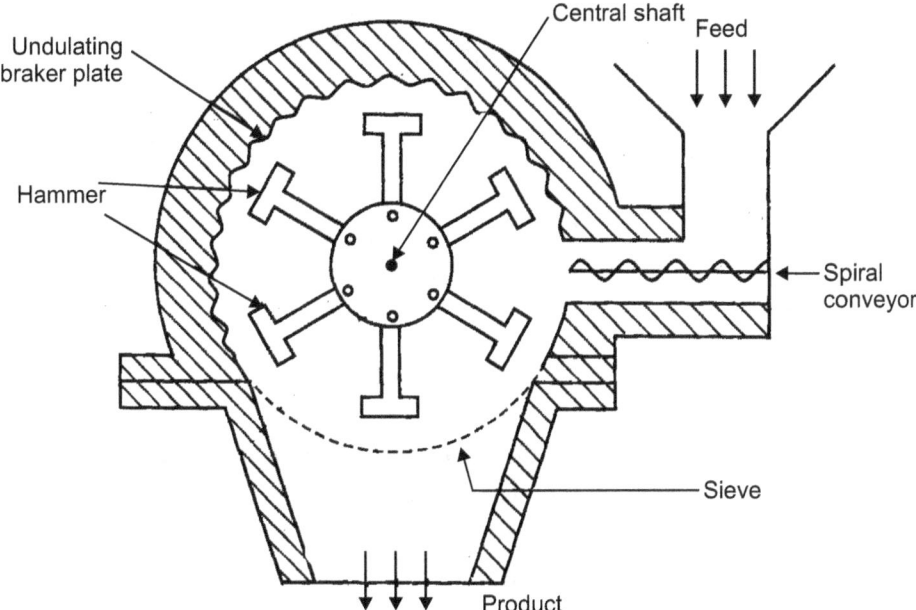

Fig. 9.31: Hammer mill

4.   Ball Mill:

The ball mill is very widely used machine for fine size reduction. The size reduction is achieved by two mechanisms.

    1.   Impact of balls when they fall over the material.

    2.   Shearing: When the balls slide over each other and give a rubbing action.

Construction :

The ball (conventional) mill consists of a cylindrical vessel made of stainless steel, porcelain or rubber. The diameter of the vessel varies and it may be upto 3 meter, however, in pharmaceutical industries it does not exceed 1 m. The diameter of the balls depends on the diameter of mill and for a mill of 1 m. diameter. The diameter of balls should be about 7.5 cm. The balls should occupy about 30 to 50% of the volume of the vessel. The speed at which ball mill is rotated is a very important factor. If it is operated at very low speed the balls only slide over each other and the impact is not obtained while if it is operated at very high speed the balls are carried over along the periphery in the vessel and size reduction is achieved. The minimum speed at which centrifuging takes place is called as **Critical speed.** When the ball mill is prepared at high speed which is about 2/3 of the critical speed cascading takes place i.e. balls are carried upwards to a definite height and then they fall along the diameter of the mill giving impact over the material as well as the slide over each other and give the shearing effect. If the balls are of the same size it takes a long time to get fine powder as well as the product is not uniform in size, if the balls of different diameters are taken a fine product uniform in size is obtained in a shorter time.

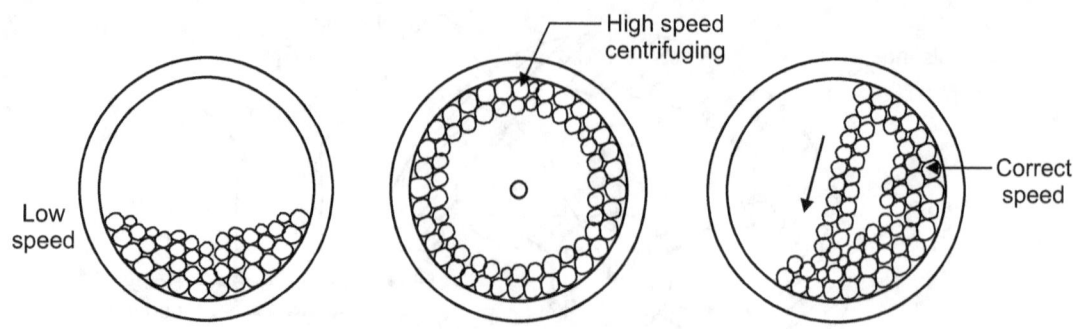

Fig. 9.32: Working of ball mill

Modification of cylindrical ball mill is called as **Hardinoe conical cylindrical ball mill.** In this ball mill, a part of mill is cylindrical the remaining being conical. The advantage of this machine is that the balls are different diameter under segregration. The bigger balls are present in the cylindrical part while the smaller balls are present in the conical part. Due to this fine powder is achieved in a shorter time and the product is more uniform.

In both these types of ball mills in industry, the material is felt by means of a spring conveyor from the one end of mill. The other end of a mill (discharge end) is provided with a coarse sieve and the product comes out through this sieve. If necessary the product is passed through a separator or classifier, which separates the fine particles from the coarse particles. The coarse particles may be ceased back to the ball mills for further size reduction. This operation is called as close circuit operation. When the product is not subjected to size separation it is called as open circuit operation.

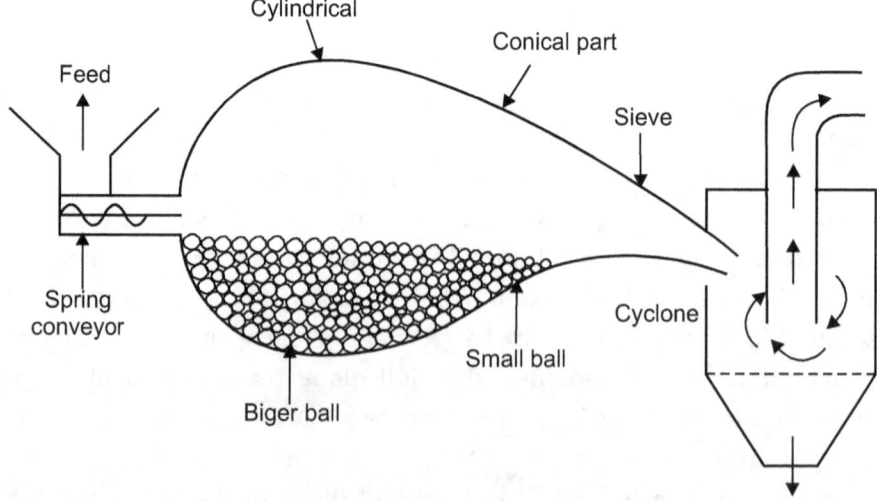

Fig. 9.33: Hardinoe conical ball mill

Advantages of Ball Mill:

(a) Grind variety of materials.

(b) Completely closed, therefore it can be used for continuous compound.

(c) It is equally suitable for dry grinding and wet grinding.

(d) They are cleaner than other mills. Easy installation, low operative cost.

(e) It can be used for continuous operation or a classifier can be used in conjunction with the wires.

Disadvantages:

(a) The contamination for the material is relatively more.

(b) Soft and sticky material sometimes form a cake which is unvariable.

(c) Very noisy machine.

5. Fluid Energy Mill:

1. Micronizer:

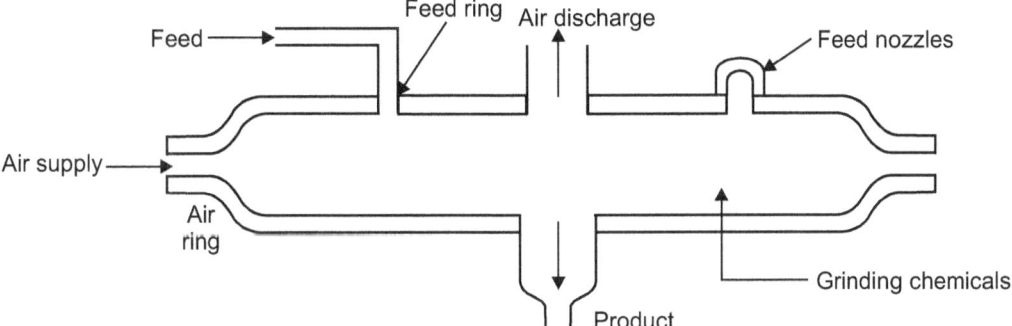

Fig. 9.34: Micronizer

The fluid energy mills differ from machine in that there is no noising part in this machine. The micronizer consists of two plates, the user plate has got a central opening for the air discharge and it also possess a circular feed ring along its circumference. The material to be grinded is suspended in air or water and it is introduced into the feed

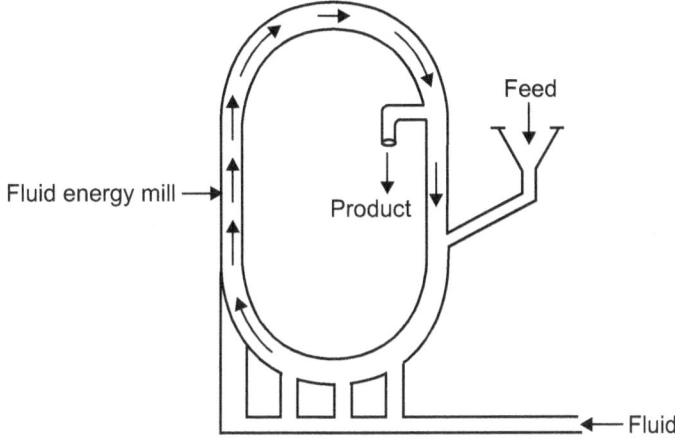

Fig. 9.35: Fluid energy mill

ring. The lower plate possess a central opening for the removal of the product. When the two plates are fixed together they form a cylindrical space. i.e. grinding chamber. The feed is introduced from the feed ring into the grinding chamber by means of nozzle which are arranged tangentially and pointing downwards, the air or water is passed under pressure through the air manifold into the grinding chamber by means of horizontal tangentially arranged nozzles due to the higher velocity of the fluid. The particles colloid with each other with a surface of grinding chamber and they break due to impact. The air is removed in the upward direction while the product pass down.

It consists of a loop of pipe which has a diameter of 20 to 200 mm. The diameter depends on the height of loop which may be upto about 2 mm. A fluid usually is injected at high pressure through nozzles at the bottom of loop. Solids are introduced into the stream. The size reduction takes place because use of impacts and attritional forces occurs between particles.

Advantages of Fluid Energy Mills:

1. Product is smaller almost of colloid size.
2. No additional cooling system is required.
3. No contamination of product.
4. Close control of particle size and of particle size reduction.

This method is used where fine powders, are required. e.g. antibiotics, sulphonamides and vitamins.

6. Wet Grinding : (Levigation)

The size reduction is carried out by suspending the feed in some liquid in which material is insoluble. The mills generally used are fluid energy mill, colloidal mill etc. Wet grinding is of limited application. Since, it requires a material that is already of small particle size and is insoluble in the liquid used.

Advantages :

1. Product contains less fines.
2. Capacity of plant is large.
3. Problem of dust eliminated.
4. Useful when screening and sieving is necessary.
5. For product in the form of suspension, the size-reduction and mixing operations are combined.
6. Materials are easy to handle.

Table 9.3: Selection of Degree of size reduction

Sr. No.	Degree of Size reduction	Typical methods	Mill used
1.	Large piece	Cutter or compression mills	Cutter mill or Roller mill.
2.	Coarse powders	Impact mills	Hammer mill.
3.	Fine powders	Combined impact and attrition mills	Ball mill.
4.	Very fine powders	Fluid energy mill	Micronizer and Jet-O-Mizer.

Grading of Powders:

Standards for powders for pharmaceutical purposes are mentioned in the British pharmacopoeia. B.P. states that the degree of coarseness or fineness of powder is differentiated and expressed by their size of the mesh of the sieve through which the powder is able to pass.

Table 9.4: The B.P. specified five grades of powder

Sr. No.	Grade of powder	Sieve through which all particles must pass	Sieve through which not more than 40% of particles pass
1.	Coarse	10	44
2.	Moderately coarse	22	60
3.	Moderately fine	44	85
4.	Fine	85	Not specified
5.	Very fine	120	Not specified

Thus, the coarse powder is defined as "the powder of which all the particles pass through a No. 10 sieve and not more than 40 percent through a No. 44 sieve". This is usually referred to as a 10/44 powder.

Other grades are expressed in a similar way.

Edge runner mill:

There are two heavy wheels, either of stone or metal, connected by a shaft. The wheels rotate at its axis in a shallow, circular plan. The material is fed into the centre of the pan, and is worked outwards by the action of the wheels. Scrappers are provided to scrap the material constantly from the bottom of the vessel and feed it to the wheel, where it gets crushed to powdered. Size reduction is due to crushing and shearing. It gives particles comparable with a disintegrator. It has little use in Pharmaceutical industry.

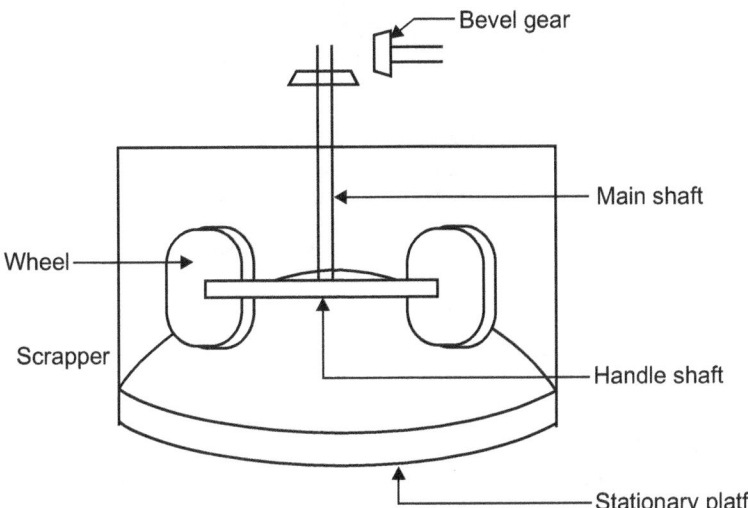

Fig. 9.36: Edge runner mill (side view)

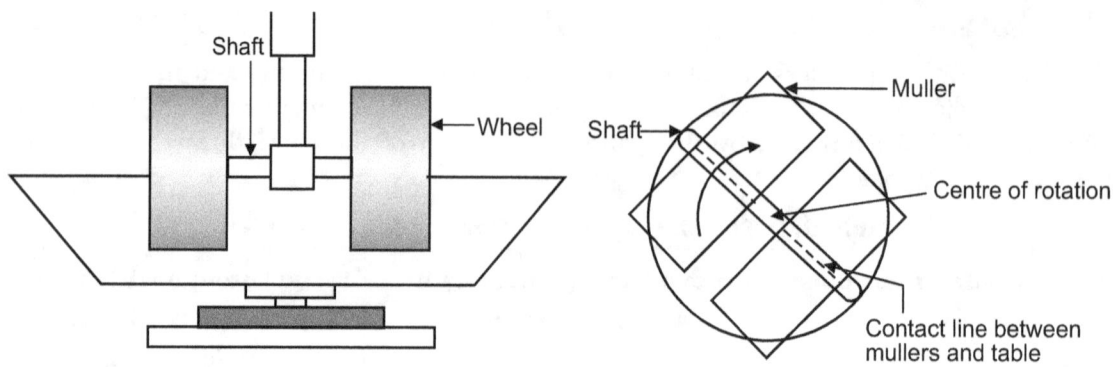

Fig. 9.37: Edge runner mill

End runner mill:

It is a modified form of the pestle and mortar used in the laboratory. This gives size reduction due to crushing by compression and shearing. As shown in the Fig. 9.38, it consists of a steel mortar and a steel pestle. The mortar is fixed on the rotating wheel, operated on an electric motar. As the mortar rotates (unlike the laboratory pestle and mortar), the pestle placed in an off centre position in the mortar also rotates. Thus, it accomplishes shearing and crushing of the material at the point of contact with the mortar. The material is continuously scraped and fed into the grinding path. This mill provides moderately fine powder and operates successfully with fibrous materials, bark, woods fruits, leaves, etc. wet grinding, with very viscous material such as ointments, and paste, is also possible.

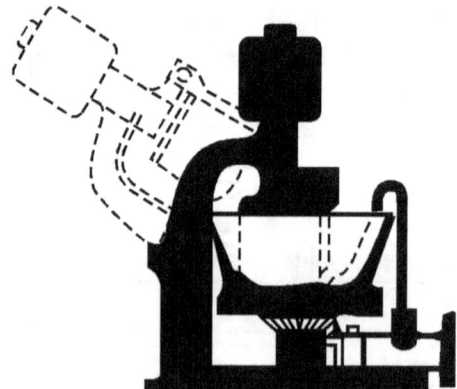

Fig. 9.38: Tilting end runner mill

(C) SIZE SEPARATION

Standards for powders for pharmaceutical purposes are laid down principally in the British Pharmacopoeia which states that the degree of coarseness or fineness of a powder is differentiated and expressed by the size of the mesh of the sieve through which the powder is able to pass.

Table 9.5: The B.P. specifications of fine grades of powders

Grade of Powder	Sieve through which all particles must pass
Coarse	10#
Moderately coarse	22#
Moderately fine	44#
Fine	85#
Very fine	120#

Since particles that will pass through a 120 sieve will also pass through a 10 sieve. Hence, the very fine powder meets the same definition as a coarse powder, clearly a limit must be placed in **"fines"** in the coarser grades of particles and it is obvious that this can be done by placing limits for two sieves for each powder – a large sieve through which all particles must pass and a smaller sieve through which the particles will not pass.

Because of this, the B.P. specifies a second, smaller size of sieve for coarser powder but states that not more than 40% shall pass through. This means that the objective is to obtain a powder with all the particles between specified maximum and minimum size but, because of particle size reduction difficulties, atleast 60% of the powder between those size is acceptable.

Table 9.6: The relevant grades of powder and sieve numbers

Grades of Powder	Sieve through which all particles must pass	Sieve through which not more than 40% of particles pass
Coarse	10#	44%
Moderately coarse	22#	60#
Moderately fine	44#	85#
Fine	85#	Not specified
Very fine	100#	Not specified

Thus, the full definition of coarse powder is that it is powder, all the particles of which pass through a No. 10 Sieve and not more than 40% through a No. 44 sieve.

For convenience, this is usually referred to on a 10/44 powder. Other grades are expressed in a similar way.

A better idea of the degree of divergence of these powders can be obtained by comparing the areas of the particles, based on maximum particle size for each grades, that is, on the upper and coarser limit. Coarse powder is represented on unity and the other grades are shown in the following table.

Table 9.7: Comparative account of powder size

	Type of Powder	Comparison of Powder Size
1.	Coarse powder	1
2.	Moderately coarse powder	1/6
3.	Moderately fine powder	1/24
4.	Fine powder	1/90
5.	Very fine powder	1/200

The British Pharmacopoeia makes two statements with regard to these **"official"** grades of powder in practice.

1. It is required that, when a powder is described by a number, all particles must pass through the specified sieve.
2. When a vegetable drug is being ground and sifted, none must be rejected.

Sieves (Screen): Any discussion of the performance of size separation equipment, of crushing and grinding equipment, involves a determination of the amount of material of different size present. The only general and practical method for this is to determine the fraction of the sample that will go through a screen with given openings. It has been the custom in the past to specify screens merely by the number of **meshes per unit inch.** Thus, a screen analysis may show the weight – percentage of the material that passes through 10 mesh and remain on 20 mesh through 20 and on 30, through 30 and on 40, etc.

Table 9.8: Variation of Screen openings with mesh and wire diameter

Mesh	Wire diameter in.	Clear opening in.	Mesh	Wire diameter	Clear opening in.
30	0.017	0.0163	20	0.032	0.0180
30	0.014	0.0193	22	0.028	0.0175
30	0.012	0.0213	26	0.020	0.0185
30	0.010	0.0233	28	0.018	0.0171
30	0.008	0.0253	30	0.015	0.0183
			35	0.011	0.0176

Standard Screens: Various sieve scales have been proposed, in which both the diameter of the wire and the number of meshes per inch are specified so as to give a definite ratio between the openings in one screen and the next succeeding screen in the series. One comment set of standard screens (sieves) is tyler standard screen scale.

Sieves and Sifting:

A feature of the modern pharmaceutical industry is the increased use that is being made of materials in a fine state of sub-division. Numerous methods have been developed for sifting powders and determining their particle size. Of these sieving is undoubtedly the most common, being applicable to practically all powders from about 40 µm upwards.

1. Sieving :

In the U.K., the British Standard Sieves are extensively used both for scientific work on powders and for separating them into fractions on a commercial scales. In Europe, the **German DIN** (Deutche Industrienomen) is widely used. But different standards are used for German, American and other sieves. It states that a sieve has a certain mesh is meaningless unless the diameter of the wire constituting the mesh is also specified. This will determine the size of the opening. Clearly the opening will always be smaller than the measurement suggested in the mesh designation.

Table 9.9: Wire Mesh Sieves

Sieve No. (mm)	Preferred Average Wire Diameter (mm)	Tolerance for Average Aperature Size (mm)	Approximate Sieving Area. (mm)
3.35	1.25	0.10	33.
2.00	0.90	0.060	48.
1.70	0.80	0.051	48.
1.18	0.63	0.035	43.

Table 9.10: Perforated Plate Test Sieve

Sieve No. mm	Preferred Plate thickness mm	Minimum width of bridge mm	Tolerance on Nominal Aperature Size mm	Sieving Area %
6.70	1.0	1.3	6.70	47

Alpine Airjet Sieve:

In recent years, the Alpine Airjet Sieve has been developed to extend the range of conventional sieves which tend to block at practicle sieves below about 80 μm. The action of the sieve depends on a jet of air instead of mechanical vibration. Its purpose is to fluidize the powder, thereby preventing blocking of the mesh and at the same time cushioning the particles from impact with Tar mesh which, is the core of soft powders, artificially produces fines.

The apparatus consists essentially of a metal housing into which the sieve mesh is fitted. Powder is placed on tar mesh which is then covered by a close fitting lid and is fluidized by an upward jet of air directed on to its cover surface through a rotating slit. A vacuum is simultaneously created in the interior of the housing so that the undersized powder is swelled through the sieve into a paper filter from which it can be recovered if required.

Advantages:

1. It is rapid.
2. It produces closer and more reproduceable size cuts, is not subject to the clogging which occur in hand. Vibration sieving at small sizes in particular, gives true result.

Classifiers and Sifters:

Most commercial classifiers and sifters are based on the principle of sieving. Thus, in the Pascal Turbine Sifter there is a cylindrical screen which is divided into two three compartments, in each of which there is a turbine heater, which drives an air current through the screen and carries the fine powder with it. This is drawn off from the base of the machine. The air is recirculated and the coarse material is discharged from a spout at the side. Brush sifters employ brushes to separate the fine and coarse particles on the sieves mesh and one useful for **greasy** and **sticky powder** such as **waxes** and **soaps.** One design has three circular brushes mounted on a triangular structure. The sieves are mounted on a delivery funnel of stainless steel and enamel and the whole unit is supported on a wheeled trolley for ease of movement.

In recent years there has been an increasing demand for pharmaceutical powder like **Griseofulvin,** and aspirin in an extremely fine state of sub-division i.e. less than 10 μm and this has necessitated the use of essentially centrifugal classifiers. One example is the cut rock classifier.

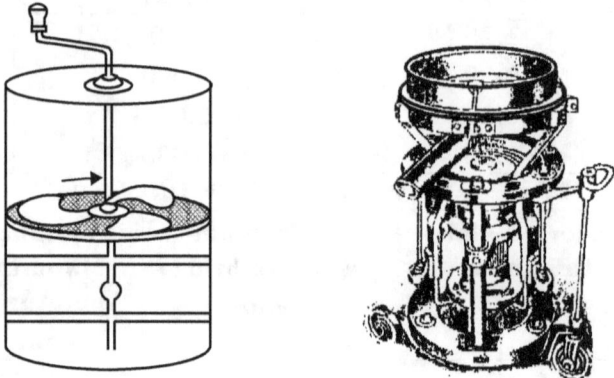

Fig. 9.39: Classifier and Sifter

Particle size distribution :

When the number or weight of particles lying within a certain size range is plotted against the size range and mean particle size is so called **frequency distribution curve.**

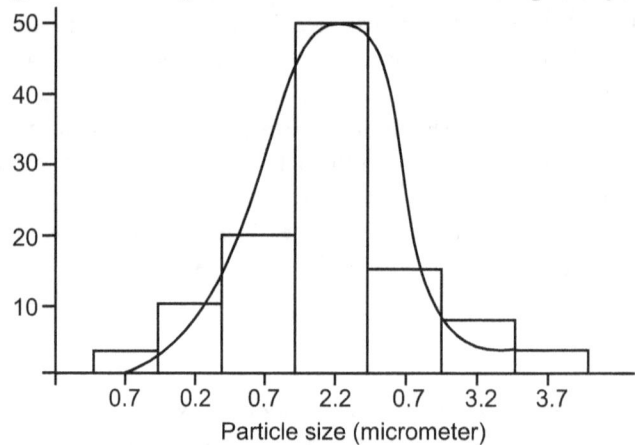

Fig. 9.40: Particle size distribution curve

Method for determining particle size :

Many methods are available for determining particle size:

1.   Sedimentation method.

2.   Determination of particle volume.

3.   Optical Microscopy.

4.   Sieving.

None of the measurements are truly direct methods. Although the microscope allows the observer to view the actual particles, the results obtained are probably no more "direct" them those resulting from other methods.

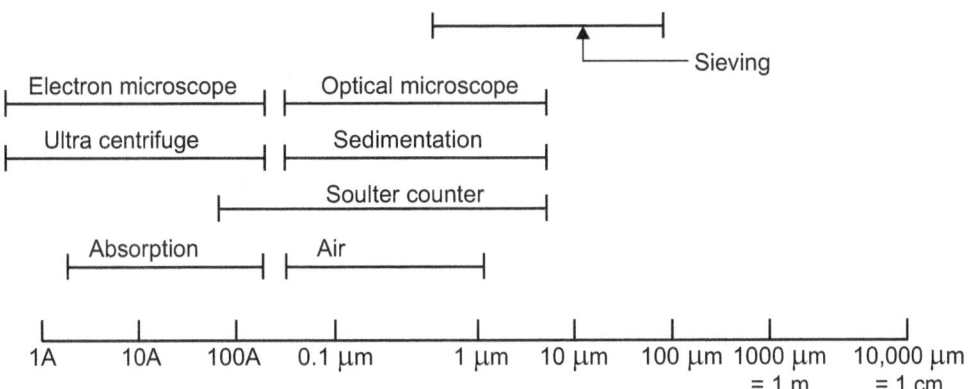

Fig. 9.41: Optical microscopy

1. The Sedimentation method: Yields a particle size relative to the rate at which particles settle through a suspending medium, this measurement is important in the development of emulsion and suspensions.

2. The measurement of particle volume, using an apparatus called the **coulter counter,** allow one to calculate an equivalent volume diameter.

3. Optical microscopy: It should be possible to use the ordinary microscope for particle size measurement in the range of **0.2 µm** to about **100 µm.** According to Microscopic method, an emulsion or suspension, diluted or undiluted, is mounted on slide and ruled cell and placed on a mechanical stage. The microscopic eye piece is fitted with a micrometer by which tar size of the particle may be extracted.

The field can be projected on to screen where the particles are measured more easily, and a photograph can be taken from which a slide is prepared and projected on a screen for measurement.

Disadvantages:

1. The diameter is obtained from only two dimension of the particle, length and breadth. No estimates of the depth (thickness) of the particle is ordinarily available.

2. In addition, the number of particles that must be counted (around 300 to 500) in order to obtain a good estimation of tar distribution makes the method somewhat slow and tedious.

4. Sieving : This method utilizes a series of standard sieves calibrated by the National Bureau of standards. Sieves are generally used for grinding coarse particles, if extreme care is used. However, they may be employed for screening material as fine as **44 micrometers** (No. 325 Sieve).

(D) MIXING OF POWDERS

In small scale work, it is better to use hand mixing methods.

Spatulation:

Small amount of powders with same range of particle sizes and densities may be mixed with the help of spatula, the powders being placed on a tile.

Trituration:

This is carried out in a mortar. In case of combination of small amount of one drug, with a large quantity of a diluent it is better to triturate first with one volume of drug, with equal volume of the diluent and then adding twice as much diluent and continue the trituration. This procedure i.e. additioning twice as much diluent as there is material in the mortar is continued until the total bulk of powder is in the mortar.

By the term trituration, it is meant the pestle be moved (with pressure) in circle, starting from the centre, reaching the periphery and returning of the pestle to the centre. This cycle is repeated several times or until the mixing is satisfactorily completed.

Shifting is useful where free flowing light powders are desired.

Tumbling:

Tumbling is carried out in a wide mouth closed container. It is obvious that this procedure avoids pressure gradient. The powders are required not to occupy more than half or less than half the capacity of container. The container is rotated in such a manner that during the motion the powder particles float in the air. Tumbling is used for mixing powders with density differences.

Special problems in handling the medicinal powders:

Hygroscopic Powders:

Powders which absorb moisture from the atmosphere are called **hygroscopic powders.** Some powders absorb moisture to such a great extent that the powders go into solution. Such powders are called **deliquesent powders.** Remedy lies in dispensing these powders in granular form in order to reduce surface area of powders and to expose less area to the air. If powdering is necessary, it may be carried out in dry mortar.

Efflorescent Powders:

Some substances lose their water of crystallisation on exposure, particularly to dry atmospheric conditions such substances are said to effervescent. Such powders may lose water of crystallisation during trituration causing the powder to become pasty. This difficulty can be overcome by using corresponding anhydrous salt or by drying the crystalline form to constant weight when such steps, as above are being taken the dose is required to be adjusted.

Eutectic Mixtures:

Many substances, when combined with other powders turn into liquid or give rise to a pasty mass. This is undesirable when powders are being dispensed. Such combinations i.e. which liquify are known as Eutectic Mixtures.

Examples:

Acetanilide, antipyrine, menthol, camphor chloral – hydrate phenol, salol, thymol and acetylsalicyclic acid.

When two or more of these are combined liquification occurs. Liquifaction is avoided in the following ways :

1. If each substance is in sufficient quantity, dispense each separately.

2. Alternatively use starch, talc or calcium phosphate as an absorbent powder equal in proportion of liquifiable substances. Each liquifiable substance is triturated with equal quantity of absorbent powder. The second liquifiable substance is separately triturated with the absorbent powder and then both the mixtures are lightly mixed.

Extracts:

Sometimes extracts are prescribed with other powders. The extracts in the form of powders are available in the market. When it is necessary to use a pilular extract in powders, dilute it with lactose and gently heat it to powder form and then use it.

Explosive Powder Mixtures:

These are generally a mixture of oxidising and reducing substance. For example, a combination of Potassium chlorate and tannic acid is an explosive mixture particularly so when pressure is applied. In trituration, there is a pressure gradient. In order to avoid explosion the substances should be powdered separately and then combined by mixing lightly.

Mixing and Homogenization of Powders:

The term mixing is defined as *"the process in which two or more ingredients in separate or mixed conditions are treated so that every particle of any one ingredient is as nearly as possible adjacent to a particle of each of the other ingredients".*

Mixing is one of the most common pharmaceutical operation employed in the preparations of various types of formulation. The intentions of mixing are:

1. To ensure uniformity of composition so that smallest quantity of sample taken from the bulk material represents the overall composition of the mixture under process and

2. To promote or initiate physical or chemical reactions like diffusion, dissolution etc.

Mixing in general is classified as under:

1. Positive Mixing or Miscibility:

Wherein two gases or two miscible liquids mix completely. All that is required of the mixing equipment is that it shall accelerate the diffusion process.

2. Negative mixing or immiscibility:

Wherein the phases differ in density and will separate unless continuously differ. The phases may be either liquid in liquid or solid in liquid. This is particularly demonstrated by suspensions of solids in liquids.

3. Neutral mixing:

Wherein neither mixing nor demixing takes place unless a force is exerted on the system. It is exemplified by mixing of solids with liquids when the concentration of the former is higher than the latter.

The mechanism of mixing: The mechanism of mixing is explained by the following methods :

(a) **Convective mixing:** It is the bulk movement of groups of particles from one part of the powder bed to another.

(b) **Diffusive mixing:** It is the mingling of particles as individuals. The distribution of particles is over a freshly developing surface.

(c) **Shear mixing:** As a result of forces slip planes are set-up.

Rate of mixing: As a result of process of achieving uniform randomness and thus, its rate is proportional to the amount of mixing done. In the early stage of mixing, the particles change their path of circulation and find themselves in different environment. Thus, the rate of mixing is very fast. While at the end of mixing process particles do not find different environment and the rate reaches to zero.

Mixing of Solids:

It is a neutral type of mixing. The degree of mixedness will increase with the length of time for which mixing is done, with the variation in particle size or density in two powders the mixing can even be negative. Since the law of diminishing return gets applied to this system is a economic time of mixing.

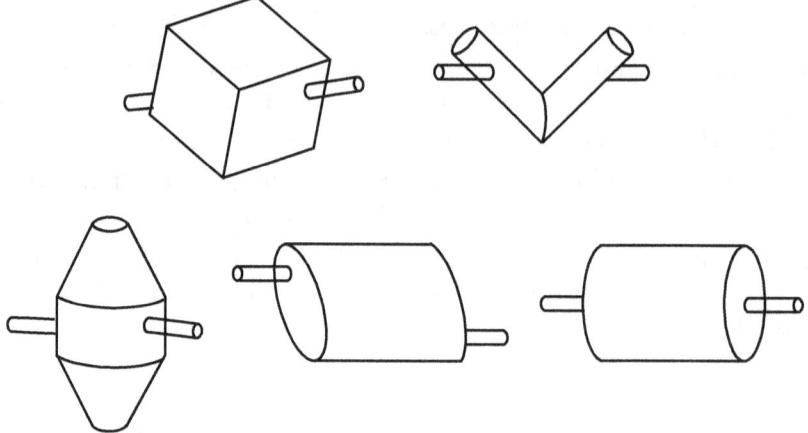

Fig. 9.42: Different forms of tumbling-drum mixers

Factors which control the mixing are as under:

1. Volume:

The mixer must allow sufficient space or volume for dilation of the bed, over-filling of the mixer reduces the efficiency and may also prevent mixing.

2. Mixer mechanism:

The type of mixer selected must provide suitable shear forces to bring about local mixing and convective movement.

3. Duration of mixing:

Mixing should be carried out for optimum time as the degree of mixing will reach the equilibrium therefore, optimum time for any particular system should be followed or also the segregation may occur.

4. Handling of the mixed products:

Handling of the mixed products should be done in such a way that its segregation is minimised. The vibrations or transports are the factors which may cause segregation.

Following are the few physical properties which affect the mixing of powders and need to pay more attention than before undertaking any sort of solid mixing:

1. Density:

If the components of mixing differ in density the heavier material will go to the bottom which will result in the improper mixing of the ingredients. To bring the proper uniformity during mixing, charging and operating in a mixer proper attention should be given to the density.

2. Particle size:

Variation in the particle size lead to the segregation, as smaller particles can fall through the voids between the large particles.

3. Particle shape:

Spherical particles are ideal for mixing as irregular shapes can become interlocked thus decreasing the risk of segregation once the mixing has been achieved.

4. Particle attraction:

Some particles exert attractive forces like electrostatic charges and may tend to segregate.

5. Proportion of mixing materials:

The percentage of materials is to be mixed play a very important role in mixing. The usual method is to mix the components in lesser amount with equal quantity of the diluent. This is to be followed in the ascending orders which ensures the best possible mixing.

On large scale powders are mixed in Mixers, a typical of which is shown below.

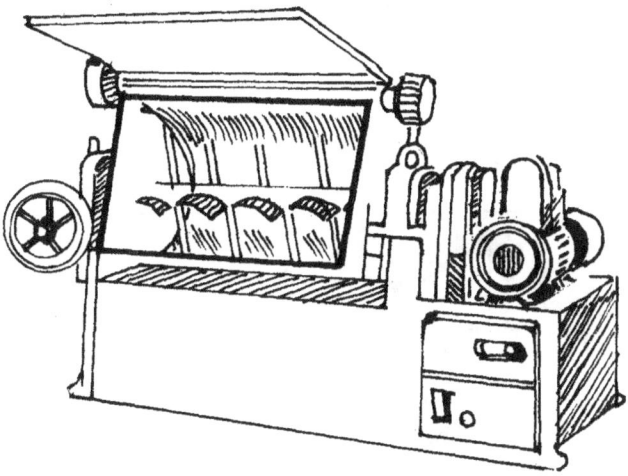

Fig. 9.43: Powder Mixer

Double arm mixer or kneader:

These are suitable for all types of viscous semi-solids pastes, ointments, chewing gums and even the smokless powders. This consists of rectangular trough or bowl with the bottom shaped in the form of two semi-cylinders, wherein two parallel agitator blades are mounted horizontally in bearing in the end walls. These agitators force the material to travel up at the side and knead in the centre of the tough. Thus, the folding, kneading, tearing or mixing takes place. Kneaders may be of flow lapping agitator type or tangential agitator type. The choice of their selection depends upon the material to be mixed. However, for lighter material the over lapping type of kneaders are used and for heavier special tangential agitators are used. The double arm mixer may be tilting or non-tilting type. Normally, non-tilting type are quite big and have a bottom discharge wall or gate for emptying the container.

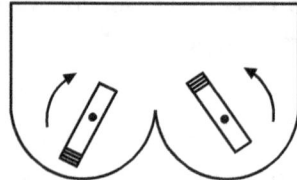

Fig. 9.44: Sigma blade mixer

Mixing Equipments

Although size reduction equipments are used for mixing purposes, some special machines are designed for mixing of pharmaceutical powders.

1.   Ribbon mixer:

It consists of a trough mounted on a stand. In the trough, a ribbon like conveying scroll is attached to a shaft. The ribbon may be continuous or interrupted. The shaft is operated by an electric motor. The trough is semicircular, with a lid. It can be tilted on the stand to remove the material. When the motor is started the material gets mixed due to convection and shear. Two ribbons, with opposite direction may sometimes are attached to the shaft. A mixture of high homogeneity can be produced by prolonged mixing, even when the components of a mixture differ in particle size, shape, density or have a tendency to aggregate.

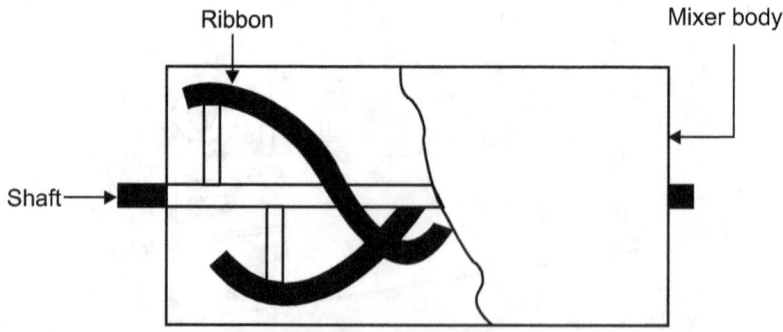

Fig. 9.45: Ribbon mixer

2. Paddle mixer:

It comprises of a semicircular trough, containing a number of paddles mounted on the shaft at diverse angles. The shaft rotates alongwith the paddles, lifting the material filled in the trough in an irregular fashion. Convection and shear mixing is the predominant mechanism in this mixer.

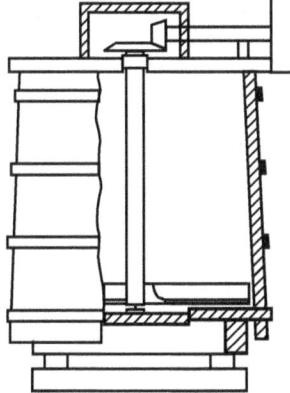

Fig. 9.46: Paddle mixer

3. Impact mixer:

The working of this mill (Hammer mill) has been discussed earlier in this book. This mill is used for mixing and grinding of materials.

4. Agitated Powder Mixer:

Mixing of powders is difficult due to variation in densities, particle size, physical form and the bulk used. This problem is more serious when diluent is used with potent medicament (low bulk). In mixing process, the particles should move relative to one another to ensure homogeneous mixture. Hence, localised shearing is necessary to move the particles, bulk of the material should also come in the region of shear.

During mixing process no pressure should exert on the powder. Pressure results in cake formation and hence homogeneous mixing becomes more difficult.

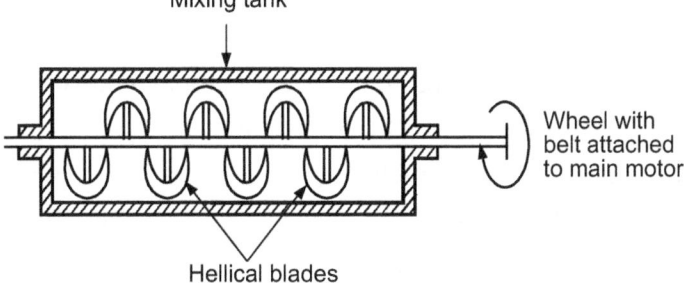

Fig. 9.47: Agitated powder mixer

Powder mixing is a neutral process and when the process is stopped the mixture remains in steady state unless further agitated.

Mechanism of powder mixing is either convective or diffusive. Convective mixing results movement of bulk of particles while diffusive mixing is a result of movement of individual particles. However, both the types give homogeneous mixtures.

Various tumbling drum mixtures give good mixing of powder. The efficiency can be increased by fitting internal baffles in the drum. Baffles act as agitator resulting homogeneous mixing of powder. One of the agitated powder mixer is shown in Fig. 9.45.

The helical agitator mixer do not exert pressure on the powder but only shift bulk of powder or particle in the drum to cause proper mixing.

5. Planetary mixer:

This is also used for semisolid mixing. It consists of an anchor type of paddle, revolving in a cylindrical pot with a hemispherical base. The paddle rotates on its axis and the axis also moves around. The paddle thus gets scraped from the wall and thrown to the centre to the pan. This facilitates the mixing process.

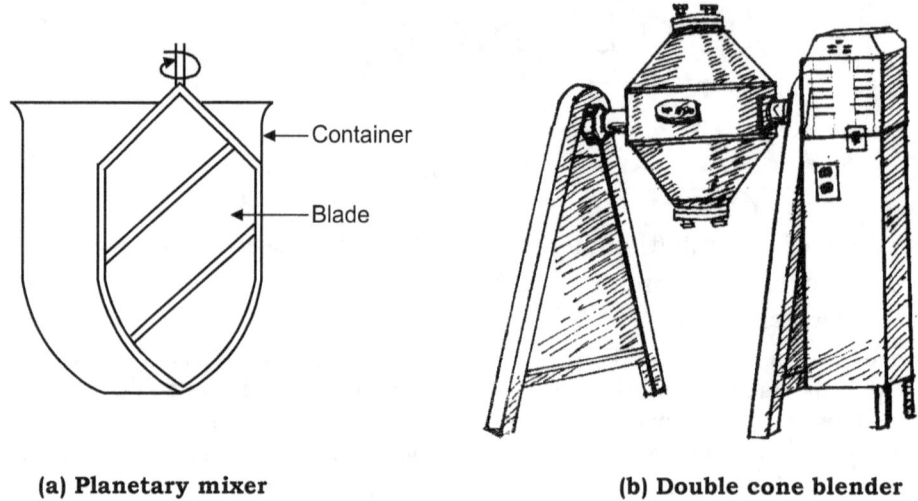

(a) Planetary mixer   (b) Double cone blender

Fig. 9.48: Mixers

6. Double Cone Mixer:

This type of mixer is designed in such a way that the vessel imparts movement to the material of mixing by tilting the powder until the angle of surface exceeds the angle of response. Thus, powder bulk or particles slide and get mixed in the vessel.

Various shapes are available in this type of mixer. It rotates on central shaft. Shape may be cylinder, cube, double cone, V shape or Y shape with or without baffles or agitator.

During the process of mixing particles of powder hit each other and wall of the mixer resulting mixing action. However, speed of mixture is very important. It should run at critical speed. Too high or too low speed will definetely affect the mixing process. Over loading mixer with powder material should be avoided. There should be sufficient room for powder to move in drum. Critical time for mixing can be set by withdrawing the samples from mixer at interval of time and analysing it for homogenicity.

(E) GRANULE MANUFACTURING

Granulation is a process that converts powdered materials into aggregates called granules.

Granulation:

Apart from basic need of granules in the manufacture of tablets, since,

1. Fine powder does not flow uniformly from the hopper of the tablet machine die.

2. The tablets produced by using only fine powder vary widely in weight.

3. Mixture of powders in the formulation may cause separation of light and heavy particles, resulting un-uniform tablets in contents and weight also.

4. Fine powders produce "capping" in tablets.

5. "Sticking" is the outcome of using only powders during compression.

To overcome all the above technological difficulties it is necessary to convert the powders into the granules for compressed tablets.

Since, several tablets are official in several pharmacopoeias apart from many more unofficial tablets available in the market, the process of granulation has received the attention of most of the manufacturers to develop the granulation as a very important and separate department in the tablet manufacture.

Granules other than the tablet compressing are very essential:

(b) For highly hydroscopic chemicals as they cannot be used alone in their own way and are mixed with inert substances like starch and lactose and are converted into suitable forms and kept away from chemical and therapeutic degradation.

(c) Dry extracts are available in the market in the form of granules only.

(d) Volatile oils are to be added to the formulations for their better availability or intention in the form of granules only. Hence, granules are to be prepared on the industrial scales.

Granulated opium and Granular pepsin are official products in IP while Bournvita, Proteinex and Complan are the granular patented products in the market.

Essential Granule Properties :

The following are the essential properties of the granules :

1. They have uniform distribution of all active ingredients in the formulation.

2. They should contain particles which approach spherical shapes, spheres have minimum inter particulate friction so possess excellent fluidity and free from static charge.

3.   They should possess ingredients with or without other additives which are compressible. Compressible components of the formulation confer sufficient physical strength to the tablets to withstand the damage due to mechanical forces during process.

4.   They must present range of particle sizes with both coarse and fine particles, fines tend to improve the fill of the die and fill the intergranule spaces by forming physical bonds upon compression.

By observing the above properties of granules one can compare the reasons as to why the materials must be in the form of granules and not in fine powder for preparation of compressed tablets. The reasons are summarized below.

Granules:

1.   Granules flow easily and do not give variation in the tablets produced.

2.   Granules are of uniform composition and segregation is not a serious problem. But to improve the fill certain proportion (5 to 15%) of fine material is essential.

3.   Granules pack down rapidly hence transmit the pressure compression force readily. Upon compression granules inter particular bends are formed and sound tablets are produced.

4.   The granules being heavier do not blow out of the die and do not clog the lower punch.

The Granulation processes:

It is obvious that successful tableting depends upon uniform flow of materials from hopper to the die. Fine powders are usually difficult to compress owing to their poor flow properties. The degree of mix is fixed within granules and the desired size of the granules can be choosen in order to impart the essential flow properties and uniform filling of the die.

The methods of granulation are:

1.   Dry granulation;

2.   Moist granulation and

3.   Granulation by preliminary compression.

1.   Dry Granulation:

This method is suitable for the tablets containing only one ingredients and available in crystalline form. A limited number of substances can be directly compressed either alone or with the addition of other essential pharmaceutical aids such as disintegrating agents or lubricants. If the crystals are larger they can be reduced to smaller size by crushing so as to pass through suitable sieve (No. 20) for average size by tablet to produce particles of uniform and required size. Then, dry them to remove surface moisture.

Aspirin, Ferrouos gluconate, Yeast and salts such as Sodium chloride, Potassium bromide as treated in this way.

This method is newly used when the formulation contains mixture of two or more crystalline substances because it gives wide variation in content of active substances in the tablets.

2.   Moist Granulation :

This is one of the methods of granulation still most widely used where the substances are stable in presence of moisture. It requires more time and labour. The granules prepared by this popular method meet with all the physical requirements for the compression of good tablets. This method consists of a number of steps carried out in the following order.

1.	Weighing	5.	Drying
2.	Mixing	6.	Dry screening
3.	Granulation	7.	Lubrication
4.	Screening the damp mass	8.	Compression.

The active ingredients, diluents and the disintegrates are placed in powder mixer and mixing is carried out until uniform dispersion of powder blend is attained. The powder blend may be shifted through a screen of suitable size to remove or to break up lumps. Solutions of granulating agents or binding agents are added to the mixed powder under continuous stirring, to render it coherent mass. The approximate way of determining the desired point is to press a portion of the mass on the palm. If the ball crumbles under moderate pressure the mixture is ready for the next stage of processing.

For large quantities mass mixers of sigma blade type can be used.

This coherent mass of suitable consistency is forced through a 6 to 8 mesh screen which may be done manually for small batches or by means of mechanical granulations or communiting mills for large quantities.

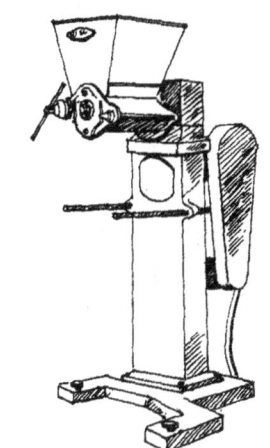

The communiting mills employed usually one oscillating granulator, fitzpatrick mill, and Reitz extractor. The oscillating granulator consists of hopper feeding to a chamber containing a powerful oscillating rotor, which forces the material through a screen. Screens are of various mesh specifications and are inter-changeable.

Fig. 9.49: Oscillating granulator

For continuous production Reitz extractor is used which consists of a screw mixture with a chamber where the powder blend is mixed with granulating fluids or binding agents. The wet coherent mass is gradually extruded through a perforated end plate forming threads of the wet granulation.

The wet granules are then subjected to drying. Drying is accomplished by tray dryer.

Special Methods of Granulation:

(a) Air suspension technique:

The air suspension technique was described by Wurster in 1959-60, for moist granulation. It consists of fluidized chamber with centrally placed atomiser above the bed. Finely grounded powders are suspended in the stream of air within the chamber and mixed. By means of a pump the granulating liquid is sprayed through atomiser directed downwards on the suspended powder to form the agglomerates. The size of granules produced as the solvent evaporates can be controlled by monitoring the factors such as the volume and temperature of the granulating liquid, and the time of granulation.

Once the granules are produced, the additives such as lubricants, disintegrants are introduced into the fluidized chamber which are dispersed throughout the granules by the short turbulent cold air stream.

(b) Spray drying process:

This is also one of the processes employed for wet granulation. The components of the tablet formula, such as diluents, disintegrants, binders and lubricants are either suspended to form a slurry or dissolved in a suitable vehicle according to their chemical nature. The slurry is pumped to an atomizing wheel under constant stirring to maintain uniform dispersion. The atomizer whirls the slurry or vehicle into a stream of hot air. The hot air, removes liquid carrier, resulting in formation of spherical solids that fall at the botton of the dryer. Thus, it forms base.

The drug or active ingredients are mixed with this base in a suitable proportion before compression. If the drug is stable to the operating temperature and vehicle used, it may be incorporated in the slurry alongwith other components.

DRYING OF GRANULES

Tray Drying:

The granules to be dried are spread in thin layers on the trays, and raking these trays in drying cabinet. The drying is effected by circulating hot air currents and thermostatic control. An alternative drying method which is much faster than tray drying is fluidized bed drying.

Fluidized Bed Drying:

In fluidized bed drying, the bed of granular solid particles is partially suspended in an upward moving warm air stream and granules are frequently agitated. The granules are lifted upward and fall back in random manner due to continuous fluidization. Moreover, the other excipient can be blended in drying granulation directly in the fluidized bed.

Generally, for batch size of 25 kg to 200 kg the average drying time required is 20 to 40 minutes depending on capacity of dryer.

Fluidization has better temperature control and minimum degradation of ingredients during drying cycle. It is economic while greater uniformity is residual moisture content is achieved, which further contributes to the reduction in static charges on the particles.

ENVIRONMENTAL CONTROLS

Environmental conditions play very effective role in the dosage formulation such as tables, capsules, injections, granules, powder, syrups, tinctures and other pharmaceutical dosage forms. There are number of environmental parameters which affects the quality of products. These factors are light, dust, temperature, humidity, insects, ventilation, air and contamination.

Light: Number of products are sensitive to light and they can change their properties and affects the therapeutic efficacy. e.g. chloroform gets converted in phosgene gas due to effect of light. Some other drug products such as nimesulide, ascorbic acid, chloramphenicol etc. are light sensitive drugs.

Dust: During the formulation of granules, powder mixing, reducing particle size, punching of tablets, dust is produced. Mostly, it is harmful for the health and toxic to the person working in such atmosphere, e.g. sulphur dust is very harmful to the human health. Some products such as sulphonamides, histamines, aspirin also produce allergic reactions.

Humidity: Some chemicals, reagents and drug substances are highly sensitive to the moisture. Both low and high humidity reduce the quality of the product and some times changes its physical as well as chemical nature of the products e.g. camphor, menthol, sodium chloride are affected by humidity and changes their states. If a powder material is completely free from humidity, it creates problem in tablet compression. Capsule shell also becomes brittle due to low humidity and sticky due to high humidity.

Temperature: Temperature and humidity are linked to each other and hence, it is essential to maintain it in the manufacturing unit and during storage. The products should be stable and maintain its efficacy in the environmental conditions (at NTP).

Insects: Due to sticky nature of materials or insects attracting materials, it gets contaminated by the insects. Hence, it should be protected from the insects by covering the material, closed container or closed environment.

Ventilation: Without ventilation, cross contamination and incompatibility occurs. It should be maintained properly during the working hours.

Air: Fresh air circulation is necessary for maintaining ideal condition of products as well as for the safety of the working personnel in the field.

Contamination: It is a very serious problem in the formulation as it cannot be identified easily. Hence, care should be taken to protect from the contaminations. It may be microbial, chemical or may be of other type.

Pouch Filling Machine:

It provides tamper resistant packaging along with high degree of environment protection useful for filling pharmaceutical powders, granules, liquid (liquid shampoo) etc.

The machine is available in two forms verticle and horizontal sealing pouches.

The pouch size varies in length 50 mm to 200 mm and width from 30 mm to 160 mm which can accommodate 0.5 g to 50 of material depending upon the bulk density of the product to be packed.

The vertical form fill and seal machine is available for producing $^3/_4$ side sealed sachets capable of handling all types of free flowing powders or granules.

It consists of following main parts :

1. Film laminate
2. Cup filler
3. Metal collar
4. Mandrel
5. Longitudinal sealer
6. End sealer.

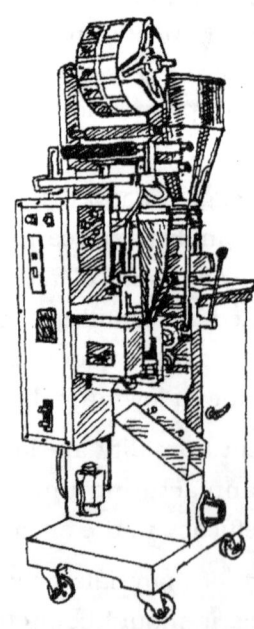

Fig. 9.50: Pouch Filling Machine

The film is drawn over a metal collar and around a verticle filling tube which drops the product into the package formed by the machine. Sometimes the metal filling tube also works as mandrel, controlling the longitudinal pouch size and thus promotes the sealing. The end sealer moves up the film tube at a fixed distance and finally seal the packet. The top sealing of the pouch becomes the bottom seal of the next one and thus, it continues.

The output of the machine varies from 20-100 pouches per minute. Additional options like conveyor, over printer, product level control, liquid filter, and others can also be provided with the machine. Thus, by using this machine one can save time, it is easy to handle, economical and also help in maintaining the cleanliness in the premises.

Chapter ... 10

BIOLOGICAL PRODUCTS

(A) IMMUNOLOGY

Introduction to Immunology:

A large number of preparations of microbial origin are used in the management of infective diseases. These preparations are usually used for protection or immunization against diseases caused by bacteria and viruses but are also used, though less frequently, for the treatment and diagnosis of such diseases. *The power to resist the effects of the invasion of pathogenic microbes is called* **immunity** *and the lack of ability to resist infection is called* **susceptibility**. *All immunological preparations are* **biological products** *of a predominantly protein nature.* With one exception if they are to be effective they must be administered parenterally since, their oral administration results in inactivation of the preparation. The exception is poliomyelitis vaccine (oral) which contains live viruses capable of multiplying in the gut.

Since, the immunological preparations are considered as medical preparations a brief survey of the available types is given here.

The concept of immunity is diagrammatically presented hereunder:

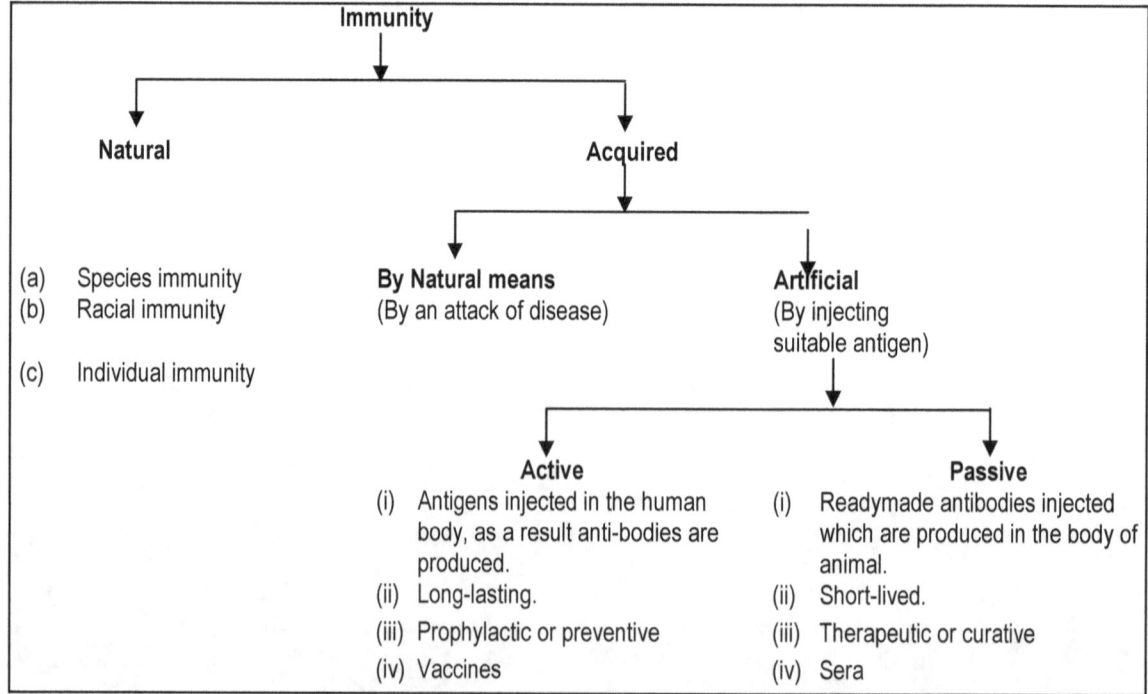

Active immunity is produced by injecting antigens into the body which stimulate the production of **antibodies.** A substance in response to which antibodies are produced is an **antigen.** Antigens derived from micro-organisms are administered in the form of **vaccines.** These may consist of living or dead micro-organisms which are weakened or attenuated or sterile extracts or filtrates of cultures of micro-organisms containing the toxins produced by the organism. Vaccines, whatever their nature, produce immunity without the clinical effect of the disease. Active immunity is characterized by being slow to develop. The production of an adequate antibody level often requires several injections of the vaccine. The first injection produces a primary response with a low level of immunity but appears to train the body in antibody production so that the second injection produces a high level of immunity. The interval between the injections may have to be several weeks to produce an adequate secondary response. Active immunity, once produced, is lost only slowly and the antibody level in the blood is capable of rapid restoration by subsequent booster doses or exposure to the relevant infection. Active immunization is, therefore, a prophylactic measure used to protect an individual likely to be exposed to a particular infective disease.

Infection and Body Defences:

Now it is a common knowledge that these micro-organisms are universal in nature. They are found every where in water, soil, in the body, in the tissues etc. Not that all are dangerous and deadly. Nevertheless some of them are beneficial to the human race in so many ways. Those, which cause disease are referred as pathogenic others are non-pathogenic. Majority of the diseases are caused by the infection of human body by these microbes, (few-illustrations are given below) may be bacteria, virus, fungi etc. The infection may be transferred from person to person by various means for example by direct or indirect contact through food and water supplies, by inhalation of infected dust or droplets of moisture, by direct contamination of wound or by the agency of animal carriers most often insects.

Table 10.1: Diseases and causative organisms

Name of the Disease	Causative organisms
Tuberculosis	*Micobacterium tuberculosis*
Diphtheria	*Corynebacterium diphtheriae*
Typhoid	*Salmonella typhi*
Small pox	*Variola major*
Cholera	*Vibrio cholerae*
Tetanus	*Clostridium tetani*

Infection may be avoided by practicing personal hygiene and sanitation, water treatment, fumigation, insect and flies eradication and immunisation.

The result of infections depends on several factors such as:

1. **Route of infection:** For example: *Cholera vibrios* if do not get an entry in the alimentary tract will not cause the disease. For tetanus infection the route may be an injured tissue.

2. The number of infecting organisms: This may have pronounced effect. More the number more the chances of infections. Though this cannot be the rule. Entry of lesser number of bacteria can also result in disease.

3. The attacking power or the virulence of the micro-organisms i.e. their capacity to produce toxic substances or toxins responsible for causing the disease.

These toxins are of two types:

(i) **Endotoxin**, which remain in the cell of bacterium and is given out when it disintegrates.

(ii) **Exotoxin** is poisonous substance which diffuse through the bacterial cell wall into the medium in which bacteria are growing.

These toxins can be rendered harmless by way of chemical treatment, heating at elevated temperature and by prolonged storage at room temperasture. Such harmless toxins are referred as **toxoid** or **anatoxin** and can serve as antigen. Likewise, the virulance of bacteria can also be checked and controlled by way of repeated cultivation in the laboratory or growing the organisms in adverse conditions not conductive to their growth viz., incubating at higher temperature growing in a medium devoid of nutrients having unsuitable pH etc. Thus, a bacterium can be rendered avirulent or attenuated or weakened (loosing its power attack). Different strains of bacteria may have varying degrees of virulence as was the case with small-pox.

Classification Immunological Preparations:

The official immunological preparations are classified as under:

1. Producing active immunity (containing antigens).

The antibodies to which immunity is due are produced by immune individual in response to stimulation.

I. Bacterial vaccines:

(a) (i) Living bacteria, e.g. Bacillus Calemette and Guerin (B.C.G.) Vaccine.

(ii) Dead bacteria, e.g. Pertussis vaccine.

(b) Bacterial toxoids: e.g. Diphtheria vaccine.

(c) Mixed vaccines. e.g. Diphtheria and tetanus vaccine, Diphtheria and Pertussis-vaccine.

II. Viral and Rickettsial vaccines:

(a) Living viruses, e.g. Poliomyelitis vaccine (oral) and rickettsial.

(b) Inactivated viruses e.g. Poliomyelitis vaccine (inactivated) and rickettsiae, e.g. Typhus vaccine.

2. Diagnostic preparations (containing antigens), Schick test toxin, Tuberculins.

3. Producing passive immunity (containing antibodies)

The antibodies are received from another individual or animal by transference.

Antitoxic sera, (e.g. Tetanus antitoxin).

Antiviral sera, (e.g. Rabies antiserum).

Antibacterial sera, (e.g. Leptospira antiserum).

Storage of Immunological Preparations:

Immunological preparations invariably loose potency on storage. The rate of deterioration varies with different products and can be controlled to some extent by the conditions of storage used. The recommended storage conditions are always printed on the lable of the preparations and should be observed.

In general, the preparation become inactive fairly rapidly at room temperature (about 20°C) and storage in a refrigerator to ensure a reasonable life. Bacterial vaccines, bacterial toxoids and antisera should be stored in the dark at temperatures between 2°C and 10°C: under these conditions they retain their potency for one year or more. Viral and rickettsial vaccines usually require even more careful storage and their storage conditions are discussed later in the appropriate section of this chapter.

1.   Preparations Producing Active Immunity:

I.   Bacterial vaccines:

(a)   These are most commonly, suspensions of bacterial cultivated on suitable medium and killed in such a manner as to preserve their antigenic activity while destroying their pathogenicity. Sterilisation is carried out using minimal heat treatment or slow chemical inactivation. Vaccines containing living bacteira are prepared from attenuated strains which are non-pathogenic to man but stimulate immunity to pathogenic strains of the organism.

Bacillus Calmette   Guerin vaccine, (B.C.G. Vaccine)

Cholera vaccine,   vibrio cholera vaccine),

Pertussis vaccine,   whooping cough vaccine)

Plague vaccine

Note:

B.C.G. vaccine contains living cells of an attenuated strain of *Mycobacterium tuberculosis*. It is available in a liquid and a dried form, the latter being reconstituted immediately before use. When stored in the dark at temperature 2°C and 10°C the liquid form retains its potency for only 14 days while the dried form is stable for 12 months from the completion of manufacture. All the other bacterial vaccines are sterile suspensions of the appropriate organism.

(b)   Bacterial toxoid vaccines (Bacterial Toxoids):

Immunity against infections caused by organisms, which produce exotoxins can be achieved by infecting suitably modified preparations of these toxins. The toxins can be obtained by cultivating the organisms under suitable conditions in a fluid medium and removing the bacteria using a bacterial filter, the filtrate contains the toxins. Because of their high toxicity, however, the unmodified toxins are converted by chemical treatment to toxoids in which specific toxicity has been reduced or removed but which remains antigenically effective. The conversion of toxin to toxoid is usually done by treatment with formaldehyde and the product is known as a **formal** toxoid or **antitoxin**. The toxoid may be further purified by precipitating it with alum, flocculating it with the corresponding antitoxin or adsorbing it on aluminium hydroxide or hydrated aluminium phosphate. The precipitate or floccules are separated, washed and resuspended in a suitable solution isotonic with blood.

The official bacterial toxoids are:

Diphtheria vaccine, (Diphtheria prophylatic), available as

(a)   Formal toxoid,

(b)   Alum precipitated toxoid,

(c)   Purified toxoid aluminium hydroxide,

(d)   Purified toxoid, aluminium phosphate,

(e)   Toxoid – antitoxin floccules,

Tetanus vaccine, (Tetanus toxoid), available as

(a)   Tetanus vaccine in a simple solution,

(b)   Formal toxoid.

(c)   Alum precipitated tetanus vaccine,

(d)   Purified toxoid, aluminium hydroxide,

(e)   Purified toxoid, aluminium phosphate,

(f)   Staphylococcus toxoid,

Available as formal toxoid.

(c) Mixed vaccines:

Mixed vaccines are used to produce simultaneous immunisation against two or more infective diseases. They may consist of mixtures of simple bacterial vaccines, bacterial vaccines mixed with bacterial toxoids or mixtures of bacterial toxoids, the component vaccines or toxoids being prepared separately before mixing.

The official mixed vaccines are:

Diphtheria and pertussis vaccine, (Diphtheria-whooping cough, prophylatic).

Diphtheria and tetanus vaccine, (Diphtheria-tetanus prophylactic).

Diphtheria, Tetanus and Pertussis vaccine, (Diphtheria-Tetanus Whooping Cough prophylatic).

Typhoid-paratyphoid A and B and Cholera vaccine.

Typhoid-paratyphoid A, B and C vaccine.

Typhoid-paratyphoid A and B cholera vaccine.

Typhoid-paratyphoid A and B tetanus vaccine, (Typhoid-paratyphoid A and B vaccine-tetanus toxoid).

II. Viral and rickettsial vaccines:

Immunisation against effective disease caused by viruses and rickettsia is of particular importance in the control of these diseases since they are generally resistant to treatment with antibiotics and chemotherapeutic agents.

Both viruses and rickettsiae multiply only in actively growing host cells and the production of vaccines containing them is, therefore, technically more exacting than the production of bacterial vaccines. The vaccines may be prepared from selected infected tissues from suitable animals, which have been deliberately infected with the viruses or rickettsiae (e.g. rabies, smallpox and typhus). More commonly, they are prepared from cultures of the organisms in fertile eggs (e.g. influenza, smallpox, typhus and yellow fever) or from isolated tissues or cell cultures (e.g. poliomyelitis and small pox).

During the preparation of the vaccines, the cultures are usually purified by removing much of the non-specific reactions in the patient. The viruses and rickettsiae in the vaccines may be living or they may be inactivated during the preparation of the vaccine. Living vaccines are prepared with attenuated strains of the normally pathogenic organisms (e.g. poliomyelitis and yellow fever) or with non-pathogenic organisms antigenically related to the pathogen (e.g. small pox). Inactivation of the organism, when required, is carried out by treatment with formaldehyde or some other chemical or physical agent (e.g. heat), which will preserve the antigenic efficiency of those organisms.

The official vaccines containing living viruses are:

(a)   Poliomyelitis vaccine

(b)   Smallpox vaccine (vaccinum variola)

(c)   Yellow fever vaccines

The official inactivated viral vaccines are:

(a)   Influenza vaccine (Inactivated influenza vaccine)

(b)   Poliomyelitis vaccine (Inactivated)

(c)   Rabies vaccine (Antirabies vaccine)

(d)   The only rickettsial vaccine (inactivated)

(e)   Typhus vaccine

Note:

Smallpox vaccine is powder available in both a liquid and a dried form. Yellow fever vaccine is supplied only as a dry powder and the other vaccines in liquid forms.

Storage of Viral and Rickettsial Vaccines:

Special care must be taken in the storage of some viral vaccines, particularly those containing living virus. *Poliomyelitis vaccine (oral)* is stable in the frozen state for two years. When thawed and stored at 0°C to 4°C it remains potent for six months but at 18°C to 20°C looses potency after seven days. *Liquid smallpox vaccine* must be stored at – 10°C to – 20°C to retain its potency for 12 months. At 2°C to 10°C it is stable for two weeks but at 10°C to 20°C in unstable after one week. *Dried smallpox vaccine* is stable indefinitely at 2°C to 10°C and for one year at 22°C. *Yellow fever vaccine* in the dry state is stable for at least one year at 4°C or below, but looses potency in few days at 20°C.

Rabies vaccine should be stored at 2° to 4°C but is stable at these temperature for only six months. The remaining viral and rickettsial vaccines (Influenza, poliomyelitis (Inactivated and typhus) are stored in the same manner as bacterial vaccines (between 2°C and 10°C). All vaccines should be stored in the dark.

2. Diagnostic Preparations:

The British Pharmacopoeia describes two preparations which are used for diagnostic procedures in controlling infective diseases.

Schick Test Toxin and Schick Control are used in the Schick test for susceptibility to diphtheria. The test toxin is a sterile dilution of diphtheria toxin in an isotonic buffer solution with the test dose contained in 0.2 ml. A positive skin reaction to the intracutaneous injection of the test done indicates the absence of specific antibodies for the toxin and, therefore, susceptibility to diphtheria. Schick control is prepared by heating Schick test toxin to destroy the toxins and is injected in the same way as the Test toxin but at a different site. A 'Pseudo-positive' reaction to the control, i.e. redness at both sites, indicates sensitivity to constituents of the Text toxin other than the specific toxin.

Storage: Schick test toxin may be stored at 2°C to 10°C up to six months without undue loss of potency.

Tuberculin, of which two forms are available, is used in diagnostic tests for tuberculosis. Old tuberculin is a sterile, concentrated extract of *Mycobacterium tuberculosis var hominis or bovis.*

Tuberculin Purified Protein Derivative:

(Tuberculin PPD) is the active principle of old tuberculin, obtained by fractional precipitation. It is supplied as a liquid, a dry powder or as sterile tablets and is more stable than old tuberculin.

In the Mantoux test, the tuberculins in graded doses are administered intracutaneously (0.1 ml) but they may also be administered by the Half multiple puncture method. A positive skin reaction to the tuberculin indicates sensitivity to tuberculoproteins and shows that the patient has been infected with the tubercle bacillus although the infection may not be active.

Storage: Old tuberculin and dried **tuberculin** PPD, stored at 2°C to 10°C in the dark, will retain their potency indefinitely. Concentrated solutions of Tuberculin PPD stored in the same way, are stable upto five years. Dilutions of the tuberculins are much less stable.

3.   Preparations Producing Passive Immunity Antitoxic Sera:

Antitoxic sera (or antitoxins) are produced by immunizing an animal, usually a horse, by a series of injections of the appropriate bacterial toxin or toxoid. When a suitable antibody titre is obtained, the animal is bled and the serum separated. Usually, the serum is then concentrated and purified by extracting the serum globulins with which the anti-bodies are associated. The procedures used involve fractional precipitation with, for example, ammonium sulphate and selective digestion with a proteolytic enzyme e.g. pepsin. The sera so prepared are termed refined sera. Refining reduces the volume of the serum which must be injected and the removal of the proteins devoid of antitoxic activity reduces the quantity of protein injection and hence the risk of serum reactions. Refined sera are also more stable than native (unconcentrated) sera.

The antibodies or antitoxins present in antitoxic sera act by neutralizing the toxins produced by the infecting organisms. They therefore, find a therapeutic use in the treatment of some infectious diseases by neutralizing the effects of circulating toxins while the invading organisms are attacked by chemotherapeutic agents.

The official antitoxin sera are:

(a)   Botulinum antitoxin (Botulinum antiserum)

(b)   Diphtheria antitoxin

(c)   Gas-gangrene antitoxin (Oedematiens)

(d)   Gas-gangrene antitoxin (septicum)

(e)   Gas-gangrene antitoxin (Vibroin-septique)

(f)   Gas-gangrene antitoxin (Welchii) (Gas-gangrene antitoxin – Perfringens)

(g)   Mixed (Gas-gangrene antitoxin)

(h)   Scarlet fever antitoxin (Streptococcus antitoxin)

(i)   Streptococcus antitoxin (Scarlatina)

(j)   Staphylococcus antitoxin

(k)   Tetanus antitoxin.

Antibacterial Sera:

Antibacterial sera are prepared by a procedure similar to that described for antitoxic sera except that the antigen used to immunize animals is a bacterial vaccine. The antibodies in an antibacterial serum appear to act by counteracting the virulence of the organism and rendering them more susceptible to phagocytosis or lysis. Antibacterial sera have been used against bacteria, which do not produce well-defined exotoxins but their use has been almost completely superseded by chemotherapy.

Antiviral Sera:

The preparation of antiviral sera by animal immunisation is generally unsuccessful mainly, due to the difficulty of finding suitable animal hosts.

Rabies antiserum is prepared in this way and is the only official true antiviral serum. It is prepared in a manner similar to that for antitoxic sera using graded doses of living or inactivated rabies virus to immunize horses or other animals.

Such other antiviral sera as available are *immune human sera* obtained from patients, who are convalescing from the virus disease (convalscent serum): from adults who have had, or been exposed to the disease in the past (adult serum) or from persons, who have been artificially immunized against the disease (hyperimmune serum). Immune human sera which have in the past been used with success include measles convalescent serum, measles adult serum, ruberola convalescent serum and smallpox convalescent serum, but these sera are now almost unavailable.

Human gamma globulin: (B.P.) It is prepared from pooled adult plasma and contains the normal antibodies likely to be found in humans, may be of value in preventing or attenuating some virus disease including measles, rubella, poliomyelitis, smallpox and vaccinia.

The antibodies in antiviral sera are believed to act by preventing the virus from entering tissue cells. They have no effect on intracellular virus and their use, which is at best of doubtful value, is mainly as a prophylactic measure.

The use of immune human sera involves a risk of transmitting homologous serum jaundice but this risk is virtually absent from the use of human gamma globulin.

(B) BLOOD AND BLOOD PRODUCTS

Blood is a important transport medium and along with circulatory system, it forms a link between internal environment of the body with the external environment. For normal functioning of body cells the interval environment must be kept within normal physiological limits (homeostasis). Blood transports materials (gases, nutrients, secretions), between external and internal environment, regulates pH, body temperature and water content of cells and protect body from foreign microbes and toxins. Thus, by these functions it helps in maintaining the homeostasis and hence, is described as a vital fluid of the body.

Anatomically, it is a fluid connective tissue and consists of the cells suspended in a fluid called blood plasma. It is heavier, thicker and more viscous than water. Its temperature is slightly higher than normal body temperature and is slightly alkaline with pH of about 7.4. The volume of blood in a adult human body is about 5.5 litres, and constitutes about 8% of the total body weight. Whole blood is composed of two portions: **Blood plasma** (55%) a watery liquid with dissolved substances and **Formed elements** (45%), the cells and cell fragments.

Blood plasma:

Its composition is as follows:

Water   –   90-92 per cent

Plasma proteins   –   6-8 per cent (albumin, globulin, prothrombin, fibrinogen)

Nutrients	–	Amino acids, glucose, fatty acids and glycerol and vitamins.
Waste products	–	Urea, uric acid, creatinine, bilirubin, ammonium salts.
Gases	–	Oxygen, Carbon dioxide, Nitrogen
Regulatory Substances	–	Enzymes, Hormones.
Protective Substances	–	Antibodies
Electrolytes	–	Cations – Na^+, K^+, Ca^{++}, Mg^{++}
		Anions – Cl^-, HOP_4^-, SO_4^-, HCO_3^-

Formed Elements:

Erythrocytes (R.B.C.) – 5 to 5.5 millions per cubic millimeter of blood

Leucocytes (W.B.C.)

Granulocytes

Neutrophils	–	3000	–	7000 per mm^3
Eosinophils	–	50	–	400 per mm^3
Basophils	–	0	–	50 per mm^3

Agranulocytes

Monocytes	–	100	–	600 per mm^3
Lymphocytes	–	1000	–	3000 per mm^3
Platelets		– 250000	–	400000 per mm^3

Including whole human blood various blood products are official in various pharmacopoeias meant for different physiological conditions. Many times blood is processed or different fractions made available are used as when they are dissolved. The names of few of them are –

(i)   Whole human blood.

(ii) Concentrated human red blood corpuscles.

(iii) Dried human plasma.

(iv) Fresh frozen plasma.

(v)   Dried human serum.

(vi) Dried human fibrinogen.

(vii) Human plasma concentrate.

(viii) Dried human thrombin.

(i)   Whole Human blood:

Therapeutically active substances collected directly from the donors directly into sterile bottles containing and anticoagulant and dextrose. The bottles (glass or plastic) receiving the blood contains 2 to 2.5 g of Di-sodium acid citrate, 3 g of dextrose and 120 ml of water for injection usually 420 ml of blood is collected at a time.

Blood contains living red blood corpuscles, which are not capable of growth or reproduction but contain complex intracellular structure and a multiplicity of enzyme and enzyme systems.

Since it is expected that the RBC of this blood should perform their basic physiological function of oxygen transport their structural and functional integrity should be nicely preserved.

All the equipments used while collecting the blood

1. Should meet the sterility norms.

2. Blood should be stored in between 4 to 6°C until used.

3. It should be used within 21 days only.

4. Its haemoglobin content should not be less than 9.7 dl.

5. It should indicate the ABO blood group both for corpuscles and serum and also the Rh group.

Since blood is fluid, circulating connecting tissue, its transfusion is a kind of homograft (i.e. transfer of tissue from one individual to another individual) and thus its introduction develops antibodies by reacting with antigens on cell surfaces, and result in rejections of RBC introduced.

Certain fatal diseases like malaria, hepatitis A, hepatitis B, syphilis, and AIDS (by way of HIV) may get transmitted along with the blood and hence blood should not be accepted from a donor if he has not been tested with **negative - results** for evidence of the above infections.

Blood transfusion is done for several disorders such as

(a) To restore the blood volume due to haemorrhage.

(b) In acute peritonitis.

(c) Certain type of shocks.

Whole human blood should be used within 21 days only if used afterwards it may result in

1. Shorter life after blood transfusion

2. Haemolysis.

3. Increased permeability to the cell membrane with toxic effects.

(ii) Dried human plasma:

Though whole human blood has many advantages is also suffers from certain demerits. To overcome these demerits dried human plasma can be used, since it is

(a) Compatible with all blood groups and specificity of individual blood group can be ruled out.

(b) Dried human plasma can be stored for long duration as compared to whole human blood.

But in real sense it is not substitute for whole blood, but only for fluid replacement. Thus, blood plasma is the only liquid part of unclotted blood and is carefully prepared from time-expired citrated whole blood.

The plasma collected from selected donors is either freeze dried and dried by any other method wherein denaturation of proteins is avoided.

The blood plasma of blood donors of different blood groups (not more than 10 in number) is collected and mixed with every precautions that it complies the test for sterility.

Dried human plasma is a light, deep cream coloured powder and should not have streaks of red or pink colour. It is readily soluble in water for injections giving cloudy solutions. It contains not less than 45 g/l of proteins. It should cause coagulation by the addition of 17 g of calcium chloride per litre indicating the presence of fibronogen.

Dried human plasma is reconstituted by dissolving in a quantity of water for injection equal to the volume of fluid from which it has been prepared. The reconstituted contents must be used within three hours.

(iii) Fresh frozen plasma:

This is prepared by centrifugation of whole human blood within few hours of its collection from the donor, then it stored in frozen state below – 30°C.

It must be labelled according to the stated blood group or pooled.

Before use it is thawed by immensing in a water bath at a temperature not exceeding 37°C. It takes about 45 minutes for thawing.

In fresh frozen plasma, the valuable, labile clotting factors are preserved.

(iv) Dried human serum:

This is prepared from the whole blood, which is allowed to clot in absence of anticoagulant. The supernatant liquid is collected by aseptic method it is clarified by filtration method.

It differs from the plasma in the respect that it does not contain fibrinogen. The liquid is dried by freeze drying method. It should contain not less than 6.5% of proteins.

All precautions should be taken as they are taken, while collecting the dried human plasma.

Fractionation of blood plasma:

Human plasma consists of the following:

(a) Albumin 55%

(b) α-globulin 14%

(c) β-globulin 13.5%

(d) γ-globulin 11.0%

(e) Fibrinogen 06.5%

Thus, a large number of constituents have been separated by fractionation. These fractions are fibrinogen, thrombin, thyrotropin and antibodies against infectious diseases. Various methods like Electrophoresis, dialysis, salting out by ammonium sulphate, and use of solvents are few of them.

Few of the above products have been described below:

1.   Fibrinogen:

It is prepared by precipitation with ethyl ether at a temperature in between 0-10°C and the normal pH of the plasma. The product is stirred well and the precipitate is collected, which is nothing but fibrinogen. It is further washed with ether, citrate saline and then redissolved in water and freeze dried. Ethyl alcohol can also be used instead of ethyl ether.

Fibrinogen can transmit hepatitis β and it is used in deficiency of Fibrinogen in pregnancy.

2.   Prothrombin:

The supernatant liquid from the fibrinogen precipitation is the base for isolation of prothrombin. This liquid is adjusted to pH 5.35 cooled to 0°C. Precipitate gets formed which is separated and constitutes prothrombin.

3.   Thrombin: The precipitate of prothrombin is washed with distilled water and further dissolved in citrate-saline solution, which is adjusted to pH 7.0 and to it are added calcium ions and the thrombokinase. The solution is filtered and dried by freeze drying method. This constitutes the enzyme thrombin.

β-globulin and γ-globulin are obtained by the further precipitation of supernatant liquid from the prothrombin separation, with ether.

Human Immunoglobulin:

Human immunoglobulin is the name given to the fraction separated from human plasma.

The antibodies formed in human being are said to composed of three classes of serum proteins named as IgG, IgM and IgA immunoglobulins. Human immunoglobulin mostly consists of IgG immunoglobulin. This fraction was called as γ-globulin earlier. IgG immunoglobulin contains antibodies against viruses and bacterial toxins specifically aginst viruses producing hepatitis, measles, poliomyelitis and Rubella and even antitoxins for mumps, diphtheria and tetanus.

Plasma Substitutes:

Due to one or the other reason it has been realised that it is very difficult to collect and store the human plasma. A contimual vigilance is a "must" in its use, to save from the transmission of diseases.

Many attempts, in the past have been made to develop plasma substitute to restore the blood volume. Substitutes of non-human origin were tried. It is felt that a ideal human plasma substitute

1.   Should have the same osmotic pressure (isotonic) as whole human blood.

2.   Should be slowly destroyed in the body (excretion or metabolised).

3.   Should be non-antigenic and non-toxic.

4.   Should be easily sterilisable.

Many compounds that have been investigated so far are the gum-acacia, dextran, and polymers like polyvenyl pyrolidone, hydroxy ethyl starch, modified gelatin etc.

The more important plasma-substitutes commercially available is the market in the parenteral form are described below.

Dextran is a group of polysaccharide produced by bacteria on a sucrose substrate and containing backbone of D-glucose units. The type of bacteria used for the purpose are known as **Leuonostoe mesenteroides** and **Leuconostoe dextranicum Fam.**

Lactobacteriaceae are used for production. Dextran is obtained by precipitation and is further purified to remove pyrogens and antigenic properties.

1.   Dextran 110 injection:

It is solution of polymer (Dextran) either in sodium chloride solution or Dextrose injection. Dextran is used in the concentration of 5 g per litre and is sterilised by autoclaving or filtration method. This injection should also pass the other general requirements as laid down for parenterals in Pharmacopoeia.

Dextran should have homogenous molecular size and also should have average molecular weight of 1,10,000.

2.   Dextran 40 injection:

Is a preparation of average molecular weight of 40,000 of small molecular size. It should also comply all requirements as specified for injections.

(C) SUTURES AND LIGATURES

Surgical dressings or Curatio is a term applied to a wide range of materials used for dressings of wounds. These are used as absorbents, supporting agents, coverings to reduce or to prevent infections.

SURGICAL DRESSINGS

The word surgical dressing is used to include all materials either used alone or in combination to cover the wound. The purpose of application of the dressing is to protect the wound and favour its proper healing. A material which holds the dressing in desired position is known as **bandage.** Fibres are used for the preparation of surgical dressings.

Surgical dressings are meant for the following functions:

1.   To reduce or prevent infections.

2.   To offer protection to healing wound.

3.   To offer mechanical support to the tissues.

Surgical dressings should comply with the following requirements as mentioned in Pharmacopoeia.

1. They should be sterilised before use.

2. They should be stored in dry well-ventilated place at a temperature not exceeding 25°C.

3. Permitted antiseptics in prescribed concentrations be used.

4. They should not be dyed unless mentioned in the monograph.

5. Adhesive products should not be allowed to freeze.

6. There should not be any loose threads, fibre-ends in dressings.

Surgical dressings are classified as:

(a) Fibres:

    (a) Non-medicated fibres:

    Absorbent cotton, wool, rayon, silk etc.

    (b) Medicated fibres:

    Boric acid wool, Capsicum wool.

(b) Fabric:

Absorbent lint, Absorbent ribbon gauze, Boric acid lint, Absorbent gauze X-ray detectable.

(c) Bandages:

    (a) Non-medicated bandages:

    Crepe bandage, Domette bandage, Calico bandage, Cotton and rubber elastic bandage.

    (b) Medicated bandages:

    Plaster of Paris bandage, Zinc paste bandage, Zinc paste ichthamol bandage.

(d) Rubber and Oil Impregnated Materials:

Belladonna self-adhesive plaster, Zinc oxide self-adhesive plaster, etc.

British Pharmacopoeia recognizes the following types of surgical dressings.

1. Fibres and related materials	i.e. Viscose, animal, wood cellulose wadding.
2. Carded products	i.e. Absorbent cotton, viscose wadding etc.

3. **Non-extensible non-adhesive,**

    woven products, i.e. Absorbent muslin, Domette bandage, etc.

4. **Non-extensible adhesives**

    woven products, i.e. Belladonna adhesive plaster, zinc-oxide surgical adhesive tape.

5. **Extensible non-adhesive products** i.e. Cotton bandage, elastic web bandage etc.

6. **Extensible adhesive woven products,** i.e. Elastic adhesive bandage, extension plaster.

7. **Non-woven products** i.e. impermeable plastic surgical adhesive tape, permeable plastic surgical, adhesive tape, etc.

Important surgical dressings are:

(i) Absorbent Cotton Wool:

It is a widely used fibre as surgical dressing. It consists of epidermal trichomes of the seeds of *Gossypium herbaceium L.* and other cultivated species of *Gossypium* (Fam Malvaceae). Each tricome consists of a single cell, upto 4 cm. In length and 15 to 40 µm in width, forming a flattened tubular band with slightly thickened rounded edges and showing 50 to 120 twists per cm.

It is widely used for wound cleansing and for pre-operative skin care. A shorter staple length and high dust containing fibre is used for routine cleansing.

(ii) Gauze:

Gauze is a fabric of plain weave usually supplied in pieces of 90 cm wide in various length and folded longitudinally. It may be available as ribbon gauze. Gauze pad consists of folded absorbent gauze.

The gauze is used to prepare swabs, pads, strips etc. which are used for pre-operative skin preparation, post-operative wound care and during surgery. X-ray detectable absorbent gauze is also available.

(iii) Lint:

It consists of a cloth of plain weave, in which the warp threads are cotton and the weft may contain cotton or mixture of cotton and viscose fibres. On one side warp has been raised from the warp yarns. These raised warp threads give fleecy, thicker and soft appearance and increased absorbency. It is used as absorbent and protective dressing.

(iv)   Bandages:

Bandages are the products used to retain dressings in place, to provide support and for application of medications to the skin.

It may be elastic or non-elastic, adhesive or non-adhesive.

(v)   Surgical adhesive tapes:

These consists of self adhesive mass spread on the supporting material which may be permeable, semi-permeable or occlusive. These tapes may be extensible, inextensible or elastic. They are used to retain dressings, to immobilize small areas or to secure tubing during parenteral therapy.

Following are the important terms used to describe Surgical Dressings:

(i)   Staple:

It is an alternative term for fibre.

(ii)   Neps:

Neps are knots or tangled masses or fibres visible to naked eye. They may be produced in cotton during growth or when it becomes damp.

(iii)   Yarn:

It is term applied to thread spun from the fibres.

(iv)   Yarn count:

It is the weight in grams of 1 kilometre of yarn. It is used as a measure of thickness.

(v)   Slubs:

Thick soft parts of a yarn are referred as slubs.

(vi)   Union fabric:

It is the fabric composed of two kinds of yarn. e.g. cotton and wool.

(vii)   Warp and weft:

The threads in a fabric running lengthwise are referred as 'warp' or 'ends', while those crossing them at right angles are 'weft'.

(viii)   Plain weave:

A weave in which the threads pass alternatively over and under the threads running at right angle.

(ix)   Twist:

It refers to the direction of twisting the fibres while spinning the yarn. Twist to the right is called 'Z' twist or right twist whereas, twist to the left is called "S" twist or "reverse twist."

(x)   Naps:

This refers to loose fluffy fibres. These are commonly observed on one surface of cotton lint, raised from the warp threads of cotton cloth of plain weave by cutting and scraping the threads. These weakened threads enable the material to be easily torn. A fabric on which naps are produced is called 'Raised fabric.'

(xi)   Selvedge:

A fabric edge woven so that it is fast and the threads do not become loose.

(xii) Snaris:

These are loops protruding from the fabric due to insufficient tension on the yarn in weaving.

SUTURES

These are the sterile threads, strings or strands specially prepared for use in surgery meant for sewing tissues together. Sutures must possess the following properties:

(a)   They must be sterile and should cause no irritation.

(b)   They should have finest possible gauge and adequate strength.

(c)   If absorbable, their time of absorption must be known.

(d)   They are intended to be used for one occasion only.

Sutures may be prepared from intenstinal tissues and tendons of animals and birds; vegetable fibres; camel hair; human hair; synthetic threads or metallic wires. Depending upon their characteristics of absorption, i.e. digestion in the tissues of the body, sutures are known as absorbable or non-absorbable sutures.

Various methods are used to sterilize the sutures (to make them free of pathogenic micro-organisms). A few of this important methods are –

1.   Chemical sterilisation.

2.   Sterilisation by irradiation.

3.   Sterilisation by heat.

Heat sterilisation involves two processes and sutures are classified into two categories depending upon heat resistance,

(a)   boilable (in anhydrous liquid)

(b)   non-boilable.

The sterilisation should not affect the properties of sutures or their utility. In irradiation mcthod, sterilisation is carried out by particles β electron or by gamma rays from cobalt 60. The recognised dose of gamma rays treatment is 2.5 megarad.

Sutures may be of the following types:

1. **Absorbable sutures:**

    (a)   Sterile catgut (small intestine of sheep, ox and appendix of deer).

    (b)   Sterile reconstituted collagen suture.

2. **Non-absorbable sutures:**

    (a)   Sterile non-absorbable sutures (silk and cotton).

    (b)   Sterile linen suture.

    (c)   Sterile polyamide suture (nylon).

    (d)   Sterile polyester sutures (terylene).

    (e)   Sterile braided sutures.

    (f)   Sterile stainless and silver sutures.

3. **Haemostatics:**

    (i)   Oxidised cellulose.

    (ii)   Absorbable gelatin sponge.

Uses:

Depending upon the physical and chemical properties and also the desired effect, various sutures are effectively used under different conditions.

Silk sutures are strong, smooth in active and also available in various diameters. The braided form is compact one and has a special advantage of not getting twisted when drawn through the body tissues. Nylon sutures are strong enough and enjoy the merit of their utility in skin and plastic surgery. Cotton sutures due to their low order of tissue reactivity are preferred, but suffer from poor tensile strength. Linen, though very much economical and quite effective, lacks in uniform diameter of practical purposes. Kangaroo tendons are specially used in harnia, while metallic sutures are used in surgery in general.

Absorbent Cotton:

Cotton wool, Purified cotton, Surgical cotton, Medicinal cotton.

Cotton consists of the epidermal trichomes or hairs of the seeds of cultivated species of the *Gossypium (Gossypium herbaceum, Gossypium barbadense)*, belonging to family malvaceae. Purified cotton or absorbent cotton consists of the trichomes as mentioned above, but freed from fatty matter and adhering impurities. It is also bleached and sterilised.

Preparation of Absorbent Cotton:

Cotton is commonly grown for the purpose of fibres in the tropical countries. The plant after flowering, bears fruits known as capsules. The fruits are 3 to 5 celled. Each capsule contains numerous seeds. The seeds covered with hairs are known as bolls. The bolls are collected, dried and taken to the ginning press, wherein trichomes are separated from seeds. Various devices are used to separate short and long hairs. The hairs with short length are known as linters and are used in the manufacture of absorbent cotton, while long hairs are used for preparation of cloth. The raw cotton obtained by this way is full in impurities like wax, fat, colouring matter, vegetable debris, etc. It is processed to get rid of most of the impurities. It is taken to the machine known as cotton opener and followed by treatment with dilute soda solution or soda ash solution under pressure for about 10 to 15 hours. The wax, fatty material and colouring matter are removed by this treatment. It is then washed with water and treated with suitable bleaching agent. It is again washed with water, dried and carded into flat sheet. It is finally packed wrappers and sterilized.

Description:

Colour	:	White (due to bleaching)
Odour	:	Odourless
Taste	:	Tasteless
Size	:	2.5 to 4.5 cm in length and 25 to 35 micron in diameter.

Extra Features:

It is free from pieces of leaves, seed coat, foreign matter and dust. It may be slightly off-white in colour, if sterilized.

Standards:

Absorbent cotton wool I.P. has the following standards:

1. Length of staples   :   not less than 1.5 cm

2. Water soluble extractive :   not more than 0.5%

3. Ash   :   not more than 0.5%

It should comply with the test for the following as mentioned in the monograph:

1. Neps,   2. Fluorescence,   3. Acidity

4. Absorbency and,   5. Oxidising substances.

LIGATURES

The threads or strings used for typing blood vessels or tissues, during surgery are known as **ligatures**.

Essential properties of ligatures are:

1.   Ligatures must be sterile.

2.   They must have adequate strength.

3.   Their gauge should be as fine as possible.

Preparation, Quality Control Tests for Catgut:

Catgut is prepared from the intestines of the sheep and has nothing to do with the cat.

For the preparation of surgical gut the first 25 feet part of the intestine of sheep is selected in the slaughter houses, after removing most of their contents. The intestines are cleaned and then soaked in water. Samples with abnormalities are discarded and cleaning operation is done several times to ensure complete cleanliness with the help of sharp knives the cleaned intestines (casings) are splitted into smooth and rough ribbons. The smooth ribbon representing the antimesentric part of intestine is selected for the further preparations of surgical gut. The submucous layer is removed from this smooth ribbon by soaking it in alkaline solution. This soaking and scrapping enhauses the tensile strength.

This is followed by hardening process in which scraped ribbons are subjected to the treatment of chromic salts. Hardening delays absorption in the body and hence this process decides the type of surgical gut to be prepared. Depending upon the gauge of the thread to be prepared the number of twists and spinning is to be controlled. Uniform gauge with good tensile strength is required to be maintained with final product. The strings are then dried in controlled humidity and properly maintained temperature. Finishing of the strings by rubbing against the abrasive surface is done to produce the uniform product of circular section, followed by gauging. Finally, the guts are sterilized by suitable method. The method of choice of sterilization is heating method. Iodine method used earlier (being lengthy) is replaced by heating. In heating method sterilization lot of care is required to be taken as the presence of moisture and high temperature may cause damage to the chemical nature of guts make them unsuitable for use.

Since the intestines of sheep are full of spore forming anasrobic bacteria, a cause for tetanus or gas gangene sterility tests are to be performed very carefully. Sterilization is done by using toluene or xylol and heating to a temperature of 160°C for several hours.

A catgut for surgical use should comply the following pharmacopoeial tests.

1.   Sterility test.

2.   Gauge

3.   Tensile strength.

Packaging of Catgut:

The Pharmacopoeial catgut is non-boilable material and is available in glass-tubes containing alcohol and small quantity of water. Non-boilable type material is ready for use. Immediately after opening the glass-tube the contents after removal from glass tubes are to be soaked in sterile spirit or few seconds in sterile salive solutions.

Kangroo tendens, silk, linen, silkworm gut, horse hairs are the other natural material which can be used to a lesser extent as they are not suitable in other respects such as tensile strength, gauge etc.

The synthetic materials such as nylon, metallic wives and alloys are the still other materials of choice with special advantages in surgery as they are non-irritant, with the high tensile strength and fine gauge.

Nylon:

Nylon (Polyamide) is one of the synthetic fibres, similar to terylene; chemically it is a polymer and made by interaction of adipic acid and hexamethylene diamine. Nylon fibres are highly lustrous to dull, white or coloured. When applied to flame, they melt with a formation of bead.

Nylon is soluble in 5 M Hydrochloric acid, 90% Formic acid, 90% Thenol, but insoluble in acetone. Solubility of Nylon distinguishes them from other fibres of biological origin.

Nylon fibres are used for the preparation of non-absorbable sutures and ligatures.

Chapter ... **11**

PACKAGING OF PHARMACEUTICALS

Packaging these days, have in its own right, become a science. Though neglected formerly, now the training in packaging has been given utmost importance in pharmaceutical companies. We in India have **"Indian Institute of Packaging"** in Mumbai which offers training and consultancy in the field of packaging. Initially, packaging was considered only to contain the dosage form, but now its aesthetic appeal and convenience are also considered important. In advertising agencies we have specialised personnel therefore for package design pharmaceutical organisations also now invest money to opt for research in package design. National Institute of Design (NID), Ahmedabad promotes the cause of packaging in a significant manner. Packaging is not only a physical activity of packing, but also an essential marketing input that helps product's identification, promotion, and gives its importance of shelf. It is also a major consideration in physical distribution of products like material handling, transportation, storage etc.

A drug product may become a useless and even hazardous if it reacts with packaging material or decomposes because of improper storage. This may happen regardless of how well it is formulated, or manufactured.

Definitions:

The **container** is the device that holds the drug and may be in direct contact with the drug. The *Immediate Container* is that which is in direct contact with the drug at all times. The *closure* is that part of the container that can be opened and closed to facilitate the access of contents and their removal.

Primary and Secondary Packaging Materials:

Package components which actually come into contact with drug or may have a direct effect on shelf-life of contents are known as primary packaging materials, where as cartons, corrugated shippers and pallets which form the outer packaging are known as secondary packaging materials.

Content and closure should never interact physically or chemically with the article placed in it so as to alter the strength, quality, or purity of drug beyond official requirements. Also they should offer certain specified degree of protection.

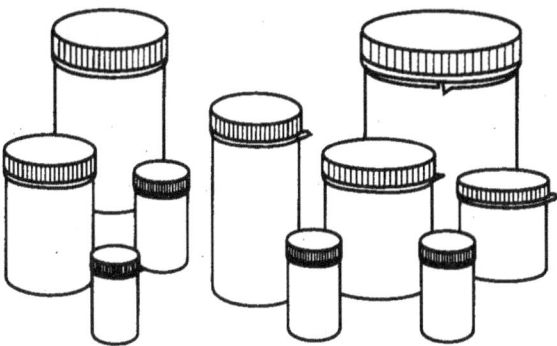

Fig. 11.1: Containers for various formulations

Following are the types of containers:

1. Light resistant containers:

It protects the contents from the effect of incident light by virtue of the specific property of material of which it is composed including any coating applied to it. If protection from light is required, a clear or colourless or a translucent container may be made light resistant by means of opaque enclosure in which case the label of the container bears statement that opaque covering is needed until the contents have been used up.

2. Well-closed containers:

A well-closed container protects the contents from extraneous solids and from loss of drug under the ordinary or customary conditions of handling, storage and distribution.

3. Tight containers:

A tight container protects the contents from contamination by extraneous liquids, solids, vapours from loss of drugs and from effervescence, deliquiscence and evaporation under ordinary conditions of handling, shipment, storage and distribution and is capable of *reclosure*. Where a tight container is specified, it may be replaced by a hermetic container for a single dose of drug.

4. Hermetic containers:

A hermetic container is impervious to air and any other gas under the ordinary conditions of handling, storage and distribution.

5. Single dose containers:

It is one which is enclosed in such a manner that none of the contents may be removed without obvious destruction of closures and the contents of which are intended for promptly after it is opened, normally it is for parenteral use.

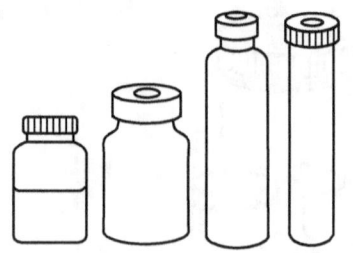

Fig. 11.2: Containers for capsules

6. Multiple dose containers:

Multiple dose container is a container that permits the withdrawal of successive portions of the contents without changing the strength, quality or purity of remaining portion, meant for parenteral use.

Types of Containers and Container Closures:

The material selected must have the following characteristics:

1. Must protect the preparation from environmental conditions.
2. Must not be reactive with the product.
3. Must not impart to the product taste and odour.
4. Must be non-toxic.
5. Must be approved by drug-department.
6. Must be adaptable to commonly employed high speed packaging equipments.
7. Must have promotional and marketing value.

Packaging Material Selection:

Today most of the containers are composed of the following materials singly or sometimes in combination.

1. Plastic,   2. Metal,
3. Glass,   4. Paper.

1. Plastic:

Plastics in packaging is most successful because of –

(a) Ease with which they can be formed.

(b) Their high quality and freedom of design and mouldability.

(c) Extremely resistant to breakage and their safety to consumer and also reduction in breakage loss during distribution.

The following plastic materials are used in packaging.

1. Thermosetting materials e.g. (a) phenol formaldehyde resins, (b) urea formaldehyde resin.

To manufacture containers they are heated in a mould under pressure (compression moulded). The process is irreversible i.e. after setting, the plastic material cannot be remelted without decomposition.

Thermosetting materials are used in packaging industry mainly for bottle and closures.

2. Thermoplastic materials: This group includes material which can be converted into an unlimited range of shapes and sizes by process such as *extrusion* and *injection, blow-moulding, injection moulding, thermoforming, extrusion, casting and callendering* etc. The advantage of thermoplastic materials is that they can be remelted without decomposition. The examples under this category are:

(a) Low density polythene:

It is used for bottles, jars, collapsible tubes, plugs and fittings, films, closures etc. The disadvantage of low density polythene is that it is *permeable to essential oils and to chloroform*. This means that the preservatives and flavouring agents may be lost in this type of container while the active ingredients can be stored.

(b) High density polythene:

It is used for bottles and jars, films and closures. Both low and high density polythenes are subject to stress cracking which depends on environmental conditions and composition of the solution stored therein.

(c) Polypropylene:

It is used for jars, bottles, rigid tubes, closures, thermoformed components etc. This type of plastic is not easily available in India. They are useful where printed containers are an advantage, e.g. for packing of tablets etc. Propylene tubes are excellent when used in the smaller diameters. Efficiency fall off as the diameter increases because the closure become less effective.

(d) Polystyrene:

Employed for jars, tubes, closures, thermoformed components etc. *Polystyrene tubes are unsuitable for moisture sensitive products.* They are used where printed container is considered an advantage.

(e) Polyvinylchloride (PVC):

There are two types: (a) Plasticised, (b) Unplasticised.

Unplasticised   :   are used for bottles, jars, thermoformed components.

Plasticised   :   PVC is used for extruded tubing and film.

PVC is resistant to oils but is rapidly plasticised by esters such as methyl salicylate. Further PVC contains substantial amounts of additives and hence we have to apply to it the same kind of criteria as we do in case of drugs. Plasticised PVC is far less prone to stress cracking than polythene and hence, this aspect requires less emphasis when dealing with PVC.

Use of Plastics in Packaging:

1.   Containers for transfusion solutions and retention enemas.

2.   Containers for eye drops.

3.   PVC tubes for eye ointments.

4. **Spray bottles:** Low density polythene squeeze bottles have been found to be quite suitable for spraying powders or liquids.

5. **Suppository packs:** Unplasticised PVC and low density polythene have been found to be satisfactory in packing suppositories.

6. Flexible Packaging.

Advantages of Plastic:

The distinctive style of package, like its counterpart the metal collapsible tube, excels in functional characteristics. Plastic tubes have a number of inherent practical advantages over other containers or dispensers. They are:

1. Low in cost.
2. Light in weight.
3. Durable.
4. Pleasant to touch.
5. Flexible, facilitating product dispensing.
6. Odorless and inert to most chemicals.
7. Unbreakable.
8. Leakproof.
9. Able to retain their shape through their use.
10. Have a unique "Suck-back" feature which prevents product ooze.

If too much product is dispensed with one squeeze, relaxation of hand pressure will permit the product to be sucked back into the tube. If this feature is not desirable for fear of contamination plastic tubes designed to avoid suck-back are available.

2. Metals:

Rigid containers are usually of tin or aluminium and are used for the following purposes.

1. **For packing tablets or capsules:** Here a plug type of polythene closure is used in preference to screw cap as former after better protection depending on product to be packed.

There are two types: (a) Plain, (b) Lacquered.

2. Shaker can for dusting powder.

3. **Collapsible tubes:** Used generally for ointment creams and pastes. Collapsible tube is an attractive container that permits controlled amount to be dispensed easily, with *good reclosure* and *adequate protection* of product. The risk of contamination of portion remaining in the tube is minimal because the tubes do not *suck back*. It is light in weight, *unbreakable* and tends itself to high speed *automatic filling operation.*

Any ductile metal that can be worked cold is suitable for collapsible tubes; common ones in use are: Tin 15%, aluminium 50%, lead 25%.

Tin is most expensive and lead is cheapest. Tin is most ductile.

Materials used for collapsible tubes:

Tin: Tin containers are preferred for foods, pharmaceuticals, or any product for which purity is a paramount consideration. Tin is the *most chemically inert* of all collapsible tube metals. It offers a good appearance and compatibility with a *wide range* of products.

Aluminium: Aluminium tubes offer significant *savings* in *product shipping* costs because of their *light weight*. They provide the attractiveness of tin at somewhat lower cost.

Lead: Lead has the lowest cost of all tube metals and is widely used for non-food products such as adhesives, inks, paints and lubricants. Lead should never be used alone for anything taken internally because of the risk of lead poisoning. With internal linings, lead tubes are used for products such as fluoride toothpaste.

Linings: If the product is incompatible with base metal, the interior can be flushed with wax type formulations or with resin solution although the resins or lacquers are generally sprayed on.

Wax linings are most often used with water-base products in tin tubes, and phenotics, epoxides and vinyls are used with aluminium tubes. Phenotics are most effective with acid products, *epoxides* protect better against *alkaline* materials.

3. Glass:

Glass is most commonly used in pharmaceutical packaging because

1. It possesses superior protective properties,
2. Economical,
3. Containers are readily available in various sizes and shapes,
4. Essentially chemically inert,
5. Impermeable,
6. Strong,
7. Rigid,
8. FDA acceptance,
9. Visibility,
10. Glass does not deteriorate with age, with a proper closure system,
11. It provides an excellent barrier system against practically every element except light. Coloured glass specially amber can give protection against light when it is required. Major **disadvantage of glass** is its fragility weight and volume occupied. Some glass also impart alkalinity which can be overcome by choice of glass tube for a given application.

U.S.P. recognises the following four types of glass:

1. Type I. Borosilicate glass: It is highly resistant glass and also chemically more inert than soda line glass (because in this alkali earth cations are replaced by Boron and / or Al and Zn).

2.   Type II. Treated sodalime glass: are made of commercially sodalime glass that has been de-alkalized or treated to remove surface alkali. The de-alkalizing process is known as *sulphur treatment* and virtually prevents weathering of empty bottles. This type of bottle becomes resistant for a period of time, to attack by walls.

3.   Type III. Regular sodalime glass: are untreated and made of commercial sodalime glass of average, better than average chemical resistance. Suitable for anhydrous parenteral a solid parenteral.

4.   Type NP (non-parenteral): General purpose sodalime glass for oral and topical products.

Coloured glass for light protection: Glass containers are available as clear flint and amber coloured. Only amber and red colours are effective in protecting the contents of bottle from effects of sunlight by screening out harmful UV rays. According to USP light resistant container requires a glass to provide protection against 2900 – 4500 A°.

Amber coloured glass is manufactured by adding Ferrous oxide or Manganese dioxide to the glass melt during manufacturing. But if the product contains ingredients subject to iron catalysed chemical reactions, amber glass should not be used.

For decorative purposes blue, emerald green and opal glass may also be obtained.

Silicone treated glass: Siliconised vials available commerically are often treated during their manufacturing by special silicones (solution of silicone in organic solvent) in which bottles are annealed. They are cooled slowly to prevent development of stresses. The advantage of such containers are:

(a)   Not melted by aqueous solution or suspension.

(b)   Foaming is reduced.

But it also has certain disadvantages: e.g. extraction during repealed sterilization, difficult to adhere label etc.

4.   Paper:

Paper is used in fabricating drug containers ranging from envelopes used on dispensing counter to hold a few tablets from the fibre drums used by manufacturer.

Paper is used as envelopes, packets, boxes, by pharmacies. Its property can be modified by using *plastics foils,* waxes or other material to improve the barrier properties. In such cases however, the extra material rather than the paper provides the protection. Use of these is based on the knowledge of stability of drug involved and storage conditions.

Recently, we in India have also started using layered chemically treated paper called tetra-pack paper for storing products like milk (Amul) and soft drinks like (Frootee).

This paper which use to get imported till now is being made in the country. It preserves the perishable contents for a reasonably good length of time till the container is not opened. It thus, avoids the refrigeration need and thus, is a great help in distribution. In future, we shall find tetra pack paper containers also for drugs and medicines in liquid form to be taken in single dose.

Unit Dose Packaging:

A number of drugs are available in the market in flexible packagings. Their chief advantages are:

1. Consumer convenience,

2. Improved package aesthetics, and

3. The added protection.

Strip packaging is very common. However, a few drugs are sold in Blister packs too.

In contrast to the *flexibility* of strip package the blister pack offers *rigidity*. The user simply pushes the drug out of the back of the blister or peels the backing off to get to the product.

The important factors which govern the choice of flexible packaging material are:

1. Heat sealing characteristics,

2. Permeability of moisture,

3. Permeability of gases,

4. Printability.

Blisters:

For unit dose packaging of tablets and capsules in a blister (Fig. 11.3) the package consists of a *transparent thermoformable plastic* material and a *heat sealable lacquered backing* material both of which are taken into account when the compatibility and protective qualities of the total package are assessed.

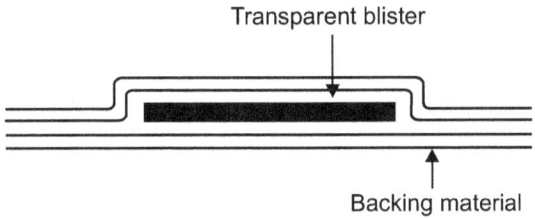

Transparent blister

Backing material

Fig. 11.3: Blister pack

Materials commonly used for thermoformable blisters:

1. (a) Polyvinyl chloride (PVC).

    (b) PVC/Polyethylene combination

    (c) Polystyrene

    (d) Polypropylene

2.   For added moisture protection
   (a) Polyvinylidene chloride (Saran) or ⎫
   (b) Polymonochlorotrifluorotheylene (Adar) ⎬ film may be limited to PVC
                                              ⎭

Backing Materials:

Backing materials are of two types: (a) Push-through packs, (b) Peelable backing materials.

Push through packs: The backing materials for push through blister packs are:

(a) Aluminium foil when it is to be sealed to plain vinyl or PVC/Adar. When using a moisture protective thermoplastic base material. e.g. PVC/Adar, it is important that the backing material be pinhole free.

Peelable Backing Materials: Manufacturers are able to offer peelable backing materials. e.g. Usually a paper/foil combination that will give a peelable seal to either PVC or Saran.

The paper surface is of exceptionally high quality to allow in-line printing on the forming equipment if required.

Blister Packaging Equipment: The moisture protection offered by various blister forming material can vary widely depending on the methods and equipment used.

Blister Packing Equipments are of two types:
1.   Intermittent motion machines.
2.   Continuous motion machines.

1. Intermitent Motion Machines:

(Hassia Model) On these machines each operation of form / fill / seal and die-cutting of the finished unit is carried out on a falt *pattern station* with the verb being moved from station to station by an intermitent motion.

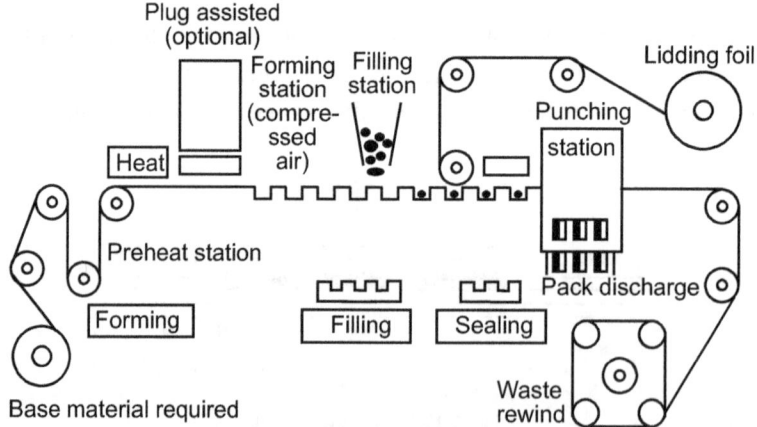

Fig. 11.4: Intermitent motion Blister packing machine Hassia – model

Continuous Motion Machines: On this type of machine all operations are carried out as part of a continuous process on cylinders. These machines can achieve higher output than the platten-forming machines, but the *depth* and *angle of draw of blister* require more critical control.

Continuous Motion Machine – *Hoffiges and Karg types.*

Process: Blister packing consists of *semirigid thermoformed plastic froy* in which there are a number of *cavities* each containing one unit and with an aluminium foil cover heat sealed over it. The process involves the passage of web of 0.2 mm PVC from a real over system of heated *roller to plateau or roller.* Here in its heat softened conditions, it is forced into cavities of suitable size and shape by *vacuum or positive pressure.* The items are fed from hopper into the cavities and then the foul cover coated with *vinyl lacquer* is sealed over it. The strips thus, formed are cut into separate trays of suitable length which may be packed singly or collectively in cartons.

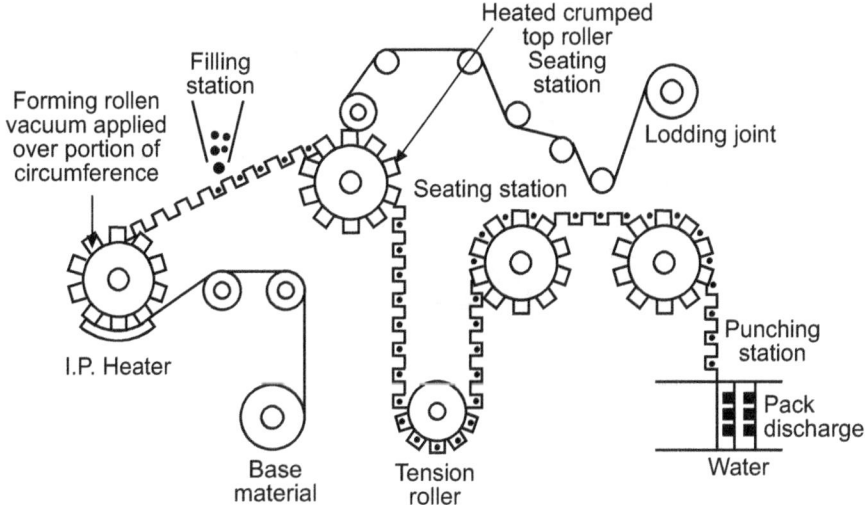

Fig. 11.5: Continuous motion Blister packing machine

Strip Packaging Materials:

Film: A plastic material upto 0.010" in thickness is considered a film.

Sheet: A material above 0.010" thickness.

Laminate film: When two completely different films are combined with an adhesive they are called a laminate film.

Composite film: When two more films are extruded at the same time and joined together, they are called a composite film.

Cellophone: Cellophone is *regenerated cellulose.* It is not thermoplastic and requires a thermoplastic coating to become a heat sealable material. It is sensitive to moisture and expands and contracts as the humidity changes.

One of the major disadvantages of cellophone is its limited shelf life, since it shrinks and gets brittle under dry conditions in the winter.

Polyester: It has good chemical resistance, usually contains no plasticizer and has good transparency. Cost is rather high but its unusual strength makes it a useful combined with other films for child-resistant unit dose packaging. Polyster has good shelf life characteristics.

Polyster is a good barrier for odors and gases and is resistant to greases and oils. The uncoated polyster film is not heat-sealable.

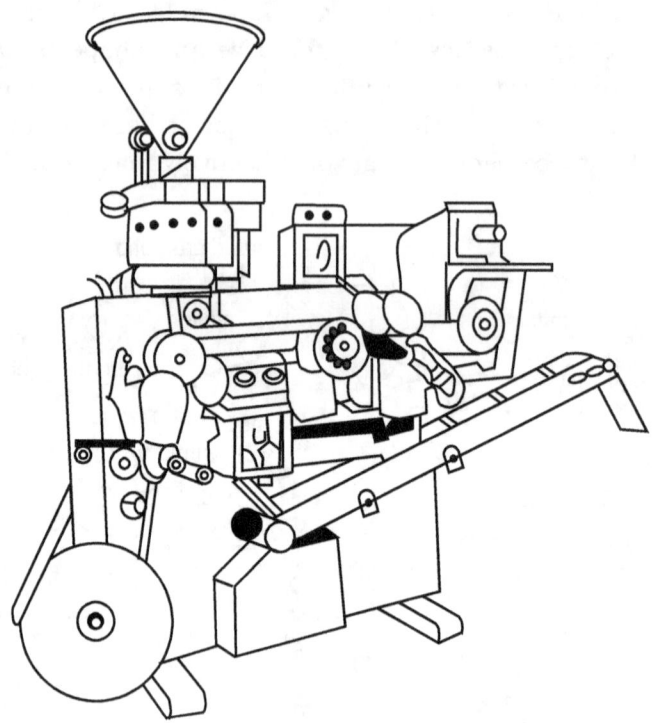

Fig. 11.6: Strip packing machine

Foil: Among the flexible packaging materials, metal foil is widely used where the ultimate protection from moisture, oxygen and light is required. The moisture vapour transmission rate and gas transmission rate are zero in the heavier gauges and near zero in gauges below 0.001" (1 mil).

Most "commercial purity" aluminium is around 99.5% pure with about 0.4% iron and 0.1% silicon making up the balance. A higher iron content increases the bursting strength, which may be an advantage in the strip packaging of tablets and capsules, but it reduces corrosion resistance of the foil.

Laminates: To achieve certain package requirements, it may be necessary to combine certain materials. These requirements may be

1. Appearance
2. Machinability
3. Strength of seal
4. Moisture and oxygen barrier properties
5. Printability and
6. Economics.

When moisture protective properties are required the most protective film should be on the outside. Usually the protective value of a laminated material is more than doubled when the coating is on proper side.

Properties of different laminates:

0.25 mm aluminium will give 100% protection against moisture, gas, odour and protection from light.

Paper lamination gives strength, toughness and improves other physical properties of a low cost to foil laminate.

Low density polythene
High density polythene,
Cellophone
PVC
} Help foil laminations to attain flexibility and resistance to cracking and wrinkling, resistance to corrosion with generally inert surface heat sealability for hermetically sealed packs

Choice of various laminates:

0.04 mm aluminium/150 gauze polythene is the commonly used laminate for strip packing in pharmaceutical industry, but it is the costliest laminate.

Cellophone/polythene is the cheapest laminate which can be used, provided the product is not affected by moisture.

For the effervescent tablets aluminium foil at high temperature accelerates gas formation, and one finds the puffed pockets of stripped table since gas cannot leak out from the foil.

Immediate cooling of strips after strip packing is must or alternate packing should be designed for effervescent tablets.

Dimensions of Strips:

1. For maximum utilisation of foil the diameter of tablets should be twice that of thickness of the tablet and the pocket size should be twice the tablet diameter.

2. For capsules the pocket size should be the

    length = length of capsules + 2 diameter of capsule

    = $(l + 2d)$

    width = 3 times the diameter of capusle

3. The minimum sealing width should be;

    (a) 4 mm from all sides of the strips | to give proper sealing

    (b) 6 mm in between the two pockets |

Strip-*width* can be calculated from the above data, depending on the number of tracks on the machine and *length* of strip will be decided on the number of tablets required in a pack.

Heat Sealing Temperatures:

Depending on the type of laminate used and the machine available one has to decide the sealing temperature.

1. The normal sealing temperature range is 125 – 140ºC depending on the nature of foil.

2. High temperature will give rise to

    (a) sticking problems (polythene etc.)

    (b) prints on the foil will become smuday,

    (c) and heat discoloration of tablets,

    (d) loss of potency in thermolabile drugs.

Comparison of Bottle/Strip/Blister Packaging:

Bottles are compact for bulk hospital packs but break and once the cap is opened, the life of the product is reduced.

1. Strips and blister packs offer more protection.

2. Strip packs give better protection but the final pack will be larger than blister or bottle pack.

3. Blister packing is very expensive.

4. The blister pack machines are costly.

6. Light sensitive and moisture sensitive drugs cannot be blister packed.

Strip Packaging:

In strip packaging, the tablets and capsules are packaged in a flexible film, a variety of laminates that are connected in a continuous strip. The strip can be rolled and placed in a dispenser type folding carton. The flexible package allow complete labelling on each pocket as well as sequential numbering on individual unit.

Child-resistant Packaging:

The consumers (patients) are to be warned to keep the medicines out of reach of children.

Almost all the solid dose oral medicines should be dispensed either in reasonable child-resistant containers or in unit dose packaging of strip or blister type.

Under very special cases of the following type it may not apply if –

(a) The original manufacturer's packs are so designed that the transfer to a reclosable child-resistant container is not required.

(b) The patients are elderly or handicapped and would have difficulty in opening a child-resistant container, while being used.

(c) Patients request specifically.

Materials for Closures:

1. Cork:

Obtained from the bark of oak growing in mediterranean countries. It is almost chemically inert and does not impart undesirable odours or flavours to the product. However, it cannot be used for many *liquid* preparations because of *mould* growth.

2. Glass:

Ideal material for making efficient and satisfactory closures but difficulty lies in making quick fix type fitting to prevent any leakage requiring skill.

Another disadvantage is that the stopper can slip out of neck of bottle easily, therefore, it is restricted to lab glassware and fancy cut glass only.

3. Plastic:

This has replaced old type of closure such as cork, rubber, metal crown cork and glass. Plastic have a property of being moulded into various shapes and hence, have become much more popular than any other types of closure. There are various types of plastic materials which can be used depending on the cost and compatibility with the type of material to be packed in the glass bottles. Plastic selected for closure must be tested for any extractable matter contained in them and for their reaction with contents of the bottle. *Plastic closures cannot be made pilfer proof unless an overseal of a metal is employed.*

4. Rubber:

At the present moment, rubber is exclusively used for closures for vails of antibiotics and multidose injectables because of its self-sealing properties and secondly because it can withstand sterlization temperatures better than plastics.

Rubber closures used for parenteral multidose containers are required to be pierced through by hypodermic needles. Hence, it is necessary to test them for hardness by a hardness tester. Further, the rubber manufacturers should be required to carry out hypodermic needle puncture test to ensure that doctors experience difficulty with closures due to their hypodermic needles being damaged on account of their undesirable hardness. Hardness test is also required while using automatic machines for stoppering vials.

Rubber closures used even for non-parentral preparation, must be free from any contamination such as dust particles. They also have disadvantage of absorbing bactericides dyes etc.

5. Metals:

Metals used as closures are mainly tin plate and aluminium but the latter is preferred because of its ductility and ease of forming into any desired shape. Further, tear off closures can be made satisfactorily only from aluminium. They have another added advantage that they can be made Pilfer-proof.

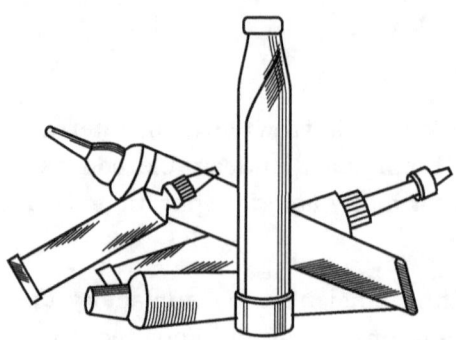

Fig. 11.7: Various types of collapsible tubes

But metal alone by itself provides a seal that will prevent leakage by evaporation of the contents of a bottle. Even for solids, a metal closure without a liner is not satisfactorily because it will not prevent deterioration from humidity, fungus or bacterial growth.

Closures are available in five basic designs.

1.	Screw-on Threaded or Lug	Many modifications of these basic
2.	Crimp-on (Crowns)	types exist, e.g. vacuum, tamper
3.	Press-on (Snap)	proof, safely, child resistant and
4.	Roll-on	linerless type etc.
5.	Friction	

1.   Thread Screw Cap:

When the screw cap is applied, its thread *engage with the corresponding thread molded on the neck of the bottle.* A liner in the cap pressed against the opening of the container seals the product in the container by overcoming sealing surface irregularities, and provides resistance to chemical and physical reaction with the product being sealed.

The screw cap is commonly made of *metal of plastics.* The metal is usually tin plate or aluminium and in plastics both thermoplastic and thermosetling materials are used. *Metal caps are usually coated on* the inside with an *enamel or lacquer for resistance against errosion.*

1.   Lug Cap:

The lug cap is similar to the threaded screw cap and operates on the *same principle. It is simply an interrupted thread on the glass finish, instead of a continuous thread, which is* used to engage a lug on the cap side wall and draw the cap down to the sealing surface of the container. Unlike the threat closure, *it requires only a quarter turn.*

The lug cap is used for *both normal atmospheric pressure and vacuum pressure closing. The cap is widely used in the food industry* because it offers a *hermatic seal and handles well in sterilization equipment and on production lines.*

2.   Crown Caps:

This style of cap is commonly used as crimped closure for beverage bottles.

3.   Roll on Caps:

The aluminium roll-on cap can be sealed securely, opened easily and resealed effectively. It finds wide application in the packaging of food, beverages, chemicals, and pharmaceuticals. The roll-on requires a material that is easy to form a aluminium or other light-gauge metal.

The roll-on technique allows for dimensional variation in the glass container.

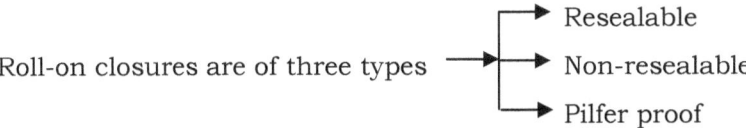

Roll-on closures are of three types → Resealable / Non-resealable / Pilfer proof

4.   Pilfer-proof Closures:

The pilfer-proof closure is similar to the standard roll-on closure except for a *greater skirt length.* This additional length extends below the threaded portion to form a bank, which is fastened to the basic cap by series of narrow *metal 'bridges'.*

When the pilfer proof closure is removed, the bridges break and *bank remains in place on the neck of the container.* The user can reseal the closure, but the detached bank indicates that the package has been opened. The torque necessary to break the bridges and remove the cap is nominal.

5.   Non-resealable Roll-on Closures:

In some packaging applications resealable cap is not desired. Non-resealable caps *require unthreaded glass finishes.* The skirts of the closures are rolled under retaining rings on the glass container and maintain the linear compression. Closures of this type have tear-off tabs that make them tamper and pilfer proof.

Closure Liners: A liner may be defined as any material that is *inserted in a cap to effect a seal between the closure and the container.*

Liners are usually made of a resilient backing and a facing material. The backing material must be soft enough to take any irregularities in the sealing surface and elastic enough to recover some of its original shape when removed and replaced. It is usually glued into cap with an adhesive, or the cap can be made with an undercut, so that the liner snaps into place and is free to rotate.

Homogeneous Liners: These one-piece liners are available either as disk or as ring or *rubbers or plastic.* Although they are more expensive and more complicated to apply, they are widely used for pharmaceuticals because their *properties are uniform and they can withstand high temperature sterlization.*

Heterogeneous Composite liners: These are composed of layers of different materials chosen for specific requirements. The composite liner consist generally of two parts: A facing and backing. The facing usually is in contact with the product, and the backing provides the cushioning and sealing properties required.

Factors in Selecting a Liner:

1. Compatibility (Chemical resistance)
2. Appearance, caliper etc.
3. Gas and vapour-transmission rates, WVTR Oxygen, Carbon dioxide etc.
4. Removal torque
5. Heat resistance
6. Shift life
7. Economics.

3. Inner Seals:

These secondary liners are affixed to the mouth of containers and require repture to gain access to the product. They are used in the drug and food industry to provide the product with *additional environment protection* and protection against contamination. Inner seals are usually composed of *cellophane or glassine paper and are applied* to the container with an FDA approved water-based adhesive.

Rubber Stoppers: The rubber stopper is used primarily for multidose vials and disposable syrings. The rubber polymers most commonly used are natural neoprene and butyl rubber.

The types of ingredients commonly found in a rubber closure are:

1. Rubber
2. Vulcanizing agent
3. Accelerator/activator
4. Extended filler
5. Reinforced filler
6. Softner/Plasticizer
7. Antioxidant
8. Pigment
9. Special Components, waxes.

When the rubber stopper comes in contact with parenteral solution if may absorb active ingredient, antibacterial preservative, or other materials and one or more ingredients of the rubber may be extracted into the liquid.

These extractives could:

1. Interfere with chemical analysis of the active ingredient.
2. Affect the toxicity or pyrogenicity of the injectable products.
3. Interact with drug preservative to cause inactivation.
4. Affect the chemical and physical stability of the preparation so that particulate matter appears in solution.

Evaluation of Packaging Materials:

Depending upon the material and purpose of using the primary packaging material the method of evaluation differs. The materials normally used for packaging Pharmaceuticals may be glass, metal and plastic, and may be used for parenteral or non-parenteral purpose.

(a) Evaluation of Glass Containers for Injectable Preparations:

Containers may be ampoules, vials, or bottles and are prepared from uncoloured glass except for the substances which are sensitive to light and should be transparent to permit the visual inspection of contents. They are prepared from Type I glass, Type II glass or Type III glass. The containers should be used once only. For evaluation unused containers be used.

The containers are to be tested for –

(1) Hydrolytic resistance by using at least 10 containers if volume is less than 5.0 ml or 5 containers if volume is 6 to 30 ml or at least 3 containers if volume is more than 30 ml.

Carry out the test as mentioned in Appendix – II of Indian Pharmacopoeia 1996 Vol. II. Volume of 0.01 M Hydrochloric acid required to neutralise the alkalinity is worked out, which varies depending upon the volume of bottle under test.

(2) Test for Arsenic: Follow the method given in Appendix-II of Indian Pharmacopoeia under containers.

(b) Evaluation of metal containers for eye-ointments:

These containers should pass the test for metal particles as described by I.P.

(c) Evaluation of plastic containers:

Plastic containers for non-injectable preparations should pass the I.P. requirements for

(1)   Leakage test.

(2)   Collapsibility test

(3)   Test for clarity of aqueous extracts.

(4)   Non-volatile residue.

Plastic containers for injectable preparations:

Plastic containers should comply the following tests for material as described in I.P. 1996.

(a)   Leakage test

(b)   Collapsibility test

(c)   Transparency

(d)   Water-vapour permeability

(e)   Extractable di (2-ethyl hexyl) phthalate

(f)   Test for barium

(g)   Test for Heavy metals

(h)   Test for Tin

(i)   Test for Zinc

(j)   Residue on ignition

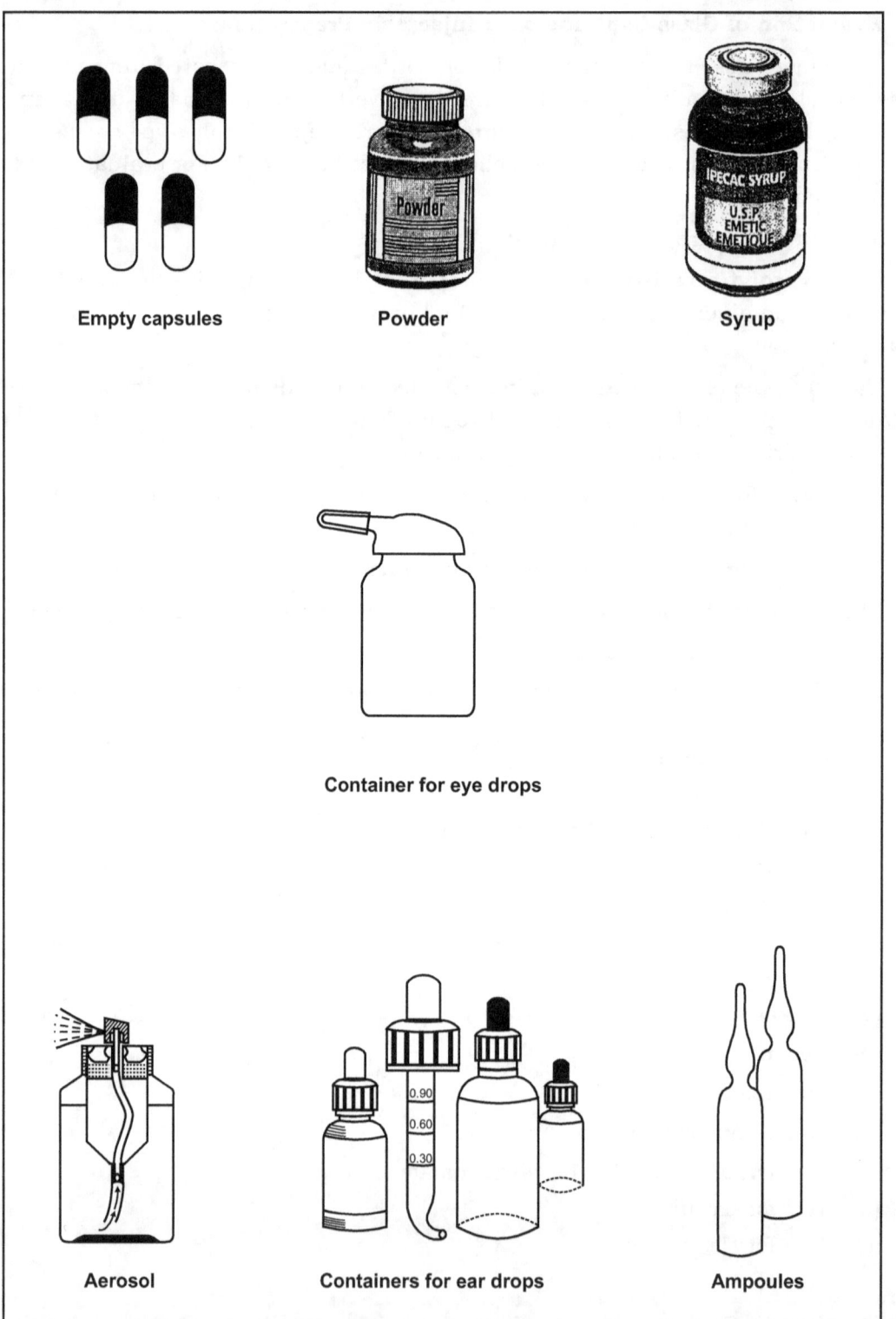

Empty capsules

Powder

Syrup

Container for eye drops

Aerosol

Containers for ear drops

Ampoules

✳✳✳

BIBLIOGRAPHY

1. Bentley's Text Book of Pharmaceutics – **Rawlins E. A.** ELBS 1979.
   Bailliere Tindale East bourn Cast. Sussex. U.K.

2. Sprowl's American Pharmacy – **Dittert L. W.** J. B. Lipincott Co. 1974. Philadelphia, USA.

3. Modern Pharmaceutics, **Gibert S. Banker and Christophere Rodes** – 1990 Marcel Dekker Inc. Newyork, USA.

4. Unit Processes in Pharmacy, **David Granderton Willian Heineman** Meical Books, Ltd.

5. Introduction to Pharmaceutical Dosage Forms 1969, **Ansel H.C.,** Lea-Febiger Philadelphia, USA.

6. General Pharmacy, **M. L. Shroff** 1975 Five Star Publiations, Kolkatta.

7. Pharmaceutics – **Aulton Michel E.** First ELBS Edition 1990, Longman Groups (FE) Ltd. U.K.

8. Pharmaceutical Formulations, **Mittal B.M.,** 1990, Vallabh Prakashan, New Delhi.

9. Remington's Pharmaceutical Sciences, **Alfonso R. Gennaro** 18th Edition 1990, Mack Publishing Co. Pennsylvania U.S.A.

10. Martindale's Extra Pharmacopoeia, 30th Edition 1993, by "The Pharmaceutical Press" London.

11. Dispensing of Medication, **Hoover** 1996, 2nd Edition Mack Publishing Co., Pensylvania.

12. Indian Pharmacopoeia, Second Edition 1966, Ministry of Health, Government of India, New Delhi.

13. Indian Pharmacopoeia, Third Edition, Vol. I and Vol. II 1985, Ministry of Health Government of India, New Delhi.

14. Indian Pharmacopoeia, Fourth Edition, Vol. I and II, 1996, Ministry of Health Government of India, New Delhi.

15. Tutorial Pharmacy, **J. W. Cooper and Colin Gunn** 1960, Pitman Medical Publishing Co. Ltd., UK.

16. British Pharmacopoeia, 1993, Her Majesty's Stationery Office, London, U.K.

17. Theory and Practice of Industrial Pharmacy, **Leon Lachman, Herbert A., Lieberman, Joseph L. Kanig Z.,** Third Indian Edition 1990, Varghese Publishing House, Mumbai 400014.

18. Hand Book of Drug Laws : **Salim Malik.**

19. Pharmaceutical Dosage and Drug Delivery Systems, **Ansel H.C.** – Popovich and allen Williams and Wilkins.

✱✱✱

INDEX